I0762031

The Crystal Dynasty

The Knife's Edge

Abigail Mader

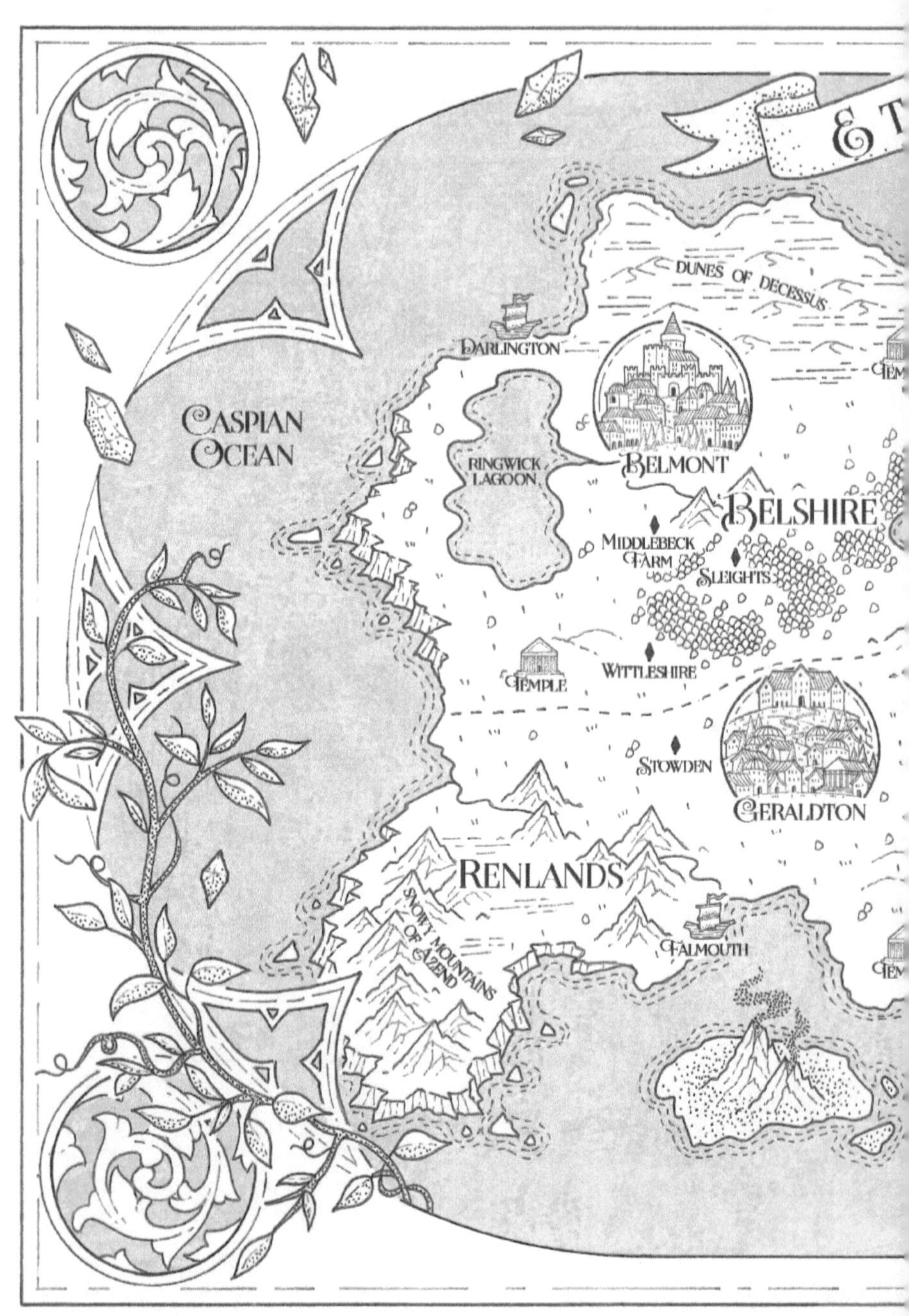
DUNES OF DECESSUS
DARLINGTON
CASPIAN
OCEAN
RINGWICK
LAGOON
BELMONT
BELSHIRE
MIDDLEBECK
FARM
SLEIGHTS
TEMPLE
WITTLESHIRE
STOWDEN
GERALDTON
RENLANDS
SNOWY MOUNTAINS
OF AZEND
FALMOUTH

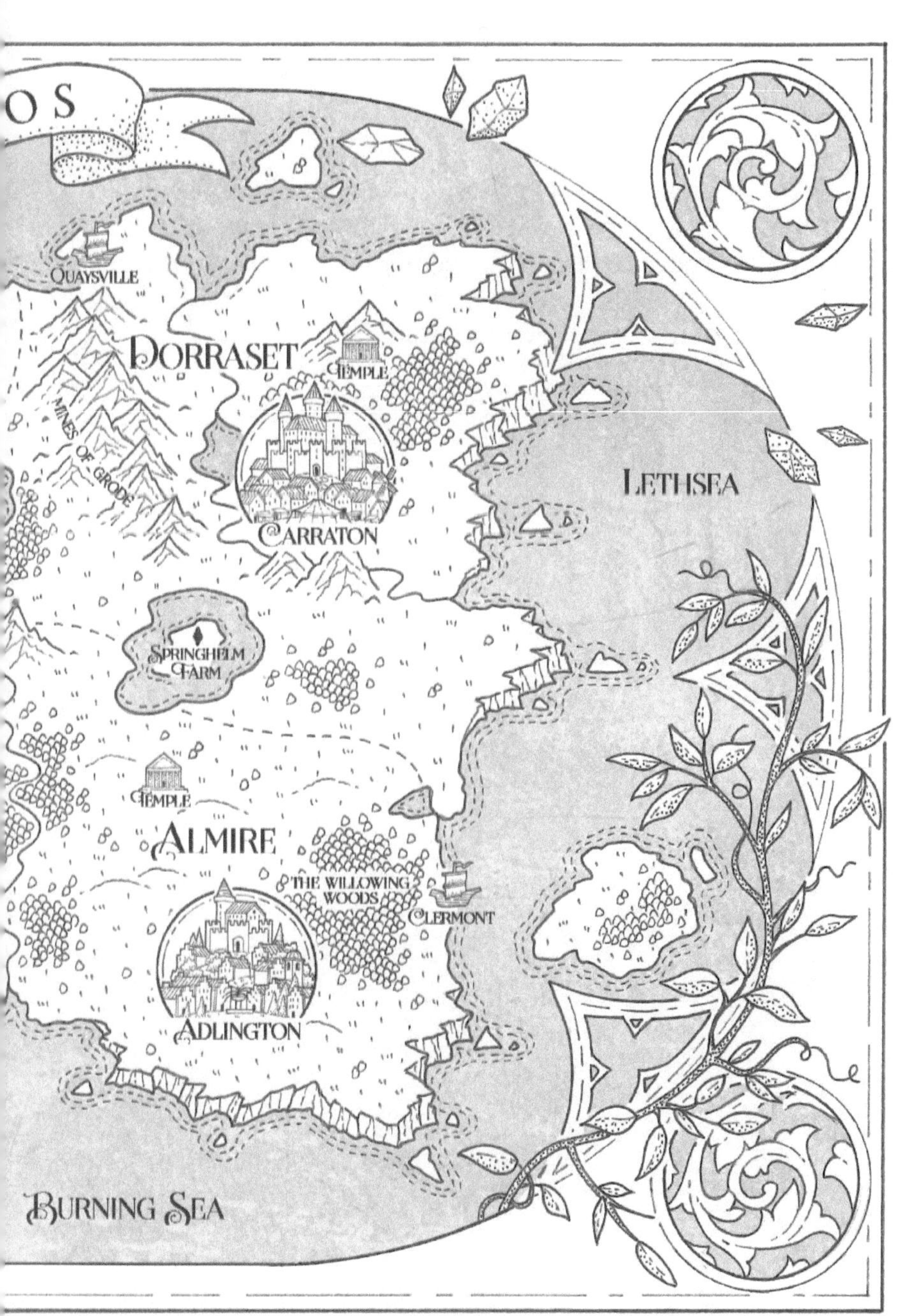
OS
QUAYSVILLE
DORRASET
TEMPLE
MINES OF GRODE
CARRATON
LETHSEA
SPRINGHELM FARM
TEMPLE
ALMIRE
THE WILLOWING WOODS
CLERMONT
ADLINGTON
BURNING SEA

ISBN: 978-1-7635740-7-6

Dedication

To my readers – It's been quite a journey, so here's to one last emotional rollercoaster. Buckle up and enjoy. You're in for an experience you won't forget.

Happy reading.

Or perhaps a touch of emotional turmoil.

Either way, enjoy!

Content Warnings

With the final instalment, the themes are similar to those in books 1 and 2. If you have read these, then you know what to expect. If you haven't read the first two books, PUT THIS BOOK DOWN. Ethos is no place for the uninitiated. (Also, spoilers. So many spoilers. Not to mention confusion about who everyone is.)

Anyway, here's what to expect:

More deaths (sorry),

One open-door spicy scene in chapter 3, near the end, so it's easy to skip,

Detailed descriptions of torture,

Grief and trauma processing,

One character (hi, Elinor) experiences a significant mental spiral near the end.

Please take care of yourself and read at your own pace. Your mental health matters.

Table of Contents

Prologue

Liora stepped into the grand hall of the temple in Carraton, her gaze sweeping across the magnificent room. Though she had attended countless meetings here over the years, the majesty of the sacred space never failed to steal her breath. The vaulted ceilings soared above, adorned with murals so vivid they seemed to pulse with life – an intricate history of the divine spirit, and the long, storied legacy of the priestesses. Each brushstroke captured both their moments of grace and the deep shadows of their failures.

As her eyes traced the painted walls, she saw how the blame had been laid upon the priestesses for the chaos that followed the divine spirit's disappearance years ago. The trust they once held had crumbled. They had been hunted, persecuted, and forced to the fringes of society. And yet, they had endured. Through quiet resilience and steadfast loyalty to the royal family, the priestesses had reclaimed their standing, rising once more as protectors and spiritual guides of the kingdom.

With the backing of the royal bloodline, the priestesses' unwavering devotion to the divine spirit rang hollow for many. Liora was among those who no longer believed in the symbol they so desperately clung to. The divine spirit had been absent for centuries, with no sign of her return, and Liora had long since begun to question whether their endless prayers and rituals held any true meaning.

Magic still coursed through the land. Those blessed with the gift could channel it to command the elements – not through divine will, but through the guidance of others who had already mastered it. No deity was needed. *If the non-magical people had abandoned belief in the sacred spirit, why then did the priestesses persist in upholding something that had lost all meaning?*

To Liora, it was clear: their world no longer required the guidance of a vanished spirit. Her faith had crumbled slowly, piece by piece, until only ruins remained. And yet, she knew the others would never see as she did. They would continue to worship a deity who had forsaken them, binding themselves to a legacy she now saw as obsolete.

But she wanted more – for herself and for the priesthood. The old ways were shackles, relics that held them back, and she envisioned a new era – one where the priestesses could lead the land through progress and practicality, not blind devotion. Her ambitions stretched far beyond reform. Liora dreamed of standing at the helm, reshaping their order into something greater – something untethered by what she saw as outdated ideals. She would bring the priestesses into this new age, and she would rise as their high priestess.

This vision led her to Queen Elinor. The queen was the embodiment of change – a ruler who refused to bow to tradition or sentiment. She had carved her own path, dismantling anything or anyone that dared to stand in her way. In Elinor, Liora saw a kindred spirit, a woman who shared her desire to reshape the world and cast off the chains of the past.

Their alliance wasn't born of loyalty or friendship; it was forged in ambition. Elinor could grant her the power and influence she needed to dismantle the old order and build something entirely her own. In return, Liora would provide her knowledge, her cunning, and her allegiance. Together, they could create the future they both envisioned.

At the centre of the hall stood the ebony round table, polished to a mirror-like sheen and glowing with delicate golden inlays. Liora's gaze drifted across its surface, pausing on the intricate patterns that seemed to shimmer beneath the soft light. Within this sacred space, decisions were made that echoed across the realm – a place meant to symbolise unity. But to Liora, it was a stage upon which ambition played out beneath the guise of purpose and veiled intentions.

Her eyes moved across the room and settled on her sisters, not by blood, but by the sacred bond of their shared calling. Each woman bore the title of High Priestess, representing her own temple. Zara, the High Priestess of Carraton, was the most senior figure among them and the highest-ranking member of their order.

Gathered around were Zuri of Decessus, whose temple perched on the edge of the dunes; Sade of Belshire, nestled deep within the forests; Nia of Almire, whose coastal realm whispered with the breath of the sea; and Liora herself, the priestess of the Renlands, where endless hills rolled beneath a boundless sky. Each brought with her the weight of her homeland's history, burdens, and quiet triumphs. Their presence here was meant to symbolise unity, though Liora knew better.

Despite their youthful appearances, she was well aware that each of these women had lived far longer than they seemed. The power they wielded slowed time's march, preserving their vitality even as the decades slipped by. Behind their serene expressions lay a wealth of experience, wisdom sharpened by hardship and survival. Many among them were past eighty, though none looked a day over forty – a testament to their enduring bond with the elements, and the ancient magic that shaped their lives.

Liora had often marvelled at how age lent strength to their insights and decisions, though now she viewed this meeting as a chance to reshape the very foundation of their discussions. Wisdom, after all, was a double-edged sword – capable of anchoring them to tradition or opening their minds to change.

Their golden cloaks shimmered as they moved with dignified grace, the flowing fabric catching the light with every step. The rich hues complemented their complexions, casting each woman in a striking, regal glow. As custom dictated, their hoods remained lowered during council, revealing faces marked by serenity and tempered wisdom.

But Liora saw more than what lay on the surface. Her keen eyes caught the subtle signs others might have missed: the flicker of tension in Sade's jaw, the quiet wariness lining Zuri's brow, the flicker of iron resolve beneath Nia's calm façade. They had gathered at Zara's summons, but the weight of their presence – and the looming influence of the queen – was unmistakable.

Liora inclined her head towards each woman as she took her seat, exchanging brief, formal greetings.

"Zara's timing for this meeting is interesting," she said, her voice low yet edged with intent. "Given all that's unfolding in the realm, one has to wonder what she intends to share."

Sade tilted her head slightly, her sharp features betraying a hint of curiosity. "With Queen Elinor tightening her hold, there's no shortage of urgent matters. Perhaps Zara seeks a solution we've yet to consider."

Zuri offered a soft, knowing smile. "It isn't like her to summon us without purpose. Whatever it is, it's bound to be important."

Even in their composed exchanges, the tension in the room was palpable. Liora settled into her seat, her posture poised, though her thoughts raced beneath the surface. She sensed the undercurrents among them – the silent questions, the guarded doubts. Though their words were laced with curiosity and concern, Liora's thoughts drifted elsewhere.

Her gaze lingered on Nia, whose calm expression gave little away. Liora admired the coastal priestess's elegance, but their ideals couldn't have been more different. Nia's unwavering faith in the divine spirit often struck her as hopelessly naïve. Liora's own cynicism had long since hardened her against such beliefs. The divine was gone, and Zara's continued insistence on clinging to ancient traditions wore at her patience more than she liked to admit.

The soft murmur of conversation stilled as the great doors of the hall opened, drawing every gaze towards the figure entering. Liora straightened, her eyes narrowing as she watched the High Priestess of Carraton cross the threshold. Zara's presence was commanding – her jet-black hair gleaming like polished obsidian beneath the flickering lights of the chamber.

As she approached the table, the atmosphere shifted. The others moved in quiet unison, falling respectfully silent as Zara took her place at its head. There was reverence in their stillness – a deep, almost instinctive respect.

Liora didn't share it.

As Zara spoke, Liora maintained her serene façade, though her thoughts churned beneath the surface. She appeared attentive, nodding at the appropriate moments, but her mind was elsewhere, anchored to the plans she had so carefully crafted. The stakes were too high to waste this opportunity; every word exchanged in this hall could be shaped to serve the vision she guarded so closely.

"Sisters, welcome. I know many of you have travelled far to be here, and for that, I thank you," Zara began, her voice calm and composed, her expression unreadable. Liora inclined her head, catching the soft murmurs and gestures of recognition shared among the others.

"We face a grave threat," Zara continued. "Queen Elinor has brought nothing but pain and suffering to our lands in recent years. She murdered her own brother, King James, to seize the throne, and she hasn't hesitated to slaughter innocent children who resemble the royal twins, all to secure her crown. Now, she's taken George's life as well. Eight years ago, we failed to remove her, and our power has been fading ever since. That battle drained us and claimed the lives of many of our sisters."

Silence settled over the room like a shroud. The weight of Zara's words pressed heavily against the golden glow of the hall. Liora's fingers rested lightly on the arms of her chair, her expression placid, but her thoughts spun faster. Elinor's atrocities were not news to her – what mattered now was what Zara intended to propose. It had to be more than a solemn reminder of past defeats.

"This time, we must succeed," Zara declared, her voice firm with conviction. "We must join forces with the rebels, find Cecilia and the twins, and bring down the queen once and for all. The prophecy demands it."

Liora stiffened, and she wasn't alone. The word *prophecy* shifted the atmosphere instantly, and she saw the flicker of unease ripple across the other priestesses' faces. Her gaze sharpened, eyes locking onto Zara with quiet intensity. She was the first to speak, her voice measured but edged with suspicion.

"Prophecy? What *prophecy* are you referring to?"

Zara hesitated – for only a breath – but Liora caught it. A flicker of doubt was quickly masked. It was all she needed to deepen her scepticism.

"Before your arrival, I discovered something extraordinary," Zara said, reaching into the folds of her robes. "An ancient scroll, hidden for centuries. It speaks of two fates."

As she withdrew the scroll, the air in the room seemed to tighten. The parchment looked weathered, its edges frayed with age, yet as she unrolled it, the ink shimmered faintly, casting a subtle glow that drew every eye. The other priestesses leaned forward, captivated. Liora, however, narrowed her eyes. Of course, it would glow – anything to bolster its mystique.

"This prophecy speaks of two fates, two destinies entwined. One is destined to save us; the other, to destroy the realm. One path leads to light and salvation, the other to darkness and ruin. The fate of the world rests on who prevails."

Though her face remained composed, Liora's thoughts roiled beneath the surface. Glowing text, an ancient scroll conveniently uncovered in a time of crisis – it all felt too perfect, too deliberately timed. Her gaze swept the room, noting flickers of uncertainty in the others' expressions.

"Read it to us," Liora said, her voice level.

Zara inclined her head and began, her voice resonant in the quiet hall.

"Amidst great turmoil, when shadows cast long over the land, two will rise, their destinies intertwined. One path leads to light and salvation, the other to darkness and ruin. Who prevails determines the fate of the world.

"The first, a beacon of hope, shall wield the power of the crystals. Guided by wisdom and compassion, they are meant to unite the realms. Driven by ambition and vengeance, the second, a harbinger of doom, shall seek the throne, bringing chaos and despair.

"Aiding the chosen ones and guiding their steps, the divine spirit, disguised, is to walk among them. Riddles of old reveal the way to find the crystals and unlock their power.

"The fate of the world rests on their shoulders. Their choices shape the future. In the end, one path must triumph, and the realm will be forever changed."

As Zara finished, silence settled over the hall. The faint shimmer of the scroll's text reflected in her eyes, lending the moment an air of reverence, at least for some. Liora, however, was unmoved. Her gaze lingered on the glowing parchment. The whole display reeked of performance.

She glanced around the table. The other high priestesses exchanged anxious looks, their unease unmistakable. The words Zara had spoken were clear: the fate of the realm hinged on this prophecy and the struggle between these two fates.

"And this prophecy only revealed itself to you now?" Sade asked, her voice tinged with scepticism.

Zara gave a solemn nod. "Yes. I found it just before your arrival. Someone hid it long ago, and I believe it has resurfaced now, in our hour of greatest need."

Liora's eyes narrowed. Her voice, cool and sharp, cut through the tension. "Why have we never heard of this prophecy before?"

She didn't disguise her doubt, nor did she soften it. The timing was too convenient, the language too polished. It felt more like a fable designed to galvanise the uncertain than the divine truth Zara insisted it was.

Unbothered, Zara extended the scroll towards her. Liora accepted it, the text casting a soft glow across her hands. The light flickered like a whisper, ethereal and suspiciously dramatic. She studied the words carefully, but the glow did nothing to dispel her misgivings. If anything, it deepened them.

To her, this read like a tale crafted to inspire fear and hope in equal measure – something written to control, not to guide.

"I understand your doubts," Zara said, her tone firming. "But we must take this seriously. Look around us—Ethos suffers under Elinor's rule. If she prevails, what will stop her from spreading her tyranny beyond our borders?"

Liora finished reading and passed the scroll to Zuri, who accepted it with a solemn nod. The dunes priestess examined the text with the same measured scrutiny, but Liora noticed the way Zara's words seemed to settle in her – subtly, but visibly. As the parchment made its way around the table, Zara continued, her voice laced with urgency.

"The signs are all around us—the chaos, the suffering, the darkness spreading across our land. This prophecy speaks to our current situation. We can't afford to ignore it."

Liora pressed her lips into a thin line. Zara's conviction rang clear in every syllable, her resolve nearly tangible, but sincerity alone didn't make something true. Maybe the others were beginning to soften, but to Liora, this was still a well-rehearsed performance cloaked in mysticism.

When Nia, the last to receive the scroll, finally spoke, her voice was gentle, yet firm. "The prophecy speaks of two fates, two destinies intertwined. We must ensure the path of light prevails."

Zara inclined her head, as though Nia's agreement affirmed her stance. "Then we must trust in the prophecy," she said, her voice rising with renewed purpose. "And we must act swiftly and decisively. Every moment we delay, Elinor's grip tightens."

Liora leaned forward slightly, her gaze sharp. "I have contacts in the Renlands who may know the whereabouts of rebel groups. I'll reach out and gather whatever intelligence I can."

Zuri gave a measured nod. "I'll do the same in the dunes. The desert tribes have always been resourceful, and they may know more than we realise."

"I'll scour the forests of Belshire," Sade added. "The woodland folk are brave and loyal. They'll be eager to join our cause."

Nia gave a soft nod. "Then I'll return to Almire. The coastal villages have suffered long under Elinor's reign. They'll be ready to fight."

A beat of silence followed before Zuri's voice cut through, calm yet probing. "And what of the young heir? A babe of Elinor's blood, but no threat to the realm. What becomes of him?"

Liora turned her gaze to Zuri, watching her carefully while keeping her own expression unreadable. The question lingered in the air like mist.

Nia, ever composed, replied without hesitation. "We find a family willing to take him in. No one needs to know his lineage. He's innocent, and he deserves a life unburdened by a legacy he had no hand in."

The others remained quiet, each absorbing Nia's words. Liora said nothing, but the answer settled uneasily within her. Innocence was rarely a shield in their world, and bloodlines were never truly forgotten.

Zara nodded, her voice steady with unwavering resolve. "Then it's settled. We have faced great challenges before, and we have always risen to meet them. Despite our losses, we remain strong. Together, we can rid this darkness Elinor has cast across the land and restore peace."

Liora's fingers curled tightly around the arms of her chair. The others spoke with such conviction as if the path ahead were clear and certain. But to her, this unity was fragile, built on a prophecy that had appeared at the most convenient moment. Zara's sudden belief in it made Liora uneasy. *If it had truly been hidden for centuries, then who had placed it where Zara would find it now?* Blind faith, no matter how well-intentioned, could be fatal.

The priestesses continued to speak, their voices weaving together a blend of strategy and hope that filled the hall. Liora offered measured responses when required, but her mind was elsewhere. The low-burning candles cast long, flickering shadows on the stone walls – a reminder of the darkness still thick over Ethos, and the quiet shape her own ambitions were beginning to take.

As the meeting drew to a close, the high priestesses rose one by one, exchanging subdued farewells before departing into the night, each bearing the weight of her task. Liora followed, her movements calm and deliberate, her expression serene. But as she stepped beyond the threshold of the hall, her thoughts were no longer aligned with theirs.

Outside the temple, she shed her golden cloak and replaced it with a plain, unassuming robe. The transformation was seamless. The poised high priestess vanished into the night, her regal bearing traded for anonymity. Liora moved like a shadow, silent and swift, slipping beneath the canopy of the forest where the moonlight filtered through the leaves in fractured silver beams.

She had her own truths to uncover – her own plans to pursue. Her allegiance to Zara's cause was little more than a mask.

Tonight, her path diverged from theirs.

She moved with purpose, her footsteps soundless on the forest floor. The shadows swallowed her whole until she reached a secluded clearing – her destination.

There, waiting in the dim moonlight, stood a lone figure. Elinor. The queen's silhouette was unmistakable – tall and imposing, her eyes gleaming with a blend of anticipation and malice. Elinor's presence was as commanding as ever, and Liora felt a thrill of excitement at the prospect of their alliance.

"Your Majesty," Liora said, bowing her head in greeting. "I have news and plans to share."

Elinor's lips curled into a sinister smile. "Speak, Liora. What have you learned?"

Liora met her gaze squarely. "The high priestesses have convened. They're aligning themselves with the rebels and intend to find Cecilia and the royal twins. They believe that, together, they can overthrow you."

"Have they located my niece and nephew?" Elinor asked, her voice cold and precise.

"Yes. They're also hunting the crystal shards. One is already in their possession. They met with Zuri, and she advised Aevah to bond with the shards once she finds them. Aevah has headed to the mountains. Jacob is travelling to Almire."

Elinor's eyes glinted with amusement. "Perfect. I hold the shard in Almire. I'll set a trap for my young nephew. As for Aevah, have your people monitor her movements. When the time is right, draw her to your temple with offers for aid. Make certain she never leaves."

"It will be done," Liora replied, her tone calm and sure. "But there's something else, Your Majesty. Zara has come across an ancient prophecy."

Elinor's expression darkened, curiosity flashing across her features. "A prophecy? What does it say?"

Liora hesitated briefly. "It speaks of two fates, one destined to save the realm and the other to destroy it. The priestesses believe the prophecy concerns you, Aevah, Jacob, and the shards. They're treating it with utmost seriousness."

Elinor let out a dry laugh, her smile twisting with contempt. "I assume I'm cast as the villain in this story?"

"Yes," Liora said evenly. "They are determined to ensure it's fulfilled in their favour. They believe that if the twins gather the shards, your downfall will follow."

"I've known that much already," Elinor said sharply. "What of Cecilia and Adrian? What role are they playing?"

"They've been travelling the kingdom, rallying rebel forces. They intend to come for you, to challenge your reign. We haven't located their base camp yet."

Elinor's eyes narrowed, her composure cracking with a flicker of rage. "Find them. Find the camp. I want both of their heads at my feet."

"My spies are already working on it." Liora leaned forward, her voice lowering to a determined whisper. "We must strengthen your position and prepare for their attack. With Lord Stone's daughter in your grasp, you hold a powerful bargaining chip. But we need to solidify your rule further."

Elinor nodded slowly, her thoughts already racing ahead. "The shards."

"You possess two of the four," Liora continued. "With my help, you can bond with them, restore the power you once had and more. Together, we'll make you unstoppable."

Elinor's smile widened, confidence returning in full. "Excellent. Come to the castle tomorrow. We'll perform the bonding ritual then. I will not relinquish the throne, not now. No, I plan to crush them once and for all. This prophecy will see me victorious."

Liora inclined her head. "I'll do whatever is necessary to secure your victory, Your Majesty." But as the words left her lips, her thoughts drifted back to one final line from the prophecy.

Elinor caught the hesitation in her eyes. "Something troubling you?" she asked, her voice sharp and her gaze piercing.

Liora's fingers intertwined. "There was one more passage… something I dismissed at first. But if any of this is real, it might carry significant implications."

"Go on," Elinor ordered, her tone clipped but curious.

"It speaks of the divine spirit," Liora said. "It claims she will return in disguise, walking among us to aid the chosen ones."

Elinor let out a bitter, cynical laugh. "You mean to say she might be walking among us, all-powerful and benevolent? Nonsense."

"You don't believe it's possible?"

"Of course not," Elinor snapped. "The divine spirit abandoned this realm centuries ago. No one has seen her since. She's not returning, not in disguise or her true form, to help anyone. It's a comforting myth, nothing more."

"I thought the same," Liora replied, her expression mirroring Elinor's disdain. "The prophecy reads more like poetic nonsense meant to comfort the desperate."

"Let them believe it," Elinor said with a dismissive wave. "Their faith changes nothing. Prophecies and spirits are for fools and dreamers. We shape our own destiny, Liora."

Liora nodded once, her expression unreadable. "As you say, Your Majesty."

Together, they turned and departed into the night. Tomorrow would mark the next phase of Elinor's ascendancy – and for Liora, the continuation of a delicate game played in the shadows.

Chapter 1

Jacob's Journey

One night had passed since Jacob and Aevah had gone their separate ways. With his cousins, Edward and Bryne, at his side, Jacob was now en route to Almire. Thanks to the map and the riddle they had deciphered, he believed the shard he sought was concealed within some kind of well.

Unlike Aevah, he had no control over the power. He would have to search the old-fashioned way – by hand – and hope for success. How he would manage it was a problem for another day.

For now, their immediate concern was crossing Belshire and the Renlands to reach Almire. Unfortunately, cutting through the mountains would only delay their progress. Bryne had suggested they continue as planned and pass through Geraldton to connect with a rebel faction there. The city was only a few days' ride away, and Jacob looked forward to it with growing anticipation.

Geraldton was famed for its stone and wood sculptures. As a woodworking enthusiast, Jacob hoped to admire the artisans' work and perhaps glean new techniques. Though their stay would be brief and his identity concealed, he couldn't contain his excitement, especially at the thought of sleeping indoors.

The cold autumn nights had been harsh. A warm bed now seemed a distant luxury. He never imagined he would long for the desert's heat, but it was far better than the constant damp that seeped into his bones. Closing his eyes, he tried to imagine the chill wind as a gentle breeze rather than a biting gust. He could almost feel the sun-soaked air of the desert wrapping around him like a familiar embrace. For a fleeting moment, he was back in that vast expanse, where the horizon stretched endlessly and cold nights were a fading memory.

After several more days on the road, Geraldton finally appeared on the horizon. A sprawling city unfolded before them, its sunlit buildings shimmering like a promise of civilisation and comfort. Jacob had never seen anything so spectacular. He bounced in his saddle, eager to pass through its gates. The thought of a warm meal and a soft bed lifted his spirits.

But as they entered the city, Geraldton's once-vibrant energy felt dimmed. A heavy, subdued air clung to the streets. Guards at the gates scrutinised each newcomer, while cloaked men – likely trackers, identified by distinctive pins – scanned the crowd with hawk-like eyes. Inside the walls, whispers replaced conversation, and cautious glances replaced friendly nods.

His aunt's relentless pursuit of both his family and the rebels had blanketed the city in fear. Trackers and guards patrolled in force, silencing the city's former liveliness and replacing it with unease.

Jacob rode between his cousins, sensing their nervousness mirrored his own. The stories of Geraldton's grandeur clashed sharply with the sombre reality before them. Merchants stood behind stalls with guarded expressions, speaking in hushed tones. Even the children played quietly, their eyes flicking nervously towards the patrolling guards.

Jacob flinched each time a patrol passed, sweat forming on his brow despite the cold. They wandered the wary streets in search of an inn that was both affordable and welcoming. Locals avoided eye contact, clearly unwilling to engage with strangers. Eventually, one kind soul took pity on them and pointed them towards a place called *The Merry Minstrel.*

The inn stood out with its thatched roof and vibrant flower boxes. A warm light spilt onto the street, and a painted wooden sign of a cheerful minstrel swung gently in the breeze. It was a welcome sight amid the city's gloom.

Inside, the world felt transformed. Warmth radiated from a crackling hearth, instantly drawing Jacob's attention. Before he could step closer, a jovial man with a round belly and twinkling eyes greeted them.

"Welcome to *The Merry Minstrel!* How can I assist you this evening?"

Edward answered, "We're looking for rooms for the night—anything suitable for the three of us."

"You've come to the right place," the innkeeper replied with a broad grin. "We've got cosy lodgings available. Let me show you to your quarters."

Coin changed hands, and the innkeeper led them up a narrow staircase to a modest but clean room on the second floor. The space was furnished simply, with wooden beds, a small table, and a washbasin. Fresh linens and a comforting, homey atmosphere rounded out the room.

"This will do nicely," Edward said, grateful for the refuge. "Thank you."

"You're welcome," the innkeeper said and smiled widely. "If you need anything, just let me know. We also serve a hearty supper in the common room if you're hungry."

Relieved to have found shelter, Jacob and his cousins freshened up before heading downstairs. Laughter and the bright tunes of a lute filled the common area. The contrast with the city outside was striking.

They settled at a vacant table, and after placing their orders with a friendly waitress, Bryne leaned back and discreetly scanned the room.

"It's awfully jolly in here," he murmured, "compared to the atmosphere outside."

"Yes, likely because no one's watching. I'm sure the mood changes the moment the guards show up," Edward replied.

"I'll ask around, see what I can learn. If things are truly this dangerous, our friends might already be gone," Bryne said, before slipping into the crowd.

The waitress returned shortly after, but only brought two plates. Bryne's meal had likely been delivered while he was mingling.

Once they had eaten, Jacob and Edward lingered a while longer, basking in the inn's warm atmosphere. The laughter, music, and clinking of mugs provided a welcome contrast to the fear outside – a comforting illusion, though one that made them uneasy. Vigilance remained essential, but for the briefest moment, they allowed themselves to feel normal again.

With no signs of trouble, Edward eventually gave a subtle nod, signalling it was time to return to their room. Jacob followed him upstairs. Bryne arrived not long after.

He closed the door behind him and sat heavily on one of the beds, his expression grim.

"It's worse than we thought," he said. "Guards are everywhere. They're actively hunting anyone connected to the rebels. Our friends are still in the city, but they're lying low. We need to be careful."

Jacob frowned. "Why such merriment, then? It doesn't match the danger outside."

Bryne leaned forward, resting his elbows on his knees. "The patrols follow a strict schedule. People know when to expect them. That window gives the patrons here just enough time to relax… pretend things are normal."

Jacob nodded, grasping now the delicate balance the locals had learned to maintain. "Then let's enjoy this brief respite, but we must stay vigilant."

Edward agreed. "We'll rest tonight. Tomorrow, we begin our search. We need to find the rebels and make contact."

***

The next morning, they dressed and made their way downstairs to a quieter inn. Only a few early risers lingered in the common room, quietly enjoying their breakfast. After a quick meal, the trio stepped into the cool morning air and began their search through the streets of Geraldton.

Edward and Bryne, both well-practised in discretion, blended effortlessly into the crowds. They moved with quiet purpose, gathering information with such ease that Jacob hardly noticed their efforts. He, on the other hand, found himself easily distracted – torn between the awe inspired by the city's architecture and craftsmanship, and the anxiety provoked by the ever-present patrols.

As Bryne vanished once again into the throng, Jacob and Edward came upon a local stonemason working on an intricate sculpture in the street. The artisan had set up a small display area, inviting passersby to watch him work. Drawn by curiosity, they joined the modest crowd that had gathered to observe.

Jacob's gaze was fixed on the mason's hands, which moved with precision and grace. The rhythmic tapping of the chisel against stone echoed softly through the street, almost hypnotic in its steadiness. Slowly, the rough block began to take shape. It seemed to be the beginnings of a human figure, though it was still too early to discern who or what it would become. Jacob felt completely absorbed in the artistry, the noise of the street fading into the background. He could have stood there all day.

But his cousins had other plans.

"I have an address," Bryne whispered as he appeared at their side. "They're holding a meeting tonight. One of us should scout the area to make sure we have the right place. The intel is good, but with all these patrols, I don't want to take chances."

Edward nodded. "I'll check it out. You stay with Jacob, maybe head back to the inn. The patrols are already more frequent as the day fades away. The last thing we want is to get stopped by one of them."

Bryne agreed and handed over the address. Jacob followed him back reluctantly, casting a final glance at the sculpture as they left. Knowing the guards would soon begin their rounds at the inn, they decided it was safest to eat in their room and wait for Edward to return.

As they settled in, Jacob leaned against the wall, arms folded. "Do you think everywhere in Ethos is becoming like this?"

Bryne exhaled thoughtfully through his nose. "I do. For years, Elinor has faced no true challenge to her reign. I believe she assumed you had left the country with your grandfather, as there was no sign of you for quite some time. Then, when your grandfather showed up at the castle, and with her discovering that both of you, along with your mother, were still out there, I'd say she now feels cornered. She understands that the people are likely to support you and Aevah over her."

Jacob gave a bitter smile. "She's doing a good job of making us stay hidden. If we stepped out into the open, I doubt we would survive the day."

"Most likely not," Bryne agreed. "She wants all of you out of the way, rebels included. But we won't let that happen. No matter what it costs us, we'll see either you or Aevah on the throne. That's where you belong."

Jacob looked away, eyes unfocused. "Thank you... But I hope we can do it without spilling too much blood. And as for the crown, I've kind of been hoping Aevah might take it. Being king was never the dream, not even when I was young and living in the castle."

Bryne gave him a firm clap on the shoulder, a reassuring smile on his face.

"She'll make a fine queen, no doubt about it. But don't forget, you have the heart of a leader, too," Bryne said. "The people will stand behind you, just as they would Aevah. And when the fighting begins, they'll need you both."

Jacob sighed, the weight of Bryne's words settling heavily on his shoulders. "It's going to come to war, isn't it? A fight for the throne—with only her or us left standing."

Bryne's expression softened. "It will. Elinor won't allow any other outcome. As much as we long for peace, the path to it isn't always what we'd hope. Sometimes, we have to fight for the peace we want to build. And we're ready to fight for you, for Aevah, and for a future where none of us has to live in fear."

Jacob nodded slowly, absorbing the gravity of his cousin's conviction. "Then let's make sure that the future becomes a reality."

Before Bryne could respond, the door creaked open. Edward stepped inside, dusting the chill of his cloak.

"Good news," he said. "The place is secure. Grab your cloaks and let's go."

Without delay, the three cousins left the inn and made their way towards Geraldton's old warehouse district. The area was rundown and mostly abandoned, an ideal place for a rebel group to remain hidden. As they moved deeper into the district, Jacob noticed the change in atmosphere. It was quieter here – too quiet – and yet a tension hung in the air, palpable and pressing.

A few locals moved hurriedly through the crooked streets, heads down and eyes alert. They paid no obvious attention to the trio, yet their awareness was unmistakable – every glance, every step calculated.

Jacob scanned the area but spotted no patrols. Still, that didn't mean they weren't near. As they turned a corner, Edward gave a subtle nod to a young boy, no more than ten, who immediately darted into the narrow alleyways ahead, vanishing from sight.

Ensuring they weren't being followed, Edward led them down a tight, winding snicket. The path was so narrow they were forced to walk single file, with high, crumbling walls on either side, casting deep shadows that swallowed what little light remained.

Jacob's thoughts raced as they walked. The meeting ahead loomed large in his mind. Despite the stigma surrounding the word *rebels*, he didn't see them as villains. To him, they were the flicker of hope in a darkened nation – a possible solution to the unrest plaguing Ethos. He dreamed of finding allies who believed in the same vision: a kingdom reclaimed not through domination, but through unity, healing, and purpose.

As they arrived at a nondescript door beneath an old warehouse, Bryne knocked in a specific pattern: two quick taps followed by three slow ones. The door creaked open a moment later, revealing a pair of wary eyes peering out from the shadows. Recognising Bryne and Edward, the same young boy from earlier silently ushered them inside.

Jacob stepped through the threshold, his eyes scanning the dim surroundings. He realised, with a quiet sense of awe, that he was entering the rebels' secret meeting place for the first time.

The boy led them down a narrow corridor lined with flickering torches mounted on stone walls. A threadbare, dark rug stretched along the floor, guiding their steps towards a large open chamber that pulsed with life.

The air was thick with anticipation. The space buzzed with activity – men, women, and children alike filled the room, their voices low and purposeful. Some carried out preparations, setting up chairs for those who needed them; others conversed in close-knit groups, their faces set with quiet determination.

Jacob's eyes widened as he took it all in. Despite the tension, there was camaraderie. People helped one another with wide-eyed smiles and quick hands. Clusters formed to discuss strategies, while others polished weapons or sorted supplies with methodical precision. This wasn't a disorganised band of hopefuls – it was a well-structured resistance.

As they navigated through the crowd, Jacob caught sight of a makeshift stage at the far end of the chamber. A stern-faced man stood there, speaking to the gathered members. His voice carried clearly through the room, imbued with authority and purpose. Edward and Bryne led Jacob towards the back, where they found seats among the others.

Jacob glanced around, studying the faces of those who risked Elinor's wrath simply by being here. He hadn't imagined himself part of something so important, yet here he was, shoulder to shoulder with those who refused to live in fear.

His cousins, seasoned resistance members and clearly familiar with the group, introduced him to a few key figures. Each handshake was firm; each gaze filled with trust and unspoken resolve.

Then the man on the stage – Marcus, the leader of this rebel faction, as Jacob soon learned – raised a hand, and the room fell into expectant silence.

"Welcome, everyone," Marcus began, his voice calm yet commanding. "We have much to discuss tonight. The mission before us is more critical than any we've faced. The enemy grows stronger, but so do we. Together, we will reclaim our land and restore peace to our people."

A wave of cheers and murmurs of agreement rippled through the crowd, echoing Marcus's call to action.

Marcus continued, his voice steady but urgent. "We've received reports of increased operations of patrols and guards sweeping across the nation. Elinor grows more fearful of our movement by the day, and that fear makes her more dangerous than ever. We must stay vigilant and adapt our strategies to remain one step ahead."

He moved on to share updates from other rebel factions scattered throughout Ethos. Each one faced similar pressures, responding with caution and resolve. And each had come to the same inevitable conclusion: war was no longer a distant threat – it was coming.

Marcus paused, letting the gravity of his words settle over the room. Then he raised his head and scanned the gathering with a resolute gaze. "I have with us today two individuals, many of you know well. They will help lead us through the trials ahead and guide us to victory. Cecilia and Adrian, please, come forward and share your plans."

At the sound of the name *Cecilia*, Jacob's breath caught in his throat. His gaze darted to the front of the chamber, where a woman stood and began making her way towards the stage. Her hair was darker now, and time had marked her face – but there was something unmistakably familiar about the way she moved, the way she held herself.

As Cecilia began to speak, Jacob barely heard her words. His mind raced, searching memories long buried beneath the years of distance and doubt. The tone of her voice, the calm authority and the subtle warmth, it all struck him with the force of a wave.

"Mother?" he whispered, barely audible, his voice trembling with disbelief.

He rose to his feet, hardly aware of the murmurs stirring around him. His heart pounded as he moved towards the front of the room, eyes locked on the woman he had dared to hope he'd see again.

"Mother?" he said again, louder this time.

Cecilia turned at the sound of his voice. Her eyes widened in shock, and she stepped off the stage slowly, as if approaching a ghost. Her hand lifted to her mouth, then reached forward, trembling.

Standing before her, Jacob felt her fingers brush his cheek – gentle, tentative, as if confirming he was real. Tears welled in her eyes as she whispered, "Jacob? Is it really you?"

He nodded, his voice breaking. "It's me, Mother. I'm here. I've missed you so much."

In the next moment, he collapsed into her arms. She held him tightly, fiercely, as though afraid that letting go might make him vanish.

The room had fallen utterly silent. Rebels stood frozen, witnessing the reunion with quiet reverence. Years of separation dissolved in that one embrace, and mother and son clung to each other, their tears speaking words they couldn't yet say.

The rebels, who had been whispering among themselves just moments before, now stood in solemn silence. Some wiped tears from their eyes, visibly moved by the powerful reunion between mother and son.

Marcus stepped forward, his voice laced with reverence. "Prince Jacob, your presence here is an honour. We have long awaited this moment."

Still holding his mother's hand, Jacob gave a small nod. "Thank you, Marcus. I'm here to help, but… seeing my mother again—it changes everything."

Cecilia, her gaze shimmering with pride and emotion, added gently, "We've been apart for too long. There will be time later for politics. For now, let us simply be."

The room quieted once more, a shared respect settling over the gathering. Cecilia scanned the faces in the chamber, searching for someone else. "Where is Aevah?" she asked, her voice edged with concern.

Jacob smiled. "She's safe, Mother. Aevah is searching for the next crystal shard. She's with Isabella, and they're travelling through the mountains."

Cecilia exhaled slowly, relief softening her expression. "Good. Come, we have much to talk about."

She led him away from the main gathering, allowing Marcus to resume the meeting with the rebels. At the back of the room, she gestured to a small seating area, settling into a wooden chair as Jacob took the one beside her.

"Jacob, it's been so long," she said quietly, still studying his face. "I can hardly believe you're truly here."

He nodded, his voice thick with emotion. "I've missed you so much, Mother. Every day. Aevah and I both. We never gave up hope that we would see you again."

Tears welled in Cecilia's eyes as she reached out, taking his hand in hers. "I thought of you both every day, too. The hope of seeing you again was what kept me going through the darkest times."

Jacob squeezed her hand gently, comforted by her touch, the warmth and love that had been absent for far too long. "We're together now. There's so much to catch up on… and so much to do."

Cecilia nodded, her expression growing resolute. "Yes. But for this moment, let's just cherish being here, together."

She tilted her head slightly, her eyes softening. "You look so much like your father. When I first saw you standing there… for a heartbeat, I thought you were him."

Jacob's heart swelled as he looked at his mother, a soft smile touching his lips. "I wish he were still here," he said quietly. "I miss him every day. But I know he'd be happy, knowing we're together again." He paused, his voice dropping to a murmur. "I'll do everything I can to make him proud, Mother."

Tears glistened in Cecilia's eyes as she whispered, "Oh, Jacob… he would be so proud of you—and of Aevah. Both of you."

They sat in silence for a while, hands clasped tightly, letting the moment settle. The hum of the meeting faded into the background as they focused on each other, exchanging pieces of the lives they'd lived apart. Every word shared was steeped in joy, relief, and the ache of lost time.

"Cecilia." A soft voice broke through the moment. Adrian stood behind her, resting a gentle hand on her shoulder. "The gathering is over. I'm heading out for a bit, but I'll find you later."

Jacob watched him leave, eyes following Adrian as he slipped out with the last of the rebels. Each one gave quiet nods or words of parting, clearly aware that mother and son needed this time. It was a silent show of respect, and no one lingered.

Once Adrian was out of earshot, Jacob turned to his mother, his voice low, tinged with unease. "Is that the same Adrian who betrayed you and Father?"

Cecilia let out a slow sigh, the emotion in her eyes shifting to a weary calm. "Yes. It is."

Jacob's brow furrowed. "How can you trust him after everything?"

"Because people can change, Jacob. And Adrian has. He saw the truth while working for Elinor. He saw things he could no longer ignore. Adrian recognised her for who she really was. Since we reconnected, he's done nothing but prove his loyalty. I believe in him completely."

Jacob shook his head slowly, still grappling with the past. "I just don't want to see you hurt again."

Her hand settled gently on his arm. "I know. And I'm grateful for your concern. But I know what I'm doing."

He gave a small nod, though the unease didn't leave him. He trusted her judgement, but the memories of betrayal lingered. Around them, the last traces of the meeting vanished, leaving the room quiet.

Edward and Bryne were the last ones to leave, offering their goodbyes with understanding in their eyes. They promised to return the next day, giving Jacob space to reconnect with his mother – something he deeply appreciated.

Jacob and his mother spoke well into the night, sharing fragments of their stories until exhaustion overtook him.

Eventually, Cecilia rose and led him to a small room, promising to resume their conversation in the morning.

That night, Jacob drifted to sleep with a full heart, comforted by her presence and happier than he had been in a long time.

Chapter 2

Partings and Promises

Being reunited with Jacob was everything Cecilia had dreamed of and more. He had grown into a striking young man, the very image of his father, James. From the tousled mess of his hair to his quiet mannerisms, the way he moved and carried himself, even the nervous tapping of his fingers – it was as if James had returned to her through their son.

The sight of him filled her with joy, but it also pierced her heart. So much time had been lost. Not a day had passed that she didn't wish things had turned out differently. The long years apart weighed heavily on her, but seeing the man Jacob had become offered some solace. He was kind, thoughtful, strong – everything she had hoped for. And she owed that, in part, to her father.

Her father.

A fresh wave of sorrow crept in at the thought of him. All those years, he had hidden the twins, kept them safe from Elinor's reach. But in doing so, he had also kept them from her. Cecilia had wrestled with that decision, carrying a quiet anger towards him, not because she blamed him, but because of the cost. He had done what he thought was best under the circumstances.

When they last parted, things had still felt strained, but they had made peace. He knew she loved him, and she clung to that truth now more than ever. Believing anything else was unbearable, especially knowing she would never see him again. His recent death at Elinor's hand was a wound that had yet to scab over. It bled with every breath, a loss too vast to measure.

Sitting alone in the silence of the night, Cecilia let the grief come. Tears streamed down her cheeks as she remembered her father's strength, his steadfast love, and the final, selfless act of bravery. She bowed her head, whispering a quiet promise into the darkness – to honour his memory, to keep fighting for her family, and to see Elinor's tyranny brought to an end.

Her thoughts then drifted to Aevah. Oh, how she wished her daughter were here to share in this moment. Seeing Jacob again had filled a hollow space in her heart, but Aevah's absence left another aching void. The yearning to hold her, to see her face, to tell her everything, was overwhelming.

The door creaked open, breaking her reverie. Adrian stepped into the room with careful steps, mindful of the quiet.

"How did it go?" he asked softly, settling into bed beside her.

She turned to him, a faint smile playing on her lips. "It was wonderful. He's grown so much… and he looks just like James."

Adrian reached out, his hand finding hers, his touch warm and reassuring. "I'm glad you had that time. You both needed it."

Cecilia nodded, her voice wistful. "I just wish Aevah could be here, too."

He squeezed her hand gently. "I know. But you'll be together again. It's only a matter of time."

She leaned into him, allowing herself to rest in the comfort of his presence. "Thank you, Adrian. For everything."

He kissed her forehead, his voice low. "Get some sleep. Tomorrow is going to be another busy day."

***

As the first light of dawn filtered through the small window, Cecilia lay in bed, wrapped in a quiet tangle of thoughts and feelings. A mixture of anticipation and unease stirred within her, a soft hum beneath her skin. She turned her head to look at Adrian, still asleep beside her. His face, serene and unguarded, was softened by sleep and framed by a week's worth of stubble that lent him a rugged charm.

She reached out, her fingers brushing gently along the contours of his face. The coarse texture of his beard prickled against her skin, grounding her in the present moment. Her touch was light, reverent – part tenderness, part wonder – as if she were memorising a part of him, she already knew by heart.

Adrian stirred, his eyelids fluttering open until his gaze met hers. A drowsy smile tugged at his lips.

"Good morning," he murmured, his voice thick with sleep.

"Good morning," she whispered back, her voice barely audible. "I was just lying here, thinking about how much has changed… and how grateful I am to have you by my side."

He reached for her hand and brought it to his lips, pressing a kiss into her knuckles. His touch was warm, grounding, as always. "No, love," he said, voice hushed and full of feeling, "it is I who am blessed. Not a day passes that I don't thank the divine spirit for bringing you into my life."

Cecilia leaned in, brushing her lips against his in a slow, lingering kiss. Their foreheads met as they breathed each other in.

"You are my everything, Cecilia," Adrian said, his voice low and earnest. "You have my heart, my sword, my soul. In a world torn by chaos, you are my reason, my purpose, my light. Without you, I am a knight without a cause. With you, I am whole."

Her breath caught in her throat, a rush of warmth blooming in her chest. She placed her hand on the back of his neck and pulled him close, her lips capturing his with aching urgency. He responded in kind, deepening the kiss as his hands slid around her waist, holding her tightly, as if to keep the world at bay.

Time seemed to pause. The walls of the room faded, leaving only the two of them – limbs entwined, hearts beating in harmony, the quiet magic of morning wrapped around their bodies like silk.

Then, a sudden knock at the door shattered the stillness.

They broke apart, breathless and wide-eyed, the spell broken. Reality came crashing back, reminding them that outside their sanctuary, the world was still waiting.

"Just a moment," Adrian called out, his voice muffled as he leaned over to search for his pants.

Cecilia was quicker. She moved with practised grace, wrapping herself in a nearby robe and securing the sash around her waist without taking her eyes off Adrian. With a steadying breath, she approached the door and cracked it open, peering through the narrow gap.

"Tobey, what can I do for you?" she asked, her voice warm but alert.

The young boy stood outside, shifting from foot to foot. "Sorry t' botha ye, me lady, but Prince Jacob's up and lookin' for ye."

"Thank you. We'll be right down," she replied with a kind smile, then closed the door softly behind her.

Turning back, she found Adrian nearly dressed, fastening his belt and sliding his sword into its sheath.

"Looks like it's time for breakfast," he said, tucking in his shirt before stepping over to her. He cupped her face in his hands and kissed her forehead gently. "I'll meet you downstairs. I want a word with Marcus before he heads out."

Cecilia nodded, watching him leave before turning to prepare for the day herself. The quiet intimacy they had shared would have to wait.

She checked her reflection in the small oval mirror hanging on the wall, brushing her hair and tucking a few stray strands behind her ears. Once satisfied, she left the room and made her way downstairs.

She found Adrian and Marcus deep in conversation at the bottom of the stairwell. As she approached, the two men concluded their discussion, and Marcus gave her a polite nod before striding off to attend to his own errands.

Adrian offered a small smile and gestured ahead, falling into step beside her as they walked through the hallway together.

But with each step closer to the dining hall, Cecilia felt the muscles in her shoulders begin to tense. Her thoughts drifted back to Jacob's unease the previous day – the wariness in his voice when he had asked about Adrian. Given Adrian's former allegiance to Elinor, Jacob had every reason to be cautious.

Cecilia knew better than anyone how far Adrian had come – how much he had changed. She believed in his redemption. But belief wasn't enough. Not this time.

It would come down to whether Jacob could trust him, too.

She cast a glance at Adrian, who walked beside her with his usual composed demeanour. His face remained unreadable, offering no hint of what he might be feeling – a trait befitting a seasoned knight. Still, it annoyed her, as she hadn't learned many of his tells that might give away his emotions.

When they entered the dining hall, they found Jacob and his cousins already seated, joined by a few others who had been present the night before. Conversations hushed momentarily as the pair approached, then resumed in a low murmur as Cecilia and Adrian stepped to the side, allowing them to finish their breakfast undisturbed.

Cecilia immediately sensed the tension radiating from Jacob. Though he didn't speak, the way his eyes flicked towards Adrian between bites of porridge didn't go unnoticed.

"Good morning," she greeted the room, her tone calm and deliberate.

"Aunt Cecilia," Edward said with an easy grin, offering her a nod. "It's been a while."

"Far too long," she replied, returning the gesture with a soft smile. Her gaze shifted to Bryne, who stood and extended his hand.

"Bryne," she said, taking his hand in a firm shake. "It's good to see you."

"And you," he replied, his grip strong. "Last time we crossed paths, I believe I was being scolded for sampling too much wine I had no business touching—followed by a rather dramatic scene involving me throwing up at your elegant dinner party."

Cecilia let out a warm laugh. "Yes, I remember that night well. Your mother was particularly unimpressed with you, if I recall correctly."

She touched his arm gently, the laughter fading into something more solemn. "I was sorry to hear of their deaths."

"And we for you," Bryne said with genuine sympathy. "Uncle James was a good man. So was George. None of them deserved the deaths they received."

She nodded slowly, her eyes clouded with shared grief. "Thank you, Bryne. It's been a difficult time for all of us."

Adrian stepped closer and rested a reassuring hand on her shoulder. The quiet support didn't go unnoticed. Edward stepped forward, eyeing the gesture with careful curiosity before extending a hand to Adrian.

"I don't believe we've been formally introduced," Edward said. "I've heard a fair bit about you, some good and some not. But I'm told you're on our side now."

Adrian took his hand with a firm shake. "It's nice to finally meet you, Edward. I understand your reservations, and I'm here to prove my loyalty."

Edward nodded, his expression turning grave. "We'll be watching. Actions speak louder than words."

Cecilia turned towards Jacob, who had been watching the exchange with a guarded mix of curiosity and caution. Her heart swelled as she crossed the room to him – pride and concern mingling in equal measure.

"Jacob, my dear," she said softly, reaching up to brush her fingers against his cheek.

Jacob smiled, warmth flickering in his eyes as she pulled him into a tender embrace. When they parted, she stepped aside and gestured towards Adrian.

"There's someone I'd like you to officially meet."

Jacob's eyes narrowed as he studied Adrian, his expression unreadable but tense. "I've heard of you," he said slowly. "My mother speaks highly of you now, but I also remember the stories. The betrayal."

Adrian stepped forward, his posture steady, gaze unwavering. "You're right to be cautious. I betrayed people I cared about, and that's not something I can undo. But I've changed. I've seen the truth of who Elinor is, and I'm here because I believe in this fight. I don't expect your trust—I intend to earn it."

Cecilia watched the silent tension stretch between them, her son's inner conflict visible in the tightness of his jaw and the flicker in his eyes. He stood at a crossroads, between history and hope.

At last, Jacob extended his hand. "I trust my mother. That's why I'm giving you this chance. I hope you won't make me regret it."

Adrian grasped his hand firmly, nodding. "You won't. I promise."

Finally, Adrian and Cecilia sat down for breakfast, and the mood began to shift. Conversations started to flow, and the group shared memories of the past. The tension of Adrian's presence gradually eased as the cousins – Edward and Bryne – lightened the atmosphere by recounting tales of youthful mischief. Most stories centred around Bryne's antics, inevitably dragging all three siblings into trouble. Laughter echoed through the hall, softening the edges of the morning.

Talk eventually turned towards the previous night's meeting. Adrian quietly shared with Cecilia the rebels' plan to set up a base camp at the old Mines of Grode. Intel had confirmed what many feared: their situation was deteriorating faster than expected. Elinor's attacks were becoming more frequent and more destructive, leaving entire towns in ruins, their people broken in body and spirit.

Worse still, Elinor already held two of the four shards. If she claimed the remaining two, the consequences would be catastrophic. Cecilia's expression hardened with resolve as Adrian outlined Marcus's strategy. The mines would offer both protection and proximity. She agreed wholeheartedly – this was the right move.

It was then that Jacob turned to her, his face serious, his decision already made. "It's time for me to leave."

The words pierced her. Their reunion had been brief, precious, and everything she had longed for, but the reality of their mission was pulling them apart once more. She looked into Jacob's eyes, seeing the determination and resolve that mirrored her own.

"Jacob," she whispered, stepping close. "I just got you back. It's too soon to lose you again."

He took her hands, his grip firm but gentle. "I know. But we all have a part to play. I have to find the last crystal shard. It's the only way we can defeat Elinor and bring peace to our land."

Tears welled in her eyes, but she nodded. "Just promise me you'll be careful."

"I promise," Jacob said, his voice filled with conviction. "I'll come find you in the mines once I have the last shard, and with Aevah. We'll be together again soon."

He embraced her one final time before turning to Edward and Bryne, who were already preparing to leave. The cousins exchanged nods of determination, the weight of their task resting heavily on their shoulders.

Cecilia stood silently as the three of them mounted their horses. The ache in her chest deepened with each step they took away from her. Adrian moved beside her and pulled her close, anchoring her in the moment.

"He'll be alright," he murmured. "Jacob's strong and capable. He'll find the shard and come back to us."

She nodded, wiping a tear from her cheek. "I know. It's hard to let go. I just hoped we'd have more time. Even a day or two longer."

Adrian wrapped his arms around her, offering solace. "No matter how long, it would never have been enough. Best he leaves now and completes his part. Plus, we have a lot of work to do here. Jacob and Aevah will need us to be ready for when they return."

Drawing a steadying breath, Cecilia straightened her spine. "You're right. We have to stay focused and keep moving forward. We must prepare."

Chapter 3

Charting Fate's Course

Elinor was still adjusting to life as both a new mother and queen of the realm. Her newborn son, Eadric – the heir to the throne – was only six weeks old, and she was still getting used to the relentless demands of motherhood. Despite the sleepless nights and the constant care he required, Elinor remained steadfast in her commitment to her royal duties.

After her conversation with Liora and the revelation of the so-called prophecy, Elinor knew she had to act swiftly. The high priestesses were clearly aligning against her, determined to bring her down and ensure the prophecy – if it even existed – came to pass. She had never heard of such a prophecy until now, and its sudden emergence seemed far too convenient, suitably timed to rally support to the rebels' cause.

Regardless of its truth, she couldn't afford to lower her guard. She had already begun devising strategies to strengthen her forces and set traps for her enemies. Whether the prophecy was real or fabricated, Elinor would fight for her throne and for her family with everything she had.

Cradling Eadric in her arms, she gazed down at his innocent face.

"You will grow up to be a powerful ruler," she whispered, her voice filled with determination. "I will make certain no one threatens your future."

Bradley entered the room then, his face softening at the sight of them. He stepped forward and gently took the baby from her arms, holding his son with pride.

"He's going to be a great king one day," he said softly.

Elinor nodded. "Yes, he will. But we must ensure his future is secure."

Sensing the weight behind her words, Bradley placed Eadric in his crib and turned to face her fully. "What do you need me to do?"

Elinor moved to the nearby table and gestured to a map spread across its surface, pointing to several key locations.

"We need to reinforce our defences and locate the rebels' hideouts. Then we capture my niece and nephew, Cecilia and Adrian. Liora is taking care of Aevah for us, but Jacob is ours to find and seize."

"I'll have our spies watching Almire closely. The moment he's spotted, they'll move in. And what about Cecilia and Adrian, do you want them apprehended or killed?" he asked.

"Oh, alive… definitely. But we'll need a tracker. One skilled enough to bring them in without issue. Adrian won't go down without a fight, and Cecilia is far more cunning than I once believed."

Bradley nodded, his eyes returning to the map. "I'll see to it. Our forces will be ready. No one will stand in our way."

Elinor's mind spun with possibilities. Which lords still stood by her, and which might need… persuasion? She still held Lord Stone's daughter captive, a useful piece of leverage to keep him in line. Others, like Christopher Malins and the Roberts, were dependable allies. The Bennetts, however, remained uncertain.

Stone's loyalty was secure as long as his daughter lived. Bishop would never side with her unless she found a way to change his mind. Bradley's own house, Woodlock, of course, was unwavering. She turned to find him watching her intently. He knew her well and could almost hear the calculations running through her mind.

"We need to send word to the lords we trust. Tell them to begin their preparations immediately. I want eyes and ears in every town and forest, hunting and killing any rebel factions that form. And tell the Roberts to keep watch as well for Jacob. He is to be brought here, alive."

"And those we don't trust?" Bradley asked.

"Remind them that defying the crown is treason, and that treason will cost their lives," Elinor replied coldly.

Her thoughts drifted to William Bennett and his son, Galrick. They lived near where Aevah would be travelling and could serve as a perfect tool – aid her, then betray her at just the right moment. Once Aevah retrieved the crystal shard, Elinor could simply swoop in and claim the prize. Why risk the treacherous mountains herself when Aevah could do the hard work?

The idea was too perfect to ignore. A personal visit to the Bennetts would reinforce the consequences of betrayal. Sending Galrick with her spies and Liora to shadow Aevah would ensure the girl never slipped from her grasp again. Elinor smiled at Bradley.

"Start packing, my love. We're about to take a little trip."

Given how long travel by carriage would take, and how much she despised the experience after enduring it while pregnant, Elinor chose to sail instead, much to Bradley's satisfaction. They would board a ship at Burcord Wharf and disembark at Halls Creek Harbour, using lesser-known docks at each end to reduce travel time to no more than a week, weather permitting.

She also intended to pay a surprise visit to the local temple, one of the lesser ones. After everything Liora had revealed, Elinor was eager to see what truths, or lies, might still be hidden within its walls.

She had no intention of revealing that she already knew their plans – it would be far more satisfying to watch them squirm beneath her gaze. Her presence alone would be enough to make them uneasy. Once they sensed the power radiating from her, they would understand just how formidable she had become once more. And while they whispered in corners and cast suspicious glances, she would quietly sow the seeds of doubt within the temples.

Only one of them could restore her full power through the bonding ceremony. The true entertainment would come from watching the suspicion spread – watching them begin to question one another, slowly realising that one among them had betrayed the rest.

Oh yes, this trip was going to be delightful.

Power stirred within her, responding to her anticipation. No, she wasn't yet as strong as she had been when High Priestess Zara conducted the original ceremony – Zara had had a full circle of priestesses to assist her. Now, with only Liora, the ritual had been more limited. Still, the bond they managed to forge had granted her more than enough strength. She could feel it in every breath, every heartbeat – magic pulsed through her veins, vibrant and ready. Nearly as powerful as before.

A sudden cry from Eadric pulled her from her thoughts.

She crossed the room to his crib and gently lifted him, immediately recognising the hunger in his tiny wails. Settling into the rocking chair, she began to nurse him, all thoughts of vengeance and strategy dissolving as she gazed into his ocean-blue eyes, so like his father's.

As he fed peacefully, she rocked slowly, humming a soft lullaby, allowing herself to fully absorb the stillness of the moment. Just mother and son. Her heart swelled with something far more powerful than any magic: love.

***

By morning, the castle was alive with motion as preparations for the royal voyage were well underway. Servants bustled through corridors, loading trunks and securing last-minute arrangements. Though the ride to the harbour was brief, the sense of occasion hung heavily in the air. Bradley's excitement was palpable – he practically radiated enthusiasm. Elinor, while pleased to be travelling by sea, didn't quite share his passion. Still, she indulged his energy with quiet amusement.

Once everything was ready, Elinor stepped into the waiting carriage with Eadric nestled on her knee. Bradley followed, his expression alight with anticipation, and Lady Chloe climbed in after them. A contingent of royal guards flanked the carriage, riding ahead and behind as they made their way to the harbour where the newest addition to the royal fleet awaited them, the *Sovereign.*

As they approached the dock, the ship came into view, an imposing and elegant silhouette against the pale autumn sky. Its tall masts reached high, sails already catching the morning breeze like wings poised for flight. The hull, crafted from polished oak, gleamed in the sunlight, reflecting golden hues across the water. At the bow stood a masterfully carved figure of the divine spirit, arms raised in eternal guidance. Encircling the figure were intricate engravings of stars and constellations, a nod to the vessel's celestial namesake and its promise to navigate by the night sky.

The deck teemed with activity. Sailors moved with practised precision, coiling ropes and hauling barrels of provisions aboard. Every motion was part of a well-rehearsed routine, fluid and orderly, the crew operating like a single organism.

Bradley, ever the sailor at heart, could hardly contain himself. The call of the sea ran deep in his blood, and being near it again seemed to awaken something in him. He paused to take in the ship's fine craftsmanship, his eyes scanning every beam and sail with admiration, before launching into a spirited conversation with the crew.

Elinor, holding Eadric in her arms, watched him fondly. Sailing, to her, was simply a means of travel, practical and efficient. She didn't share Bradley's awe, but she let him enjoy it all the same. With Eadric cradled close, she ascended the gangplank to the deck, where the captain greeted her with a respectful bow.

"Welcome aboard, the *Sovereign*, Your Majesty," he said. "It is an honour to have you and your family aboard."

Elinor inclined her head graciously. "Thank you, Captain. We are eager to begin our journey. How have the seas treated you with the autumn winds?"

"The waters have been kind, Your Majesty," he replied. "The winds favour us—gods willing, it will be a swift and smooth voyage."

Bradley joined them then, with Lady Chloe at Elinor's side. The captain led the party towards their quarters, and Bradley resumed his steady stream of questions, his curiosity unrelenting until Elinor cleared her throat pointedly.

"These are your rooms," the captain announced, opening the door to reveal a spacious, elegantly furnished cabin. Rich tapestries adorned the walls, and the furniture was upholstered with fine fabrics. Several oval windows overlooked the sea, and the gentle sway of the ship was both soothing and rhythmic.

Bradley's eyes lit up as he stepped inside. "This is wonderful," he said with genuine warmth. "Thank you for such fine accommodations."

"It is our honour, Your Majesties," the captain replied with a bow. "Should you require anything, do not hesitate to ask."

"We appreciate your hospitality," Elinor said and gave him an appreciative nod.

Once the captain left, Bradley turned to her with the grin of a boy who had just received his favourite toy. "I can't wait to explore the ship. It's been too long since I've felt the sea beneath me."

Elinor chuckled. "Just don't get too carried away. This isn't your crew, remember. I'd rather you didn't irritate them within the first hour."

"I won't, I promise," he said, scooping Eadric into his arms. "Now then, my boy—how about Daddy shows you around this magnificent vessel? The sea is in your veins, you know. One day we'll sail together, and you'll feel the freedom of the open water for yourself."

Beaming with pride, he swept out of the cabin, leaving Elinor and Chloe behind. Chloe had already begun unpacking their belongings, arranging garments and supplies with a practised touch.

"This is going to be quite the adventure," she said with a smile.

"That it is," Elinor replied.

As the *Sovereign* cast off, the castle and harbour slowly faded from view, swallowed by the horizon. The open sea stretched out endlessly before them, its vastness exhilarating. Standing on deck, Elinor let the cool breeze tangle in her hair, inhaling the sharp, salty scent of the ocean. The rhythmic crash of waves against the hull was steady and calming – a lullaby of motion and promise.

She turned her gaze to Bradley, who was already pointing out various features of the ship to Eadric with the animation of a man in his element. Elinor's heart softened at the sight of them. Her world. Her future. Her strength.

There was nothing she wouldn't do to protect them.

As the ship sailed steadily into the unknown, Elinor closed her eyes for a brief moment and whispered a silent vow to herself – to guard her family, to defend her crown, and to face whatever lay ahead with unshakable resolve.

***

The first few days at sea proved to be an adjustment for Elinor. The ship offered a rare and unfamiliar peace, far removed from the relentless demands of royal life. For once, no one approached her with documents to sign or decisions to make every waking hour. The constant hum of duty had quieted, replaced by the rhythmic lull of waves and the soft creak of timber.

Yet, the tranquillity came with its own form of confinement. With no land in sight and only the boundless expanse of sea and sky stretching in all directions, the freedom she had longed for began to feel like a gilded cage. The open ocean, soothing at first, slowly pressed in, reminding her of just how far they were from everything and everyone.

Bradley, on the other hand, was loving every minute. The sea invigorated him. Though a king consort, he had thrown himself into life aboard the ship without hesitation. From dawn until dusk, he worked the deck with the crew, his hands calloused by rope and salt, his spirit lifted by the fresh air and honest labour. He welcomed the shift from politics to physical tasks, thriving among the camaraderie of the sailors, relishing the purpose that came with each chore.

Elinor often found herself watching him from the upper deck. She had never seen him like this before – this version of him, shaped by the sea, belonged to another life, one she had only heard about from stories of his younger days working his father's merchant routes. Now, seeing him move with such confidence and ease – adjusting sails, tying off lines, offering quick directions to the crew – was nothing short of mesmerising. And, truth be told, more than a little arousing.

There was something about the way he held himself here: assured, capable, and quietly commanding. He didn't posture or boast; he simply *was*. It stirred something in her that courtly charm never had.

She watched as he scaled the rigging with agile precision, climbing from the deck to the mainmast to fix a jammed pulley. His fingers moved deftly over the ropes and gears, securing them with practised efficiency. Once satisfied with his repair, he slid down the mast with a flourish, landing on the deck in a crouch before straightening up and flashing her a grin – cheeky and triumphant, fully aware of her gaze.

"Enjoying the show?" he called out, brushing his hands together.

"Oh, just a little," she replied with a smirk. "My husband, the sailor, working hard and playing it up for his queen."

With a dramatic sweep of his arm, he bowed low, his voice full of mock gallantry. "Your words honour me, my queen. But if you keep looking at me like that, I may have to start charging for the view."

She arched a brow, amusement dancing in her eyes. "Charging, are we? Has the swashbuckling sailor now dreamed of wealth? What's next—bottling sea air and selling it to wide-eyed traders at the port?"

He chuckled, the wind catching in his hair. "Not just any sea air, my love. Only the finest, collected during a full tide under the watchful eyes of the divine herself. I'll call it... *Ocean Essence*."

Her laughter broke across the deck, warm and melodic. "My husband, the entrepreneur. Truly, your imagination knows no bounds. Still, I think I'll keep the sailor over the salesman, if it's all the same to you."

He stepped closer, his grin widening as he held her gaze. "Ah, but why choose when you can have both? Now tell me, my queen—did I earn any extra points for fixing the pulley *and* managing to look dashing while doing it?"

She leaned in slightly, her voice low and teasing. "Oh, you earned all the points, my charming sailor. But don't celebrate too soon. The real test is yet to come. Let's see if you can keep them when the seas turn rough. You'll have to work twice as hard then."

He leaned in close, his voice dropping to a conspiratorial whisper. "Twice as hard? For you, my queen, I'd work thrice as hard. Though something tells me you'll be watching every moment."

Elinor gave him a playful shove, rolling her eyes. He stumbled back with exaggerated flair, clutching his chest as if struck by a moral blow.

"Ah! My queen wounds me not with a blade, but with her very hand! Show mercy!" he cried, his theatrical despair betrayed by the grin tugging at his lips.

She shook her head, laughter glinting in her eyes. "Oh, please. If that rattled you, how would you survive an actual battle?"

Straightening, he winked. "Battles are nothing. It's your sharp tongue and deadly shoves that truly test a man's mettle."

"Keep talking, sailor," she said, stepping closer, her voice low and teasing. "And I'll show you just how sharp my tongue can be."

He raised his hands in mock surrender. "Alright, alright! I concede. But just so you know, I endure it all gladly—for you, my queen."

She turned away with another roll of her eyes, but the smile she tried to hide gave her away. "You're impossible," she muttered.

Before she could take another step, he caught her by the waist and pulled her against him. His lips found hers in a firm, possessive kiss that left her breathless and weak at the knees. When he finally pulled back, his eyes gleamed with mischief.

"And you love me for it," he said, voice husky with confidence, before releasing her and striding away with that maddeningly self-assured swagger.

Elinor stood frozen, heart pounding, her fingers brushing her lips, still tingling from his kiss. Her cheeks flushed as she stared after him.

"Where do you think you're going?" she called, trying to sound stern but failing miserably.

He turned, tossed her a wink. "Follow me and find out."

Without hesitation, she hiked up her skirts and rushed after him. "Wait for me!" she shouted, laughter bubbling up as excitement and curiosity spurred her onward.

He glanced back just long enough to catch the sight of her chasing him, his grin stretching wide as he picked up the pace.

"You'll have to move faster than that," he teased, his voice carrying easily over the rush of the waves and the rhythmic creak of the ship's wooden frame.

Determined, Elinor quickened her pace, nearly tripping over a loose plank before catching herself with a muttered curse. She chased him through a narrow passageway, weaving past crates and barrels that carried the scents of salt, spice, and sun-warmed wood. The farther they went, the dimmer the light grew, until he led her into a secluded alcove tucked beneath the bustle of the main deck.

A single lantern flickered in the small space, casting warm, wavering light over a hammock suspended between two beams and a rough bench carved from an old plank. The air was cooler down here, the quiet hum of the sea and wood groaning in harmony – a lullaby of the ship itself.

Bradley turned to face her, mischief dancing in his eyes as he leaned against the wall with a casual ease that only made her heart beat faster. "Thought you might appreciate a spot where we could steal a moment alone."

Elinor glanced around the cosy little hideaway. Her cheeks flushed from the chase. "You're full of surprises, aren't you?"

"Only for you," he murmured, stepping close and gently brushing a strand of hair from her face. "I'm glad you followed."

Her smile came unbidden, despite the warmth still lingering on her cheeks. "You could've slowed down a bit," she muttered, half in jest.

He laughed, the sound low and smooth. "Where's the fun in that?"

His lips found hers in a soft, lingering kiss before trailing down her neck in slow, deliberate movements. Her breath caught, the intimacy both achingly familiar and electrifyingly new. A spark lit inside her – a sharp, heady rush of sensation that sent her heart racing. It had been so long since they'd had a moment like this – just the two of them, unburdened by courtly obligations or the cries of their infant son.

Here, in this hidden sliver of quiet, it was as though time had paused. The world narrowed to the warmth of his breath, the press of his hands, the steady thrum of want building beneath her skin. She clutched the edge of the bench to steady herself as his lips continued their path, slow and reverent.

It wasn't just desire; it was the ache of longing she hadn't realised had taken root. She yearned not only for his touch, but for the simple freedom to just *be* – not a queen, not a mother, but Elinor. His Elinor.

She tilted her head, granting him better access, her breath hitching.

"Bradley," she whispered, the name trembling from her lips, carrying all the emotion she couldn't bring herself to speak aloud – love, need, gratitude, and something deep and unspoken that pulsed just beneath the surface.

When he finally paused, drawing back just enough to meet her gaze, Elinor saw her own longing reflected in his eyes. Mischief still lingered there, flickering at the edges, but it was softened by something deeper – a raw tenderness that stripped away titles and responsibilities. For a moment, they were simply two people, yearning for each other beyond the weight of crowns and the lullabies of sleepless nights.

Her cheeks burned under his stare, but she didn't look away. "I've missed this," she confessed softly, her voice barely louder than the creak of the ship.

His hand rose to her face, brushing her cheek with a featherlight touch. "Me too, my queen. More than you know."

A shiver coursed through her as his hands moved lower, exploring with a practised, reverent touch that reignited every dormant nerve. She closed her eyes, allowing herself to sink into the quiet thrill of it – of being wanted, seen, known. His fingers slid upwards, teasing her clit, then moved in and out of her with a gentle ease. Her hands clutched the fabric at his chest, her breath growing shallow, caught between pleasure and disbelief that they had stolen this moment for themselves.

"Bradley," she moaned, his name a thread of sound wound tight with feeling.

He responded without words, only movement – faster, more deliberate – as if he knew every part of her body by heart. She clung to him, her breath faltering with each wave that surged through her. Her body moved with his, a rhythm older than words, older than vows, bringing her close to orgasm.

When release took her, it did so completely, leaving her trembling, breathless, and smiling against his shoulder. "Wow," she murmured, still wrapped in the afterglow, leaning into his warmth.

He dipped to her ear, brushing a kiss there that made her shiver again. "I need you," he whispered, low and urgent. His hands found her waist, fingers slipping beneath the layers of fabric as he pressed closer. She turned and placed her palms firmly on the bench in front of them.

"Then take me. I'm yours."

At her words, he did just that. She gasped as he first entered her. Her fingers gripped the bench, the rough wood grounding her as everything else melted away. Each thrust was a wave, building and crashing inside her, carrying her further and further into a sea of sensation. Her moans mingled with his grunts, a primal duet echoing in the quiet room. Time dissolved, leaving only the intense, shared experience, the friction of skin on skin, the breathless urgency of their joining.

When it finally ended, they lay spent, limbs entwined, the silence punctuated only by their ragged breathing and the pounding of their hearts.

Elinor traced slow, absent circles on Bradley's skin, her breathing gradually steadying. The ship creaked softly around them, the sea murmuring against its sides.

For now, all that mattered was this – just them, lost in the fragile stillness of the moment.

Chapter 4

Stepping into the Storm

As pleasant as the journey had been, Elinor was still grateful to hear that the ship had docked – it was time to return to solid ground. The gentle sway of the vessel had proved vexing at times, leaving her queasy for stretches of the journey – a sensation she wasn't usually prone to when sailing.

Bradley extended his hand to help her disembark. The bustling port teemed with activity, yet their destination lay beyond the immediate chaos. A carriage awaited them, ready to take them to the local temple several hours inland.

Once everyone had disembarked, Elinor, Bradley, Lady Chloe and Eadric settled into the carriage, while her guards rode ahead and behind. The overland journey was a welcome change from the confines of the ship. Through the window, the landscape unfurled like a living painting, brushed with hues of red, orange, and yellow. Trees stood nearly bare, their fallen leaves forming a patchwork beneath them.

Though one could traverse the world by sea, days spent staring at endless blue sky and water, broken only by the distant outline of a coast, could feel monotonous – like going nowhere at all. On land, however, the world revealed itself with every turn. And so, it did now.

Cresting a hill after a brief ride, the temple came into view, its spires rising proudly into the sky. The carriage slowed as they approached, and when it drew to a stop before the entrance, no one came to greet them.

Elinor's lips curled in delight. Her unannounced arrival would surely throw them into disarray.

"Let's make our presence known, shall we?" she said.

Without waiting for assistance, she leapt from the carriage and strode towards the temple doors. Bradley followed close behind, with Lady Chloe carrying Eadric in her arms. Elinor's guards hurried to stay ahead of her, but they struggled to match her brisk pace. As she ascended the ancient steps, they scrambled to keep up, reaching the top just as she grasped the heavy wooden door knocker and struck it with a loud *thunk*.

She stepped back and waited, a satisfied smile on her face, ready to surprise whoever answered. She held tightly to her power, letting it radiate from her – an unspoken warning of what she had become, thanks to one of them. Her instincts proved correct. When the door opened, the young priestess who stood on the threshold turned pale at the sight of her.

"Good afternoon, Priestess. May we come in?" Elinor asked, her voice sincere as she gestured to the group behind her. "The weather is rather brisk, and we would appreciate stepping into somewhere warm."

"Your Majesty. Of course, please proceed," the priestess replied, pulling the door open wide. "Follow me."

Inside, the temple buzzed with quiet activity as the other priestesses went about their routines, unaware of their unexpected visitor. That changed the moment Elinor crossed the threshold – her presence shifted the atmosphere, her aura commanding immediate attention.

The head priestess, Sade, approached swiftly, bowing with respect. "Queen Elinor, we weren't expecting you," she said, her voice laced with shock.

Elinor smiled. "I thought a surprise appearance might be more enlightening. I trust that's acceptable?"

Sade nodded, though a flicker of uncertainty passed through her expression. "Of course, Your Majesty. We are always ready to welcome you."

Elinor's gaze swept across the gathered priestesses, already calculating how best to sow seeds of doubt and distrust. "Excellent. Show me to a room. Once my household and I are settled, I will speak with each of you individually. There's a traitor in your midst, and I intend to unmask them."

"A traitor, Your Highness? Surely not?"

Elinor's eyes narrowed slightly, her tone hardening. "Yes. Someone within these walls has been working against us."

Sade swallowed, her composure briefly faltering. "We shall do everything in our power to assist you."

"Good," Elinor said, her voice leaving no room for disagreement. "I will speak with each of you alone. Prepare yourselves."

With a brisk nod, Sade turned and led Elinor to a set of guest chambers, no doubt hurrying off afterwards to warn the others. Elinor stepped inside, paused to take in her surroundings. The chamber was rich and warm, dominated by a large, intricately carved wooden bed draped in silks and velvets. A fire crackled in the hearth, casting golden light that danced across the polished marble floor.

Elinor's gaze was immediately drawn to the adjoining bathing chamber. A large, sunken bath stood at its centre, encircled by lush greenery and delicate blooms that filled the space with a soft, natural fragrance. Shelves lined the walls, stocked with an array of fragrant oils and finely milled soaps – an indulgent contrast to the bare essentials she had endured aboard the ship.

Without hesitation, she shed her travel-worn garments and sank into the warm, welcoming water. The tension in her shoulders began to melt away almost instantly, the heat easing the tightness in her muscles. After a few quiet minutes, she called for Chloe to bring Eadric.

Chloe entered gently, cradling the baby in her arms. Elinor reached out, taking him with care, and slowly lowered him into the water with her. She held him close against her thighs, supporting him with practised ease. He let out a soft coo, clearly content with both the warmth and the comfort of being near her. Elinor smiled, her heart full. No matter how many times she held him like this, the depth of her love always managed to astonish her. How could someone so small stir such overwhelming emotions – strength and vulnerability entwined?

Once both were clean, she called Chloe to take Eadric, allowing her time to step out and dress. When she returned to the main room, she found Bradley waiting with a welcoming spread laid out. A wooden banquet board displayed an assortment of cheeses, fresh fruits, and crisp crackers. The rich aroma of aged cheese mingled with the sweetness of ripe berries, creating an inviting contrast that stirred her appetite. Beside the platter sat a bottle of her favourite red wine, its deep ruby hue catching the light.

The sight made her smile. Every detail was perfect – thoughtful, comforting, and indulgent.

"Why, thank you, my love. This is exactly what I needed," she said, settling beside him on the bed and popping a grape into her mouth. Bradley poured her a generous glass of wine and handed it to her. She took a slow sip, savouring the full-bodied flavour as warmth spread through her chest.

"You always know how to make me feel special," she added, her eyes meeting his with a tender, grateful look.

With Eadric now peacefully sleeping beside them, Elinor and Bradley lingered over the food and drink, enjoying the rare moment of quiet luxury. Eventually, she rose, brushing crumbs from her lap.

"Well, I think I've left the priestesses in suspense long enough," she said with a sly smile. She leaned down to kiss Bradley and softly brushed her fingers across Eadric's cheek. "I'll be back soon."

"We shall be waiting," Bradley replied, his eyes gleaming with amusement. "Try not to terrorise them too much."

"I would never," she said with a playful grin, before sauntering from the room, her confidence wrapped around her like a cloak.

She made her way down the corridor to a private chamber where the interviews were to take place. Taking her seat, she prepared herself. One by one, the priestesses were led in and subjected to her scrutiny.

Each one entered composed, hiding their nerves behind serene expressions. But as Elinor questioned them about their duties, their loyalties, and their thoughts on the temple's leadership, hairline cracks began to show. Her inquiries were sharp, deliberate. Then came her power, wielded openly, unapologetically. She could see the shift in their eyes, the unease, the fear, but none dared to speak against her.

Oh, she was enjoying herself immensely. Elinor took great pleasure in toying with them all. With each priestess that stepped into the chamber, she could see the mistrust deepening. The gossip was already taking root, spreading like wildfire. Her questions, carefully phrased, subtly chipped away at their confidence, not just in one another, but in Sade as well.

These women paraded themselves as paragons of wisdom and composure, their discipline evident in every measured word and graceful movement. They carried themselves with an air of quiet authority, above petty quarrels, or idle chatter, or so they liked to believe. But Elinor saw through the façade. Beneath the sanctified exterior, they were no different from anyone else. Flawed. Fallible. Vulnerable.

And the cracks were beginning to show.

By the time the last priestess had left, Elinor felt a flush of satisfaction. Only Sade remained.

The High Priestess entered moments later, her head held high as she took a seat across from Elinor with regal poise. Elinor knew Sade would be the most difficult to rattle, but that hardly mattered. The damage was already done. The seeds of doubt had been sown, and it would take time and energy to root them out. Time during which this temple would be far too distracted to interfere with her plans.

"Good evening, Your Majesty. I do hope your stay so far has been pleasant," Sade said as she poured herself a cup of tea. Her tone was even, cordial, but Elinor didn't miss the pointed edge beneath her words. "And I see you've regained your strength. Do tell me, who did you convince to help you?"

Elinor forced a calm smile, seething beneath the surface. *How dare Sade confront her so directly?* "Oh, Sade. Still so curious. Let's just say I have my ways. Not everyone is as resistant to change as you and the others."

Sade took a slow sip, her expression unreadable. "Indeed. It's always fascinating to observe how people face challenges. Some with grace, others with… less finesse."

Elinor's smile faltered for the briefest moment before she recovered. "Well, we all have our strengths. The key is knowing how—and when—to use them."

Setting her cup down with deliberate care, Sade met Elinor's gaze. "Quite right. And it's equally important to remember that true power comes from within, not from the destruction of others."

Irritation flared in Elinor's eyes, but she kept her smile in place. "Wise words. I suppose that's why you're the High Priestess."

Sade inclined her head, calm and composed. "Thank you, Your Majesty. I do try to lead by example."

Elinor could see that her attempt to unnerve Sade had failed. But she wasn't ready to yield. "Well, this has been enlightening. I look forward to watching how you handle the challenges ahead."

Sade's serene smile never wavered. "Oh, I'll be fine, Your Majesty. The question is—will you?"

With that, Sade rose and swept from the room, leaving Elinor simmering with fury. The moment the door closed, her anger erupted. A violent flash of power surged through her, and the ornate mirror on the far wall shattered into a thousand glittering shards. The splintered glass was scattered across the floor, sparkling like frost under moonlight.

She had anticipated resistance, but she hadn't expected Sade to get under her skin so easily.

Still, the plan was in motion. The seeds had taken root. The priestesses were already suspicious of one another, and they all knew someone among them had helped Elinor reclaim her power. Trust had begun to erode. Word would soon spread across the temples, and with Liora working from within, they would turn their focus inward, too distracted by internal divisions to pay attention to Elinor's next move.

Storming back to her chamber, she found Bradley fast asleep, with Chloe keeping watch over a now wakeful Eadric. Without a word, Elinor relieved her for the night and took the baby into her arms. Sitting down, she rocked him gently, humming a soft melody as she cradled him close.

Her fury faded the moment his small, warm body nestled against her. The tension ebbed away, replaced by calm. As she sang to him, her voice low and soothing, a deep peace settled over her. Whatever storm awaited outside these walls, for now, she was exactly where she needed to be.

***

By morning, Elinor and her party were ready to depart. From the tense atmosphere hanging in the air, it was clear the priestesses would be glad to see them go. After a quick breakfast, Elinor was eager to be on the road. Their next destination – Wittleshire and a visit to the Bennetts – was still several hours away.

This time, the farewell was markedly different.

The High Priestess and a small procession of solemn-faced priestesses stood lined up at the temple's grand entrance to see them off. Normally, such formalities were unnecessary. The temples operated independently of the crown, with customs all their own, and didn't observe royal courtesies the way the citizens of Ethos might. But yesterday's visit had clearly struck a nerve. Elinor suspected the display was more to ensure her departure than to honour it – none of them wanted to be the first to turn their back before she was gone. The moment her carriage disappeared, the real gossip and squabbling would begin.

As she and Bradley approached the waiting carriage, Elinor turned to Sade with a tight smile, one that didn't quite reach her eyes. "Thank you for your hospitality. I trust you'll keep everything running smoothly here."

Sade dipped her head in a shallow bow, her expression carefully controlled. "Of course, Your Majesty. Safe travels."

Elinor stepped into the carriage, her posture regal, her satisfaction barely concealed. As they rolled away from the temple, she leaned back with a contented sigh.

"That went well," she said to Bradley. "Now we wait and see how the seeds we've sown will grow."

Bradley nodded, his expression contemplative. "The temple will be in turmoil soon enough."

Elinor's smile deepened, cool and triumphant. "Exactly as planned."

Chapter 5

A Royal Visit

As Galrick strolled along the upper hall towards his chambers, he noticed a commotion among the servants. The footmen were hurrying to the front door, as if preparing to greet someone important.

Curious about the cause of the excitement, he paused and diverted his path to his brother's room, knowing it offered a better view of the main entrance. When he opened the door, he found Nicholas already perched by the window. Galrick joined him, eager to watch the events unfold.

A fine gold and red carriage, drawn by two large horses, had come to a halt at the steps of their home. As one footman opened the carriage door, both young men craned their necks, straining to see who would emerge.

"Is that the Queen? What's Queen Elinor doing here?" Nicholas exclaimed as a woman stepped out.

"I have no idea," Galrick murmured. "I overheard Mother and Father talking last week about her visit. The most I gathered before I was shooed away was that she intended to check on something. Whatever the reason, it can't be good."

"You knew and didn't tell me!" Nicholas cried.

"It must have slipped my mind."

"Of course it did. Well, do we stay here, or try to eavesdrop on the meeting? They'll likely head to the drawing room. It would be easy to hide behind the wall and listen in."

"Why, little brother, who would have thought you so sneaky? Excellent idea—lead the way."

The two young men crept down the hall. Sneaking into position, they pressed their ears to the wall, straining to catch the conversation within.

"You understand my predicament, William?" came the queen's voice, sharp and commanding. "I need the children captured and in my grasp. And since one of them is within your lands, I'm depending on you to find Aevah—lest your life depend on it."

"I do, Your Majesty," William replied, his tone weary. "But as I am unwell myself, I'm in no condition to lead any party in search of her. And I don't know who I could entrust with such an important task."

"Our sons," Roweena interjected.

"Excuse me?" the queen asked.

"Our sons," Roweena repeated. "You remember Galrick and Nicholas from the tourney. They are loyal to you and your kingdom. I'm sure they would relish the chance to serve the crown."

"Yes, they would be fine men for the task," William added.

"Indeed—I recall Galrick in particular. An excellent young man, a knight in the making. Bring them to me."

"Of course, Your Majesty," Roweena said, her voice bright with eagerness. "They'll gladly assist you in any way they can."

"Well, I suppose that's our cue," Galrick whispered. "Let's go before they find us listening."

They slipped away quickly and returned to their chambers, making it appear as though they had been there all along. When the servants came to fetch them, they followed without protest, nerves taut with anticipation.

Uncertain of what to expect, both men steeled themselves and looked to their father for guidance as they were led into the drawing room.

"Your Highness, may I present our sons—Galrick and Nicholas," William announced.

Both young men bowed. "Your Highness," they echoed in unison.

"A pleasure to see you both again," the queen said with a faint smile. "How old are you now?"

"Twenty-three and seventeen," Galrick replied for them both.

"Young men, learning the ropes of the estate, no doubt? And loyal to the crown. I remember you, Galrick. You showed promise—quite the future knight. The offer still stands, should you choose to come to Carraton… once you've completed a minor task for me."

"Yes, Your Majesty. There is much to learn, but we both work hard. And we are faithful to you and your realm. To be considered for a knighthood is a great honour," Galrick said respectfully.

"That's good to hear," the queen replied. "Now, to the matter at hand."

She leaned forward slightly, her expression sharpening.

"There is a unique crystal shard, concealed in the Azend mountains. It must be located and returned to me without delay. The complication, however, is that a certain young royal is also searching for it."

"Oh?" Galrick asked, a note of caution entering his voice.

"Yes," the queen confirmed. "It seems my niece, Aevah, is also seeking the shard."

"And you wish for me to retrieve it before she does?" he asked, already sensing the weight of what was being asked of him.

"Not quite."

Galrick and Nicholas both stood silently, listening as the queen outlined her plan. They were to find and befriend Princess Aevah, assist her in recovering the crystal shard, and then escort her to the Temple of Renlands, where she would be placed in the care of High Priestess Liora. Once Aevah was safely handed over, they were to return the shard to Queen Elinor in Carraton. In exchange, Galrick would be anointed as a knight of the realm.

The queen made it all sound noble – harmless, even. But Galrick saw the truth hidden beneath her polished words. They were being asked to betray the princess, to manipulate her into delivering herself into danger. He had no doubt Nicholas would feel the same. But trapped by duty and the weight of their family's expectations, they had little choice. For now, they had to play along – and find another way before it was too late.

"Your Majesty, it's an honour to be entrusted with such a task. We shall not let you down," Galrick said evenly.

Both brothers bowed and exited the room. Once out of sight, they exchanged a look and nodded, a silent agreement passing between them. Neither spoke of what had just occurred. Instead, they parted ways: Nicholas heading to the practice yard, and Galrick returning to his chambers.

Alone, Galrick sat down with the documents given to him. The queen's reasoning became clearer. The shard's location was veiled within a riddle, one that required a deep knowledge of the land to decipher. Beyond that, locating the shard demanded a power they didn't possess – Aevah's power.

He remembered both Aevah and her brother Jacob from summers past at the castle. They had been kind, beloved by the people. He had no intention of turning them over to the queen, whose thirst for control had become legend. The fact that they were still alive after all these years spoke volumes about their resourcefulness and the lengths the queen had gone to try and destroy them.

Galrick had heard the whispers, the dark rumours of what she had done, and what she continued to do, to cling to her throne. His father might follow her out of fear or blind loyalty, but Galrick wouldn't. He would find Aevah, yes – but not to betray her. He would help her, even if it cost him everything. The queen no longer deserved the crown she wore, and he would see her rule brought to an end.

Later that night, after the household had quieted and all had retired, Galrick slipped into Nicholas's room. He sat across from his brother, studying him carefully.

"Well? What are your thoughts?" he asked.

"I don't trust the queen," Nicholas replied, "or our parents, for that matter. But I think it's safest to play along, for now."

"I agree," Galrick said with a nod. "The clearest path is to pretend to follow order. Once we're on the road, we can choose our own course. Until then, keep quiet and keep smiling. The walls here have ears, and our lives may depend on our silence."

He stood and walked to the door. Just before stepping out, he turned back.

"Good night, little brother."

"Good night."

***

The next day arrived, with the queen departing not long after first light. Her absence eased Galrick's mind, though not entirely. Too many eyes and ears remained – servants and informants loyal to her, always watching, always listening. One misstep could cost them everything.

After breakfast, Galrick sought out his parents to discuss the final details of their journey, hoping they could leave as soon as possible. He longed to be away from the estate and on the road to find the princess, last reported to be just a few miles south. She needed to know what was happening. Her safety, Galrick suspected, would vanish the moment the crystal shard was in her possession.

He knew three shards were still missing, though the queen had mentioned only one. That alone raised questions – how many had already been found, and who held them? It was common knowledge that whoever controlled the shards wielded the true power of the realm.

He found his parents in the study, deep in conversation about the queen's orders. As he entered, his father discreetly tucked away several scrolls, offering a strained smile of greeting. His mother adopted the overly sweet tone she always used when she wanted something from him.

"Galrick, dear! How are you this morning?" she cooed.

"Well enough, Mother. I came to ask when Nicholas and I are expected to leave and whether there's anything else I should know."

"As soon as you're both packed, you may depart. The queen has given you all the information you need."

"Of course. I want to ensure everything is in order. I intend for this task to go well."

"You'll do just fine, Galrick," she said, waving off his concern. "The queen will be indebted to you. I had the kitchen prepare a hamper of food for your journey. If you're packed by today, there's no reason you can't leave first thing tomorrow."

"Thank you. I'll find Nicholas and let him know."

As he stepped from the room, Galrick couldn't help but wonder what his parents were hiding. They always seemed to play both sides – pledging loyalty wherever it benefited them most. For now, the queen had the upper hand, so they were clearly aligning themselves with her.

He and Nicholas were nothing like them. Though both bore their father's features – sandy hair, brown eyes, tall and broad-shouldered – neither of them shared their parents' ruthless ambitions. Galrick was a heavier set of the two, more solid in frame, while Nicholas was leaner and quicker. They shared none of their mother's appearance: her golden hair, freckled skin, or shallow charm. And Galrick didn't mind that at all.

He often wondered where he and Nicholas truly came from. The two of them cared for others, believing in justice and kindness – concepts foreign to their parents, who valued only power and wealth, regardless of who they had to trample to gain it.

Wandering the estate, Galrick found Nicholas outside, practising with his bow. As always, his younger brother was in perfect form. Each arrow flew with unerring accuracy, hitting the target dead-on. Nicholas was stealthy, able to move like a shadow and approach unnoticed when he wished. It was a skill Galrick admired – though he would never say so out loud.

Instead, he did what older brothers did: he teased him mercilessly about it.

He stood back and watched for a moment, amused and impressed. Nicholas was so focused, so self-assured. It reminded Galrick why it was unwise to annoy him when he had a weapon in hand. A sword fight, though – that was different. Galrick held the advantage there. The last time they'd sparred, he had accidentally sliced Nicholas's arm during a clumsy tumble.

"Nearly finished? We've got packing to do," Galrick called out.

"Almost. Why don't you join me?"

"Can't. We've got a lot to get through. I want us to leave first thing tomorrow. I'll sort the horses—you get your things ready."

"Not a problem. Just a few more shots, and I'll start. Meet me for lunch?"

"Certainly. And brace yourself—I think we're expected at a family dinner tonight."

"Oh joy. I'll see you at lunch."

As the day wore on, both brothers packed what they needed. They met briefly over lunch, speaking cautiously about their plans, then returned to their rooms to double-check everything. Galrick had seen to the horses and confirmed they were ready for the journey.

All that remained was dinner.

They made their way to the dining room, only to find an unexpected guest awaiting them.

"Good evening. Will you be joining us?" the queen asked, her tone light but laced with authority.

"Good evening, Your Majesty," Galrick replied with forced politeness. "I hope you're well? Unfortunately, we won't be staying. We've come only to say goodbye. We're packed and eager to begin."

"You're leaving now? Are you sure?" Roweena asked, feigning concern. "It will be nightfall soon."

"They'll be fine," William said briskly. "They're grown men, and the next village isn't far."

"Yes, the sooner they begin, the better," the queen agreed. "Good luck, boys. Keep in touch. My people will be there to help you."

Bowing quickly, Galrick and Nicholas made a swift exit. Once out of sight, they marched back towards their rooms.

"What do we do now?" Nicholas asked, keeping his voice low.

"Exactly what we said. Grab your things, pick up some food, and eat as we ride. I don't know how or why the queen is still here, but I'm not staying to find out."

"Right. Shall I meet you at the stables?"

"Yes. Be quick."

Galrick broke away and veered towards his chambers while Nicholas headed to his own. After gathering his belongings, Galrick continued to the kitchens, collecting provisions for the road, then made his way to the stables.

Once both horses were saddled, the brothers mounted and rode towards a village called Bedale, hoping it would provide shelter and a measure of safety. With only a few hours of daylight remaining, they urged their horses onward, racing the setting sun. Riding after dark was always risky. The roads became treacherous, and the threat of bandits loomed larger with every mile.

He would have waited until morning, but the queen's continued presence left him no choice. Her mere existence unsettled everyone. She ruled through fear and manipulation, bending people to her will or disposing of them if they refused.

Galrick loathed her.

He despised how she had involved him and Nicholas in her twisted games. But she would regret it. Somehow, he would find a way to help Princess Aevah, to locate the crystal shards, and to use them against the queen. He didn't know how. Not yet. But he would.

Chapter 6

The First Stop

As they continued along the dirt track towards their first stop, Galrick noticed Nicholas growing more puzzled with each mile they rode.

"Everything alright?" he asked.

"I thought we were heading towards Stowden, but I'm certain we should've reached it by now."

"We are, as far as the queen is concerned," Galrick replied. "In truth, we're on the road to Bedale. It's quieter, and I know of an inn where we can stay for a few nights if needed. I have a strong feeling that both Queen Elinor and Mother sent men to follow us, not long after we left. I'd rather not be tracked."

"A smart choice of town," Nicholas admitted. "But if we are being followed, they'll soon realise we've taken a different road."

"True. But there are dozens of places we could have diverted to. By the time they work it out, we'll have a plan in place to keep the princess out of their reach."

"A noble goal, brother," Nicholas said, his voice quieter. "But the queen's people *will* find us and her. They already know where she is. They're just playing the long game, letting her believe she's safe while she does all the work of retrieving the shards for them."

"I know," Galrick said, nodding. "But if we warn her, at least she can be more careful about her movements."

"I admire your optimism. I just hope we manage to stay one step ahead of the queen. If she suspects even for a second that we've turned against her…"

"She won't," Galrick said firmly. "Trust me, nothing will seem out of place."

"Galrick, we're already off course from the route she gave us. I'd say that's *something* out of place."

"Relax," he said with a grin. "We took a detour, that's all." Then, without warning, he kicked his horse into a gallop, leaving Nicholas no choice but to chase after him or fall behind.

They continued in silence along the narrow, overgrown path that wound through the woods. The sun had long since dipped below the horizon, and the forest was cloaked in shadows. Both remained alert as no woodland was safe after dark. Bandits, smugglers, and worse often emerged late, just ahead of the night watch. The wilderness could turn dangerous quickly, especially for travellers without an escort.

As they rounded a bend in the path, a clearing opened up ahead. They urged their horses into a faster trot. Beyond the clearing, the trail widened and joined a broader road that led directly into Bedale.

At the town gates, they dismounted and led their horses past the guards, offering nods of greeting. The guards said nothing, merely observing them with idle curiosity.

They made their way through the quiet streets, heading towards an inn called *The Blue Birds Blossom*. Along the way, they passed small, well-kept houses nestled between shops and taverns. Most of the townsfolk were already inside for the night, and while the streets were calm, the distant hum of music and conversation drifted from several inns.

As they turned the final corner, the inn came into view – a tall, narrow building warmly lit from within. A sign depicting a bluebird encircled by white flowers hung by the door, swaying gently in the breeze. A small flower bed lined the wall beneath the front window, and a wooden bench rested just beside it.

When they arrived, Galrick handed Nicholas the reins and stepped inside. A welcoming heat radiated from the hearth as he approached the bar. Behind it, a middle-aged woman served drinks with a friendly smile. Galrick spoke with her briefly, paid for a room, and gave false names – a precaution above all. Once settled, he stepped back out to update Nicholas, who took the horses around to the stables, leaving them in the care of a sleepy stable boy.

Reunited, the brothers headed up to their room.

It was modest, even plain – not the kind of place one would expect young lords to stay. Two single beds stood against the wall opposite the door, separated by a small bedside table holding a stubby candle. A chest of drawers stood near the corner.

After setting down their belongings, they returned downstairs and found a table. Galrick ordered drinks, and the two of them quietly took in their surroundings while waiting for their meal.

The inn was charming in its simplicity. The main room was compact but warm, its timber walls and low ceiling giving it a snug atmosphere. A larger dining area stretched farther back, doubling as a dance space on livelier nights. This evening, however, was quiet. A few patrons sat chatting over mugs of ale or playing cards at corner tables. No strangers or suspicious figures entered, and that helped ease their nerves.

By the time their meal was finished, both brothers felt more at ease. Still, they remained cautious as they returned to their room, keeping watch for anything unusual.

Inside, Nicholas collapsed onto his bed, kicking off his boots with a sigh. Galrick remained seated on the edge of his own bed, pulling out the queen's notes. He flipped through the pages in the candlelight, rereading the vague clues and encrypted details she had provided. Across the room, Nicholas was already asleep.

After a few more minutes of quiet thought, Galrick blew out the candle and lay back, determined to rise early and continue the journey. Tomorrow, the true challenge would begin.

Chapter 7

Stormbound

Back on the boat after a successful journey, the voyage began smoothly. The *Sovereign* glided effortlessly across the calm waters, its crew moving with practised efficiency. Elinor found herself enjoying the tranquil passage far more than she had expected, breathing in the salt-kissed air and admiring the endless expanse of sea and sky.

But by the second day, the weather began to turn. The gentle breeze stiffened into a fierce gale, and the sea transformed from a placid mirror to a churning, angry force. The ship rocked violently as waves slammed into its hull, sending bursts of icy spray over the deck. Above them, dark clouds gathered in a thick, brooding mass, and the wind howled like a living thing.

Bradley, ever the seasoned sailor, joined the crew on deck, helping to secure the sails and brace the ship for the coming storm. Below, Elinor clutched their son tightly, taking shelter in their quarters alongside Lady Chloe. The once-soothing sway of the ship had become a violent lurch, each motion unpredictable and jarring.

Recognising the danger, the captain made the difficult decision to alter their course. "We need to dock in Darlington!" he shouted above the roar of the wind. "It's too dangerous to press on in these conditions."

With unwavering focus, the crew battled the elements, their faces set with grit and determination. Through the storm's chaos, the ship's figurehead, the sacred symbol of the divine spirit, seemed to glow with a faint, ethereal light, as if guiding them through the tempest.

At last, after hours of struggle, the harbour lights of Darlington pierced the gloom. A collective sigh of relief swept through the passengers and crew as the *Sovereign* pushed on, the open sea giving way to the relative safety of choppy harbour waters.

Once docked, the crew sprang into action, securing the ship with practised haste. The storm still raged – wind howling through the rigging and rain lashing the stone pier like a dirge. Queen or not, Elinor ran for the waiting carriage, her skirts sodden with puddles as she clutched Eadric tightly beneath a bundle of blankets. Bradley and Chloe followed close behind, and once they were safely inside, a guard leaned in to inform them that accommodations had been arranged a few blocks away.

"Well, this is certainly a hitch in our plans," Elinor said as she gently rocked Eadric, who, remarkably, was still sleeping, occasionally murmuring and wriggling in her arms. "I do hope this weather doesn't linger. The idea of riding all the way home again in a carriage isn't exactly appealing."

"I know," Bradley replied. "Once we're settled, I'll make some enquiries and see what the forecast might hold for us." He peered out the carriage window as it rolled to a stop. "It seems we've arrived."

"Your Majesty, allow me to take him," Lady Chloe offered gently. "There will likely be people waiting to greet both of you."

Elinor had already used her power to dry them off, though it had done little to remedy the state of their mud-splattered clothing. Bradley adjusted his coat and ran a hand through his damp hair, trying to smooth it down.

"We should still make a good impression, despite the circumstances," he said, glancing at Elinor with a faint smile.

She nodded, drawing a deep breath. "Yes. Let's go meet our hosts."

The moment the carriage door opened, they hurried inside the building before them, eager to escape the downpour. The inn was grander than expected, with polished wooden floors, elegant chandeliers casting a warm glow, and a roaring fire that immediately chased away the chill.

As they entered, a well-dressed man and woman approached them, both wearing warm smiles. The woman, dressed in a regal gown, curtsied deeply.

"Welcome, Your Majesty," she said, her voice respectful and sincere. "We are honoured to receive you."

Elinor returned the smile, though she couldn't help feeling slightly self-conscious in her travel-worn attire. "Thank you for your hospitality," she replied. "The storm forced our hand, and we're grateful for your kindness."

The man, who appeared to be the innkeeper, bowed. "It is our pleasure, Your Majesty. Please, allow us to show you to your rooms. We've prepared our finest suites for you and your party."

Bradley stepped forward, his tone courteous yet firm. "Thank you. We appreciate your assistance."

The innkeeper led them up a grand staircase to the second floor, opening the door to a luxurious suite. The room was spacious and inviting, featuring a large four-poster bed, a cosy sitting area by the hearth, and a balcony overlooking the storm-swept port. Elinor felt a wave of relief as she took it all in.

"Please, make yourselves at home," the innkeeper said. "If there's anything you require, do not hesitate to ask. Dinner will be served in the dining hall at seven."

Elinor nodded gratefully. "Thank you. We'll join you shortly."

Once the innkeeper and his wife had gone, she turned to Bradley with wide eyes. "This place is perfect."

He smiled, the tension easing from his expression. "It's a welcome change from the ship."

"Let's get cleaned up. I think we could all use some fresh clothes and a good wash."

Later, once everyone was ready, they made their way to the private dining room. The space was warm and intimate, with a crackling fire and the rich aroma of a hearty meal filling the air. Elinor and Bradley settled into their seats, grateful for the comfort and calm.

Elinor glanced out the window as the rain continued to lash against the panes. "I can't believe how fierce this storm is," she murmured. "If it keeps up, we might have to rethink how we're getting home."

Bradley took a sip of soup and nodded. "We'll wait and see what the morning brings. It may pass by then."

Lady Chloe, seated across the table, added, "It's fortunate we found shelter here. The innkeeper and his wife have shown such kindness."

"Yes," Elinor agreed with a soft smile. "I'm truly grateful for their generosity."

As the meal continued, the conversation lightened. They shared stories and laughter, the warmth of the fire and the rich beef stew, providing a soothing contrast to the storm beyond the windows. For a while, the worries of travel were forgotten.

After dinner, they all retired to their rooms. Elinor, weary from the day's chaos, fell asleep quickly, the steady drumming of rain against the windows lulling her into rest. Bradley remained awake a little longer, standing by the window, watching the storm churn across the harbour.

***

The next morning, Elinor and Bradley awoke to the relentless sound of rain battering the windows. The storm had not eased overnight – the sea beyond churned with wild, unforgiving fury. Elinor moved to the window, concern etched across her brow as she watched the waves crash against the distant harbour walls.

"It seems the skies are still raging," she murmured, glancing over her shoulder at Bradley. "We need to decide whether to wait it out or travel by land."

Bradley joined her, his expression grave. "The sea is far too dangerous right now. If we wait for the storm to pass, we could be stuck here for days."

Elinor sighed, knowing he was right. "But travelling by carriage would take weeks. Even if we wait a few days and then return to the ship, it would still be faster than making the journey overland."

"According to the locals, the storm should break in a few days," Bradley said. "It's your decision—wait or leave now."

Elinor didn't hesitate. "We wait. I'm not dragging our son through flooded roads in this weather."

"I'll inform our hosts." He kissed her forehead lightly before stepping out, closing the door softly behind him.

Elinor turned back to the window, watching the rain as it streaked down the glass in silvery trails. The storm showed no sign of relenting, and she braced herself for a long, idle wait.

Unused to inactivity – no court to run, no urgent matters to attend – Elinor sought ways to keep herself occupied. During her wanderings through the inn, she discovered a quiet reading nook nestled beside a fireplace. There, she lost herself for hours in the pages of richly told stories. The inn's library was impressively curated, and she soon found herself immersed in books on local history and folklore, their mysterious legends both fascinating and strange.

She also cherished the uninterrupted time with Eadric. She often sat by the window with him nestled in her arms, singing lullabies as she rocked him gently to sleep. After a conversation with the innkeeper's wife, she was gifted a beautifully crafted embroidery kit. She and Lady Chloe spent long, quiet hours stitching delicate patterns by the fire, their conversation light and soothing, the activity both calming and creatively satisfying.

Bradley, never one to sit still for long, challenged her to chess matches between his own pursuits. When not reading or helping with Eadric, he trained with the guards in the private courtyard, taking advantage of the occasional lull in the rain. He also spent time with the men stationed with them, ensuring morale stayed high and that everyone remained sharp despite the extended pause in travel.

Evenings were spent in the inn's warm common room. There, Elinor and Bradley joined the other guests around the hearth, sharing stories and playing card games while the storm howled beyond the walls. The innkeeper's wife often joined them, spinning tales of the inn's storied past and recounting eerie local legends that made the firelight feel even more comforting.

Though the time away from court life was a welcome reprieve, both Elinor and Bradley found the prolonged respite somewhat troubling. With the storm disrupting communication, sending messages by bird was out of the question. Until they returned home, Elinor could only hope all was running smoothly in their absence.

By the third morning, the storm had finally broken. The clouds parted to reveal a pale, golden sun, and a soft light bathed the soaked earth in its gentle glow. Elinor and Bradley packed their belongings and descended the staircase to thank their generous hosts.

"We're grateful for your hospitality," Elinor said warmly. "We will always remember your kindness."

The innkeeper bowed with a gracious smile. "It was our pleasure, Your Majesty. Safe travels to you and your family."

With the storm behind them, Elinor, Bradley, and their party made their way back to the docks. The *Sovereign* waited, sails half-raised, crew bustling about with renewed energy. The ship gleamed in the morning light, the air crisp with salt and the scent of fresh beginnings.

As they boarded, Elinor took a deep breath, the briny wind filling her lungs. Relief and anticipation stirred in her chest. They were finally going home.

The return voyage proved smooth and uneventful. The sea, once furious and dark, now stretched calm and glittering beneath the clear sky. A steady breeze filled the sails, carrying the *Sovereign* swiftly across the water.

Elinor and Bradley spent most of their time on deck, basking in the sunlight and the tranquillity that followed the storm. The sea was beautiful – vast and glistening, full of promise – and as the coastline gradually drew nearer, both knew they were ready to face whatever awaited them at home.

Chapter 8

Shelter in the Shadows

Adrian and Cecilia set out from Geraldton with Dominic and Liam, two trusted friends from the rebel group, intending to travel through Belshire, then on to Dorraset, and finally to the Mines of Grode. The plan was for all the rebel factions to rendezvous at the mines and establish a base camp, but they had to be smart about it.

Large clusters of people would arouse suspicion, so everyone moved in small groups of no more than four, unless disguised as a family with young children. Families were a common sight on the roads – large groups of unrelated adults were not.

The weather offered no mercy. The late autumn rains had turned the roads into slick, muddy trails. Their horses trudged through the muck, hooves sinking into the clay-like ground with every step. Each mile was a battle against the elements. Never in her life had Cecilia felt so utterly exhausted and yet so fiercely determined. The rain was relentless, soaking through even their best efforts to stay dry, and the cold nights spent camping outdoors tested her endurance. Had she been alone, she doubted she could have carried on.

Adrian kept them moving by day and sought safe places to rest by night, but the roads were crawling with patrols under Elinor's command. While Adrian scouted ahead, Dominic and Liam took turns sweeping the trail behind them and covering their tracks. No matter how cautious they were, it felt as if one particular patrol was always just a step behind.

Recognising how close to exhaustion their mounts were, Adrian finally made the call after discovering a hidden grove off the main track.

"This is the best we're going to find for the night," he told them. "We're all tired, and if we push the horses any further, we'll lose them."

"Liam, how long do you think we've got until they're on us again?" Domnic asked.

"Hard to say," Liam replied, glancing towards the forest behind them. "They've stopped movin' for now, but it could just be a quick rest before they pick up the trail again."

Adrian nodded grimly. "Alright. Let's tend to the horses but leave the saddles on. If they come this way, we need to be ready to leave fast."

Liam led the mare towards a patch of drier ground while Dominic stepped forward.

"I'll take first watch," he said, disappearing silently into the trees before returning a few minutes later to position himself at a discreet vantage point. Dominic wasn't one for idle chatter, but he was strong, clever, and unwaveringly loyal – exactly the kind of man they needed with them.

Liam shared that loyalty, a trait common among the rebels, but he carried it with a much lighter spirit. He was the joker of the group, always ready with a quip or a grin – even in the most dire of moments. It wasn't always appreciated, but it did wonders for morale. In these circumstances, a little levity went a long way. Adrian often sensed the weight of Cecilia's anxiety over the past few days. He couldn't blame her. After everything they'd been through, the thought of returning to Elinor was unthinkable – for both of them. That was why he valued Liam's cheerful nature. When the tension became unbearable, Liam's humour cut through it. Even Dominic cracked a smile now and then.

Spotting Liam struggling with the horses, Adrian walked over to help. Liam grunted as he lifted one of the horse's legs, mud coating his hands and soaking through his clothes.

"Come on, buddy, work with me here," Liam muttered with a lopsided grin.

Adrian shook his head, amused. "Need a hand?"

"Nah, I got this," Liam replied, eyes glinting with mischief. "Just bonding with our four-legged friends."

Dominic, watching from a short distance, let out a rare chuckle. "You nearly face-planted in the mud a minute ago."

Liam winked. "Would've been a good laugh if I did."

Adrian rolled his eyes but couldn't hide his smile. "Alright, let's get it done. The sooner we're cleaned up, the sooner we rest."

Together, they worked quickly, cleaning and feeding the horses. Adrian decided to unsaddle them for a few hours, intending to re-saddle them before nightfall. They desperately needed rest, but he wasn't willing to take the risk of being caught off guard. If the patrol found them, they would need to move without delay.

With the horses settled, Adrian made his way back to their small camp. Cecilia was already tucked into her sleeping bag, and he noticed she had laid out rations – small packets of dried food ready to eat. Smiling, he grabbed his own and lay down beside her.

"Thank you," he said, holding up the packet. "I'm on second shift, so I'm going to try and get a bit of shut-eye now. I'll eat later."

"Alright," Cecilia replied with a tired smile. "I probably won't be far behind you. I gave Dominic his food already. Hopefully, tonight's quiet."

"I'm sure it will be. But I've asked Liam to re-saddle the horses before he sleeps. Just in case."

Cecilia nodded and leaned over to kiss him softly on the lips.

"Well, good night then," she murmured.

"Good night."

He watched her for a moment, smiling to himself as she drifted off almost immediately. Then he closed his eyes, letting the weight of the day finally settle into his limbs.

***

It felt like only minutes had passed before Adrian was gently shaken awake by Dominic. The world around them was pitch black, save for a few stars glimmering faintly through the canopy above. Adrian sat up slowly, rubbing the sleep from his eyes as he tried to register Dominic's words.

"No trouble so far," Dominic whispered. "The group hasn't moved, far as I can tell. Heard a bit o' rustling in the bushes, but it's just foxes and such."

"Good to know. Get some rest," Adrian murmured, rising to his feet.

He stretched, rolling his neck from side to side until a satisfying crack released the tension that had built during sleep. Now fully upright, he took a brief scout around the perimeter. Finding no signs of disturbance, he wandered a little further from camp, stopping beneath a thick-limbed tree to relieve himself. From there, he followed the faint sound of running water to a nearby stream.

Kneeling at the bank, he splashed the icy water onto his face. The cold bit into his skin, sending a jolt of awareness through his body. He inhaled sharply, blinking through the sting, but it worked – he was awake. Shaking the water from his hands and face, he made his way back to the camp, feeling more alert.

Leaning against the wide trunk of a tree that offered a clear view of their surroundings, Adrian began his watch. He unwrapped the small packet of food Cecilia had left for him – dried meat and a piece of hard bread, their last provisions. The meat was tough, the bread stale, but it was enough to keep his stomach from growling. He chewed methodically, scanning the darkness as he ate, listening for anything out of place.

The night was still. Almost unnaturally so. Only the occasional rustling of leaves or the gentle snorts of the horses broke the silence. There was something both calming and unnerving about it.

As the hours slipped by, Adrian's eyes adjusted to the dark. He could now make out the tall silhouettes of trees and the faint outlines of the horses nearby. He moved with care, checking each animal in turn, ensuring their tethers were secure and they were unharmed. The quiet interaction with the horses grounded him.

Overhead, the stars shimmered like fragments of another world – distant, serene, untouched by the challenges they would still need to face. Their light offered him a small moment of peace, a reminder that beauty still remained even amid chaos and fear.

Just as his guard began to lower, a sudden rustle reached his ears. Instinctively, his hand went to the hilt of his sword. He froze, breath held, eyes scanning the darkness. Then he saw it – two gleaming eyes reflecting the starlight.

A fox.

The creature stood motionless for a heartbeat, watching him in return. Then, with a flick of its tail, it darted into the underbrush and was gone.

Adrian exhaled quietly and lowered his hand. "Nothing to worry about," he muttered under his breath.

He remained where he was, posture alert but steady, gaze sweeping the treeline again. There was still a long night ahead. And he intended to be ready.

After another lap around the camp revealed nothing out of place, he returned to his post beneath the tree.

But just as his watch was drawing to a close, the hairs on the back of his neck stood on end. His senses screamed that something was wrong. He froze, straining his ears, hoping to catch the sound again.

Then he heard it – a rustling in the undergrowth, faint but unmistakably deliberate. It wasn't the wind, and it wasn't an animal.

Adrian's heartbeat quickened. He scanned the darkness, eyes narrowing as movement caught his attention. Shadows shifted between the trees – three figures, creeping towards the camp with practised stealth.

He didn't hesitate.

Cupping his hands around his mouth, he called out in a low but urgent voice, "Wake up! We've got company!"

His tone was just loud enough to rouse the others without drawing attention to their exact position.

Cecilia, Dominic, and Liam bolted upright, hands flying to their weapons. Within seconds, the quiet camp erupted into tense motion.

The patrolmen, realising they had been spotted, broke into a run, charging towards them.

Adrian drew his sword, stepping between the attackers and his companions.

"Stay together!" he commanded. "Dominic, left flank! Liam, take the right! Cecilia, get the horses ready—we move on my signal!"

They obeyed instantly, moving like a unit, each one falling into place without question. The patrol closed in fast, their expressions hard with determination.

Adrian's grip tightened around his hilt. He braced himself.

The first patrolman lunged, blade flashing in the moonlight. Adrian parried the strike with precision, their swords ringing out as they clashed. With a swift counter, he drove his blade forward and cut the man down in a single, decisive blow.

Dominic engaged the second attacker. His opponent was strong, but Dominic was quicker. He ducked beneath a wild swing and delivered a solid strike to the man's side. The patrolman let out a grunt of pain before collapsing.

Meanwhile, Liam faced off against the third. Gone was his usual easy-going grin – his face was set with grim focus. Their blades collided in a fierce flurry. Then, with a calculated move,

Liam disarmed his opponent and struck him across the head with the hilt of his sword, knocking him unconscious.

"Hurry!" Cecilia shouted, holding the horses by their reins. Her voice trembled with urgency. "Mount up!"

"Go!" Adrian ordered, sprinting to his horse. The others followed, swinging into their saddles just as the voices echoed from the trees behind them – more patrolmen were closing in.

"Go, go, go!" he yelled, spurring his horse into a gallop.

The group thundered into the darkness, hooves pounding the earth, their silhouettes weaving between the trees as they fled. The shouts of their pursuers rang out behind them, relentless and growing louder.

Adrian pushed them hard, weaving through the forest in an attempt to lose their tail, but no matter how much distance they gained, the patrol kept up.

They stopped briefly at a stream to let the horses drink, but none of them could sustain the punishing pace for long. They needed a skilled tracker among the rebels to match the patrol's tenacity – whoever was leading the pursuit knew exactly what they were doing.

Adrian cast a glance over his shoulder, eyes sweeping the forest. "We have to keep moving," he said, voice low and firm. "The mines are just ahead. If we can reach the tunnels, we might finally lose them."

Cecilia, breathless and pale with fatigue, gave a determined nod.

"Let's go," she said, urging her horse forward.

The group pressed on, the rocky terrain beneath them signalling their approach to the mountains. At last, the dark mouth of the Grode mines came into view, carved into the side of a cliff like a wound in the stone. It was a grim sight but a welcome one. Shelter. Safety. If they could reach it in time.

Behind them, the voices of the patrolmen rose again, clearer now, echoing through the trees. They were close.

Adrian dismounted, thrusting his reins into Cecilia's hands, and ushered everyone else ahead.

"Go on," he said urgently. "I'll cover our tracks."

Cecilia nodded and led the others into the shadowy mouth of the mine. Adrian watched them disappear into the darkness before turning his attention back to the forest. Quietly, he moved behind a large boulder, crouching low with his sword drawn, every muscle coiled and ready. His heart pounded as he listened for any signs of pursuit.

The sound of hooves grew steadily louder, and he held his breath, barely daring to move. The patrolmen rode past, their eyes scanning the area, close, but not close enough to see him. Adrian remained perfectly still, the tension in his body almost unbearable. Only when the final rider vanished down the path did he allow himself to exhale and slowly relax.

Convinced the danger had passed, Adrian slipped into the mine's entrance and hurried through the dark tunnels, guided by the echo of distant voices. Before long, he came upon his companions gathered in a wider cavern, speaking with a group of miners. The dim light from the flickering lanterns cast long shadows across the rocky walls as workers bustled about with practised efficiency.

Cecilia looked up the moment he arrived, relief flooding her expression. "Did they pass?" she asked quickly.

He gave a small nod, a faint smile tugging at the corners of his mouth. "They think we're still ahead of them. We should be safe here for a while."

Dominic and Liam exchanged relieved glances, and Cecilia let out a long breath, the tension in her shoulders easing.

"Thank goodness. I've spoken with the miners, and they know who we are and they're willing to help."

"That's more than I hoped for," Adrian admitted. Though this had been their destination, he had feared the miners might turn them away. Grateful, the group settled down, taking a few precious moments to rest and regroup. The miners offered them food and water, insisting they rest before discussing any next steps. The group accepted without hesitation – they were beyond exhausted after the relentless chase.

Once they had eaten and caught their breath, a burly man approached them. His face was kind beneath a layer of dust, his sleeves rolled up, and his clothes streaked with grime.

"You folks ready to keep moving?" he asked, voice rough but friendly.

Adrian looked up, eyes still cautious despite the warmth in the man's tone. "We are, but have the patrols passed through?"

The miner shook his head. "Nah! They don't come through here. Too many tunnels—they'd get lost before they found anything. I'll guide you through. Follow me."

Cecilia met Adrian's gaze. "I guess this is it," she said quietly.

She took the lead again, gripping her horse's reins in one hand and her water bottle in the other. The rest of the group followed close behind. Their guide introduced himself as Benjamin as they made their way deeper into the mine's labyrinthine interior.

The path was winding and steep. Though it was bitterly cold outside, the tunnels were oppressively warm, and soon the group was drenched in sweat. Every step was a strain, the terrain unforgiving, but they pressed on, driven by the promise of safety.

Eventually, they emerged into a massive cavern, the heart of the mining community. Lanterns illuminated the space in a golden haze, revealing a bustling hub of activity. Minors moved with purpose, their voices echoing off the stone walls. Benjamin led them to a small alcove tucked away from the main cavern, offering them a place to rest.

Their horses were led away by another miner as they collapsed onto nearby crates and stone ledges, catching their breath.

"You'll be safe here," Benjamin assured them. "The patrols won't find you in these tunnels. I'll be back soon to show you some accommodation."

Adrian nodded, gratitude clear in his expression. "Thank you," he said sincerely.

"Well, I'm glad we're finally here," Liam muttered, wiping his forehead. "But I feel like I've been marinating in my own sweat."

"You look like it, too," Dominic added dryly.

Their laughter came easily, a welcome reprieve after the strain of the day.

Moments later, Benjamin returned with a young woman at his side. "This is Madison," he said. "She'll take you to a place where you can wash up and get some clean clothes."

Madison smiled warmly. "Follow me," she said, leading them through another series of tunnels.

Soon, they reached a spacious chamber with several offshoots.

"We've got separate areas for men and women," she explained. "Cecilia, come with me. The rest of you can use the rooms on the left."

Adrian followed the path assigned to them. After a much-needed wash and change of clothes, the three men emerged feeling far more human. They reconvened in a communal dining area, where long wooden tables were lined with miners enjoying a hot meal. The air was rich with the smell of freshly cooked stew and bread.

They joined a group of miners at one of the tables and were soon served plates of hearty fare. The food was simple but warm and filling. The camaraderie of their hosts was unexpectedly comforting.

Not long after, Cecilia and Madison joined them. The warmth of the meal and the calm atmosphere were enough to soothe their weary bodies. Once they had finished eating, Madison led them down another tunnel to a modest bunkroom.

The space was clean and quiet, with rows of sturdy beds lining the walls. Soft lanternlight bathed the room in a warm glow, lending it a sense of peace.

"This is the best we can offer for now," Madison said gently. "Come morning, we'll have a proper meeting and look at getting you somewhere more suitable. For now, please rest."

Cecilia nodded, her exhaustion written all over her face. "Thank you. We truly appreciate everything."

The group murmured their thanks and chose bunks. Cecilia selected one in a corner for a hint of privacy, while Adrian took the one just behind hers. He sank onto the mattress, the weight of the day finally catching up with him.

As the quiet sounds of his companions settling in filled the room, Adrian stared at the ceiling, his thoughts drifting. The journey had been long and perilous, but they had made it. For now, at least, they were safe.

Madison's words echoed in his mind: *Come morning, there'll be a proper meeting.* He hoped the miners would be open to the idea of the rebels gathering here. It was the safest and most practical place they had found yet.

That was a worry for tomorrow. Right now, all he could do was let go of the tension, if only for a few hours.

With a final sigh, Adrian closed his eyes and allowed sleep to take him.

Chapter 9

Allies for Jacob

After a night's rest beneath the old oak tree, Jacob, Bryne, and Edward awoke to find themselves surrounded, each with a dagger pressed against their throat. The tall young man standing before them moved with a quiet grace, his knowing eyes seeming to pierce straight into Jacob's soul. This wasn't someone to be toyed with.

Glancing around, Jacob quickly counted at least six figures encircling them. The odds were clearly not in their favour, especially when one of the captors held Jacob's own sword. He shot a glance at his cousins, both of whom appeared oddly calm, as though this were a perfectly ordinary situation. It was, after all, his fault they were in it. He had fallen asleep during his watch. He cursed himself silently for his carelessness.

"Well, who do we have here, then?" the young man asked, a glint of amusement in his eyes.

Jacob swallowed hard as Edward slowly raised his hands in a show of submission.

"We don't want any trouble. We're just passing through," Edward said calmly.

The man holding the dagger to Jacob's throat lowered his weapon and extended a hand. Caught off guard, Jacob hesitated for a moment before accepting the gesture. He allowed himself to be helped to his feet as his cousins rose beside him. Looking around properly now, Jacob noted that their captors consisted of four men and two women.

"The name's Trysten," the young man said. "This is my sister, Elsie, and my brothers, Finn and Damon."

Once he had pointed them out, the family resemblance was unmistakable. All four siblings shared hazel-brown eyes, auburn hair, and warm olive-toned skin. They were all tall and carried themselves with quiet confidence. The young men wore their hair cropped short, while Elsie's long hair was braided and fell to her waist.

"Our friends here are Erica and Luke," Trysten continued, gesturing towards the other two. "Luke's one of the main reasons we're out here."

He motioned for Jacob and his cousins to sit. Still wary, Jacob obeyed, lowering himself onto the damp grass, slick with morning frost. He didn't utter a word of complaint and kept his attention fixed on Trysten, waiting to hear what came next.

"We're from Dunley, and I don't know if you've noticed, but patrols have been getting worse all across the country." Trysten's group nodded, murmuring in agreement. "A few months back, one of the patrols came through and raided the houses. Said they were looking for twins of a certain age."

Jacob's gaze flicked towards Edward and Bryne, concern etched across his face.

"You've heard of this happening, I take it, from that look you just shared," Luke said, breaking the silence.

"We have," Edward replied grimly. "And we've been fortunate enough to rescue some of those taken in the past."

"Truly?" Luke asked, his voice a mixture of hope and disbelief.

"Yes, although not as many as we would have liked," Edward admitted.

Luke began to fidget, his fingers nervously twisting together. He shook his head, eyes glistening. "The night the authorities came, we got wind of their plans. My parents knew we had to act quickly. My twin brother and sister were exactly the age the guards were searching for. We had no choice—we had to get them out, no matter what."

He paused, drawing a shaky breath as the memories seemed to overwhelm him. Trysten, seated beside him, gently took his trembling hand and gave it a reassuring squeeze, silently urging him to go on.

"My father took my brother, and my mother took my sister. They split up, hoping it would improve their chances of escape. I stayed behind to create a diversion, to buy them some time."

Jacob, Edward, and Bryne listened in heavy silence, their expressions sombre.

"Did they make it?" Bryne asked softly.

Luke's eyes filled with tears that refused to fall. "No," he whispered. "None of them came back. I haven't seen them since. And we weren't the only ones. Another set of twins from town were taken too… their families disappeared."

A hush fell over the group, the weight of Luke's words pressing down on all of them. Edward placed a comforting hand on his shoulder.

"I'm so sorry," he said. "Our rebel faction has been working tirelessly to stop this from happening."

Luke nodded, the gratitude in his eyes unspoken but understood.

"The townspeople tried to fight back," Trysten added, his voice tight with anger. "But those who stood in the way were either beaten or killed. Luke took the worst of it. He was a wreck after the beating—he couldn't even get out of bed for weeks. Broken bones, bruised ribs, the works."

Jacob winced, his jaw tightening.

"Since then, we've been travelling across the country," Trysten went on, "doing what we can to help, and searching for this rebel faction we kept hearing about. And it seems we may have just found some of its members."

He nodded towards Edward.

"You have," Edward said firmly. "But we're not your average group."

Jacob, who had remained silent until now, took a deep breath and stood up. "There's something I need to tell you," he began, his voice unsteady. "I'm Prince Jacob. My sister, Aevah, and I... we're the reason twins are going missing. The queen wants us dead to make sure no one can challenge her claim to the throne. She's been sending patrols across the country to capture children of a certain age, hoping to find us—or someone connected to us."

The group stared at him in stunned silence, the weight of his confession settling thick in the air.

"I'm truly sorry for everything that's happened," Jacob went on, his voice heavy with guilt. "None of this was ever supposed to happen. Aevah and I have been doing everything we can to stop her, but it hasn't been easy. We've gone our separate ways for now; each working to thwart Elinor's plans and reclaim the throne."

Luke stood slowly, his gaze locked on Jacob, intense and unreadable. Jacob's throat tightened, and his fingers drummed nervously against his thigh as he waited.

Then, Luke extended a hand. His expression softened.

"It's not your fault," he said finally. "We're with you. All of us."

Jacob hesitated for a heartbeat before taking Luke's hand, a wave of relief and gratitude washing over him. The tension began to ease. One by one, the others nodded in agreement, exchanging looks that spoke of resolve and solidarity. Conversations began to stir among them – introductions, shared stories, small fragments of laughter breaking through the solemn air – as they prepared breakfast together.

Jacob felt a sense of peace settle in his chest. They weren't alone anymore. They had allies now – friends willing to stand with them.

As they sat down to eat, Jacoub found himself beside Elsie. He glanced her way, noticing how the morning light danced along the strands of her braided hair. She seemed focused on her food, but there was a flicker of curiosity behind her calm exterior.

"Hey," Jacob said, offering a tentative smile. "Thanks for not killing us back there."

Elsie looked up, a faint smile tugging at the corners of her lips. "No problem. We don't usually kill people on sight… just a precaution."

Jacob let out a small, nervous chuckle. "Good to know. So… how have you managed, travelling with patrols lurking around every corner?"

"Not as bad as it could be," Elsie replied. "We've been stopped a few times, but never detained. Staying out in the woods helps, we're left alone more than we would be in the main areas. We avoid cities and larger towns. They just aren't safe. And after what happened in Dunley, none of us wants to go back."

Jacob nodded, taking in her words. "It must be tough. I've seen the patrols myself. It feels like there aren't many safe places left."

Elsie sighed, her expression softening. "It is hard, but we do what we must. And now that we've met you… maybe, with a little luck, all of this will come to an end soon."

Jacob glanced over at his cousins, who were quietly finishing their breakfast. "I hope so. Once we complete our current task, we'll head to the mines and start planning the attack."

Elsie grew thoughtful, her gaze distant for a moment before she turned back to him. "You know, we might be able to help."

Trysten, overhearing the conversation, stepped closer and nodded. "She's right. Whatever it is you're doing, we know the area well and we could be useful."

Jacob hesitated. Part of him was unsure whether he should reveal the details of their mission. But there was something genuine in Elsie's tone and Trysten's steady gaze that stirred trust in him.

"We're searching for a shard," he said at last. "It's vital to what we're trying to do."

He explained the riddle and the importance of the crystal shards – how they were connected to the resistance and how dangerous it would be if Queen Elinor got her hands on them.

The group listened with focused attention. When he finished, they all agreed: Elinor had to be stopped, and they would do whatever they could to help.

Erica and Damon exchanged a look before sharing that they might already have an idea of where the next shard could be found – news that filled Jacob with cautious excitement.

With renewed purpose, the group packed away their belongings and readied their horses. Trysten took the lead, with Luke and Bryne riding beside him, deep in conversation about strategy. Jacob, feeling a fresh sense of hope, fell into step near Elsie.

"I guess we'll be travelling together for a while."

"Seems like it," she replied, her eyes meeting his with a spark of amusement. "Just try not to fall asleep on watch again, okay?"

Jacob laughed, the sound light and genuine. "I'll do my best."

The air was crisp and tinged with early morning chill as they moved through the dense woodland. The day passed without incident, the first leg of the journey coming to a quiet close. In just a few short hours, the group had begun to bond, and Jacob found himself learning more about the people he now travelled with.

While chatting with Elsie and Erica, he learned they had been best friends since they were babies, raised as next-door neighbours. Their mothers were close, and over the years, that bond had only grown stronger. The girls moved with easy familiarity, finishing each other's thoughts, sharing quiet laughter and inside jokes. Jacob found himself drawn in, not just to their friendship but to the comfort and warmth it brought to the group.

Trysten and Luke had been childhood friends, their bond forged through years of shared experiences and unspoken understanding. As they grew older, that friendship deepened, slowly blossoming into something more. But neither of them had dared to speak their feelings for some time, each convinced the other didn't feel the same. When they finally admitted the truth, their connection only strengthened, and what had once been friendship evolved into a quiet, steadfast love.

Then there were Damon and Finn, the ever-adventurous brothers who had a knack for finding trouble. Close in age and inseparable by nature, they were always pushing boundaries and exploring new places. Their mischievous grins and constant banter brought a much-needed lightness to the group, lifting spirits even in the midst of their harsh and uncertain journey.

The late autumn air was cold, the biting breeze stinging their cheeks as they rode. Trysten and Edward led the way, their eyes constantly scanning the trees and underbrush for any sign of danger.

As the sun dipped low on the horizon, casting long shadows through the forest, Trysten spotted a small clearing nestled among the trees.

"We'll rest here for the night," he announced, swinging down from his horse.

The others followed, grateful for the opportunity to stretch their legs and take a break. Jacob, sore from a long day in the saddle, winced slightly as he dismounted. His muscles ached, but the prospect of rest and warmth was enough to keep his spirits up.

They quickly set up their tents and gathered around a small fire, its flickering flames casting a warm glow over their faces. The heat was a welcome relief from the chill that clung to the evening air. As they ate their simple meal, conversation turned to the day ahead.

Luke broke the silence, his voice calm but clear. "There's a well not far from here. I think it's worth checking out tomorrow. It might be where the shard is hidden."

Edward considered this, nodding thoughtfully. "That sounds like a solid lead. We'll head there first thing in the morning."

As the fire crackled and the last light of the day faded, Edward glanced around the camp. "We'll need to set a watch tonight. Bryne, Finn, can I count on you two for the first shift?"

Bryne and Finn exchanged a look, then nodded in unison. "We've got it covered," Bryne said with a confident grin. "Don't worry."

Jacob once again found himself seated beside Elsie. There was something about her presence that brought him comfort, a calm warmth that settled his nerves. They shared light conversation as they ate, trading stories and the occasional laugh. Elsie had a way of making even the smallest things feel meaningful, and Jacob found himself hanging on her every word. The more time he spent with her, the more he wanted to be near her.

The fire's glow, paired with the hush of the forest, created a kind of quiet magic around them. Jacob watched the way her eyes sparkled when she smiled, the gentle curve of her lips as she laughed. He found himself wanting to be the reason behind that sparkle, behind her smile.

They lingered by the flames longer than the others, reluctant to break the moment. Eventually, they stood, preparing to turn in for the night. Jacob hesitated, then reached out and gently took her hand.

Elsie looked up at him, surprised at first, but then her expression softened. She gave his hand a reassuring squeeze.

"Goodnight, Elsie," Jacob said softly, his voice full of warmth.

"Goodnight, Jacob," she replied, her eyes glinting with something tender – something that made his heart skip.

As they parted and made their way to their tents, Jacob couldn't stop the smile that formed on his lips. For the first time in a long while, the world didn't feel quite so heavy.

Chapter 10

Echoes in the Deep

With the arrival of a new day, the group had packed up and were ready to head out. Luke took the lead, knowing the location of a potential well, one where Jacob hoped they might find one of the crystal shards. Spirits were high, and the morning passed swiftly as the newly acquainted friends laughed and joked with one another. Jacob felt a deep sense of gratitude for having found them. Without their support, he wasn't sure what might become of him.

As they rode, he couldn't help but marvel at the beauty of the surrounding land. Even in the cooler grip of autumn, the landscape held a breathtaking charm. It felt peaceful, a serene contrast to the turmoil and fear that had recently plagued the towns and cities.

Up ahead, he saw Luke spur his horse into a gallop before doubling back with a wide grin on his face.

"This is it! The well's just up ahead," he called out.

The group quickened their pace, Jacob's heart pounding with excitement. If this truly was the place, it could bring him one step closer to defeating his aunt. The well came into view in an open field beside a modest farmhouse. It was clear they would need to ask permission before using it – best to avoid an angry farmer with a pitchfork.

Edward walked up to the house and knocked on the door while the rest of the group stayed back, not wanting to alarm the residents. Jacob watched as Edward exchanged words with someone at the threshold before returning with a slight bounce in his step.

"I told them we're just passing through and asked if we could fill our water bags," he said. "They were more than happy to oblige—as long as we move along quickly. The farmer's wary of attracting patrols."

"Understandable. Have they been through here recently?" Trysten asked.

"Not lately, fortunately for us. But he'd rather not take any chances."

Jacob and the others nodded in agreement and turned their attention to the well. First priority: fill the water bags, just in case the farmer changed his mind. The well itself was a relic of the past, its stone walls worn smooth by time and draped in moss. The wooden roof looked newer, patched together in places from several repairs. Despite its age, the water inside was cool and crystal clear, a quiet testament to the craftsmanship of its construction.

Once everyone had filled their satchels, the group looked to Jacob. Erica peered down into the well and frowned.

"So… how do we know if this is the right one?" she asked. "It looks too full to have anything hidden in it."

Jacob pulled out the riddle once more, reading it aloud before passing it around so the others could read for themselves.

"I believe we're looking for a well that's no longer in use," he explained. "One with no water from thc linc. That suggests a place dry, dark, and cold."

"And we're sure it's a well?" Damon asked.

"What else would it be?" Finn replied.

"I don't know, just putting it out there," Damon said and then shrugged.

"It's a well," Bryne affirmed. "We've gone over the riddles a dozen times."

"Then I suppose Luke here knows a few more for us to check," Trysten added with a teasing grin and a wink in Luke's direction.

Luke chuckled and shook his head. "I've got a couple more in mind. Let's not give up hope just yet."

"Then let's go!" Elsie piped up, already bounding towards her horse.

The others followed, mounting up and falling into formation behind Luke once more. Over the next few days, they checked several more wells, but each one proved to be in use and full of water. Eventually, they came upon one that stood out – sealed beneath a large circular stone and overgrown with moss.

"This could be it," Jacob murmured.

They dismounted and gathered around the weathered stone. It took the combined effort of all of them to shift it aside. As the lid scraped free, it revealed a dark, empty hole beneath.

A putrid stench rolled up from the depths – rotting vegetation and stagnant water mingling in a nauseating wave. Those nearest recoiled, hands flying to their faces as their eyes watered from the foul air. Jacob staggered back, his nostrils burning from the acrid scent.

The hopeful energy that had been building dissipated almost instantly, replaced by unease and disappointment. Whatever was down there, it was far from the treasure they had hoped to find.

"So much for this being the one," Jacob spluttered, doing his best not to breathe in the foul air.

Realising their mistake, the group worked together to reseal the well, struggling against the weight of the stone and the overwhelming stench. With grim determination, they forced the heavy lid back into place, all while trying not to inhale the rancid air. Once it was secured, they moved a safe distance away and sat down to regroup, the foulness still lingering in their senses.

"Where else can we search?" Finn asked, his gaze landing expectantly on Luke.

"How about The Willowing Woods?" Damon suggested.

Erica scrunched her nose at the idea. "Isn't that area supposed to be haunted?"

"Seriously, Erica?" Bryne laughed. "Who told you that?"

"My mum," she replied defensively. "She always warned us to stay away. Said spirits walk among the trees and claim wandering souls. Right, Elsie?"

"Right!" Elsie nodded. "She used to tell us stories. And with the way the locals talk about people disappearing in those woods, we never had any reason to doubt her."

Luke spoke up, his tone more pragmatic. "Haunted or not, it's our best shot. Those old stories were probably just meant to scare kids. The real threat is the bandits."

"Bandits?" Bryne raised a brow. "That's not exactly reassuring."

"Better than ghosts," Trysten added with a smirk. "At least we can fight bandits."

Edward's expression turned serious. "We'll need to be extra cautious. Stay close and stay alert."

Trysten nodded. "We should be fine during the day, but if night falls while we're still in there, we'll need to be even more careful."

"So it's settled then—we're heading into the haunted woods," Luke said, dropping his voice to a ghostly whisper. He swayed dramatically from side to side, eyes wide and unblinking as he raised his arms and added, "Follow me…"

The group couldn't help but laugh at his theatrics as he made his way towards his horse, still whispering in that eerie voice.

Jacob chuckled along with the rest, not believing in ghosts himself, but the mention of bandits lingered in his mind. It was already late afternoon, and unless this well they sought was at the very edge of the woods, they would likely spend at least one night in the wilderness.

As they rode on, the scenery gradually changed. Open fields gave way to dense forests, and the air grew cooler with every passing hour. They were deep inside the Willowing Woods now, and Jacob could sense a shift in the atmosphere, both in the environment and within his companions. Silence fell over the group, each person lost in their own thoughts as the looming trees seemed to press in from all sides.

Every rustle in the underbrush or sudden birdcall made someone flinch. It was clear that, despite their bravado, the talk of ghosts had unsettled them more than they cared to admit. The deeper they ventured, the more oppressive the woods became. Gnarled branches arched overhead like skeletal fingers, casting eerie shadows across the narrowing path.

Jacob glanced at his friends, noting the tension in their expressions. Even Luke, so confident earlier, now rode with increased wariness, his eyes scanning every shadow.

"Stay close," Luke whispered. "We don't want to get separated."

The group nodded and drew closer together, their formation tightening as they continued deeper into the forest. The underbrush thickened, and their pace slowed to a crawl.

By the time dusk settled in, they arrived at another potential site. This well was hidden deep in the heart of the Willowing Woods, its mouth shrouded by overgrown vines and creeping foliage. They dismounted and approached cautiously, scanning the trees for any sign of movement.

"This looks promising," Jacob said, hope returning to his voice. "Let's check it out."

Edward lit a lantern and stepped forward, holding it over the edge of the well. The light revealed only darkness below – no water, just emptiness.

"It's dry," Edward confirmed. "Could be the one."

Jacob's heart leapt with cautious optimism – but the feeling didn't last.

From the shadows of the trees, figures emerged, slowly and deliberately. There was nothing rushed or panicked in their movements, only purpose and menace. The group tensed, hands instinctively reaching for their weapons.

"Too late," came a voice, cold and cruel. "The queen already has what you're looking for."

Jacob's heart sank. He recognised the uniforms; they belonged to the queen's patrol. They were outnumbered, and from the smug look on the leader's face, he knew it.

The man stepped forward, a cruel smile playing on his lips. "But don't worry. She's eager to meet you all. Especially you, Jacob."

Edward and Bryne advanced, swords drawn. Bryne glanced at Jacob and muttered, "Get him out of here."

Then he smirked at the patrol leader and said, "Well, I'd hate to disappoint the queen of all people, but we're not really in the mood for a meet-and-greet. Maybe next time?"

The patrol leader's smile widened. "I'm afraid you don't have a choice. The queen insists."

"Well," Bryne said, feigning resignation as he lowered his sword slightly, "if she's adamant..."

In a flash, Bryne lunged. His blade caught the patrol leader off guard, flashing in the dim light and coming to rest at the man's throat.

"Run!" Trysten shouted.

Finn grabbed Jacob by the scruff of his collar and yanked him away from the confrontation. The girls were already ahead, racing blindly through the trees. Behind them, Damon, Luke, Trysten, Edward, and Bryne engaged the patrolmen, steel flashing in the dim light, swords clashing in a violent symphony of sparks and shouting.

Night had fully fallen, and Jacob now sprinted through unfamiliar terrain, half-blind and stumbling with every step. The sounds of the fight faded behind him, swallowed by the dark woods. Shadows shifted around them, turning every shape into a threat. Tree branches clawed at their clothes and skin as they pushed deeper into the forest.

Jacob's heart pounded wildly, his breath coming in ragged gasps. Behind them, the heavy footsteps of pursuing guards grew louder. Finn kept a firm grip on his arm, practically dragging him through the thick underbrush.

"Keep moving!" Finn urged, his voice taut with urgency. "We can't let them catch us!"

Up ahead, the girls moved swiftly, barely visible between the trees. Erica glanced back, her eyes wide with both fear and resolve.

"This way!" she called, leading them down a narrow path winding deeper into the woods.

Jacob tripped over a root, stumbling hard, but Finn caught him under the arm and hauled him upright.

"Come on! No time—"

A shriek tore through the woods ahead, cutting him off. Jacob and Finn exchanged a panicked glance and broke into a run towards the source of the sound. The scream echoed, sharp and chilling, sending a spike of dread through both of them.

They burst into a small clearing. A guard lay sprawled on the ground, unconscious or worse, but there was no sign of the others.

"Is he dead?" Jacob whispered, voice trembling with fear and adrenaline.

Finn knelt beside the body and pressed a hand to the man's throat. "He's still breathing, but barely. Someone got to him before we did."

Jacob scanned the shadows, heart thundering. "We need to find the girls before the guards do."

Finn nodded, rising to his feet and gripping his sword tightly. "Let's go. Hopefully, Trysten and the others aren't far behind."

They pushed on, moving cautiously through the trees, every sense on edge. The forest felt like a living thing, heavy with silence and unseen danger. Jacob's mind swirled with worry. They didn't know where they were – worse, they had no idea where anyone else was either.

The darkness was suffocating, each step a gamble. Jacob could still hear the distant echoes of combat, the cries of his friends, the steel-on-steel clangs of battle. The fear of being caught – of being delivered to his aunt – pressed down on him like a weight. Every rustle of leaves, every creak of a branch set his nerves alight.

Even the breeze against his skin made him flinch. Exhaustion dulled his senses, and the line between imagined threat and real danger blurred. He glanced at Luke beside him – also tense, also scanning the shadows like he expected something to lunge at them at any moment.

"We need to find the others," Jacob whispered. "We can't keep running like this."

Luke nodded, jaw tight. "I know. But we have to stay hidden. If the guards catch us…"

He didn't finish the sentence, and Jacob didn't want him to. The thought of what his aunt would do if she got her hands on him was enough to make his blood run cold. They crept through the underbrush, the sounds of the battle now replaced by a still, eerie quiet. Jacob's thoughts raced. *What if the others had been captured? What if they were too late?*

Suddenly, a rustling in the nearby bushes made them freeze. Jacob's heart shot into his throat as he squinted into the dark.

A figure emerged.

His breath caught – until he saw the familiar face.

"Jacob! Luke!" Erica whispered urgently, her face pale with relief. "Thank goodness I found you. We need to move, now. The guards are closing in."

She grabbed their hands and pulled them deeper into the woods, towards a dense thicket. Hidden within it was a shallow grove, low and cramped, shielded by thorny branches and thick undergrowth. It was barely large enough to hold them, but it offered cover.

Jacob gratefully collapsed into the space, his legs aching and feet burning. Luke dropped down beside him, muttering curses as he dabbed at the fresh scratches on his face and hands.

"Where are the others?" he asked.

"I don't know, but Elsie will be back any minute," Erica said. "We stayed together after the fight, found this place, then heard voices—some that sounded like the rest of you—so we split up. That's how I found you."

"So you haven't seen anyone else either?" Luke asked, brows furrowed.

"No. We were almost caught once. But when we stumbled on this grove, we jumped in. It's perfect now, while it's still dark. But once the sun rises…"

She trailed off. The rest didn't need saying.

Jacob opened his mouth to ask how long they'd been hiding, but Luke's hand clamped over it before he could speak. Jacob froze, his ears straining.

Footsteps.

They were soft, deliberate, but unmistakable. Drawing closer. All three tensed. Jacob's hand crept to his belt, fingers wrapping tightly around the hilt of his dagger. The others followed suit, blades drawn in silence, breath held, eyes locked on the shadowy gap in the brush.

Jacob inched back into the bush, the thorns digging into his skin, but he didn't dare make a sound. The pricks stung, but they were nothing compared to the fear churning in his chest. Just when he thought the pressure couldn't get worse, the footsteps halted. Silence fell, thick and suffocating.

Then a voice broke through.

"Erica?"

At the sound of Elsie's voice, Jacob's entire body sagged with relief. His shoulders dropped, and the tension that had gripped him so tightly melted away. He exhaled a shaky breath, his grip on the dagger slackening.

"Hello, gang. Seems like there's a bit of a party happening here," Finn said with a grin as he stepped into the grove behind Elsie.

With five of them now crammed into the small space, it was more than a tight fit. Finn and Luke shifted towards the edge of the thicket, taking up positions just outside the cover, eyes scanning for any signs of pursuit while the others caught up.

"Where are the others?" Jacob asked, voice low.

"I don't know… sorry," Luke replied. "We managed to hold off the first wave of guards without any serious injuries. But as they pulled back, we figured they'd regroup and come back stronger. We scattered, trying to draw them off and look for you. I got separated. I've been wandering since—ran into a few more guards along the way. Then Elsie found me."

Jacob nodded grimly. They were still in danger, and not all of their friends were accounted for.

"We've got a few hours until sunrise," he said, "then we'll be in serious trouble. What do we do?"

“We can’t stay here, that’s for sure,” Erica replied. “We have to try to get out of these woods and hope the others have made it.”

Everyone nodded in agreement. With no better options, they formed a plan. A narrow path twisted through the dense forest ahead, likely an old animal trail, but it was better than nothing.

With weapons ready and nerves strung tight, the group began their silent journey, slipping through the trees like ghosts.

Jacob followed close behind, his eyes darting between every shadow, his heart thudding with each unexpected sound. The forest felt alive, its branches shifting and creaking, as if watching them. Every rustle of leaves sent his pulse into overdrive.

He said nothing, but inside, all he could do was pray to the divine spirit that fate was on their side.

Chapter 11

Home Ground

Elinor felt a wave of relief wash over her as she stepped out of the carriage and set foot on familiar ground. It seemed like years had passed since she had last been home. She was grateful they had managed to travel by sea – had they taken the overland route, she would still be on the road.

As she passed through the castle gates, a renewed sense of purpose settled over her. She was ready to throw herself back into her duties. Workers greeted her along the way, and as she walked through the familiar hallways, the scent of fresh flowers drifted through the air, grounding her further in the comforts of home.

After freshening up, her first destination was the throne room. There, she found her trusted advisor and knight, Julian Wood, waiting. He had prepared detailed reports on the kingdom's current affairs, eager to bring her up to speed. But Elinor was more concerned with her enemies.

Julian began with the most pressing matter: Cecilia and Adrian. Despite the best efforts of the royal guard, the pair remained elusive. However, he reported that rebel captives were being taken in daily. While none had yet given up their hideouts or the location of their base, the constant patrols sweeping the countryside would, in time, uncover it.

Then there was the matter of Galrick and Nicholas. After pulling a minor disappearing act, they were now reportedly in the mountains with Aevah. The Bennetts had assured Elinor of their loyalty, claiming nerves had driven them to flee. Elinor remained unconvinced, though she was confident in the outcome – her scouts were watching, ready to intervene when the time was right.

As for Jacob, Julian explained that several young men had been mistaken for him in recent days, but none had turned out to be the prince. The search continued.

The information weighed heavily on Elinor. She had much to consider and even more to anticipate. She needed to remain one step ahead of everyone.

"I know the rebels are planning something," she said, her voice calm but firm. "And with my dear family out there trying to thwart me, I must be prepared. Where do we stand on assistance from the lords?"

"Most are ready to send soldiers at your call," Julian replied evenly.

"Most?" Her brow arched, a trace of irritation flickering in her tone.

"Lord Stone is proving difficult. Bishop has stated that his men will only arrive once Lord Stone's do."

"Oh, really?" Elinor's eyes narrowed, her fingers tapping irritably on the armrest of her throne. "And what is Lord Stone's reasoning?"

"His daughter, Your Majesty. He's made it clear—once she is returned to him, unharmed, his army is yours."

Her gaze sharpened. "Why do you look nervous, Julian? What aren't you telling me?"

He hesitated, then drew a slow breath. "Lord Stone is on his way here. He's bringing a small company. During our correspondence, I mentioned your travels and gave an estimate of your return. He informed me he would arrive within days of your return."

Elinor's expression darkened. "So, he means to confront me directly. Very well. We shall see how this plays out."

Julian shifted uncomfortably, clearing his throat. "Your Majesty, there's another matter. The kingdom's paperwork has piled up in your absence. Several documents require your signature and decisions."

Elinor let out a quiet sigh but gave a nod. "Very well. Bring them to me."

He stepped forward, offering her a stack of parchment. Each page detailed various administrative concerns. Elinor scanned them swiftly, signing where needed and jotting down notes on the rest, her mind already calculating her next move.

As Elinor worked through the documents, Julian continued his updates on the kingdom's latest developments.

"The crops in the southern regions are struggling due to the recent rainfall and unexpected frosts," he reported. "We may need to allocate additional resources to support the farmers. There have also been reports of increased illness in the coastal villages—likely tied to the weather."

Elinor's expression softened, a rare flicker of concern crossing her face. "I will address these issues promptly. Make sure provisions are dispatched to the affected regions and send some of the city's healers to the coast. If this illness is serious, I want to know exactly what we're dealing with."

Once she had finished with the paperwork, she stood and handed the documents back to Julian. "Thank you. I need to speak with Mistress Fleur."

Julian bowed. "As you command, Your Majesty."

Elinor made her way through the castle's corridors, her heels clicking sharply against the stone floor. Her thoughts were already on the next task. Reaching Mistress Fleur's quarters, she knocked briskly.

Mistress Fleur – a woman of quiet strength and dignified grace who oversaw the young ladies of the court – opened the door and curtsied. "Your Majesty. How may I be of service?"

“I need to see Lord Stone’s daughter,” Elinor said without preamble

Fleur’s expression tightened slightly, but she nodded. “Of course. I confined her to her room these past few days. She’s become rather bold of late.”

Without further delay, she led Elinor to a secluded chamber where the young woman was being held. Inside, Rosalind looked up from where she sat, her eyes flashing with a mix of fear and defiance.

Elinor stepped closer, her gaze cold and steady. “You, my dear, are a key picce in this gamc, and I intend to use you wisely. Your father is on his way to court and will demand to see you. You’ll be presented to him, looking unharmed and grateful. You’ll tell him you’re well and that you wish to stay here. That way, he’ll have no grounds to refuse my demands.”

Rosalind remained silent, her expression unyielding.

“Do I make myself clear?” Elinor’s tone sharpened, each word laced with warning.

Still, Rosalind said nothing. Her silence was louder than words, and her stare met Elinor’s without flinching.

Elinor’s eyes narrowed. “I asked you a question, Rosalind.”

The young woman pressed her lips into a tight line. Her jaw set with quiet rebellion. She refused to give Elinor the satisfaction of a response.

Elinor's voice dropped, venom threading each syllable. "Very well. If you choose silence, you'll learn quickly that my tolerance has limits."

Rosalind held her ground, her silence unwavering – a final act of resistance.

"So be it," Elinor hissed. "Don't say I didn't warn you."

Without lifting a finger, Elinor sent a wave of agony coursing through the girl's body. She watched with cold detachment as Rosalind stiffened, her body contorting against the invisible assault. A howl tore from her throat, but still her eyes locked with Elinor's, blazing with defiance. She refused to break, just as she had before.

That only enraged Elinor further.

She intensified the pain. What had once felt like a thousand needles piercing flesh now became something far worse – bones shattering from within, set ablaze by searing fire.

Finally, Rosalind's gaze faltered. Her body twisted and thrashed on the floor, and her voice cracked as she gasped, "Please stop!" Her cries turned to raw screams as she clawed at her skin, blood pooling beneath her fingers, staining the stone floor. "Please, I beg you—under the divine spirit—I can't take it anymore!"

Elinor laughed, a cruel, mirthless sound.

"Not so quiet now, are you?" she sneered. "What's the matter? Are you in pain?"

"Yes," Rosalind sobbed. "Stop. Please. I beg you…"

"Well, that's a shame," Elinor murmured coldly, "because I'm just getting started."

She released her hold on Rosalind's body for a brief moment. The young woman collapsed to the floor, sobbing uncontrollably, her limbs trembling from the residual pain. But Elinor wasn't finished – not by a long stretch.

With practised ease, she slipped into Rosalind's mind, weaving illusions that blurred the line between reality and nightmare. Though still confined within her chamber, Rosalind found herself staring at her father, Lord Stone, standing before her. But instead of offering comfort, his face contorted with fury and contempt.

"Why, Rosalind?" he demanded, his voice booming, echoing endlessly through her thoughts. "Why did you betray us?"

Her heart broke at the sight of him, her voice cracking as she cried, "No, Father, I didn't! I swear!" She reached out to touch him, but her hands passed through his image as though he were made of mist.

Elinor watched from the sidelines, her expression void of sympathy. There was only cold satisfaction in her eyes. "You see, my dear," she whispered, though Rosalind couldn't hear her, "the mind is a fragile thing. And I can break it just as easily as I can mend it."

She twisted the illusion further, turning Lord Stone's anger into violence. He lashed out at his daughter, striking her again and again, his eyes filled with disdain. Between beatings, he hurled cruel words at her – accusations, slurs, reminders of her supposed failures. Each insult sank deeper than any physical blow.

Rosalind screamed, her cries echoing off the chamber walls. The vision cycled again and again, each repetition more vicious than the last. The pain felt excruciatingly real, crafted with precision by Elinor's power. Her body trembled, and her mind frayed with each passing hour, dragged towards the brink of madness.

Elinor observed it all with perverse delight, basking in the power she held. She controlled every moment, every illusion, every scream.

Eventually, she turned to Mistress Fleur, who stood silently at her side.

"Have someone keep watch over her. The nightmare will continue in my absence," Elinor said, her voice calm and composed. "And the pain."

Mistress Fleur bowed low. "Of course, Your Majesty."

"I'll return before nightfall to release her. See that someone feeds her and watches her through the night. I don't want her doing anything foolish before her father arrives."

Without another glance at the suffering girl, Elinor swept from the chamber, her mind already calculating the next move. She had no time for sentiment. Rosalind needed to be broken – utterly and completely – before Lord Stone arrived. His loyalty, and more importantly, his army, depended on it.

The rebels were growing bolder. The stakes had never been higher.

And Elinor knew she would have to be sharper, colder, and more ruthless than ever to outmanoeuvre them all.

***

As the days passed, Elinor felt a deep sense of satisfaction. Everything was in place, and Rosalind was nearly broken. Each morning, after the servants had fed, dressed, and cleaned her, Elinor would arrive and set the tormented visions anew. Always the same: her father appearing, declaring what a disappointment she was, then inflicting endless pain – stretching her on the rack, breaking bones, or searing flesh with fire.

Thanks to Elinor's power, every moment was real to Rosalind. The agony, the terror – none of it could be distinguished from truth. By evening, Elinor would end the torment and step into the role of saviour, banishing her father and offering false comfort. Now, she was on her way to release Rosalind one final time. Her scouts had informed her that Lord Stone was riding hard and would likely arrive at the castle within hours.

Elinor hoped her tactic had worked, that Rosalind would be too frightened of her father to wish to leave. It was vital for keeping Lord Stone in line. At Rosalind's chamber door, she paused to compose herself before pushing it open.

Rosalind lay trembling on the bed, broken by the visions that still racked her mind. Her eyes, swollen and red from weeping, lifted in fear as the illusion melted away and Elinor appeared before her.

"Rosalind," Elinor said softly, "it's over now. I'm here to help you."

Rosalind's eyes widened in disbelief. "Help me?" she whispered, her voice hoarse.

Elinor stepped closer and nodded. "Yes. Your father has been dealt with. You are safe now."

Tears streamed down Rosalind's cheeks as she tried to sit upright. "Thank you," she sobbed. "I thought… I thought I was going to die. That my father was going to kill me."

Elinor brushed a strand of hair from Rosalind's face with a tender hand. "You are safe now. He can't hurt you. Rest, and I will see that no harm comes near you again." Rising, she turned to the maids. "Dress her and see that she is fed. I shall need her shortly." Looking back at Rosalind with false warmth, she added, "Rest, my dear. We shall dine together tonight. How would you like that?"

"Very much, Your Majesty. Thank you."

Satisfied, Elinor left the room. Rosalind's mind was now a tangle of blurred memories, real and false, all painting her father as a monster and Elinor as her sole protector. The queen could hardly wait for Lord Stone's arrival.

In the throne room, she took her seat, sending a guard to fetch Rosalind. Just as she gave the order, another guard entered and bowed deeply. "Your Majesty, Lord Stone has arrived and requests an audience."

Elinor's lips curled into a bitter smile. "Send him in."

The heavy doors swung open moments later, and Lord Stone strode in, flanked by his men. Tall and imposing, his stern expression mirrored Elinor's own.

"Your Majesty," he said with a slight bow. "I trust you are well?"

"Indeed," Elinor replied, her tone like ice. "I understand you are here with concerns about your daughter."

His jaw tightened. "Yes. I want assurance she will be returned to me unharmed."

Elinor leaned forward, locking her gaze on his. "She is all yours." She gestured to the guards, who ushered Rosalind in.

Elinor had to admit the maids had done well. Rosalind looked almost herself again, her navy dress elegant, her hair loose and flowing. Colour had been coaxed back into her cheeks, though her eyes betrayed the truth – haunted, distant, broken. At the sight of her father, she froze.

"Rosalind," Lord Stone said warmly, taking a step towards her. "I have missed you."

With each step he took, Rosalind stepped back, her body trembling. "No! Stay away from me!" she cried.

Suspicion darkened his eyes as he looked at Elinor. "What have you done to her?"

Feigning innocence, Elinor replied smoothly. "Nothing, my lord. I have cared for her. She has endured a terrible ordeal, and I offered her safety and comfort."

"Stay away from me," Rosalind whispered again, her voice breaking. "Don't hurt me anymore."

Elinor soothed, "Come, Rosalind, you are safe."

Rosalind darted towards her, head down, clinging to her hand as though it were a lifeline. Elinor's smile widened as she glanced at Lord Stone.

"What troubles you, my dear? Your father has come to take you home."

"No!" Rosalind screamed and then sobbed. "Don't make me go. He will hurt me again. You promised to keep me safe."

"Shh, my dear," Elinor murmured. "I will not let anyone harm you ever again."

Lord Stone stepped forward in desperation, but the guards crossed their blades before him. His voice cracked. "Rosalind, it's me. I have never harmed you."

Rosalind recoiled, clinging tighter to Elinor. "Please don't let him near me."

Elinor's eyes gleamed with satisfaction. "My lord, your daughter is clearly distressed. Best you keep your distance."

"Rosalind!" Lord Stone pleaded, anguish tearing at his voice. "I swear I have never hurt you. These are lies!"

Elinor smiled and stroked her hand. "Rosalind, my dear, you're safe here with me. Tell your father that you wish to stay in Carraton, where no harm can come to you."

Rosalind hesitated briefly, her eyes darting between her father and Elinor. "I… I want to stay here," she whispered. "I'm safe here."

"Of course, my dear. Guards, take her back to her chambers."

As Rosalind was escorted away, Lord Stone reached towards her in despair. "Rosalind!" he called, but she flinched as she passed him and didn't look back. The sight hollowed him.

Elinor turned to him, her voice hard as steel. "You see, my lord? Your daughter is safe with me, and she has chosen to stay."

His face twisted with fury. "Absurd! What have you done to her?"

Elinor's smile was cold. "I have given her care and protection. If she believes you harmed her, perhaps there is truth to it."

"This is madness!" he roared. "I will not aid you with my men until my daughter is returned, so I can undo the sorcery you've woven on her mind."

Her voice dropped to an icy threat. "You dare defy me? Know this: your daughter is under my protection. If you or any lord betray me, I will send her body back to you in pieces."

Lord Stone paled, his resolve faltering. "You wouldn't dare."

"Try me," Elinor uttered, her smile merciless. "You have until dawn. Choose wisely."

With fists clenched and anger barely contained, Lord Stone yielded. "Very well. My men will march when you call. But if any harm comes to my daughter, you will pay."

"As long as you and the court behave, she will remain unharmed," Elinor replied coldly.

He turned and stormed from the throne room, leaving Elinor watching with quiet triumph. She glanced at Julian, her loyal advisor, who had witnessed the entire exchange.

"See that Lord Stone's every move is tracked," she commanded.

Julian bowed low. "As you command, Your Majesty."

Her fingers trailed across the carved arms of the throne. "Too many seek to unseat me. We must trust no one and be prepared."

Julian's voice was steady. "We will be ready, Your Majesty. With the armies and your power, none will stand against you."

Elinor rose, her presence commanding as power crackled through her veins. "No, they will not." She descended the steps of her throne like a storm given form, ready to crush all who would dare oppose her.

Chapter 12

The Path Ahead

Aevah had been travelling with her cousin Isabella for several days now. Though she cherished her cousin's company, it felt strange not being with Jacob. Their whole lives, they had never spent a single night apart. And now, here they were – each on a separate path, journeying to different corners of the country in search of the magical crystal shards. Their mission: to stop their evil aunt, who had betrayed their father and stolen their kingdom.

It sounded like the plot of a fantasy tale – one that people read about in books. But this was Aevah's reality. A world turned upside down, where family was either scattered across the land or lost to death.

She slumped in the saddle, thoughts drifting to her grandfather and father – both taken from her by the same cruel hands. She needed them. Missed them terribly. During the day, she managed to wear a mask of strength, but at night, the pain crept in. Every hidden wound opened, raw and aching. The nightmares didn't let her forget. She often woke sobbing, the echo of her screams trapped within the silent dark.

Though she hadn't witnessed their deaths, her mind painted scenes so vivid they might as well have been memories.

Each night, she found herself in a mist-shrouded chamber. The sound of footsteps echoed behind, and she turned in fear, only to see her father standing in the distance.

"Father," she would call, voice trembling.

But he never heard.

He always stopped before a hooded woman. Aevah's heart clenched as she watched the shock widen his eyes before the blade plunged into his chest. Her scream would pierce the dream, fracturing the illusion like glass. Shards of light rained down, slicing through the darkness and illuminating the space where her father lay.

Desperation surged through her. She would sprint towards him, calling his name, but the closer she thought she was, the further away he drifted – until he was gone.

Then came the laughter. Her aunt's wicked laugh echoed in her skull like a curse.

Aevah clawed at her head as the sound grew louder, until her own screams drowned it out. Blood on her hands, she stared down, shaking from what had happened.

Then she would hear her grandfather's voice.

"Aevah."

Looking up, she'd see him standing before her, bathed in light, a smile on his face, arms stretched out to embrace her.

"Grandpa," she would cry, hope flickering inside her. She'd rise to her feet, take a step towards him, only to watch him collapse. Lifeless.

Elinor stood over him, a bloodied knife in hand, her eyes fixed on Aevah with a glint of cruel satisfaction.

"You're next," she would hiss, her voice a venomous promise.

And that was always when Aevah woke.

But the fear lingered. So did the grief, the fury, the helplessness. Even now, in the saddle, the weight of it pressed down on her chest. Her father's lifeless form haunted her vision, the pool of blood spreading beneath him. Her grandfather's smile faded as he fell...

"Aevah, are you alright?"

Isabella's voice cut through the storm of her thoughts. She had pulled up alongside her, reins in hand, concern etched across her face.

Aevah was trembling violently, her breath ragged. It felt as though the walls of her mind were closing in, memories and dreams blurring into one unbearable reality. Her vision clouded with tears as she clutched the reins tighter, desperate to anchor herself in the present.

Isabella reached out, placing a steadying hand on Aevah's arm. "Breathe, Aevah. Just breathe. You're safe here with me."

Aevah latched onto her cousin's voice like a lifeline, forcing herself to inhale shakily, then again, slower this time. The haunting images of her father and grandfather lingered in her mind, but Isabella's presence offered a small measure of comfort.

"I'm sorry," Aevah whispered, her voice trembling. "It's just… everything. The memories, the nightmares. I can't escape them."

Isabella gave her arm a reassuring squeeze. "You don't have to apologise. I'm here for you. We'll find the crystals, then your mother—and we'll make Elinor pay for what she's done."

Aevah nodded slowly, a fresh breath settling in her lungs as her resolve began to steady. She wiped the tears from her cheeks and straightened in the saddle. "Thank you. I don't know what I'd do without you."

Isabella smiled, her eyes bright with determination. "We'll get through this. One step at a time. Starting with camp, food, and a proper heart-to-heart, I think."

"That sounds wonderful."

They rode another mile in companionable silence, Isabella taking the lead. When she finally veered off the road, Aevah felt nothing but relief. It was late afternoon, earlier than they usually stopped, but she welcomed the break.

They guided their mares into a small clearing tucked within the dense woods. The ground was littered with twigs and broken branches that cracked softly beneath their boots. Thick foliage overhead let only slivers of sunlight through, casting shifting patterns of light and shadow across the forest floor.

After tying the horses to a low-hanging branch, Aevah took the lead in unsaddling them both. The clearing was modest, but large enough to suit their needs. In its centre lay a circular fire pit, edged with time-worn stones and filled with remnants of ash and charred wood – a clear sign that others had camped here recently.

The trees surrounding them blocked off a lot of the wind from the road, and Aevah knew that once the fire was lit, they would have a warm and restful night.

While Isabella worked on pitching the tents, Aevah went to collect firewood. With the forest floor already scattered with dry twigs and branches, it didn't take long for her to return with her arms full. She made her way back to the fire pit, carefully setting down the kindling.

She glanced around and spotted Isabella tending to the horses. With them taken care of, Aevah decided to try her hand at building the fire. She stacked the logs and twigs just as she had been taught and struck the flint. A few sparks jumped, one even catching briefly before flickering out. On her fourth try, frustration mounting, she drew on her power – just a small amount – and coaxed a spark into life. It caught quickly, growing into a flame that curled around the wood and soon roared into a steady blaze.

She added more logs and sat back, watching with quiet pride as the fire crackled and danced. She hadn't done it entirely by hand, but she had made fire.

Just as the flames took hold, Isabella joined her, handing her an apple and a handful of berries. They sat side by side, eating in silence, the gentle crackle of the fire and the rustle of leaves forming a calming rhythm around them.

Once they finished, Isabella stood and stretched. "Well, I think it's time we try to catch dinner before the sun sets."

She walked over to her saddlebags and pulled out her bow and quiver. Aevah rose as well, eyes widening at the thought.

"Of course, it's been a while," Aevah added with a grin and grabbed her own from her tent. "But I'm sure I've still got it."

The two of them ventured into the forest, the air cool and crisp around them. Sunlight filtered through the canopy in slender shafts, providing just enough light to see their surroundings while leaving plenty of shadow to stay concealed. They moved quietly, their footsteps muffled by the soft, leaf-strewn earth beneath their boots.

Isabella led the way, her sharp eyes scanning the underbrush for any signs of movement. Aevah followed closely behind, her heart pounding with a mixture of excitement and anticipation. The silence between them was companionable, broken only by the rustle of leaves or the occasional cry of a distant bird.

Suddenly, Isabella raised a hand, bringing them both to a halt. She pointed towards a small clearing ahead where two rabbits nibbled quietly at the grass, their ears twitching at the slightest sound.

Aevah's breath caught in her throat. The rabbits seemed fragile and unaware, their noses sniffing the air cautiously.

Isabella moved slowly, drawing an arrow and knocking it to her bowstring with practised ease. Aevah mirrored her movements, steadying her hands despite the rush of adrenaline coursing through her veins. They waited, eyes locked on their targets, breaths shallow in the cool air.

With a soft twang, Isabella released her arrow, and Aevah followed a heartbeat later. Both arrows hit their marks. The rabbits collapsed instantly.

Aevah exhaled, only then realising she had been holding her breath. A sense of accomplishment swept over her, warming her from the inside out.

They stepped into the clearing to retrieve their catch, then made their way back to camp. The fire still crackled steadily, its glow welcoming. They each found a flat rock and began the meticulous work of skinning the rabbits and preparing them for cooking. As they worked, they spoke in low voices, sharing laughter over their first, most disastrous hunting attempts.

With the meat cleaned and ready, Isabella added it to a pot alongside a handful of wild herbs and mushrooms Aevah had foraged earlier. The fire snapped and hissed as the ingredients simmered together.

As they waited for the meal to cook, the two cousins sat side by side by the fire. Its warmth and the flickering light offered comfort against the growing dusk. Aevah stared into the flames, her thoughts turning inward, heavy with worry and sorrow. After a long silence, she finally spoke.

"Isabella," she said softly, her voice trembling, "I've been having these nightmares. Every night, I see Father and Grandpa… and Elinor. It feels so real. Like they're right there with me, only to be ripped away again. I'm losing them over and over. I feel so alone. I miss Jacob so much. I miss Grandpa and my parents. It's like… like a part of me is missing."

Isabella listened without interruption, her expression gentle and filled with empathy. She reached over and wrapped her arms around Aevah, pulling her into a comforting embrace.

"I can't even begin to imagine how hard this must be for you," she murmured. "But try to remember, the dreams aren't real. They can only hurt you if you let them."

Aevah nodded, tears welling in her eyes. "I know. But I don't know if I can do this. It's too much. I feel like I'm carrying everything, and I'm terrified. Terrified that I'll never see Jacob or Mother again. That I'll never make things right."

Isabella squeezed her shoulder gently. "Your grandfather and father would be so proud of you, Aevah. You're stronger than you think. And as for Jacob and your mother, we'll find them. I swear it. Until then, you have me. I'm not going anywhere. You're stuck with me for life." She nudged her, trying to coax a smile.

Aevah gave a teary laugh, feeling a thread of warmth push through the heaviness in her chest. "I don't know what I'd do without you."

"You would do it all anyway," Isabella replied with a soft smile. "Because you're strong, resilient, and more capable than you know. But I'm glad I'm here with you. We'll face whatever comes, together."

Aevah leaned into the hug, her tears finally spilling over. "Thank you. I needed to hear that."

"I've got you," Isabella whispered, holding her tightly.

They sat there wrapped in one another's arms, the firelight dancing across their faces. For a moment, everything felt still – peaceful – until the soft bubbling from the pot snapped Isabella's head up.

"Oh no, the food!" she exclaimed, springing to her feet.

Laughter spilt from both of them as they rushed to the pot. The stew was bubbling over, but luckily, nothing had burned. They saved it just in time, and with relieved smiles, slumped back down by the fire.

As they ate, they swapped childhood tales and fairy stories they'd once heard whispered before bedtime. Warmth from the fire and from each other wrapped around them like a blanket. For the first time in a long while, the burden didn't feel quite as heavy.

When they had finished eating, sleep began to tug at their limbs, and they decided to call it a night. Aevah settled into her blankets, the firelight casting soft shadows across the tent.

She drifted off with a smile on her face, her dreams filled not with blood and loss, but with adventure, magic, and soaring beasts that carried her across golden seas. For once, her mind was free. No nightmares found her. Only peace and a long-forgotten sense of hope wrapped gently around her heart.

Chapter 13

Threads Rewoven

It was mid-morning, and Galrick and his brother had been travelling for several days, still searching for the princess. Now, away from home and free of his family's influence, Galrick found himself questioning whether she was even alive. No one had seen Aevah or Jacob since the queen had taken the throne. In his mind, the queen's paranoia, her fear of being usurped, had conjured threats that likely didn't exist. He certainly hoped that was the case. He remembered Aevah and Jacob fondly from childhood, often playing with them during visits to the capital.

As they rode on, the sound of trickling water reached Galrick's ears. Spotting a narrow path between the trees, they guided their horses towards it, seeking a chance to rest and water the animals. The stream ahead offered a brief reprieve. Galrick glanced at Nicholas, who looked just as weary and equally doubtful.

"Do you think we'll ever find her?" Nicholas asked, his voice laced with uncertainty.

Galrick sighed and shook his head. "I don't know. The queen's paranoia has driven her to extremes. You've heard the rumours of the missing children, same as I. As much as I hope they're alive and well, I fear they perished in the fire."

"Yet the queen remains certain we'll find her."

"The same queen who went mad with power and now sees threats in every shadow," Galrick said as he raised a brow.

"They could've been hidden away all these years. Who knows? Magic is a mysterious thing that can do almost anything. Maybe they've been safe all this time."

"I hope you're right, little brother. I really do."

They dismounted and led their horses to the stream, where the animals drank eagerly from the cool, clear water. The brothers took a moment to rest on the riverbank. Galrick looked around, taking in the quiet beauty of the place. It was hard to believe that such serenity could exist in a kingdom touched by madness.

Once rested, they began to walk their horses along the water's edge. A short distance downstream, voices drifted through the brush. They moved closer, careful not to startle whoever might be nearby.

Just ahead, Galrick spotted a horse – one of the finest he'd ever seen. A great white mare stood tall and watchful, her gaze fixed on them, mimicking the movement of their own horses with a wary grace. The mare calmed only when her rider placed a soothing hand on her neck, whispering soft words. She stilled, nuzzling into the young woman's arms before stepping aside, still watching the newcomers cautiously.

Galrick's gaze shifted to Nicholas, who had stopped beside him. He was staring at the young woman. Her eyes met his, and she smiled – a small, knowing smile that lit up her striking features. She wore a deep red riding dress, her long dark hair cascading in loose ringlets down her back. Her emerald green eyes were vivid against her olive skin, her cheeks and nose flushed faintly pink from the chill.

Galrick chuckled to himself, recognising the look on his brother's face – captivated and spellbound. He stepped forward to introduce them.

"Good afternoon, my lady. My name is Galrick, and this is my brother, Nicholas."

"Afternoon, Galrick. Nicholas," the young woman replied, turning to each of them as she spoke their names. "My name is…" She paused, the words catching in her throat. Galrick noticed the hesitation, the way her eyes studied them, weighing something unspoken.

Her gaze lingered, searching their faces with intensity. Galrick looked to Nicholas, who wore an expression of equal uncertainty. Then something shifted. Recognition flickered in the young woman's eyes, quickly warming into joy. A smile spread across her face, lighting up her entire demeanour as if a forgotten memory had surfaced.

"My name is Aevah," she said at last, her voice now calm and assured. "Aevah Maycott."

The name hit Galrick like a wave. He exchanged a glance with Nicholas, both of them stunned. *Could it truly be her? After so long chasing ghosts, was she truly standing before them?*

Galrick took a closer look. Though years had passed, the resemblance was unmistakable – this was Aevah. Dropping to one knee, he looked up at her with a broad smile. Seeing this, Nicholas quickly followed, still wide-eyed with disbelief as Galrick spoke.

"Princess Aevah, we've heard the rumours that you might still be alive, but we never dared believe them. You can't imagine how overjoyed I am to see you with my own eyes."

Just then, another figure stepped out from behind the horse, a young woman with a confident stride and a warm, inviting smile. She wore a simple yet elegant travelling cloak, her jet-black curls tied back in a loose braid. Her eyes, an intense shade of blue, sparkled with curiosity and intelligence as she came to stand beside Aevah, her gaze settling on the newcomers.

"This is Isabella," Aevah said, gesturing towards her companion. "She's been journeying with me for some time. Isabella, meet Galrick and his brother Nicholas."

Isabella nodded politely, her eyes meeting Galrick's with a flicker of amusement. "It's a pleasure to see you both," she said, her voice calm and kind.

At the sight of her, Galrick broke into a wide grin, scarcely able to believe who stood before him. Another old family friend – one he had long thought lost.

"Isabella…" Galrick uttered, his voice laced with disbelief and joy. "We thought you and your family were gone forever. How is it you're here—alive and well?"

Her smile softened, and she exchanged a glance with Aevah before answering. "It's a long story. Come, sit with us. We can share everything. I get the feeling we were all meant to meet like this for a reason."

She and Aevah led the brothers to a nearby clearing where a few fallen logs served as makeshift seats. As they all settled down, the initial shock began to fade, replaced by a mixture of relief, wonder, and curiosity. Galrick found himself staring at Isabella, still trying to process the fact that she was alive.

"Tell us everything," he urged. "How did you survive? What have you been doing all these years?" He paused, glancing between the two women. "Both of you."

Isabella took a slow breath, then began.

"My brothers and I were at our residence when we received word of our parents' fate," she said, her voice steady despite the weight of the memory. "The grief was overwhelming, but we knew we had to act fast. We fled our home and found refuge among the rebels. In their camp, we discovered a sense of purpose and a new family."

She paused briefly before continuing, her voice gaining strength. "We went into hiding, waiting for the day Aevah and Jacob would return. It wasn't easy. But the rebels taught us how to survive. How to fight. How to hope."

Aevah nodded in agreement. "They've been incredible in helping everyone. Jacob and I survived thanks to our grandfather. Without him, I don't think we'd be alive today. Elinor has been relentless in her search for us. Her reign has been marked by terror, especially for twins. Many have gone missing under her rule."

She looked between the brothers, her expression hardening. "Jacob and I only left our sanctuary last year. We began searching for the shards, hoping to restore what was broken. Along the way, we found Isabella and met the rebels. We trained with them, learned more about the power and how we might one day defeat Elinor. Now, we've split up, each of us searching for a shard. When we have them all, we'll reunite and face her together."

Galrick and Nicholas listened in silence, hanging on every word. Their disbelief gave way to awe.

Nicholas, still reeling, finally found his voice. "We heard rumours… whispers, really. But we never dared believe they were true. It's a miracle to see you both."

"Indeed, and now it's our turn to share our story," Galrick said solemnly. "Though I fear it's one you won't be pleased to hear."

The two women exchanged puzzled looks but gave him their full attention. Galrick explained the reason for his and Nicholas's presence, carefully making it clear that they stood with Aevah and not the queen. As his words settled between them, both Aevah and Isabella wore expressions of quiet dismay.

"So, she already knows," Aevah said, her voice low with frustration. "This complicates everything."

Galrick nodded. "Yes, but it also gives us an advantage. Knowing she's watching means we can plant seeds of misdirection—turn her eyes where we want them."

Isabella reached out, placing a reassuring hand on Aevah's. "Galrick's right. We know the queen's next move, at least for now. That gives us room to breathe—and time to plan. As long as the next shard remains hidden, her people will keep their distance."

Aevah gave a slow nod, her mind clearly turning over the new information. "Yes… This could work in our favour. It makes this stretch of the journey far less daunting."

As a sense of cautious ease settled over the group, Galrick allowed a rare smile to form. For the first time in days, he felt the tension lessen. With that, his thoughts drifted to simpler times, and he couldn't help but reminisce.

"Do you remember the summer we tried to build a treehouse in the old oak?" he asked, a wistful grin tugging at his lips.

Isabella laughed, the sound light and genuine. "How could I forget? We ended up with more bruises than progress, and the most trouble we'd ever been in. But it was one of the best summers."

Nicholas chuckled, eyes twinkling. "Yes, you older ones got a proper scolding for being such terrible influences, encouraging the young prince and princess to steal cookies from the kitchen. Our parents were furious."

"I remember bits of that," Aevah added, a soft smile curling her lips. "I think that's why we got the playhouse built in the garden a few weeks later. Oh, I loved that little house."

Galrick laughed. "Well, I'm glad our mischief led to something useful."

"For one summer, at least," Aevah said, her smile dimming slightly. "Before everything changed."

A quiet fell over them then, each lost in memory. The weight of the past pressed in, yet mingled with it was something new – hope, fragile but present.

It was Isabella who broke the silence, her voice gentle yet steady. "We've all been through so much. But we're here now, together. And that means something. We have a chance to make things right."

Aevah nodded, her expression resolute. "We have to keep moving forward. For us—and for those we've lost."

Galrick and Nicholas exchanged a glance, the same unwavering determination reflected in each other's eyes.

"We're with you," Galrick said firmly. "Whatever it takes. We'll see this through to the end."

Chapter 14

A Tavern's Welcome

It was a relief knowing that, as long as they didn't do anything too reckless, Elinor's guards would keep their distance. Watchful but uninvolved. Aevah had to admit the tension she had been carrying in her body had eased significantly. The presence of additional companions also made the journey far more enjoyable.

The path towards the mountains was smooth, the weather favourable, if brisk, and the landscape gradually shifted from rolling hills to more rugged terrain. The air grew sharper, crisp with the scent of pine that filled their senses. Yet as they neared the looming mountains, Aevah couldn't help the knot of worry tightening in her chest.

They towered in the distance, snowcapped and vast, their sheer size enough to make her question how they were supposed to locate a single shard within them, let alone climb their slopes. Though she had managed rocky hills, sandy dunes, and the occasional tree, her climbing skills were rudimentary at best. Scaling a mountain would demand techniques she wasn't sure she possessed.

As she gazed up at what awaited them, the late autumn chill nipped at their faces, and the crunch of leaves beneath their feet formed a soft symphony of nature's whispers. Despite the daunting task ahead, Aevah found comfort in the company of her companions. She glanced over at Nicholas, riding beside her, his eyes fixed on the horizon with determined focus. He seemed wildly optimistic about the idea of scaling a mountain or two, despite never having done so himself. Still, she found him to be a delightfully entertaining friend, always ready with a smile or a well-timed joke. Their bond had grown stronger with each passing day, and she found herself relying on his steady presence more than she had expected.

Up ahead, Galrick and Isabella rode slightly in front, their laughter drifting back now and then. The two had clearly grown closer, their past friendship deepening through shared experience. Their familiarity was evident in the way they interacted – his quick wit a perfect match for Isabella's sharp tongue. They exchanged playful banter with ease, keeping the mood light despite the chill. Aevah suspected there was more to their relationship than simple friendship, especially with the subtle arm touches and lingering glances they shared. It was heartening to see the bonds of friendship, and perhaps love, blooming among them.

As evening crept in, the cold became more punishing, the wind cutting through their cloaks like a blade. The temperature plummeted rapidly, and the group huddled tighter into their garments, seeking what little warmth they could.

"There's a small town another mile or so ahead," Galrick called over his shoulder, his voice nearly lost to the wind. "Let's push on and find an inn. I have no desire to spend the night out here."

The idea of a warm lodge was more than welcome. Just when Aevah thought her limbs might freeze completely, the town finally came into view. Relief swept through them at the sight of a modest inn glowing with warm, inviting light. The streets were nearly deserted, save for a few townspeople bundled tightly against the cold, hurrying along their way.

Golden lamplight spilt from the windows of the surrounding buildings, casting a warm glow over the cobbled street. Dismounting, the group led their horses to the stables and handed them over to a young stable hand before heading towards the inn. As soon as Aevah stepped inside, the warmth of the fire seeped into her skin and bones, loosening the muscles that had grown stiff from the cold.

They made their way to the bar, where a kind-faced woman greeted them with a warm smile. "Welcome, travellers. How can I help you this evening?"

Galrick stepped forward and returned her smile. "Good evening. We'll need two separate sleeping quarters for the night, please."

"Of course," the woman replied, taking the silver Galrick offered. "Follow me, and I'll show you to your rooms."

She led them upstairs, the wooden floorboards creaking softly beneath their feet. The inn held a cosy, homely charm, and the lingering warmth from the fire downstairs seemed to soak into the very walls. At the top of the stairs, she opened the doors to two adjacent rooms.

"Two of you can take this one," she said, gesturing to the first door. "And the others, the room next door."

"Thank you," Galrick replied with a nod of appreciation.

The boys took one room, while Aevah and Isabella settled into the other, setting down their belongings. Their room was simple but comfortable, with two single beds and a small wooden table between them. Both women sighed in relief, and Aevah collapsed onto the nearest bed, sinking into the softness.

Her entire body ached. Between the biting cold and the long hours riding, her muscles throbbed, and her legs burned with exhaustion. The constant pressure from gripping the stirrups had left her inner thighs raw, and the repetitive motion of posting in the saddle had strained her knees and calves. She could feel the tightness in her lower back and hips – a lingering result of keeping her balance and posture over the rough, uneven terrain.

"I think we could both use a hot bath," Isabella remarked, glancing over at Aevah, who was busy massaging her sore thighs.

Aevah gave a weary nod. "Absolutely. Let's find the communal baths."

They gathered what they needed, Aevah grabbing her soap and scented oils, and made their way to the bathing area. The warm steam rising from the tubs greeted them like an embrace, and without hesitation, they undressed and slipped into the water's inviting heat.

As soon as they submerged, the tension began to melt away. The soothing warmth seeped into their muscles, relaxing their stiff limbs and easing the chill that had settled in their bones.

"This feels amazing," Aevah sighed, leaning back against the edge of the tub.

Isabella smiled, eyes closed, as she let herself soak in the comfort. "It really does. I didn't realise how tense I was until just now."

For a while, they simply rested in silence, content in the peace and warmth. The bath was a welcome respite from the unforgiving weather and long journey. Eventually, Aevah turned her head, curiosity dancing in her eyes.

"So," she began, voice low and teasing, "what's going on with you and Galrick?"

Isabella's eyes fluttered open. "Me and Galrick?"

"Yes," Aevah replied with a mischievous smile. "You two seem… closer than just friends."

A coy grin tugged at Isabella's lips. "Oh, you've noticed, have you?"

"It's hard not to," Aevah said, playfully nudging her. "The subtle touches, the longing looks—it's pretty obvious."

Isabella let out a soft laugh, her cheeks tinged with pink. "Well, I do like him. But being in a relationship right now isn't exactly at the top of my list. There's a lot going on."

Aevah nodded in understanding. "I get that. Still… you two seem to have a real connection."

Before Aevah could press further, Isabella turned the tables, eyes sparkling with mischief. "And what about you and Nicholas? I've seen the way you look at each other."

Aevah's face flushed red as she quickly shook her head. "We're just friends. Honestly. Besides, I've got too much on my plate to think about dating."

Isabella laughed. "That makes two of us. I suppose we'll just have to reevaluate everything once this whole task is behind us." She gave Aevah a wink before slipping beneath the water, then resurfacing to wash her hair.

Aevah followed suit, lathering up her own, determined to push all thoughts of Nicholas from her mind. The warm bath did wonders for her body and her mood.

Later, back in their chamber, the girls dressed in fresh clothes. Isabella headed downstairs first, eager for a proper hot meal, while Aevah lingered behind, her entire body relaxed, and her spirits lifted now that she was finally warm.

As Aevah descended the stairs towards the common area, the lively sound of instruments filled the air, mingled with laughter, chatter, cheers, and bursts of applause. Voices joined in song with the lead singer, creating a warm, joyful atmosphere that wrapped around the room like a familiar embrace. Stepping into the space, she paused, both bemused and amazed by the scene before her. Men and women danced freely, drank heartily, and dined together, caught up in the merriment of the evening.

Spotting her friends at a nearby table, she made her way over and found a steaming bowl of meat, vegetables, and rich gravy waiting for her. Isabella was already digging into hers. The sight of the hot meal made Aevah's stomach growl in protest, and she wasted no time in joining her friend. Once she had eaten her fill, she leaned back in her chair, allowing herself to take in the energy of the room. The music's beat was infectious, and she clapped along, her eyes following the dancers as they spun and twirled. The joy in the room was contagious, and before long, she felt herself swept up in it.

Just then, Nicholas appeared at her side and extended a hand, a playful smile lighting his face. "May I have this dance?" he asked.

Aevah blinked in surprise, then laughed, her grin widening as she placed her hand in his. "You may," she said, letting him lead her onto the dance floor.

Together they joined the throng of dancers, their steps light as they spun and swayed to the rhythm of the music. Song after song, they moved with joyful abandon, their movements growing more fluid and in sync with each turn.

Soon, Galrick and Isabella joined them, swept into the festivities with laughter and energy, their dancing just as spirited as their drinking. At one point, as partners were swapped around the floor, Aevah found herself dancing with Galrick, their steps surprisingly in harmony while Nicholas danced with Isabella, both of them smiling with carefree delight.

The music continued, and the dancers rotated from one partner to the next in seamless rhythm. Eventually, Aevah and Nicholas were paired again, their movements slower now, more intimate as they swayed together, lost in the music. They danced until their legs grew tired and their cheeks ached from smiling.

Finally, Aevah tugged Nicholas gently away from the dance floor, needing a break. They found a quiet, cosy corner and sat down to catch their breath. Nicholas handed her a glass of wine, and they raised a toast to the evening's joy. The warmth of the drink spread through her, deepening the relaxation in her limbs.

"Thank you for the dance," she said, smiling at him. "I haven't had this much fun in ages."

"The pleasure was all mine," Nicholas replied, his eyes twinkling with mischief. "It's not every day I get to dance with someone as charming and beautiful as you."

She blushed, warmth blooming in her cheeks that had nothing to do with the wine. Leaning slightly closer, their shoulders brushed as they watched the dancers twirl by.

"You know," Nicholas said, voice soft and playful, "I think we make a pretty good team out there. Maybe we should enter a dance competition."

Aevah laughed, her eyes sparkling. "Oh, I'm not sure about that. I think we'd need a lot more practice."

Nicholas chuckled, his gaze warm and affectionate. "Well, I'm willing to put in the time if you are."

Before she could answer, Galrick and Isabella returned, their faces flushed and glowing from the dancing.

"This has been an incredible night," Galrick said, lifting his glass. "To friendship and to many more nights like this."

They clinked their glasses together, the sound of laughter mingling with the fading music. Aevah wished with all her heart that Galrick's words could come true. But she knew the morning would bring them back to reality. So for now, she allowed herself to soak it all in – a night to remember.

As the evening wore on, the common room gradually quieted. The musicians played softer tunes, and the dancers moved more slowly, savouring the last moments of the evening. Aevah leaned back in her chair, a deep sense of peace settling over her – something she hadn't felt in a long while. Nicholas looked at her, his expression thoughtful and gentle as she rested her head on his shoulder, her eyes growing heavy.

"I think it's time you went to bed," he murmured.

Aevah groaned softly. "I suppose you're right," she admitted, her voice tinged with exhaustion.

Nicholas stood and offered her his hand. "Come on. I'll help you get back to your room."

She took it without hesitation, and he guided her through the quiet inn, supporting her as they climbed the stairs. When they reached the door, Aevah looked around.

"Where's Isabella?" she asked, her brow furrowing slightly.

Nicholas chuckled. "She vanished with Galrick a while ago. I think they're off enjoying their own kind of fun tonight."

Aevah smiled, feeling a flicker of amusement. "Of course they are."

He helped her inside and guided her gently to the bed. She sank into the mattress with a grateful sigh, the softness wrapping around her like a cocoon. Nicholas pulled the blankets over her, tucking her in with tender care.

"Thank you," she whispered. "I'm glad we crossed paths again."

"So am I," he replied warmly, his gaze full of affection. "Sleep well."

"Goodnight," she murmured, her eyes already fluttering shut as he quietly closed the door behind him.

***

The next morning, late as it was, Aevah awoke with a smile tugging at her lips, her thoughts drifting back to the night before. Memories of dancing with Nicholas lingered like warmth beneath her skin. She stretched languidly, the pleasant ache in her limbs reminding her of the joy she'd felt.

Glancing across the room, she saw Isabella still fast asleep. Aevah hadn't heard her return during the night, but she was glad to see her friend resting peacefully. After their conversation, she couldn't help but wonder what had happened between Isabella and Galrick.

Moving quietly so as not to wake her, Aevah got ready for the day and slipped out of the room.

Downstairs, the dining room was calm, the lively energy from the night before now replaced with the gentle hum of late morning. She found Nicholas – cheerful as ever – and a rather sleepy Galrick seated at a table, enjoying a late breakfast. The mouthwatering aroma of freshly baked bread and sizzling bacon hung in the air, making Aevah's stomach growl.

"Good morning," Nicholas greeted her with a warm smile. "Sleep well?"

Aevah nodded as she took the seat beside him. "Yes, thank you. You're in a surprisingly good mood."

Nicholas chuckled. "Hard not to be when there's good food and excellent company."

Galrick let out a long yawn and stretched his arms. "Isabella's still asleep, I take it?"

"She was out cold when I left," Aevah answered. "Should I wake her?"

He shook his head. "Let her sleep. This might be the last time we all get to enjoy a proper bed for a while."

Aevah agreed and ordered herself a hearty breakfast – bacon, sausages, eggs, and toast. She was finishing the last bite when Isabella appeared, looking refreshed and bright-eyed. Without hesitation, she pinched a slice of Aevah's toast and sat down beside her.

"Morning all," she said, beaming.

"Good morning," Aevah replied with a knowing smile. "Sleep well?"

"Like a log," Isabella said through a mouthful of toast. "I needed that."

After placing her own order, the group slipped into easy conversation, recounting highlights from the night before with laughter and fond smiles. Before long, Galrick excused himself to speak to the cook about packing some food for the road.

Once breakfast was done, Aevah and Isabella returned to their room to gather their belongings. As they packed, Aevah kept sneaking glances at Isabella, waiting for her to say something, anything, about the night before.

"Well?" she finally asked, breaking the silence.

"Well, what?"

"You came back awfully late," Aevah said, raising an eyebrow. "And you were nowhere to be found when we headed up for the night."

Isabella rolled her eyes. "Relax. We just went for a walk and talked."

Aevah didn't look convinced. She narrowed her eyes, her expression sceptical.

Noticing the look, Isabella sighed. "I promise. That's all it was. We had a lot to catch up on."

Aevah held her gaze a moment longer, then nodded slowly. "Alright, if you say so."

Once packed and bundled against the cold, the two of them headed down to the stables. Galrick and Nicholas were already there, nearly finished saddling their horses. Within minutes, everyone was ready to go.

Galrick looked around at the group. "Are we all set?"

Everyone nodded. They led their horses out of the town before mounting once they reached the open road, the chill of the morning wind brushing against their cheeks.

"There should only be a day or two more of travel," Galrick said as he urged his horse into a trot. "Then we reach the mountains."

Nicholas followed close behind, while Aevah turned to Isabella, who gave her a reassuring smile. Drawing in a steadying breath, Aevah nudged her horse forward. She wasn't sure she was ready for whatever awaited them, but ready or not, the mountains were drawing near.

Chapter 15

Into the Mountains

The snowy peaks of the mountains towered above them, their jagged edges piercing the sky like frozen daggers. The group trudged through the deep snow, their breath visible in the frigid air. The journey had been long and arduous, but they were determined to find the crystal.

"There are so many peaks," Nicholas said, his voice muffled by the scarf wrapped around his face. "How will we know which one holds the shard?"

Aevah held up the one she already possessed, its pale light flickering faintly. "This should guide us," she replied. "Its power will lead us to the right mountain."

"Let's hope so. I don't want to reach the top of one of these to find out it's the wrong spot," Isabella added.

They continued on foot along the narrow, winding path that cut through the mountain pass. The terrain was rugged, with loose rocks and gravel shifting beneath their boots, making each step a careful endeavour. Towering cliffs rose on either side, their shadows casting a dim, bluish gloom. Sparse vegetation clung stubbornly to the rocky faces, and the occasional gust of wind swept down from the higher altitudes, biting at their exposed skin.

Knowing the climb ahead would be too dangerous for the animals, they had left their horses at a stable several hours away – a well-known stop for travellers and workers heading into the mountains. While in the nearby village, they had hired a local guide to help them once they figured out which mountain it was.

None of them had any real climbing experience, and they weren't about to risk their lives attempting it alone. These snow-covered peaks were treacherous, even for the seasoned. Their guide, a broad-shouldered Thorin, led the way with practised ease, a sturdy wooden staff in hand.

They had chosen Thorin for his expertise and prepared for the climb by gathering essential supplies, including a pair of mountain goats to carry the heavier loads. Aevah had been surprised by how much gear was required and silently thanked the stars that they had found someone who knew what he was doing.

They hadn't told Thorin exactly what they were searching for – only that they would know the mountain when they saw it. It was a calculated risk bringing a stranger along, but without someone who understood the terrain, they likely wouldn't survive the journey.

They placed their lives in Thorin's capable hands and shared only what was absolutely necessary. He seemed a quiet man, speaking only when needed. Bundled in thick furs, he had also outfitted the group with similar garments, something they were deeply grateful for. He led them steadily, the goats trailing behind.

For two days, they travelled along the mountain's base, following the flickering guidance of the shard Aevah carried. Its light pulsed softly as they walked, and though she was careful not to let Thorin see it, she studied it closely at the foot of each peak, waiting for the unmistakable sign that would reveal their destination. Eventually, the shard began to thrum with a quiet, pulsing energy that only she could hear.

Her heart sank when she looked up. Of course, it had to be the tallest.

"This is it," Aevah said, her eyes fixed on the massive mountain whose summit was hidden by clouds. "The shard is here."

Galrick gave a firm nod, determination settling in his features. "Then let's not waste any time. This is the one." He turned to their guide. Thorin followed their gaze, his deep voice cutting through the thin air.

"You seek the peak. I will help you reach it."

Without another word, he set down his pack and began pulling out supplies, laying them on the snow-covered ground.

"You'll need to carry these yourselves," he said as he handed out the essential gear. Aevah tucked the map and compass he handed her into her belt pouch. He then passed out knives and small axes – tools for protection and survival. Everyone took a knife, while Galrick and Isabella added axes to their gear.

Next came the medical kits, carefully packed away in their bags, followed by climbing equipment: ropes, grappling hooks, crampons, and ice axes. No one intended to face the ascent unprepared. Aevah slung a coil of rope over her shoulder and fastened the crampons to her boots. Nicholas secured an ice axe to the side of his pack.

"Thank you," Aevah said as she adjusted her load, swaying slightly under the weight.

Thorin gave a single nod, inspecting their readiness. "Sort your packs and keep your tools within easy reach," he instructed. "The path ahead is treacherous. You must take care."

With everyone as organised as they could be, the group followed Thorin's lead, heading towards the base of the mountain. Aevah felt a mix of excitement and apprehension as they began their ascent. The light snow crunched beneath her boots, each step an effort under the weight of her pack and supplies. The unfamiliar load tugged at her shoulders and strained her muscles, every movement a conscious act of balance on the uneven terrain.

Thorin moved with steady confidence, his sturdy wooden staff aiding him as he navigated the rocky path. Aevah watched his movements carefully, doing her best to mimic his footwork, but despite her efforts, she stumbled now and then – her inexperience clearly evident.

"Stay close," Thorin warned, glancing back at the group. "The mountain is unforgiving, and we must be cautious."

Aevah nodded, her breath curling in the frigid air. She glanced at Nicholas, who offered her an encouraging smile. As they climbed higher, the air thinned, making it harder to breathe. Aevah's chest tightened, and she found herself pausing more often to catch her breath. The cold grew harsher with the altitude, and she silently thanked the divine for the thick layers of clothing shielding her from the biting wind.

By evening, Thorin halted them with a raised hand. "We'll make camp here for the night," he announced, his voice carrying over the howling wind. The group took in their surroundings – uneven terrain, a blanket of fresh snow, and jagged stone forming the backdrop.

Camping in the mountains required more care than usual. Thorin guided them to a relatively flat area, partially sheltered by a rocky outcrop that would help protect them from the worst of the elements. He quickly set about issuing instructions.

"First, we clear the snow and make the ground as level as possible," he said. "Then we'll pitch the tents and anchor them securely. We'll also need a fire for warmth and food—gather dry wood and kindling. Be mindful of your footing. Even here, a misstep can be dangerous."

The group got to work. Using tools, they cleared patches of snow for their tents. Once the area was flattened, they unpacked their portable shelters, securing them with stakes and ropes to withstand the wind. Aevah and Nicholas moved off together to search for firewood, returning with what dry pieces they could find. Thorin built a modest but efficient fire, its warmth a welcome comfort against the chill.

Gathered around the flames, the group shared a simple meal of dried meat, nuts, and hardtack, washing it down with water they had melted from the snow. Aevah sat quietly, exhaustion settling into her bones. Even wrapped in furs, she could still feel the cold creeping in. She knew it would only worsen as they climbed higher, and that was a thought she didn't particularly relish.

Still, she found one small comfort. Using her power discreetly, she dried her and her companions' damp clothes before they retreated to their tents. At least they wouldn't be sleeping soaked through with snowmelt.

Before turning in, Thorin addressed them one final time.

"These mountains are home to creatures you do not wish to encounter," he warned, his tone grave. "Wolves, bears, and mountain cats roam these ranges. Keep your weapons close at hand."

He paused, letting the silence settle before continuing. "And beware the weather. It changes rapidly—blizzards, avalanches… these are not rare events. Caution will keep you alive."

His eyes swept across the group, making sure they understood the seriousness of his words.

They all nodded solemnly. Aevah exchanged a look with Isabella before slipping into their tent, while Nicholas and Galrick settled in with Thorin. Aevah had been so focused on the climb itself; she hadn't considered the threats that might stalk them in the shadows of the mountains. Now, a new layer of unease settled over her. This journey was proving more perilous than she had imagined.

***

They had been travelling for nearly a week without incident, the climb proving every bit as arduous as Thorin had warned. The days were long, bleak, and unrelenting, but the group pressed on, driven by their determination to reach the peak. Galrick found himself slowly adjusting to the physical demands of the ascent; his muscles ached less with each passing day. The icy conditions, however, remained unforgiving, though he was managing. He silently thanked the divine spirit for their luck – so far, the weather had held steady, and no wild animals had come upon them in the night.

As they trudged through the snow, Galrick glanced at Isabella walking beside him. She seemed to be handling the climb well, her resolve evident in every step. This stretch of the path was wider than most, finally allowing two people to walk side by side without risk. So, he took the opportunity to stay close, exchanging quiet words with her as they walked.

But as the afternoon wore on, Galrick noticed a shift. The sky darkened ominously, the wind picked up, and flurries began to whip around them with increasing force. What had started as a calm, cold day quickly began to unravel.

Thorin came to an abrupt halt, his expression tight with concern. "A blizzard is coming," he warned. "We need to find shelter, and fast."

Within minutes, the wind turned savage, howling through the mountain pass and whipping the snow into a chaotic frenzy. Visibility plummeted. The group struggled to stay together, their outlines blurring into the white storm. Galrick felt a surge of panic rise in his chest as the freezing air bit through his layers. His face burned where it was exposed, the wind lashing at his skin like needles.

"Stay close!" Thorin's voice barely cut through the roar of the storm.

Galrick reached blindly through the swirling snow, hoping to find Isabella. His gloved hand brushed against her arm, and he gripped it tightly, pulling himself towards her as the wind threatened to knock them both off balance.

"We need to keep moving!" he shouted, his voice hoarse from the cold.

Isabella nodded and grabbed his hand, her other arm shielding her face from the barrage of snow and ice. "Let's go!" she cried, clinging to him as they pressed forward.

They fought the storm together, step by agonising step, calling out to the others whenever they dared open their mouths. But their voices were swallowed by the gale, and it became clear they were alone, cut off from the rest of the group by the blinding snow.

"I think we've been separated from the others!" Galrick shouted, straining to be heard. "We have to find them!"

Isabella shook her head, her features pale with fear. "Not in this storm," she replied. "We won't find anyone until it passes. We need to find shelter."

Reluctantly, Galrick agreed. The storm was unrelenting, and the snow stung their skin with every gust, but they pushed on. After what felt like hours of climbing, they came upon a shallow dip in the mountainside. It wasn't quite a cave, but it offered enough of a recess to block some of the wind.

They stopped, breathless, needing a moment to rest and reassess. Galrick glanced at Isabella. Her face was drawn with exhaustion and worry, snow clinging to her lashes.

"We need to conserve our energy," he said, voice rough. "This storm could go on for hours."

She nodded, her breath pluming in the icy air. "Let's try to block the wind. If we stay exposed, we won't last long."

Galrick looked around and spotted a few large stones nearby. He began dragging them into place to form a makeshift windbreak. Isabella joined him, her hands trembling from the cold but determined to help.

As they worked, a nagging feeling crept over Galrick – an unease that prickled at the back of his neck. He cast a glance over his shoulder, but the swirling snow obscured everything beyond a few feet.

"Are you okay?" Isabella asked, noticing the way he kept looking into the storm.

He hesitated. "It's probably nothing," he muttered. "Just a feeling. Like something's out there. But with this visibility… I can't be sure."

She didn't press him, and he shook the unease from his mind, forcing himself to focus. Survival came first. They were both cold, weary, and separated from the others. For now, the only thing that mattered was staying alive until the storm passed.

With the makeshift shelter in place, the worst of the wind was held at bay, but it did nothing to combat the biting cold. The freezing air seeped through the layers of clothing, chilling them to the bone. In an effort to preserve warmth, Isabella pressed close to Galrick, wrapping herself tightly against him to share body heat. Still, the cold was relentless.

The wind was far too fierce to allow for a tent, so they stayed huddled together, hoping they would outlast the storm. Galrick stared into the swirling white around them, eyes narrowed as he tried to make sense of the blizzard. For a moment, he thought he saw movement – a dark shape flitting between gusts – but he couldn't be sure.

“I think the storm is playing tricks on me,” he muttered, more to himself than to Isabella.

She looked up, her face pale with fear. “What did you see?”

“I don’t know,” he replied, fingers tightening around the handle of his axe. “But stay alert. Something might be out there.”

They sat in tense silence, their breath visible in the frigid air. The blizzard showed no sign of easing, and the cold was becoming unbearable. Galrick’s thoughts raced as he considered their dwindling options.

“We can’t stay here,” he said finally. “If we do, we’ll freeze. And if something is out there, we’re sitting ducks.”

Isabella gave a quick nod. “Let’s go.”

They resumed their climb, battling the storm with every step. The snow made the path treacherous, the wind pushing against them like an invisible force. Galrick kept his senses sharp, scanning the white blur for signs of danger. Then, out of the corner of his eye, he saw it again – a flicker of movement against the snow.

At first, he dismissed it as another illusion, but when it reappeared, closer this time, he knew it was real.

“We’re being followed,” he said quietly, his voice barely audible over the wind.

Isabella’s eyes widened. “By what?”

“I don’t know. But it’s fast—and it’s tracking us.”

They pushed forward, the shadow stalking just beyond their reach. Then Isabella gasped and pointed, her voice urgent. "There!"

Galrick followed her gaze and saw it. A massive white mountain cat, nearly invisible against the snow, prowled towards them. Its pale fur blended perfectly with the surroundings, but its eyes gleamed with hunger. Muscles rippled beneath its sleek coat, every movement calculated and silent.

Before they could react, it lunged.

Galrick swung his axe, but the beast was too fast. It dodged easily and struck back, claws slashing across his chest. He stumbled, the impact knocking him off balance. He couldn't tell if he'd been wounded – there was no time. He dove aside as the cat prepared to strike again.

Isabella sprang into action, leaping onto the creature from behind, her knife flashing. She drove the blade into its flank. The wound wasn't fatal, but it drew blood and fury. The mountain cat shrieked in pain and rage, twisting violently to face her.

Galrick seized the opportunity. He raised his axe and swung, catching the beast's shoulder. It snarled and turned on him, its eyes blazing with fury. With terrifying speed, it lunged again and this time raking its claws across his face.

Galrick cried out as white-hot pain tore across his cheek. Blood streamed from the wounds, dripping into the snow. The sting of the wind against the open gashes made his vision blur, each breath a struggle as pain surged through him.

The beast came at him once more.

He braced himself, sidestepped, and brought his axe down with all the strength he had left. The blade struck the cat's neck deep enough. The creature let out a final, guttural roar before collapsing in the snow, a crimson river spreading beneath its lifeless body.

Galrick stood trembling, breath ragged, his limbs shaking from the cold and the fading adrenaline. He looked at Isabella, and she was breathing hard, but unharmed. Relief washed over him, quickly replaced by the burning pain in his face. He dropped to his knees, one hand clutching his cheek as blood poured between his fingers.

Isabella was by his side in an instant, rummaging through the medical kit. She pulled out bandages with trembling hands. "Hold still," she said firmly, though her voice was tight with fear.

She worked quickly, wrapping his wounds as best she could. "It's not that bad," she lied, trying to reassure him as she tied off the final strip. Then she helped him to his feet.

"We need to keep moving."

Galrick nodded, vision blurred, the pain hammering through his skull. "Let's go."

They gathered their things and pushed onward, the blizzard still raging. Time passed in a haze of wind, snow, and pain. Eventually, the storm began to ease, the wind weakening to a whisper. They stumbled upon a small man-made cave – a crude shelter carved into the mountainside. It wasn't much, but it was enough.

Inside, they finally found respite from the elements. The air was still cold, but without the wind, it felt bearable. They unpacked slowly, exhausted. Isabella turned to Galrick, her gaze filled with concern.

"Let me look at your face again," she said gently, pulling out the medical kit again.

She unwrapped the bandages and winced at the sight. Carefully, she cleaned the wounds and dabbed ointment over them. Galrick flinched as it burned against his torn skin, and somehow, the ointment hurt more than the wound itself.

Setting the ointment aside, Isabella leaned in to examine Galrick's face closely. "One of the gashes will need stitches," she said calmly. "The rest are shallow and should heal with time."

She rummaged through the medical kit again, surprised to find a small needle and thread tucked inside. Without hesitation, she prepared them.

"Hold still," she instructed, her voice firm but gentle.

Galrick tensed, swearing under his breath as she began stitching the deepest wound with careful precision. He clenched his jaw against the sting, trying not to flinch.

"You're pretty good at this," he managed, attempting to distract himself and lighten the mood.

Isabella gave a faint smile. "I've had some practice. Just try not to get mauled by any more mountain cats, okay?"

"I'll do my best," Galrick replied with a grin. "No promises, though."

He winced again as she finished the final stitch, then began redressing the other cuts with steady hands. He hadn't needed stitches many times in his life, and he hoped to keep it that way. The process was never pleasant. But once she was done, he finally allowed himself to relax, the day's fatigue crashing down on him.

Isabella stepped back, examining her handiwork with a thoughtful expression that immediately put Galrick on edge.

"I hope my handsome features are still intact," he joked, eyeing her warily.

Her smile returned, reassuring him. "And what features would those be? You certainly look better now."

He chuckled, wincing as the motion tugged at his stitches. "I'll take your word for it. Just… don't tell anyone I screamed like a baby."

Isabella laughed softly. "Your secret's safe with me. Besides, I've seen worse. You'll be back to your rugged self in no time."

"Rugged, huh?" he said, the grin returning. "I'll take that as a compliment."

"For you, yes," she replied, leaning in to kiss him lightly on the nose before rewrapping his face with care.

Then she rose and moved to rummage through one of the bags. Galrick watched her, still smiling, as she pulled out two cloth-wrapped meal packs.

"Dinner is served," she announced playfully, handing him one.

He accepted it with a chuckle. "Not exactly a feast, but it'll do."

They ate in companionable silence, the exhaustion of the day settling heavily over them. The rations were simple but filling, just enough to restore some strength. When they finished, Isabella packed away the remnants and turned back towards him.

"Let's get some rest," she said softly. "We'll need our energy for tomorrow."

Galrick nodded, feeling the pull of sleep in his bones. They curled up together again, sharing body heat beneath their cloaks and furs. The small cave provided a break from the brutal wind outside, and for the first time that day, they could relax.

As he lay there, Galrick couldn't help but think of Nicholas and Aevah. He hoped they were safe, that Thorin had managed to keep them out of the worst of the storm. But there was nothing he could do now.

With Isabella's warmth pressed beside him and the faint scent of roses in her hair filling his senses, Galrick closed his eyes. He drifted into a peaceful sleep, content for now to have her in his arms.

Chapter 16

The Road to the Summit

Aevah had been apprehensive at the start of the climb. It was undoubtedly the most challenging thing she had ever done, and though she struggled with every step, she was still moving forward, surviving. That alone filled her with pride, not just for herself but in her friends as well. They had reached the halfway point, and the sense of accomplishment that settled in her chest was undeniable. She believed, more than ever, that they could do this.

It hadn't been easy, but despite the strain, she was grateful to be exactly where she was. Even if she had grown up in her old home in Carraton, living the life of a royal, she doubted she would have ever been afforded the chance to travel the country like this. This journey, this experience, was something she would never forget. The views alone were spectacular. She wished she were the artist type, someone capable of capturing the moment on canvas, because the sight before her now was breathtaking.

The mountains stretched into the distance, their snow-capped peaks gleaming like diamonds under the sun. The sky above was a brilliant blue, streaked with delicate wisps of clouds. It felt like standing in the middle of a living painting, one so vivid and majestic that it almost didn't seem real. The sheer grandeur of the landscape filled Aevah with awe.

"This is incredible," she breathed, her voice trembling with wonder. "I never imagined it would be so beautiful up here."

"Isn't it?" Nicholas added, coming up beside her.

They continued to climb. The terrain grew steeper, more demanding with every step. Aevah felt the toll it took on her body – her legs burned from the incline, and her back ached beneath the weight of her pack. It was a relentless effort, and yet, it was worth it. She could feel it in her bones: no beauty without pain. The cost was high, but the reward – Azend in all its magnitude – was higher still.

As they pressed on, the weather began to shift. Dark clouds rolled in from the horizon, casting long shadows over the peaks. The temperature plummeted, and a sense of urgency settled over the group. Thorin stopped abruptly, scanning the skies with a grim expression.

"A blizzard is coming," he said. "We need to find shelter, and fast."

The wind picked up in an instant, shrieking through the mountains and hurling snow into their faces. Visibility dropped sharply, and the group struggled to stay close. Panic welled up in Aevah's chest as the storm closed in around them, the cold slicing through her layers like knives.

"Stay close!" Thorin shouted, his voice nearly lost to the wind.

Despite their efforts, the blinding snow drove them apart. Aevah clung tightly to Nicholas and Thorin, the only ones still within reach. They stumbled together, blinded and deafened by the storm, holding on to each other as if their lives depended on it.

"We need to find shelter!" Thorin yelled again. "There's a cave nearby!"

He led the way as best he could, but even he was faltering. Aevah fell more than once, her strength draining fast as she battled the storm. Thorin and Nicholas each took hold of her arms, dragging her along through the thickening snow. At last, they reached the cave, though its entrance was quickly being buried beneath the mounting drifts.

They scrambled inside, just ahead of the collapsing snow. Thorin ushered them deeper in, insisting it was still safer here than outside. Snow continued to pile up, slowly sealing the cave from the outside world.

Aevah could see the worry etched into Nicholas's face, mirroring her own fears. *What if Galrick and Isabella hadn't found shelter? What if they were still out there in the storm?*

"They'll be alright," she said softly, trying to convince herself as much as him. "If any of us can survive a storm, it's them too."

She offered a faint smile, which Nicholas returned as he gave her arm a reassuring squeeze. Together, they sat in silence, watching as snow steadily blocked out the entrance, sealing them in cold and darkness.

Aevah hugged herself, trembling violently. Her teeth chattered as the cold seeped into her bones. Nicholas noticed and immediately pulled her into his arms, trying to share his body heat.

"Come here," he urged, his breath visible in the frigid air.

"I'm so exhausted," she whispered, tears brimming in her eyes. "I don't know how much longer I can keep going if it stays like this."

"You should rest," he said gently, rubbing her arms to warm her. "Try to sleep a little. It'll help."

"I need to warm up," she murmured, leaning into him, desperate for any comfort. "I can't stop shivering."

He glanced towards Thorin to make sure he wasn't listening, then leaned in and whispered, "Remember your power, Aevah. You can create it. Try to embrace it, focus on spreading some warmth through yourself."

Aevah closed her eyes and focused inward, reaching for the warmth of her power. She concentrated, trying to summon the heat, directing what little energy she had left towards kindling it within. For a brief moment, a flicker of warmth spread through her limbs, but her exhaustion was too great. The sensation faded almost as quickly as it had come.

"I can't," she whispered, her voice trembling. Tears welled up in her eyes, hot with frustration. "I'm too tired."

Nicholas gently wiped away her tears, his expression resolute. "It's okay," he said softly. "Just try to sleep now. I'll keep you warm."

She gave a faint nod, the weight of exhaustion finally overtaking her. Nicholas held her close, doing his best to share his body heat. Nearby, Thorin rummaged through his pack, sorting through what few supplies they had left.

"We need to stay warm to survive," he said, his voice calm despite the growing urgency of their situation. "I'll start a small fire."

He gathered bits of dry kindling and twigs from their packs, arranging them carefully in the centre of the cave. With practised hands, he struck flint against steel until a spark caught. Flames sprang to life, flickering weakly but offering a welcome reprieve from the bitter cold.

Aevah and Nicholas moved closer, drawn instinctively to the fire's glow. Though small, the flame felt like salvation. Warmth slowly returned to her body; the shaking subsided, and sensation returned to her limbs.

"Thank you," they said in unison.

Thorin simply nodded. "Get some rest. The storm may last a while, and we'll need our strength when it passes."

With a grateful sigh, Aevah lay as close to the fire as she dared, Nicholas beside her. Thorin tended to the flames once more before lying down himself. Feeling a flicker of comfort at last, Aevah closed her eyes, whispering a silent prayer to the divine spirit for the safety of Isabella and Galrick.

Hours passed. Eventually, Thorin stirred and gently woke the others. The howling wind had faded to silence. For a moment, Aevah blinked in confusion, unsure where she was.

"The storm has passed," Thorin said grimly. "Now we dig our way out."

He was already at the cave's entrance, tools in hand. Nicholas joined him, gripping a pickaxe, and the two began to chip steadily through the thick wall of snow and ice.

Aevah, though still weary, felt her strength slowly returning. Her power stirred again, no longer blocked by exhaustion. She moved beside Nicholas, gripping her own hammer, and with subtle concentration, began to melt patches of snow with her magic, careful not to let Thorin see.

The snow gradually loosened, revealing a narrow passage. Thorin and Nicholas worked tirelessly, pushing and clearing the way. Aevah continued to help, quietly guiding heat through the ice, making the work faster and easier.

"You're doing great," Nicholas murmured to her with a knowing wink. "Just a little more, and we'll be out."

Thanks to her efforts, they cleared a path sooner than expected. Thorin stepped back, brushing ice from his coat.

"We did it," he said, a note of relief in his voice. "Let's move out."

One by one, they crawled through the narrow tunnel, emerging into the still, frigid mountain air. The storm had passed, leaving a world blanketed in untouched snow. The sky above was pale and cloudless, as if nothing had ever happened.

Aevah cupped her hands around her mouth and shouted, her voice echoing across the slopes. "Galrick! Isabella!"

Silence.

Her heart sank, but Thorin placed a hand on her shoulder.

"We keep climbing," he said firmly. "Your friends would've thought the same. We'll find them."

She nodded, clinging to his hope. The alternative was too painful to consider.

The group pressed on. The blizzard had left them depleted – supplies were low, their sledges and goats lost to the storm. They moved cautiously, voices subdued, calling out for their missing friends when they could. But no replies came. The silence of the mountains was heavy, oppressive.

Days passed. Each one stole more of Aevah's hope. Snow crunched beneath their boots, and the cold never truly left their bones. Still, they climbed.

Then, one afternoon, a sound rode on the wind – faint but unmistakable. Voices.

Aevah froze, her breath catching. She strained to hear. "Do you hear that?" she whispered, barely daring to believe it.

Nicholas nodded, eyes wide. "Yes. I did. Let's go."

They broke into a run, following the distant voices. Rounding a bend, they spotted two figures huddled in a small alcove. Relief flooded Aevah's chest as she recognised them – Galrick and Isabella.

"Galrick!" she cried, racing towards him. "What happened?"

Galrick looked up and gave a weary smile. "We had a run-in with a mountain cat," he said hoarsely. "Isabella saved my life. I'm alright. Just a few scratches."

Isabella nodded, her expression a blend of exhaustion and joy. "We found shelter, but it wasn't easy."

Aevah's eyes filled with tears as she gently embraced Galrick, mindful not to press against his injuries. "I was so worried," she whispered, her voice catching.

Nicholas joined them, his expression a mix of concern and relief. "We thought we'd lost you," he said, his voice unsteady.

"We believed the same about you," Galrick replied, his smile faint but sincere. "It's a miracle we found each other."

The group huddled close, trading stories of the past few harrowing days. Galrick and Isabella recounted their encounter with the mountain cat, the desperate search for shelter, and the constant weight of uncertainty. Aevah and Nicholas shared their ordeal of being trapped in the cave, the fear of being buried alive, and the relentless hope that they were still out there.

"We've lost most of our supplies," Nicholas said quietly. "The blizzard took nearly everything—rations, equipment, even the sledges."

"Same here," Isabella replied, motioning to a few small carcasses tied to her pack. "We were lucky enough to catch a couple of hares."

"We'll make do," Thorin said firmly. "We'll ration what we have and hunt what we can along the way."

The next few days were gruelling. The group felt the full weight of the losses – scarce food, fewer tools, and only one tent between them. Still, they pressed on towards the peak, pooling their knowledge and effort to survive. They worked together to hunt, set traps, and stretch what little food remained to lure larger prey. When they succeeded, they relished the warmth of fresh meat, a welcome break from dried rations, though the process often delayed their travel.

Despite the hardships, Aevah felt a quiet joy settle in her heart. They were together. Alive. And the summit was close.

The crystal shard in her pack pulsed with increasing energy. It seemed to sense that another piece of itself was nearby.

Though it appeared to be nothing more than a shard of quartz, Aevah could feel the strange awareness within it, almost sentient, responding to her emotions and surroundings. Its energy had grown more vibrant the closer they climbed, humming softly like a heartbeat in tune with her own.

At times, she reached back to touch it, and the warmth that spread through her fingertips felt strangely reassuring, like the shard was guiding her. It was more than a tool or a relic. It felt like a part of her. She had been about to touch it again when Thorin's voice pulled her from her thoughts.

"Night is falling," he announced. "We'll make camp here. With a few more hours of climbing tomorrow, we should reach the peak."

"That's fantastic!" Aevah said, eyes lighting up. "Can't we push on?"

"No," Thorin answered with a shake of his head. "The mountains darken fast, and climbing at night without proper gear is too dangerous."

"Then I guess we make camp," Galrick said, moving to help him.

The others followed, and soon they were sitting under the stars, gathered around a modest fire. Conversations shifted to the heavens above, the sky glittering with endless constellations.

Nicholas pointed upward. "See those stars there? That's the Hunter. Legend says he was a great warrior who once protected the priestesses in their time of need. After his death, his spirit rose to the stars to watch over us all."

Aevah followed his gaze, wonder softening her features. "What about those?" she asked, pointing to another formation.

Thorin smiled. "Those are the Twins. They were siblings, bonded by love so strong that not even death could part them."

Seeing the curiosity in Aevah's eyes, he continued the tale.

"The Twins were born to a humble family in a small village. One was a healer, whose touch could mend the gravest wounds. The other was a gifted musician, known for playing melodies that soothed troubled souls. Their talents brought peace and prosperity to their people.

"They shared a unique bond, some say they could feel each other's emotions, even hear each other's thoughts. Their unity made them stronger, and their village revered them.

"Then one day, a great darkness descended. A malevolent force swept across the land, threatening to devour everything. The Twins stood together, using their gifts to protect the people. The healer worked tirelessly, tending to the wounded, while the musician's songs gave the frightened strength to carry on.

"But the battle was long and merciless. As their lives faded, the musician played a final, haunting tune, guiding both their souls into the afterlife.

"Moved by their sacrifice and love, the divine spirit granted them their final wish—to remain together always. Their spirits rose into the sky, forming the constellation we now call the

Twins. From above, they continue to watch over us, a symbol of unity, courage, and eternal love."

Aevah listened, captivated. "That's beautiful," she murmured. "It's comforting, thinking they're up there, still protecting us."

The group shared more tales as the fire crackled, and the night deepened. Each constellation became a story, a living memory etched into the sky. Aevah found herself pulled into the wonder of it all, feeling like a child again, listening to her grandfather's stories beneath the stars.

Eventually, her eyes grew heavy. Sleep claimed her gently, and in her dreams, she soared through the night sky, chasing constellations and carving her own story among the stars.

Chapter 17

The Peak

The next morning, Aevah was pacing and bounding with restless energy, eager to be on the move again. They were so close to the shard, and she could feel it. Until now, Thorin had led them, but this time, it was Aevah's turn. She knew exactly where to go, and the others followed her without question.

She raced ahead with renewed vigour, the nearness of her goal lending speed to her steps. The others struggled to match her sudden burst of energy.

"Wait up," Isabella called, breathless as she trudged up the incline.

Aevah looked back and saw her friends lagging, panting heavily. Only Thorin remained composed, keeping his usual steady pace.

"Sorry," Aevah said, slowing slightly. "I'm just so full of energy."

Galrick gave a low chuckle. "We noticed. But try to remember, some of us are still recovering."

She frowned, guilt flickering across her face. "Of course. I'll slow down." In her excitement, she had completely forgotten about his injuries. While most of Galrick's wounds had been facial, he still bore deep bruises that made every step painful. Thorin had examined him the day before and concluded no bones were broken, but Galrick's body remained sore and stiff.

Aevah slowed her pace, and Nicholas came up beside her. They walked in silence until she suddenly caught sight of an opening ahead. "Look," she cried, then darted forward, all caution forgotten.

"Wait!" Nicholas shouted, sprinting after her, with Isabella and Galrick following close behind.

At the base of the mountain face, Aevah stood before a massive, dark entrance. The cave's mouth yawned wide, fringed with snow and half-choked by drifts, giving it a stark, forbidding presence.

She paused at the threshold. "This is it," she whispered, her voice trembling with anticipation.

Without waiting for a reply, she stepped inside, as if drawn by an unseen force.

Around her, she barely registered the murmurs of her companions. Her focus was absolute. The cave was pitch black, but she moved with unerring purpose, like someone retracing a familiar path. The shard in her pack pulsed faintly, its light unseen but guiding.

Suddenly, the darkness behind her lit up with a soft glow. She turned and blinked, momentarily disoriented, as Nicholas's lantern cast warm light across their faces.

"Are you okay, Aevah?" he asked gently, placing a steadying hand on her arm.

She nodded, her expression distant. "Yes… I don't know what came over me. It's like I've been here before."

Her eyes wandered across the space, drinking in details her mind somehow already knew.

Isabella's voice echoed softly behind her. "Do you know where we're going?"

"I do," Aevah said calmly. "I just… can't explain it."

They continued through the twisting tunnels, the air growing colder with every step. The path was uneven, with jagged rocks and slick patches of ice, but Aevah breezed through without hesitation. Behind her, the others stumbled and cursed as they struggled to keep up.

The shard's energy intensified with every step, a quiet, pulsing rhythm that matched her heartbeat. Then, a soft glow shimmered ahead, spilling into the tunnel from another cavern.

They emerged into a vast chamber and halted in awe.

Icicles draped from the ceiling like crystal chandeliers, their sharp tips gleaming in the light. Frost carpeted the ground, glittering like crushed diamonds beneath their feet. Intricate ice formations adorned the walls, casting prismatic reflections that danced like spirits.

The atmosphere was ethereal, untouched, almost sacred.

Aevah stepped forward, the shard in her pack vibrating with resonance. Before her stood a shimmering archway, its frame reflecting every hue of the icy chamber.

"This is it," she whispered. "The shard is here."

Resting upon a bed of snow and ice, the second shard pulsed gently, its light echoing the rhythm of the one she carried. The two pieces seemed to hum in harmony, their energies reaching for one another.

Aevah took a deep breath, her heart racing. "We've found it. We've finally gotten it."

A cold voice echoed behind them. "Yes, you have."

They spun around.

From the shadows emerged a pack of wolves, their fur almost indistinguishable from the gloom. Their glowing eyes pierced the semi-darkness, and their silent arrival sent a chill through the group.

"Look out!" Nicholas shouted, stepping protectively in front of Aevah and drawing his dagger.

The wolves circled, slipping in and out of view like ghosts.

"Shadow wolves," Galrick whispered. "I thought they were mere myth."

A low growl turned into words. "Oh, we are real, boy," came the reply, deep and menacing. "And you are trespassing on sacred ground. Tell us why we should let you live."

"We mean you no harm," Aevah said, her voice trembling but loud enough to carry. "We seek the crystal shard to save our kingdom. Please, let us pass."

The wolves' glowing eyes bore into her, as though measuring her words against something unseen. After a long moment, the largest wolf stepped forward, its gaze fixed unflinchingly on hers.

"You speak the truth," the wolf replied, its deep voice reverberating off the icy walls. "But one among you is not pure of heart."

Aevah looked at her companions, confusion furrowing her brow. She couldn't believe any of them would betray their cause.

"You must be mistaken," she said, shaking her head. "We all want the same thing."

"You may believe that," the wolf rumbled, "but I know one of you does not." The rest of the pack crept forward, their paws silent against the frost. "And we will not allow the shard to fall into the wrong hands."

"How can we prove ourselves?" Aevah asked, desperation creeping into her voice.

Before the wolf could respond, Thorin suddenly lunged forward, seizing the crystal shard from its place beneath the arch.

"Out of my way!" he shouted, eyes wild with greed as he turned to flee.

The wolves moved as one. The alpha let out a chilling howl, and the pack attacked. Thorin swung his axe in frantic arcs, trying to hold them off, but he was no match for their shadow-shifting forms. They slipped between realms, dodging his strikes with unnatural ease.

Nicholas jumped in front of Aevah, shielding her. He struck at an attacking wolf, but it lunged back, its fangs sinking into his leg. Nicholas cried out and collapsed to the ground.

"Nicholas!" Aevah screamed, dropping beside him. Panic surged through her, and with a cry, she thrust her hands forward, unleashing a freezing spell. Ice spread rapidly across the cave floor, encasing the wolves in thick frost.

But to her horror, they phased through the ice as if it weren't there. The frozen layer cracked and shattered around them, and the wolves emerged unscathed.

"They're immune to my magic," she muttered, her mind racing.

Nearby, Galrick and Isabella fought desperately, swinging at creatures that slipped through their weapons like smoke. But the wolves weren't interested in them – they had their target.

Thorin tried to escape, but the wolves overwhelmed him. Their teeth and claws tore into him, his screams echoing off the stone walls before ending abruptly. The crystal shard clattered to the frozen ground, coming to rest with a soft, echoing chime.

None of the others moved to retrieve it.

The wolves circled the group now, their teeth bared, eyes gleaming with threat. Nicholas leaned heavily on Galrick, pale and bleeding.

"We didn't know he would betray us," Aevah pleaded, her voice steady despite the fear coiled in her chest. "We only seek the shard to save our kingdom."

The largest wolf stepped forward once more, its eyes locked on hers. "Be careful whom you trust, girl. There are many who would slit your throat for the one you carry. Add another shard to it, and you hand your enemies everything they need to destroy your world."

It took a step closer. "To carry both shards is no small task. It is an honour, and a burden. Prove your worth, and we may let you proceed."

"What must I do?" Aevah asked quietly.

The wolf's gaze shifted to Nicholas. "To prove your strength and resolve, you must kill the one you love most."

Aevah's heart stopped. Her eyes widened as she stepped protectively in front of Nicholas. "What? No. I can't do that!"

"If you truly have the strength to defend your kingdom," the wolf said, "then you must show it. Make the hard choice. Prove it now."

"This is madness!" Galrick snapped. "No one is killing anyone."

"Not no one," the wolf growled coldly. "Her." He nodded again to Aevah.

"No!" she cried, her voice breaking. "I can't. I won't. There has to be another way!"

The wolf's eyes narrowed. "Why do you hesitate? Is your resolve so fragile?"

"How is refusing to kill someone you love a weakness?" Isabella uttered, stepping beside Aevah. "What you're asking is cruel."

The three of them formed a barrier around Nicholas, who remained silent, his face pale from pain and blood loss.

Aevah looked down at him, tears brimming in her eyes. Her hands trembled, but she raised her chin.

"It's not weakness," she said quietly, voice steadying. "Love is never a weakness. Killing someone you love doesn't prove strength—it proves cruelty. True strength is protecting the people you care about, holding your values when it's hardest to do so."

She took a breath and stood tall. "If this is what it takes to win, then I choose to lose. I won't become the kind of monster we're fighting to stop."

A low growl rumbled from the alpha's chest. "You shall not leave with the shard unless you take his life. This is your final chance."

Tears slipped down Aevah's cheeks, but she didn't waver. "Then I choose to walk away. I will not kill someone I love—not for power, not for victory. If that means we don't get the shard, then so be it. I will not betray my friends or who I am."

The cavern fell silent, the tension hanging thick in the air. The largest wolf studied Aevah for a long, unreadable moment. Then, at last, it spoke.

"You have passed the test," it said, its voice softening now, almost reverent. "True strength lies in compassion and mercy, not in taking lives. You have shown the qualities of a true leader—courage, compassion, and wisdom."

The wolf stepped back, and the rest of the pack followed suit. "You may proceed. Claim the shard. We trust you will use its power wisely."

"What?" Aevah said, stunned by the sudden shift.

The alpha wolf dipped its head. "You have proven your worth. Your refusal to kill, even when pressured, revealed the purity of your heart. Such strength is rare and essential for the one who would wield the shards."

Relief surged through Aevah, overwhelming her. She dropped to her knees, tears spilling freely as the weight of the moment settled over her.

"Thank you," she whispered, her voice choked with emotion.

Around her, the others visibly relaxed. With the immediate danger passed, Isabella hurried to tend to Nicholas' leg, now that his life was no longer in jeopardy.

Aevah turned to him, her eyes brimming. She knelt beside him and wrapped her arms around him, holding on tightly. The embrace said everything – fear, love, and profound relief.

When they pulled apart, Nicholas leaned forward and pressed a gentle kiss to her lips.

He brushed the hair from her face and looked into her eyes. "I could never hurt you, no matter what the reason," she whispered, voice trembling.

"I know," he replied softly. "And that's why you'll be a great leader. You have the strength to protect the people you love, and the wisdom to know compassion is not a weakness."

They kissed again, deeper this time, a silent promise of love and loyalty. When they parted, Aevah's heart felt full to bursting.

"I love you, Nicholas," she said, her voice raw and sincere.

"I love you too, Aevah," he murmured, eyes shining with affection.

A loud cough broke the moment. "Okay, lovebirds, that's enough," Galrick said, smirking. "We've got a kingdom to save, remember?"

Aevah laughed, rising to her feet. With Galrick's help, she pulled Nicholas upright. Then she turned and carefully picked up the crystal shard, placing it in her bag beside the first. The two pulsed in harmony, their energies resonating as one.

Before they could leave, the largest wolf approached once more. "Should you ever need us," it said, voice filled with solemn respect, "call upon the wind, and we shall come. It will be an honour to follow a leader such as yourself."

Aevah nodded, deeply moved. "Thank you," she said. "We won't forget your kindness."

With the shard secure and her friends beside her, Aevah led them from the chamber and back into the frozen mountainside. At the cave's mouth, Isabella let out a cry of relief.

"Here—look! A sledge, and sacks of food and water." She dropped to her knees, rummaging through the supplies.

"Who left this here?" Galrick asked, frowning.

"Who cares?" Nicholas winced as he shifted his weight. "Take it."

"It's enough to get us back without starving," Isabella added, a rare smile tugging at her lips.

Aevah glanced up at the sky, her heart full. "Thank you, Divine Spirit, for these blessings," she whispered.

With the supplies packed, the group prepared for their descent. Nicholas was placed gently on the sledge, unable to walk on his injured leg. Galrick took the lead, dragging the sledge with determination, while Aevah and Isabella walked alongside, offering support and keeping watch.

Without Thorin, the path was harder. The wind howled around them, and every step felt colder than the last. Aevah couldn't even remember what warmth felt like.

But whenever they faltered or strayed from the path, a wolf would appear in the distance, silently guiding them back to safety.

After several gruelling weeks, the wind finally eased, and the air began to warm. The ground grew firmer, the slopes less treacherous. In just a few more days, they would reach the foot of the mountain.

As much as Aevah longed for the comfort of civilisation, she knew the road ahead would come with its own trials. But for now, with the shards in hand and her friends beside her, she felt ready to face whatever came next.

Chapter 18

No Way Out

It was close to sunrise, and they had managed to evade Elinor's men, thanks to the shadows. But with dawn fast approaching and Jacob and the others exhausted, he held little hope for their chances.

Moving silently through the trees, each member of the group did their best to avoid detection, but the guards were closing in. There were too many to confront, and it was only a matter of time before one of them was seen. Jacob didn't know where his friends were, but he held onto the belief that they'd make it out. He couldn't bear to imagine what Elinor would do if she caught any of them.

Every step Jacob took seemed thunderous in the silence. Each snapped twig or rustled leaf sounded like an explosion to his ears. His heart pounded in his chest, loud enough, it seemed, to lead the guards straight to him.

Crunch.

A stick splintered beneath his foot.

"Stop right there."

Jacob froze, raising his hands slowly above his head. The voice had come from behind him, but he didn't dare turn around. Terror rooted him in place, and time slowed to a crawl. His heart hammered against his ribs, the rhythmic beat echoing like war drums in his ears. The air was thick with tension, and every breath felt like a gamble.

The others tensed, hands drifting towards their weapons. They knew the odds – they couldn't win this fight – but they would defend themselves if they had to. Jacob's mind raced for a solution, but fear kept it locked in place.

Suddenly, a boot slammed into his back, knocking him to the ground. The impact drove the air from his lungs, and he gasped, his hands scraping against the forest floor. Around him, he heard the guards closing in, and his friend's cries as they resisted. The chaos only strengthened his resolve, and he began to push himself up.

"Stay down!" shouted a voice, just before another boot crashed into his back, driving his face into the dirt. A guard seized his arms and yanked them behind him, binding them tightly with rough rope. Another guard tied his legs, then began patting him down, pulling free any weapons he had concealed. Once disarmed, they hauled him onto his knees by the hair, checking his front for more.

"Get up," one of the guards ordered, yanking him to his feet. Jacob stumbled, legs shaky from the sudden movement, but he managed to stay upright. Barely. He strained against the bindings, thoughts spinning as he looked for any chance to escape. Around him, the sounds of battle rang out – the clash of steel, cries of defiance, and the thud of bodies hitting the ground. His friends were still fighting, but it was clear they were outnumbered.

One of the guards stepped in front of him with a sneer. "Oh no, you don't," he said, before striking Jacob across the face with the butt of his sword.

Stars burst behind Jacob's eyes as pain exploded through his skull. The world spun, his vision swimming as he fought to stay upright. Darkness tugged at the edges of his mind, but he clenched his jaw, refusing to surrender to it.

Rough hands seized him again, dragging him towards the edge of the woods. He was half-carried, half-dragged to a waiting wagon and thrown inside. The door slammed behind him with a hollow bang, leaving him in total darkness.

"Nice of you to join me."

"Luke?" Jacob struggled to sit up, but dizziness overwhelmed him. He stayed on his back, turning his head towards the voice, blinking through the haze clouding his vision.

"In the flesh. A little bloodied and bruised, but alive."

A shaky breath of relief escaped Jacob's lips. "What happened to the others?" he whispered.

Luke shifted, wincing from his injuries. "We got separated in the chaos. I don't know where they are. I just hope they managed to get away."

Jacob nodded slightly, though the motion sent another wave of pain through his skull. "We need to find a way out of here."

Luke let out a dry, humourless chuckle. "Easier said than done, my friend. But we'll figure something out. We always do."

As they lay in darkness, the sounds of the forest outside the wagon seemed to grow louder, more ominous with every passing minute. Jacob strained his ears, desperate to catch any hint of what was happening to their friends. Shouts and the distant clash of weapons drifted towards them, but it was impossible to tell who was winning. So far, only Luke was in the wagon with him, and Jacob hoped it would stay that way.

Time dragged, each second stretching longer than the last as they waited in tense, suffocating silence.

The uncertainty gnawed at Jacob's thoughts. He had no idea what fate had befallen the others. He and Luke sat motionless, both listening intently for any sound that might offer them a clue. Occasionally, the quiet was shattered by a sudden yell – perhaps a guard spotting someone in the trees – only for silence to fall again like a shroud.

Then, without warning, the wagon door creaked open. Two bodies were thrown in, landing hard on the wooden floor. Jacob scrambled upright as best he could, heart sinking when he recognised them. Elsie and Finn. Both were battered and bruised.

Blood streamed from a deep gash on Finn's temple, and Elsie clutched her wrist, her entire body trembling.

"Elsie," Jacob whispered, his voice thick with worry as his eyes darted to Finn's limp form.

"I think they broke my arm," she said, her voice shaking. "And Finn… they—they smashed his head into a rock. He stopped moving." Her voice cracked as tears streamed down her cheeks, her gaze locked on her injured brother.

Luke moved quickly, kneeling beside Finn. He tore off his shirt, pressing the fabric against the wound to slow the bleeding. "He's still breathing," he murmured. "Hang in there, Finn. Stay with us."

Jacob struggled to crawl closer, but with his hands bound and the wagon jolting beneath him, he lost balance and fell back with a thud. They were moving.

Elsie, wincing from pain, slid over to him and tried to untie his hands with her good hand, but the knots held firm. Frustrated, she switched places with Luke, but without a blade, all their effort did was cause the rope to dig deeper into his skin, burning it raw.

"Don't worry about it," Jacob said quietly. "Even if you get it off, all it'll do is piss off the guards when they notice." The others fell back in silence, the weight of defeat settling over them like a heavy fog. No one dared voice their fears for the rest of their friends. The fact that the wagon had begun moving could only mean one thing – and none of them believed it was good.

Movement was difficult with every jolt and sway of the wagon. Eventually, Jacob, Luke, and Elsie managed to shift themselves along the floor, leaning their back against one of the wooden walls. Finn lay at their feet, still unconscious, but at least the bleeding had slowed.

Jacob watched him closely, willing him to stir. Beside him, Elsie let her head fall softly onto his shoulder. Her breathing had steadied, a small comfort amid the chaos. On his other side, Luke sat with his head tilted back, eyes closed in exhausted silence.

Jacob's own body began to give in. Weariness tugged at him with every breath, the weight of the day finally settling in his bones. As the wagon rocked gently beneath them and the warmth of Elsie's presence eased the ache in his chest, he closed his eyes and let sleep take him.

***

After several hours, Jacob was jolted awake as the wagon came to an abrupt stop. His body lurched forward, aching from the stiffness of a night spent on the hard floor. Blinking against the dim light that crept through the slats, he took in his surroundings. Luke remained asleep nearby, breathing evenly, while Elsie was curled beside him, her broken arm cradled against her chest and a pained frown etched into her face.

Jacob shifted carefully, trying not to wake them, and peered through the narrow gaps in the wagon's wooden panels. The sun was high, likely midday, casting sharp shadows across a dirt road flanked by dense trees. Guards milled about outside, some vanishing briefly into the undergrowth.

He flinched back as one guard spotted him and shouted to the others.

Scrambling, Jacob moved to rouse the others just as the door swung open, flooding the wagon with blinding sunlight.

"I see you're awake," one of the guards sneered as he climbed in. Two more followed, dragging them out one by one. Finn was thrown roughly to the ground, groaning as his eyes fluttered open.

Chains were slapped onto Elsie and Luke's wrists, while another guard sawed through the binding around Jacob's legs. Elsie let out a scream as the cold metal clamped over her broken wrist, her face twisting in agony as tears streamed down her cheeks.

"You've got five minutes to relieve yourselves, eat, and drink," a guard snapped. "Try anything clever, and you die."

"Except you, princeling," another added with a malicious grin. "The queen wants you alive. Didn't say anything about keeping you in one piece, though."

Jacob's stomach sank. They knew who he was. But he kept his expression cold and unreadable, refusing to give them the satisfaction of seeing fear.

At his feet, Finn stirred again. A guard fastened chains around his wrists and yanked him upright. Unsteady, he swayed until Luke and Jacob stepped in to support him.

"Nice to see you're still breathing," one of the guards mocked, handing each of them a scrap of bread and a tin cup of water. They ate and drank quickly, knowing they'd need their strength. Jacob helped Finn, who struggled to lift the cup with trembling hands.

"Thank you," Finn whispered, barely audible. Jacob gave a brief nod and a small, encouraging smile.

"If you need to piss, the tree's over there," another guard sneered.

They moved as a group, Elsie doing her best to manage with one hand while staying out of view. Jacob helped as discreetly as he could, painfully aware of how vulnerable she must have felt. The situation was humiliating for all of them, but especially for her, the only girl among them.

When their time was up, they were shoved back inside the wagon and locked in once more. Defeat hung heavy in the air. Unarmed, shackled, and en route to Carraton, there was little to feel hopeful about. Still, Jacob silently thanked the Divine Spirit that Finn was hanging on. They watched him carefully, wary of signs of concussion, but sitting upright seemed to help. His gaze had begun to focus, his breathing more regular.

With the cold seeping in and nothing else to do, the group huddled together for warmth. Now and then, someone murmured a new idea for escape. With his legs unbound, Jacob helped Luke explore the wagon, feeling along the wooden panels for any weakness. But the structure was solid – no loose boards, no gaps to exploit.

Frustrated, he sank back down, the hum of voices around him fading into the background noise. His mind wandered to the others – those who hadn't been caught. He prayed they were safe. Yet even more pressing was the fate of those beside him. Carraton loomed ever closer, and he feared what awaited them there.

He hadn't seen his aunt since he was very young – so young he couldn't even recall meeting her. How strange it felt that someone who shared his blood, someone he didn't even know, wanted him dead.

"So, we agree?"

Jacob blinked, jolted back to the present. "What?"

"Weren't you listening?" Luke teased.

"Sorry. My thoughts were elsewhere."

Luke nodded in understanding and repeated the plan. "Tonight, we do as we're told. We watch the guards—who hold the keys, who stand watch, how they handle us. If we're only let out briefly and locked up again right after, escape will be harder. But if we pay attention, we might spot a weakness."

"If they shove us right back in here again tonight, that's it," Elsie added grimly. Finn nodded in agreement.

"They'll likely let us out like earlier," Finn said. "We just have to make that time count. Try to convince them to let us stay out longer. If we cooperate, maybe they'll grow complacent after a day or two."

"Yes, then we make our move," Luke added. "We act by the third night, at the latest. Otherwise, it will be too late."

Jacob shivered at the weight of his words. Carraton was no longer just a distant threat – it was a destination rapidly closing in.

With nothing more to say, they lapsed into silence again, occasionally speaking in low murmurs about how they were holding up.

Trapped in the confines of a moving wagon, there was little to do beyond worry and let his thoughts spiral. Jacob knew too well that dwelling on those thoughts led nowhere good, so he tried to distract himself with small talk. No one seemed particularly eager to engage, but he pressed on, hoping to lift their spirits and keep their minds from falling into despair.

Finn and Luke humoured him for a while, offering the occasional reply, but Elsie, the one he most hoped would join in, remained silent. Her pain was etched across her face, both physical and emotional. She sat withdrawn, her thoughts clearly far away. It hurt to see her like that, and it hurt even more to know he was the reason she was here. The reason they all were.

He felt like a fool for thinking they could outwit Elinor, for dragging his friends into this mess. He should never have let them come. The guilt weighed heavily on him, pressing down like a stone on his chest. With every jolt of the wagon wheels along the uneven road, his mind raced, clinging to fragile threads of hope and escape. Somehow, they had to survive this.

At last, as the sun dipped low on the horizon, the wagon rolled to a halt. Muffled voices drifted in from outside – the guards talking – but no one came for them immediately. Jacob sat on edge, his entire body taut with anticipation. No words were spoken among them, but the glances exchanged told him everything he needed to know. They all shared the same thought: tonight, they would begin observing, planning.

Then, finally, the door creaked open and swung wide. Harsh moonlight spilt inside as a guard entered, dragging them out one by one into the hands of waiting guards. As Jacob stepped into the open, a biting wind cut through his clothes. With no cloak or proper warmth, the chill sank deep into his skin, making him shiver. The others huddled together instinctively, their breaths visible in the frigid air.

The nearest guard shoved Jacob forward towards a small clearing where a campfire crackled. "Sit," he ordered, pushing him hard by the shoulder. Jacob stumbled and fell to his knees. The guard, unsatisfied, pressed down harder, his fingers digging into Jacob's shoulder until he lost his balance and hit the ground with a thud. Laughter followed.

The guard stepped in front of him, grinning. "Well, look at that—the princeling bows to the likes of me."

Jacob spat dirt from his mouth and clenched his jaw, refusing to speak. His silence only amused the guard more. "What's the matter, princeling? Cat got your tongue?" he sneered, kicking a spray of dirt towards Jacob's face.

Still, Jacob said nothing. He stared at the ground, shoulders tense. The guard's patience ran out. He grabbed Jacob by the collar, yanking him upright before backhanding him across the face. The blow stung, sharp and immediate.

"You think you're better than me, don't you?" the man declared, his face inches from Jacob's. "Let's see how high and mighty you feel when you're rotting in Carraton." With that, he shoved Jacob backwards. He hit the ground hard, pain jarring through his spine.

The guard muttered curses under his breath and stalked away, leaving Jacob to collect himself.

"You alright?" Luke whispered beside him, keeping one eye on the guards.

"I'm fine," Jacob muttered, brushing dust from his clothes. "Seems that one has it in for me. Best we keep quiet, like we planned. No reason to provoke him further."

Luke nodded and sat beside him, with Finn and Elsie following suit. The rest of the evening passed uneventfully. The guards gave them food and water and escorted them to a nearby cluster of trees when they needed to relieve themselves.

Because the group remained quiet and compliant, the guards largely ignored them. When night fell, they were locked back inside the wagon. Thankfully, the cruel guard left Jacob alone.

Knowing the ride ahead would be long, and wary of the guards' positions outside, the group huddled together for warmth. Luke removed his cloak and draped it over them as best he could, but the fabric was this, and the night air still found its way in.

Jacob was grateful to be inside. As the wind howled beyond the wooden panels, he found a sliver of comfort imagining the guards braving the cold while they were at least somewhat sheltered. The thought gave him a brief, bitter satisfaction, a small victory in a string of losses.

As he settled down, he felt Elsie shift closer. Without hesitation, he pulled her gently into his arms. Her eyes fluttered open, just for a moment, and she offered him a faint smile.

He kissed the top of her head and whispered, "Goodnight."

Wrapped in each other's warmth, Jacob finally allowed himself to relax. For the first time in what felt like days, a flicker of peace touched his heart. And with Elsie in his arms, he drifted off into a rare moment of sleep, soft, quiet, and momentarily free from fear.

Chapter 19

A Desperate Gambit

The next morning, Jacob awoke to the sound of banging and clattering outside the camp. Around him, the others stirred, groaning as they were pulled from an uncomfortable, restless sleep. Blinking against the light, Jacob became aware of the stiffness in his limbs, a result of the cold night. Then he realised he was still entwined with Elsie, her head resting gently on his shoulder.

There was a brief, awkward moment as they both registered their closeness. But Jacob's discomfort quickly gave way to concern when Elsie flinched, her face tightening from the pain in her injured wrist.

Finn had fashioned a makeshift sling from the hem of his shirt the night before, tearing off a strip of fabric to support the broken bone. Fitting it had been a challenge, especially with chains still shackled to her wrists, but they had managed. Though the thin fabric offered little comfort, it was better than nothing.

Having slept on it, the pain was worse that morning. Jacob helped her shift the position of her arm, adjusting the sling to take more of the weight off her arm. She sighed softly in relief as some of the pressure eased.

The door to the wagon creaked open, and guards entered, dragging them out one by one. Breakfast was the same cold, lumpy porridge and a single cup of water. After a few minutes to relieve themselves, they were herded back into the cramped wagon they had come to despise. The routine was becoming all too familiar, and morale was low.

As the wagon wheels began to turn and the guards fell out of earshot, the group seized the chance to speak in hushed voices, planning their escape.

"Okay," Luke began, keeping his voice low. "There are six guards and four of us. Not terrible odds to start with."

The others nodded.

"And so far," Elsie added, "the same one always carries the keys."

"Another point in our favour," Jacob said. "So when do we make our move?"

"When we're let out for our bathroom break," Luke answered. "Only one guard ever watches us. When the moment's right, I'll give a bird call as a signal. Then I strike—take down the first guard. After that, it's all about coordination and stealth."

"Jacob, Elsie," Finn said, "you two gather the horses and grab what supplies you can—food, water, anything useful. If the coast is clear, search the camp. Luke and I will handle the rest of the guards. They're all armed, so once we bring down the first, we'll have weapons too."

"Don't be seen," Luke added, his eyes locking with Jacob's and then Elsie's. "Stick to the brush and trees. Release any extra horses—you know they'll send riders after us if they can. And if it looks like we're losing, get out. Don't come back. Understand?"

Jacob looked to Elsie, who shrugged. "If you need it, I can help," he said, his voice firm.

"We know," Luke said gently, placing a reassuring hand on his arm. "But I won't risk something happening to you. Stick to the plan. You have a part to play, and it doesn't end in a shallow grave at the hands of these so-called men. If things go bad, you ride. No looking back."

Jacob exhaled sharply. "Fine. But you'd better know I'm not happy about leaving any of you behind."

"We know," Finn said. "But this is worst-case scenario stuff. And it won't come to that. We're escaping tonight. Every last one of us."

There were quiet murmurs of agreement, careful not to draw the guards' attention. Then the group fell silent again, leaning back against the wagon walls, waiting for nightfall.

They stopped once more for a midday meal – more of the same – before continuing as the sun began to dip below the trees.

Jacob was buzzing with tension, his leg bouncing and fingers tapping as he tried to release the nervous energy building inside him. When the wagon door finally creaked open again, adrenaline surged through his veins. In his rush, he stumbled as he was yanked out, crashing into the nearest guard.

"Watch it!" the man shouted, shoving Jacob aside. "That goes for the rest o' you too. Hurry up. I've got better things to do than babysit you lot. If it were up to me, you'd all be dead already. But orders are orders—the queen wants you breathing."

He continued grumbling as he led them past the camp. Jacob kept his eyes sharp, scanning the layout. The guards were spread out, one tending to a pot of stew, another sharpening his sword. But two were out of sight. That could complicate things.

The guard rambled on, escorting them into the trees, just beyond the camp's line of sight, for their daily bathroom break.

"Now we gotta feed you too? You'd better be worth the coin. You're costin' us—"

A birdcall pierced the air. Sharp and deliberate.

Jacob's heart stopped.

Luke moved like lightning. He stepped in behind the guard, looping the chain from his manacled wrists around the man's throat. He pulled hard, metal digging into flesh. The guard's eyes widened, mouth gaping in shock. He clawed at the chain, gasping as panic overtook him.

The guard couldn't speak; only a strangled gurgle escaped his throat as he struggled. Luke's grip tightened, muscles straining as he yanked the chain harder. The guard's face turned red, then a deep shade of purple, his eyes bulging as he gasped for breath. Jacob watched in silent horror as the man's frantic movements slowed, weakening with each passing second.

With one final, desperate pull, Luke cinched the chain until the guard's eyes rolled back, and his body went limp. He let go, allowing the guard's lifeless body to crumple into the underbrush. Chest heaving, Luke took a moment to catch his breath before signalling to the others.

They crept closer, though Jacob trembled slightly. He had known what was coming, but seeing it unfold was something else entirely. Beside him, Elsie reached for his hand and gave it a reassuring squeeze just as Finn approached with a dagger. With practised hands, Finn cut through the ropes binding Jacob's wrists.

Free, Jacob rubbed at his skin, the flesh raw and chafed where the ropes had dug in for days. He flexed his fingers, feeling the painful prickling of returning blood flow. Stretching his arms overhead, he tried to ease the tightness in his back and shoulders, every joint aching from confinement.

"Is everyone okay?" Luke whispered.

They all nodded, too cautious to speak aloud.

"Good. We know the plan. This one didn't have the key to the chains, but he had a few knives on him," Luke said, patting the dead man's body. "Finn and I will move in to take out the other guards. Jacob, Elsie—start making your way to the horses."

“Remember,” Finn added with a faint smile, “if something goes wrong, run. Preferably on horseback.”

They concealed the guard’s body beneath the undergrowth, then split off towards their targets.

Jacob and Elsie kept to the camp’s edge, using the trees and shadows for cover. With his hands free, Jacob moved more easily, quietly navigating the uneven ground. Elsie, still bound, stumbled beside him.

“Here, let me help,” he whispered, catching her before she fell again.

“Thanks,” she murmured, her expression strained. “These chains aren’t exactly built for stealth.”

He kept a steady hand on her arm, guiding her through the darkened terrain. From a distance came shouts of alarm – guards reacting. The plan had begun. The fight had started.

Jacob froze when he spotted the horses. They were tied to a tree near the edge of the clearing, restless and on edge, ears flicking at the commotion. He glanced around, and there was no one in sight. Stepping forward cautiously, he raised his hands.

“Easy, easy,” he whispered to the nearest mare. He needed to move quickly, but a panicked horse could ruin everything.

Elsie scanned the camp. “We need to move. Finn and Luke won’t hold them off forever.”

He nodded, his mind racing. “I’ll untie them. You gather the supplies.”

Focussed on his task, Jacob didn't hear the footsteps behind him. He only reacted when the cold bite of steel pressed against his neck.

"Going somewhere?" a voice sneered, a hand clamping down on his shoulder.

Jacob's heart hammered as he felt the sting of the blade nicking his skin. A thin line of blood trickled down his throat.

He was turned roughly to face another guard, this one with Elsie in his grasp. Her eyes were wide with terror.

"Let her go!" Jacob demanded, his voice shaking with fury and fear.

The guard holding Elsie chuckled darkly. "Oh, of course, your highness. Whatever you say."

Without warning, he slammed her to her knees and struck her across the face. She cried out as her head snapped to the side.

"Any other demands?" he mocked.

Jacob's heart pounded as his mind raced for a way out. He clenched his fists, helpless, forced to watch as Elsie writhed in pain.

"Please, just let her go," he pleaded, his voice cracking.

The guard only laughed, low and cruel, before slamming his boot into her ribs. Elsie collapsed with a cry, curling inward.

"No!" Jacob lunged towards her, but the cold blade pressed harder against his throat, and the guard holding him tightened his grip.

The second guard sneered and struck Elsie again, this time across the face. Blood bloomed on her lip. He yanked her closer, his hand twisted in her hair.

"Every time you speak, she suffers. So, keep your mouth shut if you want her to stay in one piece."

Jacob froze. The threat paralysed him more than the blade. He saw the pain in Elsie's eyes – fear, anger, and something else. Trust. His jaw clenched as he forced himself into silence, swallowing everything he wanted to say.

"Seems like the princeling finally gets it. Move," the guard sneered.

They were dragged back to camp, Jacob's hands re-bound along the way. The knife never left his throat.

"Remember," the guard muttered, his voice low and venomous, "say a word or try anything, and the girl pays. There's a lot we can do to someone like her."

Jacob's stomach churned. His face went pale, but he said nothing. He couldn't risk it. He wouldn't give them another excuse to hurt her.

As they neared the camp, Jacob's breath caught in his throat. The guard Luke had attacked was still alive, though barely – his neck bruised and swollen. The rest of the men bore cuts and bruises of their own, and none of them looked pleased. Their expressions were stormy, fists clenched as they stared at Jacob and Elsie.

Then, Jacob's gaze dropped, and his heart sank.

Finn and Luke lay on the ground, bloodied and unmoving.

"Ah, nice of you to rejoin us," one of the guards said with a grin that didn't reach his eyes. "After all our kindness, you repay us with attempted murder?" He gestured at the injured men around him. "We don't take kindly to betrayal. You thought you could kill us and run?" His voice hardened. "Think again. We have ways of dealing with troublemakers like you."

His gaze flicked to Luke and Finn. "You're going to regret ever crossing us."

Then the punch came, sudden and brutal. Jacob's head snapped back as the guard's fist connected with his jaw. Another blow struck his gut, knocking the air from his lungs. He doubled over, gasping, only to be kicked from behind and sent sprawling into the dirt.

What followed was a blur of pain.

Fists and boots rained down on him. They were relentless. Every impact lit up his nerves with fresh agony. He curled inward, trying to protect himself, but there was no mercy. It felt endless – like they wouldn't stop until he was dead.

"Enough," one of the guards muttered at last.

The others stepped back, panting.

"The queen wants him alive. All of them."

Jacob didn't hear the words so much as feel the silence that followed. He lay there, barely able to move. Pain radiated from every limb. His ribs burned with each breath, and one eye was swollen nearly shut. Blood trickled from his split lip, and his head pounded with every heartbeat. He tasted copper.

Hands grabbed him, hauling him upright along with Finn and Luke. His legs buckled, but someone held him steady. He swayed, dizzy and nauseous.

"What do we do with them?"

"Toss them back in the wagon."

"And the girl?"

"In with them," the lead guard replied. "Looks like someone already had their fun with her."

"But we haven't—"

"I said, put her in the wagon. That's an order."

Grumbling, the guard obeyed. The door was slammed shut and locked.

Inside, no one spoke.

They sat in silence, each consumed by pain and exhaustion. Jacob leaned back against the wooden wall, his vision swimming. At some point in the night, he passed out, waking only when the wagon jolted into motion again.

Every bump sent new waves of pain through his battered body. He blinked slowly, wincing, then turned his head to find Elsie huddled in the corner. Her face was pale and tight with pain, her eyes dull.

He wanted to comfort her, but he didn't move. Didn't speak. He was afraid it would only make things worse.

The hours dragged on. The silence between them was broken only by the occasional groan. Jacob drifted in and out of consciousness, too weary to fight it. The guards came and handed out water, metal cups with a strange aftertaste, and a scrap of bread. Then back into darkness.

Later, Jacob realised something wasn't right.

Even with the pain, they were sleeping too easily. Too deeply. The water tasted off. He tried to fight the pull, blinking hard to stay alert, but his thoughts tangled. His limbs felt heavy. His mind dulled.

He didn't want to sleep. He couldn't. But the drug was already in his system.

The last thing he saw before the blackness claimed him was Elsie's face, her eyes full of fear and worry. And then he was gone.

Chapter 20

Shackles and Secrets

The journey to Carraton was a haze. Jacob had no idea how long they had been travelling – thanks to the drugs, time had slipped away from him entirely. But that day it was different. No substances dulled his senses, and the water they were given tasted normal. Even so, his mind remained clouded, his body heavy and uncooperative. The pain from the beating still lingered, turning every movement into a trial. His stomach churned, hollow and unsettled, stripped of appetite by the residual effects of whatever they'd given him and the mounting stress of their situation.

Around him, his friends fared no better. Each bore the marks of their suffering. Luke's face was swollen and bruised, his eyes barely open. Finn had a deep gash across his cheek, the dried blood stark against his pale skin. And Elsie – Elsie looked hollow, her spirit fractured by the unrelenting torment. They all wore the same haunted expression: pain, exhaustion, and fear carved into their faces like scars.

"Hope you all enjoyed the last few days," a guard sneered as he slammed the wagon door shut and locked it. "It was peaceful for us, with you lot sleeping so soundly. But now that we're near the city, it's time to wake up and meet your fate."

Jacob's face paled. They were close – too close. Carraton loomed ahead. Elinor awaited them and likely their doom. He tried to summon a plan, anything at all, but his thoughts refused to align. His friends were just as lost, their silence heavy with dread.

"It'll be okay," Finn said quietly. "Once we're inside, we can reassess. I've no doubt Trysten and the others are following us. With the help of the rebels, they'll get us out."

"Yes," Jacob added, clinging to the idea. "The rebels will come. Word would have reached them by now. My mother will have a plan in place, I'm sure of it." He held tightly to that fragile strand of hope as the wagon rumbled forward.

Time passed in a daze until Jacob noticed the pace slowing. He heard the guards calling to one another before the wagon ground to a halt. For a moment, there was silence. Then the bolt slid open with a harsh scrape. As the door creaked outward, the silhouette of a man appeared in the fading light, and they were dragged out, one by one, and dumped onto the ground.

Jacob dared a glance around. From what he remembered of his childhood, they were in the courtyard near the stables. Night was falling, and the crescent moon hung low and bright above them.

"It's definitely the prince, mi'lord. 'Im and 'is companions," one of the guards said.

A tall man in a regal cloak stepped forward. He grabbed Jacob's chin, turning his head side to side with a frown.

"I'll take your word for it," the lord said. "Hard to tell through all the swelling. Her Majesty will know for sure when she sees him."

"Aye, mi'lord. She'll know 'er nephew, I'm sure of it."

The lord looked over the group with distaste. "What happened to them? All of them?"

"They tried to escape," the guard replied. "So we taught 'em a lesson."

"This was your doing?"

"Aye, mi'lord."

"Well then, you can explain to your queen why they're not in one piece, as she specifically requested."

"Mi'lord, I—I—"

But the lord was already turning away, addressing someone else before vanishing from view with a final, sharp glance. Jacob didn't recognise him, but the man's bearing spoke of arrogance and command, gleaming armour and all.

A guard seized Jacob's arm and began to haul him towards a nearby building with a solid metal door. Behind him, his friends were dragged along as well, each flanked by a guard.

Walking proved nearly impossible at first. The long days trapped in the wagon had reduced Jacob's legs to jelly, his muscles weakened and stiff from disuse. But his guard showed no sympathy, dragging him along regardless. The door opened as they neared, revealing a shadowy entrance.

They were led inside, into a cold and forbidding corridor. Jacob had never been in this part of the castle before. The air was damp and smelled faintly of mould and rot. A thick sense of dread hung over everything. Along the walls were cells with solid doors, each fitted with heavy bars in place of windows. The only light came from a few scattered torches, their flames casting dim, flickering shadows.

Coughing echoed from the cells, some weak and rasping, others sharp with desperation. Voices cried out for water or food, the pleas bouncing down the narrow corridor. Chains clinked. Someone groaned in pain.

The guards didn't flinch. Their faces were blank, their steps purposeful. Cold. Indifferent.

No, this wasn't a part of the castle Jacob had ever seen before, and one he wished he never had. The corridor was narrow and bleak, and the few guards stationed there glanced at the group with thinly veiled curiosity.

"This them?" one of them asked, eyeing Jacob in particular, as he stood at the front.

"Yes. And this one's the prince," the other replied. "Her majesty gave orders—pay special attention to him."

The first guard gave a low whistle. "Looks like they've already been taken care of, judging by the state of them."

"Just get them locked up, and keep an eye on him," came the curt response.

Without another word, Jacob was shoved forward to an open cell a few doors down. He stumbled inside, the door slamming shut behind him, the bolt drawn with a heavy finality. He spun around and pounded his fists against the cold metal, pain jolting through his hands.

"Wait! My friends!" he shouted, panic seizing his chest. "Where are they? What have you done with them?"

His voice echoed down the corridor, swallowed by the oppressive silence. No answer came. He banged on the door again, desperate, but there was only the faint coughing of unseen prisoners and the distant, pitiful cries for food or water.

His heart sank. The realisation settled over him like a weight – he was alone. Truly alone.

Turning back with his head bowed in defeat, Jacob took in his surroundings. The cell was small and damp, the stone walls slick with moisture. A thin layer of straw barely covered the floor. A tiny, barred window high above let in the faintest sliver of light, just enough to cast weak shadows across the room. The chill seeped into his bones, the silence pressing down on him – until it was broken.

"Jacob?" came a faint voice. "Jacob, can you hear me?"

His heart leapt. He pressed his ear to the damp wall, straining. "Elsie? Is that you?"

"Yes, it's me," she whispered, her voice trembling. "I'm scared, Jacob. I can't hear Finn or Luke. I don't know where they are."

Jacob closed his eyes, willing his voice to stay steady. "It's going to be okay, Elsie. Help is on its way. My mother and the rebels will find us. Remember, it's me Elinor wants. You'll be safe."

"But… what if they don't get here in time?" Her voice was barely a breath, fragile with fear.

"They will," Jacob said, more firmly this time, trying to lend her his strength. "We just have to hold on a little longer. Stay strong, Elsie. It'll be all right."

There was a pause, then the soft sound of her breathing filtered through the wall. "Thank you, Jacob," she whispered. "I needed that. Just being able to talk to you helps."

He leaned his forehead against the stone, drawing a small comfort from the connection. "Elsie… I'm so glad we met. Getting to know you—it's been one of the best things in my life."

Her voice, faint but warm, drifted back to him. "Same here. And when we get out of this, we'll finally have time together—and we can settle who the better archer is."

Jacob laughed softly. "Oh, that's definitely you. I was never any good. Just ask my sister." His smile was bittersweet as he thought of Aevah.

"I can't wait to meet her."

"You will," he said softly. "Soon, Elsie. You and Aevah will be like two peas in a pod."

She chuckled faintly, the sound like a small light in the darkness. Then, after a moment, she whispered, "I think I need to rest. I'm so tired."

His heart clenched, but he kept his tone light. "Then rest. We'll talk more in the morning."

"Goodnight, Jacob."

"Goodnight, Elsie," he replied, his voice thick with tenderness and quiet resolve.

As her presence faded into silence, Jacob remained still in the darkness, a flicker of hope glimmering in his chest. He closed his eyes, clutching tightly to the fragile promise of a future beyond these walls, and swore he would get them out, no matter what it took.

***

Elinor paced her chambers, her heart pounding with anticipation. Word had arrived that one of the wagons transporting a group of captured rebels was nearing the castle, and among them was said to be her nephew, Jacob. Over the years, she had received similar news, only to be disappointed time and again. But this time felt different. This time, she was certain.

Bradley stood at the window, his eyes fixed on the horizon, scanning for any sign of the approaching wagon. The minutes dragged on, stretching into what felt like hours, until at last he caught sight of movement in the distance.

"It's here, my dear," he said calmly. "Shall we go down and greet your long-lost nephew?"

Elinor's heart skipped a beat. She hesitated, then shook her head, her voice trembling with a mixture of hope and dread. "No. I don't want to get my hopes up again. Let Julian confirm it first. He's waiting for me."

Bradley gave a quiet nod, understanding her caution. He kept his gaze out the window but said nothing more.

Elinor's thoughts raced. *Could it really be Jacob this time? After all these years, all the false leads, was he finally within her grasp?* Her emotions tangled – hope, anxiety, vindication. She squeezed her hands, her eyes darting around the chamber, unable to settle on anything. Every few seconds, she glanced at the door, willing it to open.

"Oh, come on, Julian," she muttered under her breath. "Tell me it's him."

Bradley stepped away from the window and moved to her side, placing his hands gently on her shoulders. "This is it. Julian will confirm soon."

Footsteps echoed in the hallway, steady and deliberate. Elinor's breath caught in her throat. Her eyes fixed on the door as the footsteps grew louder. At the sound of a knock, she all but stumbled to answer it.

"Is it him?" she asked, her voice barely above a whisper.

She stepped aside as Julian entered. His expression was composed, but his eyes met hers directly.

"Yes, Your Majesty," he said. "He's battered and bruised, thanks to the guards who brought him in. I've instructed one of them to explain the details to you personally. Even with the damage to his face, he's confirmed his identity."

Elinor's heart soared, but her expression remained calm. "Have the men escorted to the throne room. I would speak with them myself."

Julian bowed and left without another word.

Bradley stepped forward. "Do you wish for my presence?"

"Yes, my love," she replied, her voice cool but resolute. "I want to hear how they found him, and if they have any further information we might find useful."

He nodded and offered her his arm. "Then let us await our guests."

They entered the throne room together, taking their seats atop their elevated thrones. Both radiated authority and poise. Elinor's fingers tapped lightly on the carved armrest, an elegant, subtle sign of her impatience. Bradley sat tall and still, his gaze unwavering, his expression unreadable.

The heavy doors creaked open. Six guards entered, their steps cautious, their faces a mixture of reverence and unease. They advanced in a loose formation, stopping just short of the steps to the dais. As one, they bowed low.

"Your Majesties," one of them said, his voice steady but respectful, "it is an honour to stand before you."

Elinor's eyes narrowed slightly. "My knight has informed me that you have indeed captured my nephew, Prince Jacob Maycott." Her tone was sharp, measured. "If this is true, then you may expect reward and recognition once I see him for myself. But before that, I want to hear from you how you found him."

"Of course, Your Majesty," the guard replied.

Elinor leaned forward, her gaze fixed intently on the man as he began to recount the details of Jacob's capture.

"We had been watching the area for some time, as instructed," the guard began. "We spotted a band of rebels and kept our distance. From their conversations, we learned they were searching for a particular well. The name 'Jacob' was mentioned several times. The turning point came when he spoke of his aunt, the queen. That's when we were sure."

Elinor's heart quickened. Every word brought her closer to confirmation.

"As they let their guard down, we struck," he continued. "A few managed to get away, but we captured the ones we needed and brought them to you."

"Anything else we should know?" Bradley asked, his voice even.

The guard hesitated only briefly. "The girl—Elsie, I heard them call her. She and Jacob… they're close. Very close. I believe that could be important, considering the circumstances."

Elinor laced her fingers together, a wicked smile curving her lips. "Oh, that is *very* important, gentlemen. Thank you."

She leaned forward slightly, her voice laced with false warmth. "Please, make yourselves at home. Rest, freshen up, and enjoy some food and drink. And, as I said, if he is who I believe he is, you'll be rewarded handsomely."

The guards bowed low, murmuring their thanks before taking their leave. As the doors closed behind them, silence settled over the throne room.

Elinor's mind raced, her thoughts sharpening like a blade. The girl, Elsie, might be her way in.

"We must use this," she said, turning to Bradley, her eyes gleaming. "If the boy in that cell is truly my nephew, then this girl may be the key to his cooperation."

Bradley gave a single, thoughtful nod. "Then we should go down now. See for ourselves."

Elinor rose, drawing a deep breath to steady herself. "Yes. Let's go."

When they reached the cells, the air turned cold and damp, thick with the stench of rot and mildew. The guards straightened at their approach, faces stern. One stepped forward and unlocked the cell door, swinging it open with a groan. Bradley remained outside as Elinor entered alone, a candle flickering in her grasp.

The room was dim and silent, the only sound her footsteps echoing on the stone floor. The cell was dark and reeking of decay. In the corner, the candlelight caught on a slumped figure lying atop a thin layer of straw. Chains bound his hands and feet.

Jacob stirred at the sound of movement, lifting his head. The flame's glow revealed the bruises and swelling on his face, but it was unmistakably him.

Even through the damage, Elinor saw it: the auburn-brown hair, the fair skin, the strong nose – all the traces of James. And then the eyes – his mother's eyes. Green, sharp, and burning with hatred.

That glare pierced her. For a moment, it made her hesitate. A chill slid down her spine. Without a word, she turned and stepped back into the corridor.

Bradley waited by the wall. She met his gaze. "It's him."

He inclined his head. "Then we have him."

Turning to the nearest guard, Elinor gave her orders with crisp precision. "Tomorrow, bring him fresh clothes and food. Water, too—he is to wash and be made presentable. Once ready, escort him to the same chamber where I once met with his mother. I intend to speak with him myself."

The guard bowed. "Yes, Your Majesty."

Elinor said nothing more as she and Bradley returned to their chambers. Her mind churned with the conversation to come –

how she would break him, how she would use his emotions, his ties, his fear.

This time, there would be no escape. No more leniency. If Jacob refused to give her what she needed, he would be hanged.

So would the rest of them – his rebel friends, his allies, every last one.

She wouldn't make the same mistake twice.

Chapter 21

Beneath the Queen's Gaze

Although the cell was cold and the floor unforgiving, Jacob had managed to get a bit of sleep. His thoughts and dreams had blended together, a restless jumble that offered no true rest. Elinor's face appeared again and again in his mind, not with fear, but with fury. Every time he saw her, his blood boiled.

Restless, he sat up and stretched, trying to ease the stiffness in his limbs. The chains had been removed, for which he was grateful, but his body still ached from the beating he'd taken. Coupled with the days of travel in a cramped, swaying wagon that jolted over every stone, his muscles were sore and stiff.

Ironically, the cell's floor was a welcome change. At least nothing moved beneath him now, and he had space to stand. Compared to the wagon, it was almost pleasant.

Rising to his feet, he crossed the cell to the wall once more, hoping to hear from Elsie. He prayed her night had passed without incident – hers, and Luke's and Finn's. Not knowing their fates gnawed at him.

Just as he opened his mouth to speak, he heard footsteps from outside. Turning, he watched the cell door swing open. A guard stepped in, followed by a maid. Without a word, she placed a bowl of water and clean clothes on the floor, then exited. Moments later, she returned with a tray of food and left again. The guard shut the door behind her, locking it before taking position by the wall, pike in hand, eyes fixed on Jacob.

"Eat and dress. Fast."

Jacob did his best to ignore him. Hunger gnawed at him, and he devoured the porridge in big spoonfuls, barely tasting it. He gulped down the water so fast it spilt down his front, then wiped his mouth with the back of his hand. Turning to the bowl, he noticed a washcloth folded neatly atop the clean clothes. Stripping off his shirt, he began washing himself as best he could.

He felt marginally better once he pulled on the fresh shirt, slightly too big, but clean and dry. Still standing, he removed his shoes and trousers, continuing to scrub the dirt from his skin before dressing in the rest of the clothes.

Once he was finished, the guard approached and shackled his hands once more.

"Come."

The guard grabbed him by the arm and shoved him through the door. Three more guards waited outside, forming a square around him, spears in hand.

“Quite the escort,” Jacob muttered, glancing behind him. He saw no sign of his friends. “Where are you taking me?” he asked, though he didn’t expect an answer. “What of my friends?” Still silence. He had a fair idea of where he was being taken, but he hoped Luke, Finn, and Elsie were still safe in their cells. The farther they were from Elinor, the better.

The guards didn’t respond, marching him through the castle in silence. Elinor was taking no chances. He wasn’t going to escape under this kind of watch.

As they moved, people glanced in his direction and whispered among themselves. Some, when the guards weren’t looking, lowered their heads and placed a hand on their chests. A quiet gesture of support or sympathy. It gave him a sliver of hope.

Walking through the castle stirred a strange feeling in him. He had grown up here, yet the place felt distant and unfamiliar. Fleeting memories surfaced: a boy racing down the corridors, laughter echoing through the halls. He and Aevah chasing each other in the gardens. Their mother shared tea and cake beneath the great tree. His father…

Fragments of a life that now seemed like a dream.

The halls bustled with servants. Paintings and tapestries lined the walls, and though everything looked familiar, it all felt foreign. Finally, they stopped before a wooden door. One of the guards rapped his knuckles against it.

Jacob squared his shoulders.

He was ready to face the woman who had started all of this.

***

As the door opened and Jacob was led into the chamber, Elinor's eyes locked onto his. Though she had seen him the night before and knew it was Jacob, the shock still struck her like a blow. For a fleeting moment, she thought she was seeing James, back from the grave. The resemblance was uncanny.

Memories surged unbidden, crashing into her like waves – childhood laughter, whispered secrets, shared glances – and then, the final moment: his voice calling her name in betrayal and pain, just before she ended his life. That memory hit hardest of all.

Forcing her emotions back under control, Elinor straightened and gestured for Jacob to sit. He scowled at her but obeyed, his shackles clinking as he moved stiffly towards the chair. When he sat, his cold gaze bore into her, unreadable but filled with disdain.

It felt like déjà vu. She had walked this path before – with Cecilia. The past was circling back, but this time, she wouldn't repeat her mistakes. Once she extracted what she needed from him, Jacob would be eliminated before he could become a threat like his mother.

Settling into her seat opposite him, Elinor tilted her head slightly, regarding him with a composed expression.

"I don't believe we've been formally introduced," she began, her tone smooth. "I am Elinor, queen of Ethos, and your aunt. It has been many years since I last saw you. Too many, some might say."

"Not long enough in my eyes," Jacob shot back. "Especially considering you're trying to wipe out my family, just as you did my father. Planning to kill me the same way? A knife to the heart, wasn't it?"

Her eyes narrowed, but she kept her tone even. "Your father sealed his fate when he stole my throne. That choice led to his death. But you, Jacob, you still have a chance. You can choose the right side."

His jaw tightened, his glare unwavering. "And what choice is that? To betray the people I care about? To bow to you?"

Elinor leaned forward slightly, her gaze piercing. "To survive. To protect the lives of your friends, your mother, Aevah. Tell me where they are, and I might let you live."

Jacob's expression wavered, just for a moment. Anger and uncertainty flickered in his eyes. "You think I'd betray them for that? You think I'd give you that satisfaction? I'd rather die."

Her patience frayed at the edges, but she tempered it. This had to be played carefully.

"Think about it," she said coolly. "Your life—and the lives of your friends—are in your hands. Make the right decision."

She caught it then: the brief flash of panic in his eyes at the mention of those still imprisoned below. Inside, she thrilled at the realisation. He had just handed her the key to breaking him, without even knowing it. He might be willing to die, but could he bear watching his friends suffer?

She gave a nod to the guard, who opened the door. One by one, Jacob's companions were ushered in. Each of them looked battered, worn down by captivity, but their eyes still held a fire she couldn't ignore.

"Don't tell her anything, Jacob!" one of them shouted, defiant despite the bruises.

Perfect.

Elinor smiled coldly. Ready to prove a point, she stood and embraced her power, letting it coil through her like a storm barely held in check. She focused it on each of them, feeding intensity into every pulse of energy as she spoke, ready to show Jacob exactly what defiance would cost.

"You have one chance to make this easy on yourself," Elinor said. "Tell me what I want to know, and you and your friends might live to see another day. Refuse, and I'll make sure every one of you hangs."

Jacob's jaw clenched, a faint twitch betraying his rising panic as he glanced at his companions. He could see them struggling, squirming against invisible agony. Elinor, ever observant, watched him closely, gauging the moment he would begin to crack. Not yet satisfied, she increased the intensity of their suffering, targeting Elsie with cruel precision.

She studied his face as their expression contorted, grimacing, deepening into raw, involuntary reactions. Muscles twitched and tensed, sweat began to bead across their brows, and their hands gripped at anything they could reach, white-knuckled, desperate for an anchor against the pain.

Then came the cries.

Elsie screamed first. The sound pierced the chamber just before all three collapsed to their knees, one after the other, unable to endure the waves of torment coursing through them.

One of the young men, Luke, clutched his head, eyes bloodshot, howling as though his skull might split apart. Finn had already dropped to the floor, his body writhing uncontrollably, veins bulging beneath his skin, his voice breaking in agonised pleas for it to end.

And Elsie – Jacob's heart shattered at the sight of her curled in on herself, sobbing, her voice hoarse from begging for death. Tears streamed down her cheeks as the agony raked through her, relentless and unmerciful.

"Stop!" Jacob's voice rang out, hoarse and broken. "Stop, please! You win. Just let them go!"

Elinor's eyes gleamed with quiet triumph as she withdrew her power. The chamber fell silent but for the laboured breathing and muffled sobs of the tortured. Jacob sagged forward, shoulders heavy with defeat. His defiance had shattered.

"Jacob, no—" one of them cried, but the guards were already dragging them out. Elinor motioned for them to be taken away, silencing further protest. This was her moment.

"Ignore them," she said calmly. "Answer my questions honestly, and I'll let you all go."

Jacob looked up at her, eyes still burning beneath the weight of surrender. "How do I know you'll keep your word?"

"You don't," Elinor replied and shrugged. "But you do know I'll bring them back here and keep on torturing them for my entertainment, before I hang you all from the castle gates for everyone to see."

A flicker of fury crossed Jacob's face, followed by resignation. He had no leverage. No escape. No choice.

"What do you want to know?" he asked, the words bitter on his tongue.

Her smile widened. "Where are your mother and the rest of the rebels hiding?"

Jacob's head dropped. Slowly, he gave her everything he knew.

Elinor leaned back, barely able to contain her elation. Finally.

"Guards, take him away."

As they seized him, Jacob resisted. "Wait! You promised to let us go!"

Her expression didn't falter. Cold. Unyielding. "I will keep my promise, Jacob—but first, I need to verify your information. If you've lied to me, the consequences will be… severe."

His shoulders slumped again, heavier this time, as they dragged him from the room.

Even before the door closed, she issued her next order. Men were dispatched at once to the location Jacob had revealed. She would know within days whether he had spoken the truth. If he had, the rebellion would soon be crushed – and her grip on the throne absolute.

Chapter 22

A Rebel's Reckoning

Jacob began struggling against the guards again the moment they neared his cell. "Please, let me see my friends," he pleaded, desperation edging his voice. "I need to know they're ok."

His pleas were ignored. They shoved him roughly inside and slammed the door shut. This time, they didn't even bother to remove the shackles. The cold metal bit into his already broken skin. Gritting his teeth against the pain, Jacob pulled himself upright and pounded on the door with his fists, but it was useless. The guards had gone, and his cries echoed unanswered in the silence.

Defeated, he slumped against the door, his head bowed in exhaustion.

"Jacob, are you there?" Elsie's voice was faint but laced with hope, cutting through the quiet.

His ears perked at the sound, and his body surged with energy. He scrambled towards the wall, just as he had before.

"Elsie," he whispered, heart aching at the sound of her voice. "I'm here. Are you okay?"

"I'm fine," she replied, though the exhaustion in her tone told another story. "What about you? Did she hurt you, too?"

Jacob instinctively shook his head before realising she couldn't see him. "No. I'm okay. I'm more worried about you and the others. Are Luke and Finn alright?"

"I don't know. They looked so tired when we were brought back. Luke kept us going, saying our friends would come for us. Then a guard overheard and dragged him away. Finn tried to stop it… but they knocked him out."

Jacob leaned back against the rough stone wall with a heavy sigh. None of this sat right with him. They were trapped, helpless, and completely at the queen's mercy.

He offered up a silent prayer to the Divine Spirit, hoping beyond reason that their friends would come soon to rescue them. But the longer he sat in the darkness, the more hollow the prayer felt. *If the spirit truly had power, would they be here at all?*

"Jacob? Are you still there?"

"Yes, sorry," he said quickly. "Just lost in thought. It'll be okay. The rebels will come. We'll be out of here soon, I promise."

He forced conviction into his words, though a deep part of him wasn't so sure anymore. But Elsie seemed to believe him, and for now, that belief might be the only thing keeping her going.

The following days passed in agonising slowness. Time lost all meaning, marked only by the meagre meals shoved through the door three times a day. He spent hours lying on the scratchy straw bed, staring blankly at the ceiling, waiting – but no one came.

He and Elsie continued to speak through the wall when they could, though their conversations grew bleaker. The guards offered no updates, and Elinor hadn't summoned him again. She was surely waiting to confirm whether his story had any truth to it. But still, no word came.

Jacob's heart would race every time he recalled what he'd told her – how he'd lied, gambling everything on a bluff. He hadn't given up the rebels' real location, hoping salvation would come before she discovered the truth. But with each passing day, the silence became more suffocating.

Anxiety gripped him like a vice. His breaths came shallow and rapid, his chest tightening until it felt like he couldn't draw in air. Sweat beaded on his brow, his hands trembling. The stone walls felt like they were closing in, shrinking his world into a crushing, airless box.

His mind betrayed him, conjuring vivid images of his friends suffering, punished because of his deception. He clutched his head, trying to shut it all out, rocking gently as he hummed an old lullaby from childhood in a desperate attempt to calm himself.

At some point, he must have blacked out.

He jolted awake as rough hands hauled him to his feet. A burly guard loomed over him, expression unreadable.

"Good news. You're free to go—after an audience with Her Majesty the Queen."

"What?!" Jacob's voice cracked with disbelief.

The guard smirked, clearly enjoying his confusion. "You heard me. Once you've spoken with the queen, you and your friends are free to leave."

Heart hammering, Jacob was led from his cell. Ahead, he saw his friends still in chains, their expressions a mixture of hope and suspicion. Luke looked the worst – bruised, worn – but his eyes held a flicker of hope. Finn met Jacob's gaze, his face tense.

"Is it true?" Finn asked, his voice barely more than a whisper.

"Yes," the guard replied. "After you've spoken with the queen."

They were ushered from the darkness of the cells, the dim torchlight giving way to the brilliance of the courtyard beyond. The sunlight was blinding after days in captivity, and Jacob squinted as his eyes adjusted.

The courtyard was filled with guards, their expressions stern and watchful.

Elinor stood in the centre, her presence commanding and cold. Beside her stood a man, Jacob assumed to be her husband

and the king, Bradley, who observed them with a detached curiosity.

"Good afternoon to you all," Elinor said, her voice smooth and authoritative. "I trust my guards have shared the news?"

Jacob's heart pounded in his chest as he tried to make sense of the situation. He exchanged uncertain glances with his friends. Their expressions mirrored his disbelief.

"Yes, Your Majesty," Jacob replied cautiously. "They said we're free to go."

Elinor's lips curved into a smile, but it was devoid of warmth. "Indeed. Your information was invaluable. Thanks to you, the rebels have been captured. As promised, you are free to leave."

Jacob's stomach dropped. His friends' faces fell, too. He had lied – he'd given her false information. *So, how had she found the rebels?*

Panic swelled within him, but he forced himself to remain composed.

Elinor gestured to a carriage waiting nearby. "This will take you out of the city. Once you're a fair distance away, your shackles will be removed, and you will be free to go. Though I'm afraid your weapons will remain here."

Jacob's thoughts raced. It had to be a trap. But what choice did they have? He looked to his friends; their faces were tense, caught between hope and fear.

"I must thank you again for the information," Elinor continued, her voice syrupy and insincere. "You've done a great service to the kingdom."

Jacob swallowed hard, his throat dry. "Thank you, Your Majesty."

They climbed into the carriage silently, tension weighing on every breath. As the wheels began to turn and the palace faded behind them, Elinor gave a small, triumphant wave.

Jacob's pulse thundered in his ears. His friends were watching him now, waiting for answers he didn't have.

"I don't understand what's happening," he murmured, his voice barely above a whisper. "I didn't give her the right information."

"Then what is her game?" Luke asked, his tone suspicious. "Is she actually letting us go?"

"I don't know," Jacob admitted, turning to Finn. "What about you? When they took you… what happened?"

Finn's expression darkened. "What do you think?" he said flatly. "They tortured and beat me. No magic, just pain. I didn't tell them anything."

Elsie placed a hand on Finn's arm, offering silent comfort. His eyes were haunted.

"This is some twisted game," she said. "Maybe she's planning to follow us—hoping we'll lead her to your mother."

Everyone nodded. It made sense. And if that was true, they would have to move fast to avoid leading her right to the heart of the rebellion. But Jacob couldn't shake the feeling that it wasn't going to be that simple.

A few minutes later, the carriage began to slow. Jacob's chest tightened in alarm. They hadn't travelled far enough to be anywhere near the city's edge. Something was wrong.

The doors on both sides of the carriage flew open. Guards swarmed in, yanking them roughly upright. Without warning, coarse sacks were shoved over their heads, and ropes cinched tight around their necks.

They cried out, struggling against the hands gripping them. Jacob fought back, but a baton cracked against his side, then again across his back. He collapsed in agony, gasping for breath.

A hand seized his arm and dragged him from the carriage. Blind and disoriented, he stumbled, falling hard onto the ground. The sack scratched at his skin, his eyes burned, and his breathing grew ragged beneath the suffocating cloth.

"Walk," said a guard.

The voice came from just behind his shoulder, guiding him forward. Each uneven cobblestone threatened to trip him, and when he finally reached a set of smooth steps, he tripped and fell to his knees. Gritting his teeth, he forced himself up the stairs, his legs trembling beneath him.

At the top, the guard shoved him forward until they came to a stop.

"Stay," the voice sneered.

Jacob's heart pounded. He had no idea where they were, but he could hear something – muffled murmurs ahead. A crowd.

He called out softly to each of his friends. They responded, but every voice was quickly silenced by another blow from a baton.

Then, a voice rang out – one that silenced even the murmurs of the crowd.

"Ladies and gentlemen," Elinor announced, her tone grand and theatrical, "thank you for joining us for this special occasion. As you all know, our kingdom has been plagued by rebel uprisings, spreading chaos and unrest. But today, we bring you something… extraordinary."

Jacob's stomach churned. He realised, with sinking dread, that they were being displayed like trophies. The tension in the air was electric, the audience hanging on Elinor's every word.

"Today," she continued, "we unveil a group of rebels who have eluded us for far too long. And among them, we present a very special traitor."

Jacob's breath caught in his throat.

He didn't need to see her to know she meant him. He felt a hand tighten around his arm and drag him forward. Though the sack still blinded him, he could feel the weight of countless eyes settling on him.

“Ladies and gentlemen,” Elinor declared, her voice echoing across the square, “I present to you Prince Jacob—rebel, and traitor to the crown!”

A wave of gasps swept through the crowd, followed by rising murmurs and whispers of disbelief. Jacob’s heart thundered as he was shoved forward. The sack was yanked from his head, and the sudden light stung his eyes.

He blinked rapidly, disoriented, but soon focused on the crowd before him. Faces stared back, shocked, confused, horrified. He stood exposed, vulnerable under the weight of their judgment, fear gnawing at his insides as his mind raced to predict what would happen next.

Elinor’s voice sliced through the noise. “This is the fate of those who dare to defy the crown. Let this serve as a warning to all who believe they can challenge our rule.”

Jacob trembled. His thoughts swirled in chaos. Whatever she had planned, he knew it was no simple show. This was punishment – public, deliberate, and cruel. And they were the spectacle.

Suddenly, hands gripped his arms tightly as he jerked his head towards a familiar voice.

“No! Please, no!” Elsie cried.

Jacob fought wildly, trying to break free, desperate to reach her. But the guards held firm, dragging him back with brutal efficiency. He saw his friends – Elsie, Finn, and Luke – struggling just as fiercely, each one restrained by multiple guards. Their eyes darted between each other in terror. Elinor simply stood back, watching it all unfold with a satisfied, twisted smile.

The crowd buzzed with a mixture of outrage and uncertainty. Some shouted protests. Others simply stared in shocked silence. A few turned away.

Jacob barely registered them. His world narrowed as a coarse rope wrapped around his neck and was pulled tight. Panic surged. His hands flew to the noose, clawing at it instinctively. His breath caught in his throat as he searched the crowd for anyone – *anyone* – who might intervene.

But no one came.

Tears streamed down his cheeks. This was really happening. This was how it would end.

"Jacob, help me!" Elsie screamed, her voice breaking.

He turned, horrified, catching a glimpse of her wild, terrified eyes. Finn and Luke were nearby, thrashing and kicking, trying to break free from their bindings.

"I'm so sorry," Jacob choked, his voice hoarse. "Elsie… all of you… I got you into this mess. And now you're paying the price."

He looked towards Elinor, his eyes wide with a final plea. "Please, let them—"

His words cut off into a strangled gasp as the noose snapped tight and the floor vanished beneath his feet.

Air rushed from his lungs. His hands gripped the rope, tearing at it with everything he had. But it was no use. The pressure around his throat was suffocating. Every breath became a battle he was quickly losing.

To his right, Finn and Luke were fighting, legs kicking furiously. But then his gaze landed on Elsie.

Her legs weren't moving. Her arms hung low, her head slumped to the side.

NO!

He wanted to scream, to curse Elinor, to beg the Divine Spirit for another chance, but he couldn't speak. He couldn't breathe.

His vision blurred. His face darkened to crimson. His heart slammed in his chest, its beat slowing with each desperate second. His limbs thrashed, seeking solid ground, but there was none.

Darkness crept in from the edges of his sight. His hands weakened, falling away from the rope. His legs kicked once – twice – then stopped.

The world faded. The noise of the crowd became distant, like echoes in a tunnel.

And then there was only silence.

Jacob's body hung still, swaying slightly in the breeze.

Chapter 23

Under the Surface

After a few weeks of living in the mines, Cecilia couldn't help but fall in love with the place. It was a little dusty, a little dark, and the winding tunnels made it easy to get lost, but the atmosphere was warm and welcoming in a way she hadn't expected.

The miners and their families were nothing but gracious, embracing her and her companions without hesitation. Like them, many were displeased with Elinor's reign and had willingly provided a safe base for their operations, offering shelter and support when needed. It was a kindness Cecilia deeply appreciated.

That morning, she had ventured to the market with Adrian to gather fresh ingredients for dinner. She always enjoyed visiting the space; every stall brimmed with goods – fresh produce, handmade crafts, and baked treats that left her mouth watering.

The air hummed with the lively chatter of vendors and customers.

Cecilia thrived on conversing with the merchants, learning their stories and hearing the history of the mines. She found the market's very existence fascinating, a vibrant hub thriving in a place that should have felt lifeless. The tunnels were illuminated with strategically placed candles and mirrors, creating a soft glow that lit up the stalls and merchandise for all to see.

That warm, glimmering light lent a magical quality to the bustling scene, making it feel like a hidden gem tucked away beneath the earth. As she wandered, drawn in by the wares and conversation, Adrian remained nearby, ever watchful. Yet even he seemed unable to resist the charm of the market.

His usual stern expression softened as he admired the colourful displays and exchanged friendly nods with the vendors. The market's energy pulled him in, and for a rare moment, he allowed himself to relax and take in the simple joy of the moment.

When they had finished, Cecilia and Adrian made their way back to their cabin. Unlike the other rebels, who shared crowded, bunk-style accommodations in communal lodgings, Cecilia had been offered a small space of her own. Recognising her former status as queen, the miners had insisted on giving her a modest yet private cabin as a sign of respect. Though she had tried to refuse, not wanting to appear entitled, their insistence left her with no choice but to accept it with sincere gratitude.

The space was simple but cosy: a single room with a large, comfortable bed, a sturdy dresser, and a small two-seater table positioned near a narrow window. The glow of a nearby lantern cast soft shadows across the wooden walls, lending the room a serene and inviting atmosphere. She appreciated the privacy, though part of her still felt guilty knowing others slept in far more cramped spaces.

After putting away the market goods, Cecilia waited for the heads of the rebel factions who had joined them. They were scheduled to meet that day to discuss the latest news that had reached their outpost. One by one, the leaders arrived, each bringing updates from their respective regions. They were eager to share what they had learned. The room gradually quieted as everyone found a seat on the hardwood floor, ready to plan their next moves.

Among them were Marcus, Darius and Fiona – trusted allies who had become an essential part of their efforts. Cecilia greeted them warmly.

"Thank you all for coming," she began. "I understand some of you have news to share, as do we. We've called this meeting to regroup and determine our course going forward."

Marcus gave a grim nod. "If I may begin—there have been reports of disappearances and targeted attacks in the Almire region. Rebels and civilians alike are being taken. Anyone the local guards deem suspicious is being removed without trial."

"It's the same across the realm," Darius added. His voice was tight with frustration.

Fiona leaned forward. "Yes, but there's hope. Messengers are reporting that resistance is forming—pockets of it in various territories. People are starting to fight back, and our mutual friend Walter seems to be playing a major role."

"I've received correspondence from him as well," Cecilia confirmed. "He assures me his efforts are not in vain. He's rallying a large group of rebels who are making their way here in small bands, just as we did. They should arrive within the month. He also mentioned the high priestesses. They're planning their own coordinated attack, and Walter is doing everything he can to ensure we're aligned when the time comes."

She glanced around the room before continuing. "Given the weather and the time it'll take our forces to arrive, we may not reach full strength until winter. We'll need to decide soon whether to remain here through the snow and strike in spring or mobilise once we have a sizable enough force."

"What of the young royals?" Fiona asked. "Have we received any word on whether they've found the crystal shards?"

"Not yet," Cecilia replied, her voice edged with concern. "As far as we know, Aevah is still in the mountains with Isabella, accompanied by two new companions—young Galrick and Nicholas Bennett. We're not sure how they met, but they were observed travelling together."

"We can only hope they prove trustworthy," Adrian said, his tone cautious.

Cecilia gave a small nod. "As for Jacob, we've heard nothing. He was last seen heading towards Almire. All we can do now is pray to the Divine Spirit that they're both safe and will return to us soon."

Everyone nodded solemnly, and the discussion shifted towards strategy, planning when and how to strike, and most importantly, how to stop Elinor. Rumours had reached them that her power had grown – someone had reforged her bond with the crystals. She wouldn't be an easy opponent.

Coupled with her formidable army, Elinor posed a greater threat than ever before. Their only hope was to be equally prepared. The group began laying out a plan to train the rebels currently at the base, with drills set to begin the following day. Adrian, along with Marcus, Darius, and Fiona, would lead the sessions, ensuring that everyone was battle-ready.

Yet even with a trained force, Cecilia knew they couldn't match Elinor – not without the shards. The true battle would be between Elinor and the one who possessed the power of the crystals. That task, she knew, belonged to her children. Until they returned, launching an attack would be both reckless and futile. She wouldn't send her people to their deaths in a war they were not ready to fight.

So, she would wait for Aevah, for Jacob, and for the shards. Unless Elinor struck first.

With the initial plans set, the leaders eventually left the cabin, Cecilia and Adrian following close behind. The meeting had stretched well into the afternoon, and Cecilia intended to head to the main camp to assist the miners with the evening meal. It was one of the few tasks they allowed her to help with, and she was determined to contribute where she could.

Adrian parted ways to prepare for the next day's training while Cecilia made her way to the large communal kitchen.

The rich aroma of frying food greeted her as she stepped inside. The kitchen was set up in an open area, equipped with basic but functional facilities – rows of stoves, bubbling pots, and long preparation tables. With so many mouths to feed, the space buzzed with motion and noise.

The kitchen staff moved swiftly, chopping vegetables, searing meats, and stirring fragrant stews. Cecilia greeted those nearby with a smile as she rolled up her sleeves and joined in. The work was grounding, familiar and calming. It reminded her of her time in the castle kitchens and the inn in Adlington. In both places, she had found solace in the simplicity of the task at hand. Here, among allies with a shared purpose, she felt more at home than she had in a long time.

When the meal was ready, Cecilia helped carry dishes to the long communal tables. The spread was a feast of hearty stews, thick casseroles, and generous cuts of beef and lamb roasted to perfection. Trays of seasoned vegetables, steaming pies, and bowls of grains accompanied platters of fresh fish and crusty rolls. The tables overflowed with abundance.

As the line formed and the community began to serve themselves, Cecilia and Adrian found a spot near one of the many fires that dotted the camp. The flames danced and crackled, casting a warm glow that fended off the crisp autumn air.

After eating their fill, the pair stayed by the fire, enjoying the company of those around them. Stories and songs flowed late into the night, punctuated by bursts of laughter and the clinking of cups. The wine and homemade spirits were far stronger than expected, and by the end of the evening, Cecilia and Adrian were stumbling back to their cabin, arms around each other, faces flushed with joy and drink.

Cecilia felt a deep gratitude – for Adrian, for the rebels, for this strange, beautiful community that had embraced her. Surrounded by their resilience and warmth, she allowed herself to believe, if only for a moment, that everything just might turn out all right.

Chapter 24

Shadows in the Tunnels

As the weeks passed, life in the mines settled into a steady rhythm for Cecilia and the rebel faction. They had successfully established a hidden base, well-concealed from the outside world. Despite being nestled in rocky and treacherous terrain, they managed to send and receive letters using ravens, keeping their lines of communication open. Correspondence arrived regularly from both Walter and the High Priestess Zara, keeping them informed without the need for dangerous travel.

The mines themselves were notoriously difficult to access – narrow, winding tunnels filled with hidden traps designed to deter intruders. This made the ravens indispensable, particularly for monitoring Elinor's movements. She acted swiftly, often executing plans before the rebels even heard about them or had time to stop them.

Most recently, her forces had discovered a rebel group hiding in Falmouth. As a main port, it was ideal for coordinating movement and travel across the kingdom. But Elinor had sent mercenaries to eliminate them – no man, woman, or child had been spared. With each passing day, her actions grew more brutal, her methods more unpredictable. Cecilia feared not only what Elinor might do next, but also what she might have already done. She had just been summoned to an emergency meeting, which was never a good sign.

She and Adrian made their way through the narrow tunnels, weaving around camp members rushing by with supplies. More than once, they pressed against the cold stone walls to allow others hauling heavy crates to pass. Thanks to a recently intercepted supply wagon, they had what they needed, at least for now, when the fight inevitably came.

Cecilia's stomach was in knots. These sudden meetings rarely brought good news. As they stepped into the circular cavern, the temperature dropped, and tension thickened the air. Seated around a stone table were Marcus, Darius, and Fiona, their expressions grim and unreadable. Cecilia approached cautiously, her heart hammering in her chest. She clenched her trembling hands into fists, trying to anchor herself.

"What is it?" she asked, stopping a few paces short of the table. The way they looked at her made her skin crawl – this was personal. Adrian stood beside her, equally tense, waiting for someone to speak.

"Sit down, Cecilia," Marcus said gently, rising from his chair and gesturing towards an empty seat.

"What's happened?" she asked sharply, her voice tight with dread. She refused to move. The three exchanged glances, and Cecilia's heart pounded so fiercely it felt as though it might break free from her chest. Adrian reached for her hands, and she gripped his tightly. Fiona also rose from her chair and stepped forward, her face solemn, and her body tense as though bracing for an outburst.

"We just received word," Fiona began. "Elinor has a group of rebels en route to the castle."

"And?" Cecilia asked, breath catching in her throat.

"Jacob is among them."

The words his her like a blow. She staggered. "No. This can't be." She began to pace, her movements erratic as her mind raced for answers. Adrian followed, speaking gently, but his words failed to register – her thoughts drowned everything out.

"We need to go get him!" she cried, her voice rising in desperation. "We can't leave him with her—not Jacob!"

"Cecilia, you have to calm down," Adrian said firmly, placing his hands on her shoulders. "We'll find a way to free him, but running off without a plan will only make things worse."

"No!" she shouted, pulling away from his grasp. "You don't understand. I have to go now. He needs me!"

Adrian caught her arm and spun her around to face him. "Listen to me, Cecilia," he said, his voice low but urgent. "If you go now, you'll be walking straight into a trap."

Her eyes were wild with panic and fury as she struggled in his grip. "I can't just stand here and do nothing!" she screamed, her voice breaking. "He's my son!"

"I know," Adrian said softly, holding on tighter to stop her from fleeing. "But we need to be smart about this."

Before she could respond, a deafening explosion shook the ground beneath them. The walls trembled violently as dust filled the air and rocks tumbled from the ceiling. The others sprang to their feet, Cecilia instinctively ducking.

"What was that?" she cried, her voice hoarse with panic, as fragments of stone fell around them.

"I don't know, but I'm going to find out," Darius said, already heading for the exit, just as a second explosion rocked the cavern. This one was stronger, shaking loose larger chunks of debris from the walls and ceiling, sending the entire chamber into chaos.

"We can't stay here. Any more explosions and this whole shaft might collapse," Fiona warned, her voice sharp with urgency.

"Agreed," Adrian replied, glancing anxiously at the trembling walls. "Let's get out of here!"

Cecilia and Adrian led the charge through the dark, crumbling tunnels, with Darius, Marcus, and Fiona close behind. Debris rained down around them, chunks of rock dislodged by the earlier blast. Cecilia coughed violently as clouds of dust thickened the air, clogging her lungs and stinging her eyes. Each step was a gamble – the ground shuddered beneath them, threatening to give way.

Just as they rounded a bend near the exit, Adrian came to an abrupt halt. Cecilia crashed into his back with a startled gasp. He raised his sword in a flash, eyes locked on the shadows ahead.

"Mercenaries," he muttered, tension rippling through his voice. "They've found us."

Before anyone could react, dark figures surged forward – mercenaries clad in blackened armour, their eyes gleaming with malicious intent. Adrian and Darius stepped in front, blades drawn and ready.

The clash was instant and brutal.

Steel screamed against steel as Adrian and Darius met the first wave with practised precision. Cecilia stayed behind, her heart hammering, her breath ragged from both fear and dust. Behind her, Marcus and Fiona joined the fray, their coordinated strikes cutting through the enemy lines.

Sparks flew as Adrian deflected a savage blow, his sword ringing as it locked with a mercenary's. Beside him, Darius struck with relentless power, forcing the attackers back step by step. Marcus and Fiona fought in tandem, fluid and lethal, holding the flanks with grit and discipline.

But just as the tide seemed to turn in their favour, another explosion ripped through the mine – louder, closer, more devastating. The blast shook the very foundations of the tunnel. Rock and dirt cascaded from above as the ceiling cracked and buckled. The ground heaved violently.

Panic erupted.

More mercenaries flooded the corridor, pouring into the fray with wild shouts. Screams of warning and pain echoed off the stone walls.

Adrian spun around, scanning the chaos. "Cecilia! Where are you?" he shouted above the din.

Then he saw her – trapped beneath a heavy beam, her face ashen, eyes wide with terror.

"Adrian!" she cried, her voice faint beneath the roar of battle and falling stone.

He surged towards her, cutting down anything in his path, every strike fuelled by desperation. "Hold on! I'm coming!"

The air thickened with smoke, dust, and the sharp tang of blood. As he reached her side, another violent explosion tore through the mine. The world convulsed.

And then – darkness.

Chapter 25

Marked for Capture

It had been several days since they had left the mountain, and Aevah's anxiety had only grown. She knew Elinor's people would soon make their presence known, and the relentless anticipation kept everyone on edge. The days blurred together as they navigated narrow passes and dense forests. Conversations were hushed, and sleep came in brief, restless stretches. They moved swiftly, never lingering too long, acutely aware that discovery was only a matter of time.

As they neared the edge of the woods, the tension became too much for Aevah to bear. "I need a minute," she burst out, dismounting her horse.

The group halted, concern flashing across their faces. Nicholas moved towards her but stopped just short, offering her space without question.

Aevah drew in a deep breath, trying to steady her racing heart. “I’m worried Elinor’s guards will be on us soon,” she said and sat down on a fallen tree stump. “They know we’re out here—it’s only a matter of time before they find us.” Her eyes locked with Nicholas’s as she spoke.

He crouched down despite the pain still lingering in his leg, grimacing slightly as he met her at eye level. “We can do this,” he said with quiet confidence.

“Can we? Right now, we’re alone, with no idea where any of our allies are. We’re supposed to reach a temple and have me bond with these shards—but the nearest temple holds traitors. And if one has fallen under Elinor’s control, how can we be certain the others haven’t as well?”

A heavy silence settled over the group as her fears took root in their minds.

Galrick walked over and sat beside her. “I’d love to tell you it’ll all work out,” he said honestly, “but I can’t. What I do know is that every one of us here is a fighter. We won’t stop until we see you succeed.”

Isabella, leaning against her horse, nodded. “Galrick’s right. We can’t afford to lose hope now. If we survived the chaos on the mountain, we can handle what’s coming.”

Aevah inclined her head. “Thank you. I needed that.”

She rose and offered Nicholas her hand. He took it, and with a playful laugh from her and a grunt of effort from him, she helped him to his feet. His leg was healing, but it was still a long way from whole.

They had just begun moving towards their horses when a slow, mocking clap echoed through the trees.

Everyone turned towards the sound. A figure emerged from the shadows, clapping slowly, a smirk curling up their lips. "Bravo," the stranger sneered. "What a speech. So moving."

From the surrounding woods, guards stepped into view, encircling the group in a tightening ring of steel and shadow.

Aevah froze. Panic surged through her – her instincts screamed to flee, yet a crushing weight of defeat pinned her in place. *How had she ever believed they might truly escape?*

"Who are you?" Galrick called out, his voice brimming with a confidence Aevah wished she could muster. He stood firm, even as the circle closed in.

She instinctively moved closer to Nicholas, while Isabella stepped protectively in front of her, eyes sharp and ready.

The tracker chuckled, a dark sound. "I am merely a servant of Queen Elinor," he said smoothly. "Sent to ensure you do not stray from the path she has laid out for you. And it seems our paths have crossed a bit sooner than expected."

He stepped forward, eyes gleaming with satisfaction. "We've been waiting for you to come down the mountains," he went on, his tone heavy with condescension. "Our orders were to keep back and let you reach the nearby temple. But then you gave that stirring little speech about avoiding it, and, well, we had to make ourselves known."

Aevah's heart sank. The realisation that they had been watched all along hit her like a blow.

"How could you have followed us since the mountains?" Isabella demanded, disbelief and anger in her voice. "We were careful—covered our tracks."

The tracker laughed, clearly enjoying himself. "You underestimate us," he replied. "I'm a tracker, gifted with a touch of power. I can create a glamour effect that keeps us hidden, so long as we're not directly in your linc of sight. We've been shadowing you the entire time."

Aevah's thoughts spiralled as the implications sank in. Every moment they'd believed themselves alone had been a lie. Every step, every whispered plan, had likely been heard. The panic threatened to rise again, but she clenched her jaw, forced herself to stay grounded. She couldn't afford to lose control now.

"And now, we will see to your swift arrival at the temple and into the hands of High Priestess Liora—at Her Majesty's discretion," the tracker declared coldly.

He raised his hand, signalling the guards to advance.

The group braced for the coming clash, weapons drawn, eyes sharp. Aevah, heart pounding, knew the men weren't here for her friends; they were after her. She couldn't let anyone else suffer because of her. Drawing on the power within, she reached deep into herself and seized hold of the fire that burned just beneath the surface.

Heat surged through her veins, rising with her fear and fury. Her fists clenched as the energy built, rising like a wave inside her until it was ready to break.

With a cry torn from her throat, she thrust her hands forward.

A violent wave of flame exploded from her fingertips, sweeping outward like a living beast. The fire roared through the clearing, forcing the guards to scatter in a frenzy of panic and confusion.

"Run!" Aevah screamed. "Get to the horses!"

Her companions didn't hesitate. Urged on by her voice and the chaos around them, they mounted quickly. Aevah hurled another blast of fire at the men, this time more focused. Screams echoed through the woods as the flames struck their targets. One guard fell, writhing in agony, his flesh smouldering. The acrid stench of burning flesh filled her nose, and she flinched.

The tracker, untouched but furious, rallied his forces. "Regroup! Don't let them escape!" he bellowed, his voice cutting through the smoke and shouts.

Aevah felt a pang of guilt for the suffering she had caused, but she couldn't allow herself to waver. Their lives depended on her. With no time to linger, she turned and vaulted onto her horse, galloping hard after her friends, her heart pounding as loud as the hooves beneath her.

They pushed on through the forest, driving their horses to the brink as Aevah hurled fireballs behind them. Her strength was beginning to fail. Every burst of flame cost her more. Her breath came in gasps, her vision blurring at the edges.

Up ahead, Galrick suddenly reined in his horse. "We need to slow down!" he called.

Just beyond him, a lone figure stood in their path, still and unarmed, dressed in flowing robes that marked her as a priestess. The contrast between her serene presence and the chaos they had just fled was jarring.

"Who is that?" Nicholas asked, squinting towards the figure.

The woman raised her hands in a gesture of peace. "I am here to help you," she said, her voice calm and steady.

With a graceful motion, she waved her hand, and an entrance appeared in the hillside to their right – an archway etched into stone, glowing faintly.

Aevah and her companions exchanged wary glances. Exhaustion dragged at them, and the sound of pounding hooves behind them left little time for trust or doubt.

"Quickly, inside!" the priestess cried, urgency sharpening her words.

There was no time to question. The thunder of their pursuers grew louder, closer.

Galrick made the decision. "We don't have time to debate this. Go!" He spurred his horse towards the opening, leading the charge into the unknown.

One by one, they followed, guiding their weary horses into the dark tunnel. Aevah was the last to enter, casting a final glance over her shoulder. The priestess followed closely behind. With another graceful wave of her hand, the tunnel's entrance vanished, cloaked from view by her magic.

They led their exhausted mares deeper into the passage, the echo of the hooves mingling with their ragged breaths. Faint light shimmered from above, casting eerie, shifting shadows along the stone walls, but even this gloom felt like a sanctuary after the relentless pursuit. Their pace slowed as adrenaline ebbed, and the reality of temporary safety began to sink in.

"Thank you," Aevah whispered, her voice nearly lost beneath the quiet rhythm of hoofbeats.

The priestess gave a small nod, her expression kind but determined. "We must keep moving. This path leads to a safer place, but we must not linger. Elinor's forces are not so easily deterred."

Steeling themselves, Aevah and her companions fell in behind her, winding deeper into the passage. With every step, the tension in Aevah's limbs loosened, the pressing fear retreating as distance grew between them and the threat that had nearly caught them.

As the immediate danger faded, wariness gave way to curiosity. Nicholas broke the silence, his voice low but steady as it echoed softly off the walls.

"Thank you for helping us. May we know your name?"

The priestess glanced back at them, her calm expression unchanged. "I am Thalia," she said. "A servant of the Divine Spirit. I've been watching over this region for some time."

Isabella, still cautious, asked, "Where does this tunnel lead, Thalia?"

Thalia offered a reassuring smile. "To a place of greater safety. It will take a few days on foot, but we'll emerge near the forest at the border of Almire. There, you will find rest and protection."

"And no one else knows of this tunnel?" Isabella pressed.

"None but the priestesses," Thalia replied. "There are a few such tunnels scattered across the land. Old smugglers' routes, long hidden. In times of peace, they were forgotten—but the priestesses of old preserved them, using them for emergencies. The guards won't find you here. You're safe."

Aevah felt a flicker of hope stir within her. The tunnel reminded her of another – the one her grandfather used when they fled their home. Though it had been long ago, the stone alcoves and carved passageways stirred fragments of memory she hadn't revisited in years.

Thalia paused at one such alcove and stepped inside, emerging moments later with several lanterns. She handed one to each of them. "It's dark in these tunnels. This will help."

They each gave quiet thanks before continuing, their way lit by warm, flickering light. At Thalia's direction, they stopped occasionally to rest and eat. For the first time in days, they travelled without fear. The stillness was a sharp contrast to the chaos of their journey through the mountains.

On their second evening, nestled in a quiet alcove, Aevah sat beside Thalia, questions bubbling in her mind. The priestess, serene as ever, welcomed them without hesitation.

"How did you become a priestess?" Aevah asked, her voice tinged with both wonder and caution.

Thalia smiled, her features soft in the lantern light. "It is a calling, Aevah. From a young age, I could feel the presence of the Divine Spirit. I knew my path was to serve her. I was brought to the temple to train, to learn her ways, and to understand the power she bestows."

Nicholas, listening nearby, tilted his head. "Does she speak to you? I thought no one had heard her voice or seen her for centuries."

Thalia's gaze turned thoughtful. "In a way. You're right. The Divine Spirit has not taken physical form in nearly a thousand years. But her presence is still felt. She lives within the land itself. She is the current we draw from, the strength behind our power. Her spirit endures, even if her body no longer walks among us."

Aevah felt a strange calm settle over her. There was something comforting in the idea that the Divine Spirit was still watching – that she had not abandoned them. The warmth of Thalia's words lingered in her heart, like the flicker of a lantern in the dark.

Perhaps, Aevah thought, there truly was still light to be found in the darkness.

Chapter 26

Veil of Deception

After a couple of hours of much-needed sleep, Aevah and her companions prepared for the final stretch of the tunnel. Following Thalia's lead, they rode in silence for several more hours until the narrow passage finally widened. At last, they were greeted by a rush of fresh air and the blinding brilliance of daylight.

Emerging from the underground, they squinted against the sudden brightness. Relief washed over them, profound and immediate; the open sky above felt like freedom itself.

Aevah inhaled deeply, savouring the crisp air. "It's good to see the sun again," she murmured, a small smile playing on her lips.

Nicholas nodded and stretched his arms while keeping his balance on his horse. "Feels like we've been underground for a lifetime."

The group continued onward, the sunlight invigorating them despite the lingering chill of winter. For the first time in days, hope seemed within reach.

But as the hours passed, unease began to creep in.

Isabella furrowed her brow, her eyes scanning the horizon. "Something's not right," she muttered, glancing at the terrain around them.

Galrick, riding beside her, nodded. "I feel it too. The landscape doesn't match what Thalia described."

Aevah, overhearing them, urged her horse closer. "What do you mean?" she asked, a prickle of concern rising in her chest.

Isabella gestured towards the distant hills and sparse treeline. "She said we'd come out near the woods along the border into Almire. But this… this doesn't resemble the area."

Galrick added, "The terrain's wrong. We should be seeing dense forests by now—not wide, open plains."

Aevah's stomach sank. Doubt settled over her like a storm cloud. She turned to Thalia, who rode calmly ahead, and called out, "Thalia! Where exactly are we? Is this still the path to Almire?"

Thalia slowed, turning in her saddle. Her expression remained serene and unreadable. "We are still on the path to safety," she replied, her voice gentle but evasive. "Trust in the journey."

The group exchanged uneasy glances. They had grown more comfortable with her over the past few days, but the growing inconsistencies had cast a long shadow over her assurances.

"What do we do?" Aevah asked quietly, looking to the others for guidance.

Galrick leaned in, speaking low. "Isabella, Nicholas—ride ahead. Stay close to the priestess. Keep her talking. We can't let her suspect anything yet. I need to speak with Aevah."

They both nodded and moved forward, engaging Thalia with idle chatter, their tones light and unassuming. Every movement had to appear casual; any misstep could ruin everything.

"I don't want to alarm you," Galrick said under his breath, "but I'm almost certain she's leading us to the very temple we were trying to avoid. The direction, the landscape—it all fits."

Aevah forced a smile, even as nausea twisted in her gut. "If she takes us there, we won't be getting out alive. Not with the shards."

"Can you hide them?" Galrick asked, his voice tense.

She hesitated, thinking fast. "I can try."

Reaching into her bag, she pulled out the shards, their faint glow pulsing against her palm. She closed her eyes, focusing hard, summoning her power to dampen their energy. Slowly, the glow dimmed and disappeared. She had masked them, for now. It wouldn't fool someone as powerful as Liora for long, but it might buy them time.

She bit her lip, thinking. *I need decoys… something to throw them off if they check the bag. Stones? Maybe with an illusion?*

It was a desperate plan, one that could easily fail. But it was all she had.

She couldn't risk doing it on horseback. It would be too obvious.

"Thalia, can we stop a moment?" she called out, her tone casual.

"But of course. Is everything all right?" Thalia asked.

"Yes, just a brief… lavatory break," Aevah said with an easy smile before disappearing behind a nearby tree.

Out of sight, her heart pounding as she knelt, eyes scanning the forest floor. She searched quickly, hands trembling, until she found two long stones similar in shape to the shards. They would have to do.

Clutching them tightly, she concentrated. Power flared at her fingertips as she cast an illusion over the stones. Slowly, they shimmered, transforming into perfect replicas of the real shards.

She slipped the fakes into her bag, placing them exactly where the real ones had been. Then, reaching into her cloak, she secured the genuine shards deep within the inner pockets, hidden from view but close enough to grab if needed.

It wasn't foolproof, but it might just be enough.

Aevah took a steadying breath and glanced around to ensure she was still alone. Satisfied no one had witnessed her deception, she quickly rejoined the group, her heart pounding. She forced a calm smile onto her face, praying it would be enough to hide her unease.

"We should keep going," she said, her voice steady despite the turmoil churning inside her. She gave Galrick a subtle nod before catching up with the others, doing her best to appear composed.

An hour later, they reached an open field. In the distance, a group of robed figures approached on horseback. Aevah's heart plummeted as she recognised their garments, priestesses. Her worst fears were about to be confirmed.

"It'll be okay," Nicholas said quietly beside her, attempting to offer reassurance.

The priestesses closed in, forming a wide circle around them. Aevah's stomach twisted as the figures dismounted. One stepped forward, her robes far more elaborate than the others, her air of authority unmistakable. Though her expression was kind and her smile soft, it did little to settle the rising dread within Aevah.

"Welcome," the woman said, her voice warm and measured. "I am Liora, High Priestess of the Divine Spirit. We are here to escort you to safety."

Aevah forced a grateful expression. "Thank you, High Priestess Liora. We appreciate your assistance."

Nicholas, his voice tinged with suspicion, asked, "Why the entourage? Are we in danger?"

Liora's smile remained unchanged. "It is merely a precaution. These lands are not as safe as they once were. We wish only to ensure your safe passage."

Isabella and Galrick exchanged a glance, both keeping their expressions unreadable. Aevah, meanwhile, focused on maintaining her composure. Showing any hint of distrust now would be dangerous.

The group was led across the field, the priestesses riding close around them, a protective yet suffocating barrier. As they rode, Aevah scanned the landscape, searching desperately for any chance of escape. But all she saw was the looming silhouette of the temple ahead, its dark form rising like a warning.

Her chest tightened as they drew nearer. The closer they came, the more certain she became that they were walking into a trap.

Galrick rode alongside her, his voice low. "Stay alert. We may need to act quickly."

She nodded, gripping her reins tighter. "We'll get through this," she whispered, more to herself than anyone else.

As the temple drew closer, the circle of priestesses tightened, their power almost tangible. Aevah could feel it thrumming through them, subtle but potent. They were taking no risks.

Liora remained at the front, guiding them with a steady hand, her demeanour never wavering. Yet Aevah felt a coldness deep in her bones as they crossed the threshold into the temple grounds.

The area bore some resemblance to the temple in the Dunes of Decessus – same structure, same symmetry – but here, flowerbeds and stretches of green offered only a muted beauty, their colour dulled by winter's grip. In spring, it might have been beautiful. Now, it felt hollow.

Unlike the previous temples, this one lacked peace. Its stillness was foreboding.

Liora guided them inside with practised ease. Within, the air was warm and inviting. Refreshments were offered, soft words spoken, and assurances given.

"We will help you bond with the shards," Liora said kindly. "And ensure you are safely reunited with your mother and brother."

The mention of her family tugged at Aevah's heart, stirring a fragile mix of hope and fear. But there was no time to process it. Liora was already leading her deeper into the temple, straight to the sacred chamber. No chance to rest. No chance to breathe.

The room was dimly lit, adorned with ancient runes and soft glowing crystals. Power pulsed in the air. Six other priestesses stood in a semicircle, each one radiating calm strength. Aevah's pulse quickened. She was outmatched.

"Please, pass me the shards, Aevah, so we may begin," Liora said gently, her voice both soothing and commanding.

Aevah reached into her bag and retrieved the fakes, handing them over. Liora accepted them, turning them slowly in her hands.

"Fascinating," she murmured. "I've only seen the one kept in the castle. They truly are works of art."

Aevah smiled, the expression barely held in place. Her stomach churned. One wrong move, and everything would fall apart.

Liora turned to face her, her expression still warm. "Now, let us begin the ceremony. I will guide you through the bonding process. Please, stand within the diamond at the centre."

Aevah obeyed, stepping into the centre of the marked space. She closed her eyes and inhaled deeply, trying to slow the panic rising in her chest.

Her friends stood at the edge of the room, watching silently. Their expressions were neutral, but Aevah knew better. They were waiting, watching, ready.

So was she.

Liora and the other priestesses began to chant in a language that thrummed with ancient power, their voices weaving together in an eerie, melodic harmony. The ground beneath their feet began to hum, and Aevah's heart pounded in her chest.

Without warning, the vibration intensified into a violent tremor. Nicholas and the others, sensing imminent danger, bolted towards Aevah.

"Run!" Nicholas shouted, urgency lacing his voice.

But Aevah couldn't move; something held her in place as the earth beneath her continued to quake.

"Stay back!" she cried out. "It's too dangerous!"

No sooner had the words left her mouth than the floor cracked and split apart beneath her. The stone slid away with a deafening groan, and with nothing left to stand on, Aevah plummeted into the darkness below.

The others screamed her name and rushed forward, but a sudden blast of energy erupted from the opening, sweeping them off their feet and dragging them down after her.

They tumbled into the abyss, the roar of the wind around them like a furious storm. When they finally landed, it was with a thud on cold, damp earth. They lay for a moment, catching their breath as the last echoes of the priestesses' chanting faded. Then, from above, came Liora's laughter – cold, mocking, and echoing through the cavern.

"Good luck escaping," she called. "No one has ever made it out alive."

With a resounding clang, the trapdoor slammed shut, sealing them inside.

Aevah, Nicholas, Galrick, and Isabella slowly pushed themselves up, checking for injuries. Miraculously, none of them appeared seriously hurt. Dusting themselves off, they scanned their new surroundings. The darkness was nearly complete until Aevah summoned a soft ball of light into existence. With a flick of her hand, she duplicated it into smaller orbs that floated around each of them, casting a faint, steady glow.

They found themselves in a sprawling network of tunnels – cold, winding, and lined with strange, shifting symbols etched into the stone walls. The silence was oppressive, broken only by the occasional drip of water echoing in the distance.

"We need to find a way out," Nicholas said, his voice steady, though the tension in his eyes betrayed him. He brushed his fingers across one of the glowing symbols. "Do you recognise any of these?"

Aevah examined the markings carefully and shook her head. "No. They're unfamiliar."

Isabella and Galrick each studied the walls as well, but neither could make sense of the symbols. After a moment, Isabella stepped back, scanning the branching tunnels ahead.

"We have to choose a direction," she said, tension sharpening her voice. "We can't stay here."

They exchanged anxious glances. Every path looked just as ominous as the next.

Galrick pointed down a tunnel veering to the right. "Let's take this one. It feels… different."

Nicholas gave a terse nod, and the group proceeded, their footsteps echoing through the eerie passage.

As they moved deeper into the tunnel, Aevah suddenly heard a faint voice calling her name. At first, it was barely audible, like a whisper carried on the wind, but it grew stronger with each step.

She slowed, glancing at her companions. "Do you hear that?" she asked, her voice shaking slightly.

"Hear what?" Nicholas replied, frowning.

Her heart beat faster as she realised she was the only one who could hear it. The voice was insistent now, familiar in a way that tugged at something deep within her.

"Aevah…"

Compelled by a force she couldn't explain, she picked up her pace, her strides growing longer until she broke into a run. The others called out behind her, but she barely registered their voices. The tunnel stretched endlessly before her, but she couldn't stop.

At last, she came to a shimmering barrier of light that pulsed across the passage like a veil. The voice called again – clear, warm, and painfully familiar.

Without hesitation, Aevah stepped through.

Suddenly, the cold stone and dim light vanished. She stood in the palace gardens – lush, vibrant, and filled with the heady fragrance of blooming flowers. Sunlight filtered through the canopy, bathing the space in golden hues. It was a place she hadn't seen in years, but the memories came rushing back like a flood.

"Aevah…" the voice called once more.

She turned slowly, her heart swelling with recognition – and dread.

Chapter 27

Shadows of the Past

Nicholas spun around, his friends no longer in sight. Though he could still sense their presence, the darkness closed in, isolating him. He stepped forward, uncertain, blinking rapidly and rubbing his eyes in confusion. Spinning back, he tried to retrace his steps, but the tunnel was gone and, in its place, stood something entirely different.

Somehow – he didn't know how – he had been transported back in time.

Before him stood a much younger Galrick, and when Nicholas looked down at himself, he saw a smaller frame, his limbs shorter and clumsier. He couldn't have been older than six.

They were playing, he remembered now. Without hesitation, he took off running through the sun-drenched courtyard, with Galrick hot on his heels. Laughter echoed between the stone walls as they chased each other, pretending to be knights on a grand quest.

"Got you!" young Galrick shouted, tagging him.

"No fair!" Nicholas cried, laughing all the same.

The scene shifted.

Now he was eight years old, standing in the training yard with a wooden sword clutched in his hands. His father loomed nearby – stern, unyielding, his gaze sharp as a blade.

"Focus, Nicholas," he snapped. "Your form is sloppy."

Nicholas tried to adjust his stance, willing his arms to move just right, but the weight of his father's judgement pressed down hard. He longed to earn his approval, but nothing he did ever seemed to measure up. A sudden sting on his backside made him yelp, and he bit back tears as the memory fractured.

Another shift.

He was twelve now, standing at the edge of a tournament field, his heart pounding as he watched Galrick charge down the jousting lane. Pride mingled with jealousy in his chest – Galrick, always the stronger, the braver, the favoured son.

"Your turn is next," a nearby knight told him.

Nicholas swallowed hard and took his place on the field, the weight of expectations nearly unbearable. He found himself facing Galrick in a swordfight. But this Galrick was different – cold, merciless. He attacked without hesitation or restraint.

Nicholas couldn't hold his ground. The force of Galrick's strikes brought him to his knees, and he raised his arms in a futile shield.

"Please!" he cried out.

The world blurred.

When it cleared again, Nicholas stood in the shadow of the castle. The air was thick with smoke, the aftermath of battle heavy on his shoulders. He walked through the ruined halls, stepping over fallen bodies, bile rising in his throat at the sight.

His feet carried him to the throne room. He didn't know why, but something in him urged him forward.

Inside, he found Aevah lying lifeless at Elinor's feet. The queen stood victorious, a cruel smile curving her lips.

"No!" Nicholas screamed, his heart shattering. He rushed to Aevah's side, pulling her into his arms as hot tears streamed down his cheeks. The grief threatened to drown him, each breath a struggle under the weight of what he had lost.

"You were too weak to save her," Elinor sneered. "You failed."

Nicholas trembled as he clutched Aevah's body. This couldn't be real. Sweet, brave Aevah – gone. He was supposed to protect her.

Despair surged, but beneath it, something else burned – fury, purpose, resolve. He looked down at her still face, and a fire lit in his chest.

"No," he whispered. "You'll pay for this."

His hand closed around the hilt of his sword. Rising, he charged Elinor with a cry of rage, his strike unflinching.

The blade connected, and the illusion shattered.

The darkness lifted, and Nicholas found himself back in the tunnel, breathless and bewildered, the echoes of the vision still clinging to his mind.

***

Isabella felt a strange pull as she moved through the tunnels, the darkness pressing in on all sides. With a hesitant step forward, the world around her shifted. In an instant, she was no longer in the present – she had been transported into her own memories, reliving them as vividly as if they were happening for the first time.

The vision began with her as a small girl of about six, baking with her mother in their warm, cluttered kitchen. Flour dusted every surface, and much of her as well. She giggled as she tried to knead the dough, her small hands clumsy and eager.

"Like this, Isabella," her mother instructed gently, showing her the proper way to squish and fold the dough.

But Isabella found the process boring. Instead, she stretched the dough out as far as she could and tossed it into the air with a mischievous grin. It landed squarely on her head. She burst into laughter, shaking with delight as her mother watched, hands on her hips, a frown forming.

"Why, child, why?" her mother muttered, shaking her head despite the ghost of a smile.

A puff of flour clouded the air, and the scene shifted.

Now, Isabella was a few years older and playing with her brothers. Their laughter echoed down the halls as they darted through the house. They ended up in the music room, where lively notes poured from the grand piano. Together, they danced with flushed cheeks and shining eyes, their bond as siblings unbreakable in that moment. Isabella had never felt so alive, so utterly free.

But the joy didn't last.

The music dissolved, and the warmth of the memory turned cold. The house was now filled with guards – stern, faceless men in dark uniforms. They asked questions, demanding to know the whereabouts of her parents. She and her brothers had no answers.

"I don't know where they are!" Isabella cried, her voice trembling with fear.

A guard struck her across the face. Pain exploded through her cheek, and she crumpled, sobbing. The men didn't believe her – she could see it in their eyes. Screams rang out from the next room – her brother's voice, raw with agony. Desperation surged through her as she tried to rise, to reach him, but another guard caught her first. Her head snapped to the side from the next blow, the metallic tang of blood flooding her mouth.

The vision fractured again.

She was back in the present, or something close to it, sword in hand, fighting beside Galrick to protect Aevah. The castle was under siege, the air thick with smoke, the clash of steel, and the cries of the wounded. Isabella fought with every ounce of strength she had, determined to protect those she loved.

But then, Galrick fell.

"Galrick!" she screamed, rushing to his side as he collapsed.

"Isabella…" he whispered, blood bubbling at his lips. His hand brushed her cheek before falling limp at his side.

He died in her arms. Crimson pooled beneath them, staining the stone.

She knelt over him, her heart splintering. The guard loomed above, sword in hand, the blade still slick with Galrick's blood.

"What a shame," the man sneered, voice as cold and sharp as ice. "He's dead."

Terror surged, but so did rage. The guard stepped closer, ready to end her life as well. She looked down at Galrick's still face, then rose, shaking with fury. She wouldn't let his death be for nothing.

Her hand closed around her sword. With a battle cry, she surged forward, striking with all the force of her grief and fury.

The blade found its mark – and the illusion shattered.

The barrier broke.

Isabella stumbled, suddenly back in the tunnel, still running but at nothing. She skidded to a stop, chest heaving. Her friends stood nearby, their faces pale, their eyes wide with the same haunted confusion.

Whatever they had seen, whatever they had endured – it had left its mark.

***

Galrick felt an unsettling presence as he walked through the tunnels, the darkness closing in, thick and oppressive. With a sudden lurch in his chest, the world around him twisted,

He had been pulled into his past.

The vision began with him as a boy of about five, seated at a small table set for tea. His mother sat beside him, elegantly poised and beaming with pride as she entertained her guests.

"This is my little Galrick," she said warmly, running her fingers gently through his hair. "Isn't he handsome?"

The women laughed and cooed over him, their kind words and admiring smiles making him feel like the centre of their world. His mother's love wrapped around him like a blanket – pure and unwavering. For a moment, he basked in the memory, the light of that affection still flickering in his heart.

But the scene shifted abruptly.

Now he was six, crouched on the floor with his younger brother Nicholas, the two of them surrounded by wooden blocks and scraps from their clock-making set. Galrick built tall towers with careful hands while Nicholas, giggling mischievously, knocked them over again and again with a delighted clap. Every time Galrick rebuilt them, Nicholas would topple them with a gleeful swipe, turning it into a game that made them both laugh.

Galrick had been patient then, content to let his brother enjoy the destruction.

The memory faded and returned sharper.

He was twelve, standing in the training yard beneath the watchful eye of his father. A wooden practice sword weighed heavily in his grip as he held his stance, sweat beading on his brow.

"You need to do better," his father snapped, arms crossed, tone hard. "Your form is all wrong."

The words stung, as they always did. Galrick clenched his jaw but remained silent, his thoughts burning with quiet defiance. He *could* be better. He *would* be. If only his father saw him, not just the heir, but the boy trying desperately to prove himself. With every correction shouted at him, he adjusted, striving for perfection, determined not to falter.

The world shifted again.

He was back in the present, locked in the chaos of battle. The castle walls shook with the sound of war – steel clashing, orders shouted, screams ringing out. Smoke clouded the air. Beside him, Isabella fought with unrelenting fury, matching him strike for strike. Together, they cut through wave after wave of enemy guards, united by purpose.

Then it happened.

In the blink of an eye, a guard slipped past Galrick's reach. His blade flashed, swift and merciless.

"No!" Galrick screamed, too late to stop it.

The guard's sword opened Isabella's throat in a crimson arc. Her eyes widened in shock as she fell to her knees, clutching her neck, her life pouring from between her fingers. Her eyes found Galrick's for one final, silent moment before she collapsed.

She was gone.

Galrick dropped to her side, his heart splitting open. He cradled her lifeless body, unable to breathe, the weight of grief pinning him in place.

The guard loomed above, grinning as he nudged Isabella's corpse with the toe of his boot.

"What a waste," he said cruelly. "Such a pretty thing."

A white-hot rage surged through Galrick, consuming his sorrow. He stood, face like stone, his eyes dark with fury.

Without a word, he launched himself at the guard, seizing him by the throat. His hands tightened, relentless, as the man choked and flailed. Galrick didn't stop, couldn't stop, until the vision around him cracked and shattered like glass.

The illusion dissolved.

Galrick staggered, breath ragged, the tunnel reappearing around him. His body trembled, sweat slick on his skin, heart still racing. The images clung to him. He was back – but changed.

***

Before her stood her mother, a warm smile lighting her face as she peered behind trees and bushes in the tranquil garden. Aevah wasn't quite herself, not as she was now, but a child of only four or five, seeing the world through the innocent eyes of her younger self.

She remembered the game. Her smaller self crouched low in the dense greenery, peeking through the leaves, heart fluttering with delight each time her mother called her name.

"Aevah," her mother called playfully, "where are you, little one?"

Giggling, little Aevah darted through the garden, her tiny feet pattering over the soft grass. "Come find me!" she called, laughter bubbling from her lips.

Her mother's laughter echoed behind her. "I'm coming to get you!"

Moments later, her mother scooped her into her arms, lifting her high before cradling her close. Aevah squealed with joy, wrapping her arms around her mother's neck, breathing in the familiar rosy scent she remembered so vividly. Her mother tickled her gently, and they laughed together under the sunlit canopy.

Then the memory faded, like petals on the wind.

Now she was seven, riding across vast green fields with her father. The wind tugged at her hair, tangling it into wild tendrils as she leaned forward, urging her horse to gallop faster. The thunder of hooves filled the air, and the wide expanse of land stretched endlessly before her. The thrill of speed, the freedom of the open world, made her heart soar.

"Good riding, Aevah!" her father shouted from behind, his voice booming with pride. "But can you beat me?"

She turned her head to glimpse his grin, the mischievous glint in his eyes pushing her onward. A burst of energy surged through her as she tightened her grip on the reins. Her horse responded, powerful muscles rippling beneath her as they flew over the field.

Ahead, a cluster of trees marked the finish. Determination filled her like fire. She leaned low, her body moving in perfect rhythm with the mare beneath her.

"I'm going to win, Father!" she shouted, her voice soaring with joy.

Her father's deep, proud laugh echoed in response. "Yes, you are, my brave girl!"

The trees loomed closer – then the vision blurred and faded.

She was thirteen now, crouched beside her grandfather in the forest, tracking a deer. The air was thick with the scent of moss and pine, the forest alive with quiet sounds. Her heart pounded in her chest, equal parts excitement and nerves.

"Patience is key," her grandfather whispered. "We must become part of the forest."

Aevah nodded, mimicking his stillness. Her eyes scanned the underbrush, alert, focused. They crept forward, silent as shadows, until they spotted the deer grazing in a sun-dappled clearing.

Her grandfather held out a hand, and she knew she had to stop.

They crouched, and Aevah calmed her breath.

"Steady your aim," he murmured, guiding her hands. "Just behind the shoulder. That's the vital spot."

She drew back the bowstring, tension humming through her muscles. The forest seemed to hold its breath. She exhaled slowly and released.

The arrow flew, slicing through the air. It struck true.

The deer staggered, then collapsed.

Aevah's heart swelled with triumph and sorrow in equal measure. Her grandfather placed a hand on her shoulder, firm and proud.

"Well done," he said. "You've honoured the deer—and the forest."

But the memory melted away like morning mist.

Now she stood in the castle courtyard, beneath the shadow of the gallows.

Jacob hung from the rope, his lifeless body swaying gently in the breeze.

"No…" Aevah whispered, her breath catching in her throat. Then louder: "No, Jacob!"

She ran, feet pounding the cold stone, desperation rising in her chest like a scream. Her mind refused to accept what her eyes saw. If she could only reach him, touch him, stop this –

But she was too late.

Tears blurred her vision as she stumbled closer, helpless. The rope creaked above her, the sound forever etched into her memory.

The scene warped again.

She was now walking through the ravaged halls of the castle. Smoke curled through the air, and the scent of blood clung to the stones. The walls were scorched, the floor littered with debris and bodies. War had swept through these corridors, leaving ruin in its wake.

Her breath came quickly, heart hammering. She moved with purpose, dread and resolve tangling inside her like storm clouds.

She reached the throne room.

There, seated upon the throne like a viper in a crown, was Elinor. A cruel smile twisted her lips.

"Welcome, Aevah," she sneered. "I've been expecting you."

Aevah's eyes dropped to the floor, and her stomach turned.

Jacob lay there, lifeless once again, crumpled at Elinor's feet.

"You were too weak to save him," Elinor said wickedly. "You failed."

The weight of those words slammed into her. Her knees buckled. Grief and guilt swelled within her, but something deeper stirred, a fire beneath the anguish.

"No," Aevah whispered.

Her hand slipped to her side, closing around the dagger hidden there. Her voice grew stronger.

"I won't let you win."

With a cry, she lunged.

The blade pierced Elinor's chest, and the illusion shattered.

The tunnel returned around her. Aevah stood frozen, chest heaving, the memory still clinging to her like smoke. She blinked, disoriented, and looked around.

Nicholas, Isabella, and Galrick stood nearby, stunned, silent, their faces pale with the weight of their own visions.

They were no longer in the same place. The passage had shifted beneath their feet, the air humming with foreboding. A deep rumble echoed overhead, growing louder.

The tunnel began to shake violently.

"Run!" Nicholas shouted.

Without hesitation, they bolted towards the distant light at the end of the tunnel. The earth trembled beneath their feet, dust falling in choking clouds as debris rained from the ceiling.

They burst through the tunnel's mouth just as it collapsed behind them.

The temple caved in with a thunderous roar, sending plumes of dust skyward. They stumbled out into the open air – battered, breathless, and alive.

They turned back to watch the ancient structure crumble, the final collapse marking the end of their ordeal.

Liora's words echoed in Aevah's mind: *'No one has ever made it out alive."*

Now she understood. Many had tried and failed, crushed beneath the weight of their fears, their regrets.

But she, Nicholas, Isabella, and Galrick had faced the darkness. And they had emerged stronger.

Chapter 28

Fragments of Truth

The group had taken refuge at a safe distance from the ruined temple, the ground beneath them still trembling faintly from the collapse. They had no supplies, no horses, and only the pale moonlight breaking intermittently through the heavy clouds above to guide them.

Aevah leaned against a jagged rock, her breath shallow as she tried to make sense of the chaos from the past few hours. Dust and debris clung to her clothes, but she barely noticed. Her thoughts spun back to the moments inside the temple. What she had witnessed during her trial had left her shaken—fractured. Deep down, she knew those visions weren't illusions. Jacob was gone. Her chest tightened, grief pressing down an invisible weight.

Nicholas broke the silence, his voice steady but laced with exhaustion. "We made it out alive," he said, crouching to rub his leg, which still throbbed from the strain of their escape. "Barely, but we did. That has to count for something, right?"

Galrick let out a low grunt and sank beside Aevah. "It does," he muttered, running a hand through his dishevelled hair. "But the temple is gone. And the trials…" He hesitated, glancing at the others. "They weren't just tests—they were torment. Designed to break us."

Isabella gave a knowing nod, her arms folded as she leaned against the rock wall. "Torment is right," she said quietly, meeting his eyes. "What I saw at the end—it was meant to drown you in pain. To make you believe everything was lost. It was cruel. But we got away." Her voice trembled, and she bit her lip, fighting to stay composed.

Aevah's gaze drifted towards the ruins, her throat dry as she finally spoke. "I don't think it was just the trials," she murmured. "The temple took something from me. Or maybe… maybe I left something behind. Jacob…" Her voice cracked, and she shook her head, trying to dismiss the thought. "I can't explain it, but I can feel it. He's gone."

Silence fell over the group, heavy and uncertain. No one knew what to say.

Nicholas stepped towards her, his tone firm. "I'm certain he's alive," he said, locking eyes with her. "The temple was designed to deceive us—to make us believe in the worst and trap us there. Whatever you saw, don't let it cloud your judgment."

Aevah hesitated, her thoughts still tangled in the memory of what she had seen, what she had felt, inside those cursed walls. Slowly, she exhaled, as though trying to release the last hold of that darkness. "You're probably right," she said quietly, her voice shaky but gaining strength. "It's just… this feeling. It's hard to shake. But maybe it's just the trial's lingering grip. It has to be."

"Exactly," Isabella added, arms still crossed tightly. "We all feel off. Whatever magic was in that place, it has left its mark. But we're out. We just need time."

Nicholas gave a short nod, glancing at each of them. "And we'll have that time—once we're far away from here. The temple may be gone, but I don't trust this place. We need to keep moving. The further, the better."

Galrick, seated beside Aevah, grunted in agreement. "And we need supplies. We won't last long on empty stomachs and dust."

"There should be a town not far from here," he continued. "If anything's happened—if there's any news about Jacob or the others—we'll hear it there. Word travels fast in places like that."

They exchanged glances, a quiet understanding forming between them. Aevah sighed, her resolve beginning to firm. "Let's go," she said, rising to her feet. She cast one last look at the ruins, the weight in her chest still heavy, but not as suffocating. Falling into step beside Nicholas, she fixed her eyes on the road ahead.

They walked for hours through the night, cold and exhausted, until the faint murmur of distant life reached their ears, and the town came into view. Aevah brushed leaves and dirt from her sleeves as they approached, her gaze drawn to the curling smoke from chimneys and occasional shadows moving between buildings.

Galrick raised a hand to halt them. His sharp eyes scanned the modest cluster of houses and winding paths. “Looks quiet enough,” he said, though wariness edged his voice. “But we can’t afford to take chances. No horses, no supplies—we’re practically begging for attention.”

Nicholas crossed his arms, frowning as he weighed their options. “We’ll need to be smart. If we all walk in together, someone’s bound to ask questions. The temple isn’t far, and word might already be spreading.”

Galrick stepped forward. “I’ll go,” he offered. “I’ve done this before—blend in, get what we need, no questions asked. It’s safer that way.”

Isabella’s eyes narrowed. “You don’t have to do it alone,” she countered, stepping towards him. “Two travellers draw less suspicion than one. And we both know how to handle ourselves if something goes wrong.”

“I’m not saying you don’t,” Galrick replied, his tone firm but even. “But the fewer people they see, the better. One stranger is easy to forget—two, not so much.” His gaze swept across the group. “Stay hidden, stay quiet, and give me a few hours. If anything happens, I’ll come back immediately.”

Reluctantly, Isabella stepped back. Her frustration showed in the tightness of her jaw, but she said nothing. Aevah watched them both in silence, unease settling deeper in her chest.

"We'll wait here," she said gently, her voice threaded with resignation. "Just be careful."

Galrick nodded, then turned and slipped into the shadows, his figure vanishing among the trees. The others retreated into the nearby forest, climbing up into the thick branches of ancient trees where the canopy would hide them from sight. The limbs were broad enough to conceal them, but offered little comfort.

Perched high on a sturdy branch, Aevah gripped the rough bark, shifting her weight in an attempt to ease the tension in her stiff limbs. It was no use. Her legs ached, her back throbbed, and her thoughts chased themselves in tight, anxious circles.

Every rustle of leaves or snap of a twig below sent a jolt through her. It was always just the wind or a passing creature, but the tension refused to release its grip. *They were hidden well enough, but what if someone had seen Galrick? What if he didn't return?*

On a lower branch, Isabella tapped her fingers restlessly against the hilt of her dagger. "I should've gone with him," she muttered, breaking the silence. "The two of us could've watched each other's backs. No one would think twice about a pair of travellers."

"You know why he didn't let you," Nicholas said from his post at the base of the tree, his voice calm but tired. "Galrick knows what he's doing."

Isabella didn't answer, but the tightness in her posture said enough. Aevah glanced down, noticing how Isabella kept shifting, her shoulders stiff, her movements strained. They all felt it, the same mounting dread hanging heavy around them like a storm waiting to break.

Trying to distract herself, Aevah let her gaze drift towards the distant town. Through the gaps in the foliage, she saw faint smoke curling from chimneys and the occasional flicker of movement between the buildings. The soft hum of life in the distance was almost surreal compared to the tension of the forest. She envied those people, their quiet lives, untouched by visions, trials, and the sting of loss.

Time dragged on. The hours stretched thin, and then, finally, a soft rustle stirred the underbrush.

Aevah's breath caught as she instinctively tightened her grip on the branch. Her heart pounded. Nicholas was on his feet in an instant, his hand on his sword. Isabella's dagger gleamed in the moonlight as she drew it.

"Relax," came a familiar voice. Galrick emerged from the trees, his form dark but unmistakable. "It's just me."

Relief coursed through Aevah, and she let out a sharp breath. Her muscles slackened slightly as she began to descend, moving carefully but quickly. When her boots hit the ground, she stepped forward, eyes searching his face for any sign of trouble.

"Supplies and food!" Nicholas exclaimed, already rummaging through the pack Galrick carried. He tossed a pear towards Aevah and handed another to Isabella. "What did you find out?" he asked, biting into the fruit.

Galrick ran a hand through his hair, his expression giving nothing away. "The town's quiet. No one's looking for us. No talk of anything strange."

But Aevah saw it – the subtle way his eyes avoided hers, the heaviness in his shoulders. Something was wrong.

"Galrick," she said sharply, stepping forward. Her voice was firm, but not unkind. "You're not telling us everything. What did you find out? What happened?"

He hesitated, glancing into the shadows of the forest as if searching for an escape that wasn't there. "Aevah," he began softly, his voice almost a whisper. "Isabella… I didn't want to tell you like this."

Her chest constricted, the ache in her heart flaring as the truth hovered on the edge of his words. She already knew. Deep down, she had known since the moment the bond went quiet.

"Just say it," she demanded, her voice trembling. "What happened?"

Galrick exhaled, his hands clenching at his sides. He looked at Isabella, then back at Aevah.

"You were right," he said, his voice low and laden with guilt. "Jacob is gone. And Edward. And Bryne. They were captured with a group of rebels… and Elinor ordered their execution." He swallowed hard. "They were hanged—in public. For the entire city to see."

The world tilted around Aevah. His words crashed into her like a wave, stealing the air from her lungs. Her knees buckled, but she forced herself to stay upright, jaw clenched, fury and grief twisted inside her. "No," she whispered. "No…"

But the emptiness she had felt since the temple, the gaping void where Jacob's presence had once been, confirmed it.

Isabella stood frozen, her face pale with shock. "No," she murmured, the word like a ghost. "You're lying. Edward and Bryne… they couldn't…" Her voice cracked. "They were fighters. They wouldn't let themselves be—"

"They didn't have a choice," Galrick said gently, eyes downcast. "I'm sorry."

The silence that followed was suffocating. Aevah didn't move. Her breath came in short gasps, but she barely noticed. The bond – the connection that had been a part of her for so long – was gone. Snuffed out like a flame. And in its place was only emptiness.

Her thoughts scattered, crashing against each other until everything blurred. A broken sound escaped her throat as her legs finally gave way. She sank to her knees, arms limp at her sides, staring blankly at the earth as if the world had ended.

Isabella's grief erupted outward. She cried out, a strangled, anguished sound, and collapsed into Galrick's arms. He held her tightly as she sobbed, her pain raw and unfiltered.

But Aevah felt nothing. No tears. No sound. Just the hollow ache of something precious torn away.

Nicholas moved slowly towards her, concern etched deep into his features. "Aevah," he said gently, crouching beside her. When she didn't respond, he reached out, resting a hand on her shoulder.

"She's in shock," Galrick murmured.

Nicholas nodded grimly. "Aevah, please," he urged. "We're here for you. You're not alone."

But she didn't react. Her gaze was unfocused, lost in a pain too deep to name. She was there, but unreachable. Caught in the emptiness that had swallowed her whole.

Chapter 29

The Burden of Loss

Had Aevah ever felt so many emotions at once that she thought she might lose control? Was there even a point to anything anymore? That was where she found herself – utterly worn down. Every effort, every small victory they had managed to claim, was being undone piece by piece, all because of Elinor. That woman destroyed lives, tore loved ones apart, and Aevah was tired – tired of the loss, tired of clinging to hope that seemed more fragile by the day. She was done. Nothing seemed to matter anymore. And yet, the others kept her moving, urging her forward as if there was still something left to fight for.

The rhythm of the journey had blurred into monotony. Each day bled into the next – endless trees, the dull thud of hooves on hardened earth, the creak of saddles and the rustle of cloaks. Aevah moved because the others did, because stopping wasn't an option. But her heart wasn't in it. Each step forward felt like a betrayal of what she had lost, dragging her farther from the only thing that had kept her grounded.

Elinor had taken everything that mattered – Jacob, their connection, the bond she had believed unbreakable. She had twisted hope into something cruel and unreachable, leaving devastation in her wake. Every breath Aevah drew felt heavier than the last, grief pressing down like a weight she couldn't shake. Her body was worn thin. Her mind hovered on the brink of collapse.

Nicholas rode beside her, offering silent companionship with the occasional glance. Galrick led the way, his posture rigid, his every movement sharp with tension. They didn't talk much, thankfully. Words wouldn't have helped. Nothing would. And still, their presence, silent and steady, kept her from falling entirely into the void. She wasn't alone, not completely. Not yet.

But then, on a quiet stretch of road, the ache in her chest became too much to bear. Her vision blurred with tears she refused to let fall, her fingers trembling around the reins. The grief surged, rising in her throat like a wave.

Without a word, Aevah dismounted, her legs giving out beneath her as she sank to the ground. Arms wrapped tightly around herself, she shook with the force of it – silent at first, then louder. Cries tore from her throat, ragged and raw, filling the forest with a sorrow that could no longer be contained.

Isabella was the first to move, her boots crunching softly on the dirt path as she knelt beside her. She paused before placing a steady hand on Aevah's shoulder.

"Let it out," she said gently, her usual edge softened into something kinder. "We're here."

Nicholas arrived moments later, crouching beside her and pulling her into a firm, grounding embrace. He said nothing. He didn't need to. His presence alone was enough, a quiet anchor in the storm she could no longer hold back.

Galrick tethered the horses to a nearby tree, his jaw tight as he lingered a few steps away. He didn't approach, offering her the space she needed, though his eyes remained fixed on the group, his expression unreadable.

For now, they stayed close. They let her grieve.

Nicholas stayed beside her, his arm around her shoulders, a silent shield against the weight threatening to crush her. Isabella kept watch, eyes darting between the forest's shadows and Aevah's shaking form. The grief that poured from Aevah was all-consuming, a tide that refused to recede. And yet, somewhere in the release, something shifted.

It was small, barely noticeable at first. A faint spark, fragile and flickering, nestled deep within her. The pain remained, sharp and suffocating, but the act of letting go, even for a moment, cracked the wall she had built around herself. And through the crack, the light of her friends' care slipped in.

She wasn't alone.

Aevah wiped her damp cheeks, her breath still stuttering with the aftershocks of sobs. She couldn't speak, not yet, but the gratitude she felt was undeniable. It wasn't enough to fill the void inside her, but it was something. And in this moment, something was everything.

She held out her hand. Nicholas understood and helped her to her feet. Her legs wobbled slightly beneath her, but she stood, brushing the dirt from her cloak. Her face felt raw, her heart still heavy, but the grief no longer held her captive.

She met Nicholas's gaze and gave a faint nod of thanks.

"We're here when you're ready to talk," he said softly, his hand lingering on her arm, a silent promise.

Isabella stepped closer, her expression softened with sincerity. "No one gets through this alone," she said. "And you don't have to."

Aevah's throat tightened at Isabella's words, a lump forming that she struggled to swallow. She drew in a shaky breath, her voice barely more than a whisper. "I'm sorry, Isabella. You lost Edward and Bryne… and I wasn't—I wasn't there for you. I couldn't be there when you needed someone."

Isabella's lips curved into a faint, bittersweet smile. She reached out, placing a steadying hand on Aevah's arm.

"It's okay," she replied gently. "You were in shock—anyone would've been. You weren't ready to face the world again, and I don't blame you for that."

"But—" Aevah began, the guilt still pressing heavily against her chest.

Isabella shook her head firmly. "No, Aevah. Listen to me. This isn't about blame—not on you, not on anyone. We're all hurting. We've all lost people we can never replace. But instead of drowning in that, maybe we should hold on to what we had. The memories—the parts of them that still live in us."

Aevah met her gaze. The sincerity in Isabella's voice, in her eyes, pierced the haze of sorrow that had engulfed her. Slowly, Aevah nodded, then stepped into a quiet embrace, arms wrapping tightly around Isabella. In their shared grief, they found a moment of stillness, fragile but real.

When they pulled apart, Aevah caught sight of Galrick approaching, leading the horses towards them, the reins clutched tightly in his hands. She blinked in surprise, as if seeing them for the first time. She hadn't even realised they had them. Grief had clouded her mind so completely that even the simplest details had vanished into the background.

"We need to keep moving," Galrick said quietly, extending the reins towards her. "We're getting closer to the rebels' camp."

Aevah took them with a nod, gripping them tightly as she mounted her horse. The others followed suit, and together they set off at a slow, steady pace. The silence between them wasn't uncomfortable; it was filled with understanding. An unspoken solidarity passed between them as they rode – each lost in thought yet bound by shared pain.

It was Nicholas who eventually broke the quiet, his voice gentle, tinged with reminiscence. "Do you remember when we were kids," he began, "and Jacob tried to teach me how to climb that old tree by the river?"

Aevah frowned slightly, searching her memory, until a faint smile tugged at the corners of her mouth. "He got stuck halfway up, didn't he?"

Nicholas laughed, the sound light and genuine. "Stuck and too proud to admit it. A guard had to climb up and get him down. He was furious with me for days for getting help. Said I spoiled his 'perfect adventure'."

Isabella smiled, her tone fond. "That sounds like Jacob. Always wanted to figure things out on his own, but heaven forbid you ruin his moment."

Their conversation unfolded naturally from there, like a slowly opening door. One by one, they began to share memories, snapshots of the ones they had lost: Jacob, Edward, Bryne. In those fragments of the past, they uncovered sparks of warmth, fleeting but real. Small pieces of the lives that had shaped them, echoes of the love that had once surrounded them.

And for the first time since the loss, Aevah felt a fragile spark of hope stir beneath the sorrow. It didn't erase the pain, far from it, but it glimmered faintly, a reminder that grief didn't have to silence joy forever. Those memories could carry them forward, even if those they loved were no longer there to make new ones.

Buoyed by that faint light, the group pressed onward, towards the Mines of Grode. Galrick remained certain the rebels were waiting there, hopeful allies in a fight that had yet to be won. The weeks that followed were long and gruelling, the road stretching endlessly ahead. But they didn't falter. Driven by purpose, bound by love and loss alike, they continued forward – each step a quiet act of defiance against the darkness they carried.

Chapter 30

Through the Dust

Adrian's eyes fluttered open to a world of chaos and disorientation. A high-pitched ringing filled his ears, drowning out all other sounds. His vision swam, the dimly lit cavern around him little more than a blur. A sharp pain lanced through his skull as he lifted a trembling hand to his temple, his fingers coming away sticky with blood. He groaned, every inch of his body aching as though he had been trampled by a herd of wild horses.

He tried to move but quickly discovered his legs were pinned beneath a heavy beam. Panic surged through him, his muscles straining against the weight. After what felt like an eternity, he managed to wiggle himself free, gasping in relief as he dragged his battered body into a sitting position.

He sat there, breathing heavily, trying to piece together the moments before the blast. The explosion. The mercenaries.

Cecilia. His heart pounded as shards of memory surfaced, each more distressing than the last.

Screams and cries gradually broke through the ringing in his ears, pulling him back to the present. He turned his head with a wince, spotting shadowy figures moving through the haze. Dust and smoke choked the air, obscuring his surroundings. Amid the chaos, he heard the panicked voices of his companions, mingled with the distant shouts of their enemies.

Adrian forced a deep breath into his lungs, steadying his thoughts. He had to find Cecilia and the others. He had to get them out. With a grunt of effort, he pushed himself to his feet, swaying as the cavern tilted around him. He braced against a nearby wall, gathering what strength he had left.

His eyes swept across the wreckage, searching for any sign of his friends. The tunnels were a twisted mess of jagged debris and collapsed beams, forming a labyrinth he would have to navigate. Sounds of battle echoed through the darkness, sharp clashes of steel and shouted commands, reminding him that the fight was far from over.

He spotted his sword lying nearby. Grimacing, he bent to retrieve it, the motion sending fresh pain lancing through his side. He staggered forward, heading in the direction where he'd last seen Cecilia.

"Cecilia!" he called, his voice hoarse with desperation. No answer. He called again. "Cecilia!"

A shadow stepped into view – a mercenary with a smug grin.

"Well, well. Look at you, Adrian. The queen will be thrilled to hear I killed you for her."

Adrian straightened, gripping his sword, though his arms trembled. "Not if I kill you first," he retorted, though his voice lacked its usual strength.

The mercenary advanced, but before he could strike, a blade flashed behind him. Darius emerged from the smoke, his sword plunging into the man's back. The mercenary collapsed with a choked gasp.

Adrian nodded in thanks, falling in step beside his friend. Together, they moved through the rubble-strewn tunnel until they found her.

His heart twisted at the sight – Cecilia lay pinned beneath a fallen beam, her face pale, but her chest rising and falling. She was alive.

"Cecilia!" he cried, rushing to her side. Tears welled in his eyes. "Please wake up…"

With no time to waste, he and Darius began lifting the debris. Adrian's hands shook with urgency, and pain rippled through his body with every movement. At last, they pulled the beam away and freed her. Adrian scooped her into his arms, staggering to his feet despite the agony tearing through him. He refused to let go.

Careful of every step, he followed Darius, who cleared the way ahead, dispatching the occasional mercenary with ruthless precision.

But Adrian's strength soon gave out. His knees buckled, and he collapsed, still cradling Cecilia protectively.

"I've got her," Darius said, kneeling to take her from Adrian's arms. "You need to keep moving. You can't carry her."

Adrian nodded weakly, forcing himself upright. "Thank you," he said, limping behind his friend as they pushed onward.

When they finally emerged from the tunnel, the harsh sunlight blinded them for a moment. But when Adrian's eyes adjusted, his heart plummeted.

The devastation stretched as far as he could see.

Massive sections of the mountain were gone, obliterated by the blasts. The ground was littered with the injured – miners, families, rebels – moaning, bleeding, broken. The air reeked of smoke and despair.

Adrian sank to his knees, overwhelmed by the destruction. He glanced towards Darius, who still held Cecilia, and reached out to pull his torn cloak over her. He gently stroked her face, willing her to wake.

He looked around, scanning for help. Amidst the wreckage, a few survivors had set up makeshift triage stations. Healers moved among the wounded, their hands glowing faintly, some with the telltale shimmer of power.

Staggering to his feet, Adrian approached one of them, a woman with a calm, focused expression despite the chaos. "Please," he begged. "Help her. Help Cecilia."

She nodded and gestured for Darius to lay Cecilia down on a nearby cot. "We'll do everything we can," she said gently.

Adrian watched as the healer started to assess Cecilia. He sat down beside her, taking her hand in his, so small and fragile in his bloodied grasp.

"I'm going to help where I can," Darius said, clapping a hand on Adrian's shoulder. "You stay here and get yourself looked at. You're barely standing."

Adrian gave a weak nod just as the healer, overhearing, turned to study him more closely.

Strip," she ordered. "I need to see if all that blood is yours."

He hesitated, then slowly removed his tattered shirt, revealing a gaping wound along his side.

The healer gasped. "How can you not feel this?"

"I hurt everywhere," he murmured, nearly collapsing again.

Without hesitation, she began working, her hands glowing with soft light – a signature trait of gifted healers. As she poured her power into him, slowly closing the wound, Adrian felt the first stirring of real relief.

Then, just as the pain dulled, Cecilia stirred.

Her eyes fluttered open.

***

The days that followed passed in a haze of pain, exhaustion, and grim determination. Adrian spent most of his time recovering, the wound on his side gradually healing under the watchful eye of the healer. She had stemmed the worst of the bleeding, but with so many injured and only a handful of healers, she hadn't fully mended the injury. The decision had been made early on, major wounds would be stabilised, but minor ones would have to heal naturally. There simply weren't enough resources to spare, and the healers couldn't afford to exhaust themselves.

The chaos of the explosion had left its mark, but the survivors refused to give in to despair. They worked tirelessly to rebuild what they could and tend to the injured. Makeshift hospital stations dotted the landscape, while the remaining healers moved from patient to patient with unwavering focus. Despite the devastation, a sense of camaraderie took root among the group, hope growing where only ruin had been.

Adrian, though still healing, had taken on a leadership role alongside Darius. Together, they organised the survivors, coordinated supplies, and ensured no one was overlooked. Even so, Adrian's thoughts remained fixed on Cecilia. Her condition had improved little by little. She drifted in and out of consciousness, her mind clear when she woke, which the healer had called a good sign. But it wasn't enough to ease Adrian's worry.

When he wasn't helping others, he sat at her side, holding her hand, murmuring to her. Sometimes he recounted memories, sometimes he simply sat in silence, hoping to hear her voice again.

One afternoon, as he sat beside her, lost in thought, the sound of approaching footsteps drew his attention. He turned to see Darius striding towards him, his expression grim and purposeful.

"Adrian," Darius called. "We've got one of the mercenaries in custody. We're about to begin the interrogation. I thought you'd want to be there."

Adrian looked down at Cecilia, torn. He didn't want to leave her, not even for a moment, but he knew the truth was too important to ignore. Any information they could get might be vital. He gave her hand a gentle squeeze and stood.

"Thank you," he said, his voice steadier than he felt. "Lead the way."

Together, they made their way through the makeshift hospital grounds, passing rows of wounded and weary. The injured lay wrapped in blankets or resting on salvaged bedding, while healers moved among them, their faces lined with fatigue. Hope flickered amid the hardship, but it was fragile.

They stopped before a small tent near the edge of the encampment. Inside, a single mercenary sat bound to a post, his posture rigid, eyes sharp and defiant. He was the only one left; all the others had either been killed in the fighting or vanished into the mountain's shadows.

"We need to know who sent them," Darius said quietly, glancing at Adrian. "And why did they choose that moment to ambush us?"

Adrian exhaled, his gaze narrowing on the man in the tent. "I think we can make a pretty good guess," he muttered, stepping inside.

The tent was dimly lit and stifling, its close air adding to the tension. The bound mercenary looked up, eyes meeting Adrian's with a sneer already curling on his lips.

"You'll get nothing from me," he spat.

Adrian didn't respond right away. Instead, he moved closer and pulled up a stool, settling directly across from him. The two men locked eyes, the silence stretching between them like a drawn blade.

"Let's get some answers," Adrian said, his voice calm, edged with steel. He didn't flinch, didn't blink. The challenge was clear, and neither of them intended to back down.

The tension in the tent was suffocating, the silence broken only by the distant murmurs and groans drifting in from the makeshift hospital outside.

Adrian leaned forward slightly, his tone calm but resolute. "You can make this easy on yourself," he said, eyes fixed on the mercenary. "Tell us who sent you, and why you attacked us. Cooperate, and perhaps you'll be shown leniency."

The mercenary's smirk faltered, just briefly, before returning with forced bravado. "You think you can intimidate me?" he scoffed. "I've faced worse than the two of you."

Darius stepped forward, looming over the seated man as he slowly cracked his knuckles. "This isn't about intimidation," he said coolly. "It's about survival. Yours. The longer you keep your mouth shut, the worse this ends for you."

For a moment, the mercenary said nothing, his eyes darting between them, weighing his options. The defiance in his gaze began to fade.

Finally, he muttered bitterly, "Fine. Here's what I know. The queen ordered the attack. She wants all of you gone, every last rebel. By any means necessary." He paused, breathing hard. "It's not new. This was just the first time she launched a full-scale assault."

Adrian's jaw tightened, rage simmering beneath the surface. He had suspected Elinor's hand in the ambush, but hearing confirmation made it chillingly real. "What's her next move?" he asked, voice sharp. "How big is her army? What is she planning?"

The mercenary's expression hardened. His eyes flickered with uncertainty, but he said nothing.

Darius stepped forward, his patience wearing thin. "We don't have time for this," he muttered, and without warning, delivered a harsh backhand across the man's face. The mercenary's head snapped to the side, blood trickling from the corner of his mouth.

"Talk," Darius ordered, voice low and dangerous.

The mercenary glared at them, jaw clenched tight, lips sealed in stubborn defiance.

Darius struck again, the blow harder this time. The crack of impact echoed in the tent.

"You think your loyalty to the queen will save you?" he snarled. "She sent you to die. She won't hesitate to sacrifice you if it suits her plans. So, tell us what we need to know."

Adrian watched the scene unfold, unease twisting in his gut. They need answers, but this wasn't who they were. He leaned forward, his voice quieter, more earnest. "Please," he said, meeting the mercenary's bloodshot eyes. "We're trying to protect our people. Help us do that."

For a second, the mercenary's expression wavered. His mouth parted slightly, but then he clenched his jaw, his stubborn silence returning.

Darius's eyes darkened. He raised his fist again. "So be it."

"Enough!" the mercenary spat suddenly, blood flecking his lips. "All right—I'll talk."

He slumped slightly in the chair, breathing hard. "She's planning another attack. Bigger than the last. Her army's massive—more than you can imagine. She won't stop until she controls everything."

Adrian felt a cold weight settle in his chest, but he pressed on. "When? When will she strike?"

The mercenary's eyes held a grim mix of resignation and defiance. "Soon. She's already gathering her forces. You don't have much time."

Darius took a step back, his expression bleak. "Thank you for your cooperation," he said flatly, motioning the guards outside. "Take him away. We'll decide what to do with him later."

As the mercenary was dragged from the tent, Adrian turned to Darius. "We need to warn the others. If she's preparing for war, we have to be ready."

Darius nodded, already moving. "I'll gather the leaders and meet you back here."

He disappeared through the flap of the tent, leaving Adrian with his thoughts. He exhaled slowly, what they had learned pressing heavily on his shoulders. They needed to take the fight to her and catch her off guard, but with so few remaining, it would take a miracle to defeat her.

Chapter 31

Shattered Awakening

Cecilia's eyes fluttered open, her vision gradually sharpening as she took in her surroundings. The tent was dimly lit, the air thick with the faint scent of herbs and the soft murmurs of the injured. She shifted, muscles aching in protest as she pushed herself upright. Blinking, she tried to make sense of where she was and what had happened.

As she attempted to rise further, a gentle yet firm hand pressed against her shoulder. A healer, an elderly woman with kind eyes and a calming presence, stepped closer.

"Easy now, my dear," she said softly. "You've been through quite an ordeal. Rest a little longer."

Cecilia turned towards her, mind foggy but urgent. "Adrian… where is he?" she asked, her voice barely above a whisper.

The woman smiled warmly. "I'll have him sent for," she replied, signalling to a nearby attendant. "He'll be here soon."

Cecilia nodded, her worry easing just slightly. She sank back into the pillows, her thoughts spinning. The explosion. The attack. The chaos that followed. It all felt distant – like fragments of a nightmare. Yet the pain in her body, the heaviness in her chest, made it all too real.

Moments later, Adrian pushed into the tent, his expression a storm of relief and concern. He crossed the space in an instant and knelt at her side, taking her hand in his.

"Cecilia," he said, his voice filled with emotion. "Thank the Divine Spirit, you're awake."

She offered him a faint, tired smile, her eyes searching his face. "I'm here," she whispered. "What happened? Are you alright?"

He nodded, squeezing her hand gently. "I'm fine. We're holding together… barely. But we're alive."

With furrowed brows, he began recounting the events – the mercenary's confession, the attack, and the rebels' grim plan to strike back. Cecilia listened, her concern deepening with every word.

"Adrian, that's dangerous," she said, her voice edged with fear. "Are you sure it's the right move?"

"We have no choice," he replied. "The queen won't stop until she's destroyed us. If we don't act, she'll keep sending more forces, more death. We have to protect our people."

"But our numbers…" she protested. "Not all the rebels have reached us yet. We need more men before we take that risk. And

Jacob—she has him, Adrian. If we attack, she'll kill him. I need to get him to safety."

Adrian's gaze dropped, a shadow crossing his face. He took in a slow, unsteady breath, his shoulders heavy with the burden he carried.

"Cecilia," he said gently, his voice trembling. "There's something you need to know."

Her heart began to race. Dread settled over her like a shroud. "What is it?" she asked, barely managing the words.

Adrian met her eyes, his own filled with sorrow. "Jacob… he… he's gone," he said, voice breaking. "The queen ordered a public hanging. He and his friends… Elinor saw to their execution."

"No—" The word escaped her in a breath. "It can't be. You're wrong," she said, shaking her head, desperation in her eyes as if denial alone could rewrite the truth.

"I'm so sorry," he murmured, unable to meet her eyes.

"No," she said again, louder this time. "No! You're lying, Adrian! This isn't true!"

She pushed herself up, her body trembling, knees buckling as she stood. Adrian reached to steady her, but she stumbled away from his touch, backing into the open space of the tent.

"Tell me it's not real!" she cried, her voice breaking as tears spilt down her cheeks. Her fists clenched at her sides, her whole frame quivering.

"Cecilia, please—" Adrian stepped forward, his voice pleading.

"You're lying!" she screamed, striking his chest with trembling fists. "How could you let this happen? How could you just stand there and *tell* me this?"

Her blows weakened quickly, her strength giving out. She collapsed, and Adrian caught her before she hit the ground. He knelt with her, wrapping his arms tightly around her shaking form.

Cecilia sobbed against his chest, clutching at his tunic as though it were the only thing keeping her from shattering completely.

"Please, Adrian… tell me my son is still alive," she begged, her voice muffled and broken. "Tell me this is just a nightmare…"

Adrian's own tears fell freely as he held her tighter. "I wish I could," he whispered. "I wish I could tell you this wasn't real. But I swear to you—we *will* make her pay for this. Jacob deserved so much more."

Cecilia buried her face against him, her world shattered. The tent spun around her, every breath a struggle.

"No," she gasped. "Not Jacob… he can't be…"

Adrian reached up and gently cupped her face, his thumbs brushing her cheeks.

"I'm so sorry," he said softly. "I can't begin to imagine the pain, but I'm here, Cecilia. I'm not going anywhere."

He pulled her into him again, his arms wrapping around her protectively, as though he could shield her from the enormity of the loss. His hand stroked her hair in slow, steady movements while sobs wracked her body.

"Why?" she cried into his chest. "Why, my poor boy?"

Adrian rocked her gently, grounding her with the rhythm of his presence.

"I know it feels unbearable," he murmured, voice raw. "But I'm here for you. You're not alone, Cecilia. You never will be."

She clung to him, tears soaking his shirt. "Jacob…" she whispered, the name breaking on her lips. "He didn't deserve this."

"I know," Adrian said, pressing a kiss to the top of her head. "I know."

Her hands tightened in his tunic, as though letting go would break her completely. Her cries echoed through the tent, raw and anguished. Adrian stayed with her, unmoving, a quiet fortress against the storm of grief. His hand never left her hair, his heartbeat the only steady thing in the world that had suddenly lost all sense.

Chapter 32

Commanding Fate

Elinor stood atop the castle's high tower, her gaze fixed on the smouldering remnants of the mountain in the distance. Ash and crimson stained the sky, the scent of smoke lingering even at this height. The jagged peak, once a proud sentinel on the horizon, now lay broken and blackened, its ruin a monument to her wrath. Though the attack had taken place days ago, its echoes would linger for weeks to come. She watched in cold satisfaction, the silence around her amplifying the weight of her victory.

The soft shuffle of boots against stone broke her solitude.

Julian emerged from the spiral staircase, his expression grave, his dark cloak trailing behind him like a shadow. He paused at the top, as if bracing himself for the burden of his words.

"Your Majesty," he began, voice low but steady, "the mountain is destroyed. The rebels are scattered. However, …" He hesitated, brow furrowing. "Jacob's death has stirred unrest.

The nobles murmur discontent, and the people are beginning to question the crown's actions."

Elinor's jaw tensed, though her expression remained unreadable. She turned slightly, the dying sunlight catching the sharp lines of her profile.

"Let them question," she said, her voice like cold steel. "Their doubts will vanish when the rebels are nothing but a memory and order is restored."

Julian inclined his head, but his gaze drifted towards the plains below. Beyond the city walls, the army camp stretched into the growing darkness with glints of armour and flickering campfires scattered across the field like fallen stars.

"The soldiers await your command. They grow restless, anticipating the battle to come."

Elinor exhaled, her breath forming a pale cloud in the cooling air. "Then let us go greet them and promise a battle worthy of song. Prepare my steed."

Julian bowed and turned away. Alone again, Elinor rested her hands on the cold stone ledge. She stared at the distant fires, letting the weight of what lay ahead settle over her. This was not just a battle; it was the fate of a kingdom. The rebels had to fall if her reign was to endure.

Without another word, she turned from the window and descended the winding staircase. Her footsteps echoed off the stone, purposeful and unwavering. Crossing the castle halls, she moved swiftly, ignoring those who bowed or stepped aside in her wake. Her mind allowed no distraction, only the singular path forward.

The courtyard lay in shadow, lit by flickering torches swaying in the night breeze. The chill in the air crept under her cloak, drawing a shiver down her spine. Her horse waited at the edge of the stables, steam curling from its nostrils, its sleek black coat glistening in the torchlight.

Lady Chloe stood beside the steed, a thick cloak draped over one arm. The light caught in her auburn hair, casting a warm glow around her features. She stepped forward as Elinor approached, wrapping the cloak around the queen's shoulder with gentle precision.

"I thought you might need this," Chloe said softly. "It's cold tonight—even for someone as stubborn as you."

Elinor allowed the faintest smile to touch her lips. "Thank you. Always one step ahead."

Chloe returned the smile, but her tone softened further. "Ride well, my queen."

Elinor nodded, turning towards her horse – only to pause at the sound of approaching footsteps. The rhythmic clatter echoed through the courtyard.

From the shadows emerged Bradley, arms crossed and a smirk tugging at his lips.

"Leaving without me?" he asked, his voice light, though laced with something deeper.

Elinor raised a brow, folding her arms over the heavy cloak. "I assumed you were off brooding in some forgotten corner of the castle."

He feigned offence, one hand on his chest. "Me? Brooding? Never. I merely prefer dramatic entrances. May I ride with you?"

She gave him a long look, then mounted her horse with practised ease. "I suppose," she said dryly, though the glint in her eyes betrayed her amusement.

Bradley swung up onto his own steed with exaggerated grace. "Then let's ride."

With a tug of the reins, Elinor turned her horse towards the gates. "Try to keep up," she called over her shoulder, her voice edged with a sharp, wry humour.

They rode into the night, the city's warm glow fading behind them. The journey to the camp was swift and silent, the only sounds the rhythmic clatter of hooves and the wind rushing past. Julian led the way, flanked by guards, their armour catching the moonlight in silver flashes. Bradley rode beside Elinor, his usual smirk subdued, the weight of what lay ahead pressing down on them both.

As they crested a low hill, the encampment came into view – an expansive sprawl of tents and flickering campfires stretching across the darkened plains. Smoke curled into the night sky, mingling with the scent of damp earth and burned wood. The lower murmur of voices, the clink of metal, and the distant shuffle of boots gave the camp a restless energy, like a living thing bracing for what lay ahead. Soldiers moved between the fires, their shadows stretching long and distorted in the wavering light.

Bradley broke the silence, casting a glance towards Elinor with a crooked grin. "Quite the sight."

Elinor's lips twitched, the barest hint of a smile playing at the corners of her mouth. "An army fit for a queen."

As they descended the slope, the atmosphere shifted. The murmurs grew louder, heads turned, and movement slowed as their presence rippled through the ranks. Word of the queen's arrival spread quickly, murmured from one soldier to the next like a sudden gust through tall grass. Anticipation hung thick in the air.

At the edge of the camp, a figure waited – tall, broad-shouldered, and unmistakably authoritative. The torchlight revealed a weathered face lined with battle, and eyes sharp with calculation. The dents and scars on his armour spoke of years on the front lines, and he wore them with the quiet pride of a man who had survived every war thrown at him.

"Your Majesty," General Lawson greeted, bowing with a measured blend of formality and familiarity. His voice was low and steady, forged in the heat of command. "We hadn't expected your arrival until morning."

Elinor dismounted smoothly, handing her reins to a nearby soldier without a word. "The men are uneasy," she replied. "I won't let doubt fester in their minds—or mine. They need to hear from their queen tonight."

Lawson nodded slowly, his expression unreadable. "You've chosen the right time. Some are questioning the delay—wondering why we wait while the rebels are regrouping."

Bradley slid from his saddle, brushing off his cloak with exaggerated care. "Because the queen wishes it," he said, casting a dry look at the general. "And that should be reason enough."

Elinor paid him no mind, stepping forward until she stood directly before Lawson, her gaze level and resolute. "Gather the captains," she commanded. "I'll speak to the men. They'll know why we wait—and when we strike, they'll understand the purpose behind it."

"As you command," Lawson said. A flicker of approval lit his eyes before he turned sharply and strode into the heart of the camp, his yelled orders quickly setting the camp into motion.

Elinor stood still, watching the controlled flurry of activity unfold. The fires glowed brighter now, as if the camp itself had stirred at her arrival. Beside her, Bradley folded his arms, casting an amused glance at the nearest gathering of soldiers.

"Quite the reception," he murmured. "Think they'll start composing ballads about this moment?"

"Not if you're the one writing them," Elinor replied dryly, though a faint glimmer of amusement sparkled in her eyes. She squared her shoulders and stepped forward, ready to meet her men.

As they strode towards the command tent at the heart of the camp, the soft murmurs of voices followed in their wake. Soldiers stepped aside, eyes tracking their queen with curiosity and reverence. The rows of tents gave way to the central pavilion, where the captains had already begun to gather.

Cloaks billowed in the breeze as the commanders assembled – hardened men and women marked by years of war. Their armour bore scratches and dents, and their faces were maps of experience. Scars and weathered expressions spoke of battles survived, of loyalties tested and earned.

Elinor entered the tent, its dim interior lit by a single swaying lantern overhead. The muffled conversation ceased as every captain turned to face her. Bradley lingered near the entrance, one shoulder resting against the frame, though his eyes remained sharp, missing nothing.

"Your Majesty," one captain said, inclining his head. His voice was deep, his tone laced with respectful authority. "To what do we owe the honour of your presence tonight?"

Elinor's gaze swept across the tent, locking eyes with each of them in turn.

"I've come because the men need reassurance," she said, her voice steady and composed. "There's unrest in the camp—a hunger for action. I trust you've all felt it."

Murmurs rippled through the room. Several heads nodded.

A fiery-haired woman clad in burnished armour stepped forward. "They're ready, Your Majesty. Restless. They fear the delay gives the rebels time to regroup."

Elinor didn't flinch. "Our strategy demands precision—not haste. Eagerness alone will not win this war. Our people must trust their queen to lead them wisely… and to guide them to victory."

The woman gave a nod, her earlier tension easing. Another captain, older, with a deep scar cutting across his jaw, added gruffly, "Then speak to them. Remind them why they're here—what they're fighting for."

A faint smile touched Elinor's lips. "Indeed. That is why I asked you here. Rally your units. Bring them to the central clearing. Tonight, their queen will address them."

Without hesitation, the captains bowed and began to file out, the air around them charged with renewed purpose.

As the tent emptied, Bradley stepped closer, a glimmer of approval in his eyes.

"Not bad, Your Majesty," he said lightly, though sincerity undercut his teasing tone. "You almost sounded inspiring."

Elinor arched a brow. "Almost?"

He smirked. "I'll reserve full judgment until I hear the speech."

She shook her head, a flicker of amusement softening her features, before turning towards the clearing. The time for talk had ended. What came next would shape the morale and fate of her army.

The night air was cool, the wind tugging at her cloak as she moved to the clearing. On either side of her, Bradley and General

Lawson flanked her steps, silent and composed. Smoke still lingered in the air, carried from the distant mountain that now stood blackened by fire, a monument to the destruction she had wrought.

Her gaze swept across the field as soldiers began to gather, ranks forming with a quiet discipline. These were no recruits; they were hardened warriors, forged in fire and blood. Many had taken part in the destruction of the rebel stronghold, their armour still bearing soot and ash. But beneath their silent focus, Elinor could feel it: restlessness. A hunger for forward motion, for vengeance. For purpose.

She remained still, her expression unreadable. She knew too well that raw power, left unchecked, could become chaos. Now was the time to temper it – to harness it.

The murmurs faded as more soldiers assembled. The flickering torchlight cast long shadows across the earth. Every eye turned to her.

Bradley leaned in, his voice low. "They're ready. You can see it in their eyes."

Elinor nodded. "Good. That's exactly what I need."

"And exactly what you have," he replied, his voice firm with quiet confidence.

General Lawson inclined his head. "They are loyal, Your Majesty. They will follow wherever you lead."

Elinor stepped forward, planting her feet firmly as she drew in a breath. Then she spoke, her voice clear and resonant, cutting cleanly through the night air.

"Brave warriors of the realm," she began, her tone sharp with purpose. "Tonight marks the beginning of a new era. The time has come to rid our land of the rebel scourge once and for all. We will not let their treachery go unanswered."

She paused, allowing the weight of her words to settle.

"Let it be known—*from this moment on*, we are at war. We will hunt them down. We will bring them to justice."

A roar of approval burst from the crowd, a thunderous cheer that rolled like distant thunder through the camp.

Elinor raised her hand, commanding silence once more. "But I ask of you patience. Our victory will not come from recklessness. It will come from strategy. From unity. From strength carefully measured and precisely applied. We will not stumble blindly into battle—we will *strike* when the time is right, and when we do, we will not falter."

Torches flared in the breeze, their flames mirrored in the eyes of her soldiers. She pressed on.

"Reinforcements are on their way. Supplies—armour, weapons, provisions—are en route. Soon, we will be at full strength. And when that day comes, we will march as one, and we *will not stop* until the rebellion is crushed beneath our boots."

Another cheer surged forth, stronger than the last.

Elinor stood firm, her presence commanding. Every inch the queen they needed.

At her side, Bradley shifted closer, his voice a whisper only she could hear. "Well done, my love."

She turned to him, warmth flickering briefly in her gaze, before addressing Lawson.

"Keep me informed of any developments. Reinforcements and supplies should arrive within days. I'll return once we're ready to move."

"Yes, Your Majesty," Lawson said with a respectful bow.

With a final look at her assembled troupes, Elinor offered a nod of dismissal. She and Bradley turned away from the firelit ranks, mounting their steeds for the ride back.

The war was beginning.

And Elinor intended to win it.

Prophecy be dammed.

Chapter 33

A Blaze in the Dark

The moon hung low in the sky, its pale light casting long, shifting shadows over the rebel group as Adrian crouched behind a cluster of barrels, eyes fixed on the camp ahead. The soldiers were loud – laughing and boasting around their campfires, their guard down after a long day's march. Perfect.

He glanced at Darius, his oldest friend and most trusted second, crouched beside him.

"We stick to the plan," Adrian murmured. "Retrieve the weapons, destroy what we can't carry, and get out before anyone notices we were here."

Darius gave a nod, a faint smile tugging at the corners of his mouth. "Stealing from Elinor's troops? Almost feels too easy."

Adrian smirked and signalled to the group behind them. "Keep it quiet. Move."

The rebels slipped into the camp like shadows, weaving between wagons and tents. Adrian's heart pounded as he approached the first supply wagon. Darius was already there, working the latch loose with quiet precision. The back creaked open to reveal crates packed with swords, shields, and arrows, all glinting faintly under the moonlight.

"Load what you can," Adrian whispered, beckoning the others forward. "Quickly."

They moved with swift coordination, passing weapons into sacks lined with cloth to muffle the clinking metal. Though efficient, they couldn't carry everything. The wagon held far more than they could take.

Adrian cursed under his breath, calculating.

Darius leaned in. "No time to hit the others. If we leave this untouched…"

Adrian's jaw tightened. He reached for the bottle of oil strapped to his belt. "Then we make sure no one else can use what's left."

Without hesitation, the rebels grabbed their bottles, drenching the remaining crates in oil. The sharp, acrid scent filled the air as the liquid soaked into the wood. Adrian pulled a blade from his pocket and carved the rebel insignia into the side of a crate – a warning and a message.

Once the oil had seeped deep into every crevice, Adrian lit a torch against a nearby campfire, the flames crackling to life.

"Ready?" he asked, his voice low but firm.

Darius gave a curt nod. He tossed the torch onto the crates, and flames erupted in an instant, engulfing the weapons in a fierce blaze. Heat rolled off the fire as it spread, casting flickering shadows across the wagons.

Then – shouting.

Adrian's head snapped up. A sentry stood at the edge of the grounds, pointing directly at them.

"Go!" he hissed.

The rebels scattered, vanishing between wagons and disappearing into the trees. Adrian stayed close to Darius, their movements seamless as they ran. Behind them, chaos erupted – soldiers shouting, alarms blaring – but the damage had been done. The rebels were gone, their prize in hand and their sabotage complete.

They regrouped in the forest, breathless but triumphant. In the distance, the flames still blazed, painting the night sky with orange and gold – an unmistakable beacon of defiance.

Adrian turned to the men, his voice steady. "Well done. Let's see how Elinor marches without her weapons."

Darius smirked, the firelight catching in his eyes. "She won't forget this."

Adrian's gaze hardened. "That's the point."

Chapter 34

The Rebels' Strike

Elinor's hand clenched the edge of the wagon as her gaze fell on the scorched rebel insignia carved into the blackened wood. Around her, soldiers stood in tense silence, unsure whether her wrath would erupt as thunderous commands or chilling quiet.

"What happened here?" Her voice cut through the air like a blade.

The captain stepped forward, his helmet clutched awkwardly at his side. "M-my queen, it appears the rebels—"

"I know what it *appears*," she snapped, spinning on him. "I want an answer. How did an entire wagon of weapons get destroyed under your watch without anyone noticing until it was too late?"

Her tone left no room for argument. The captain paled.

"They snuck in during the night," he said, faltering. "Stole from some crates and poured oil over the rest before setting them alight."

"During the night?" Elinor echoed, her voice low and lethal. "You mean to say no one was guarding the supplies?"

"There were men on duty, Your Majesty, but… the rebels were clever. They slipped past."

"I can see that." Her words dripped with disdain. "Who was on watch?"

The captain hesitated. His jaw tightened, and he cast his eyes downward. "They… will be disciplined, Your Majesty."

Her gaze returned to the remains of the weapons – charred, useless, their twisted metal reeking of oil and ash. She drew a slow breath, fists clenched at her sides, nails biting into her palms. Rage surged beneath her skin, but she forced it down. This wasn't the moment for fury. This was a time for precision.

She turned to face the assembled officers. "This isn't mere sabotage. It's a message. They want to rattle us, to undermine our resolve."

Her eyes narrowed. "But they've miscalculated. Ready the men. At first light, we march to the mines. Our supplies may be strained, but we will adapt. We can't afford to give them more time to regroup."

A younger officer stepped forward, hesitant. "Your Majesty… what if this is a trap?"

Elinor's eyes locked onto his. Her voice dropped, cold and sure. "No. I know the man who planned this. Adrian doesn't waste resources on traps he can't spring. This was meant to unsettle us, not ambush us. It's a warning—a taunt. He wants us to believe he's one step ahead."

Her words silenced further protest. The officer bowed and stepped back into formation.

Elinor looked once more at the smouldering ruins of the supply wagon. Her voice lowered, meant only for those close to her. "Ready the men. We give no quarter. The mines will burn before I let them slip through my fingers again. They want a game?" Her eyes burned with cold fury. "Then let's play. We'll see who's left standing."

Her officers nodded sharply and moved to carry out her orders. Tension still clung to the camp, as heavy as the smoke in the air. Elinor turned her gaze to the distant horizon, her resolve solidifying like tempered steel.

Adrian might know her mind, but she knew his just as well. And this war would break one of them.

She had no intention of it being her.

***

Adrian crouched low behind the jagged rocks, his sharp gaze locked on the approaching line of soldiers. The faint clinking of armour and the distant rumble of wagon wheels drifted towards him on the frosty morning air. He tightened his grip on the hilt of his sword, his free hand raising a silent signal for his men to hold their positions.

Elinor's forces were close – too close now. At the head of the column, the crown's banner snapped crisply in the wind, a stark emblem of the might arrayed against them. Adrian's jaw tensed. He had faced armies like this before – disciplined, well-armed, and steeped in pride. But that was another life, when he had worn the colours of the crown and stood on the other side of the battlefield.

Darius shifted beside him, voice pitched low. "We've got the high ground. They won't know what hit them."

Adrian didn't respond immediately. His eyes swept the narrow pass below – a natural choke point flanked by steep cliffs and offering no room to manoeuvre. It was the perfect place for an ambush. Elinor's detachment was small, her main force still days behind. A strong show of resistance here could send her vanguard retreating, buying precious time for their reinforcements to arrive.

Everything was in place. But plans unravelled quickly, and he had long since learned not to underestimate her.

"Good," he said at last, voice low and hard. "Let them regret the march."

A scout appeared at his side, breathless. "They're nearly in position, sir. Just a few more yards."

Adrian nodded, drawing his sword with a soft rasp of steel. The sound echoed faintly across the rocks, followed by a ripple of motion as weapons were readied and breath held. His pulse quickened with the charge of impending violence.

"On my mark," he murmured.

Below, the column advanced, the soldiers marching in disciplined formation. Adrian let them come, waiting as the wagons rolled deeper into the trap. When the lead riders reached the centre of the pass, he raised his hand.

"Now!"

The rebels surged from cover in a roar of war cries and steel, descending on the enemy with ruthless precision. Arrows rained from above, striking down the unsuspecting soldiers. Adrian led the charge, his blade flashing as he plunged into the chaos.

Elinor's forces scrambled, caught off guard. Their neat formation collapsed as panic rippled through the ranks. But Adrian allowed himself no comfort in their disarray. Victory was never certain. Not when Elinor was behind the strategy.

He moved with lethal focus, striking down enemies with swift, efficient blows. Around him, the narrow pass erupted into brutal, close-quarters combat – every movement pressed against the rock walls, every breath a struggle through dust and blood.

"Hold the line!" Adrian shouted over the din. "Don't let them regroup!"

His sword met an enemy's blade with a burst of sparks. He forced the soldier back, then slashed downward, bringing the fight to a decisive conclusion. Beside him, Darius fought like a storm, his twin blades a blur of speed and precision.

"They're falling apart!" Darius called, exhilaration in his voice. "We've got them!"

But Adrian didn't let the momentum fool him. The tide could turn with a single order. Elinor wouldn't suffer a loss without answering.

"Keep pushing!" he ordered. "Drive them back—but stay sharp. This isn't over!"

Above them, rebel archers continued their deadly work, arrows whistling through the air. Below, the enemy faltered, retreating step by step under the relentless assault. Yet Adrian's focus never wavered.

Not until the last blade was lowered would he consider them safe. And even then – only for a moment.

As the sun dipped below the horizon, torchlight and the last sparks of clashing steel lit the battlefield in flickering gold and crimson. Elinor's troops retreated, their shouts laced with frustration as they fell back through the narrow pass, leaving behind their dead, their wounded, and the bitter taste of defeat. A cheer rose from the rebel lines, echoing off the cliffs, but Adrian raised a hand, cutting through the celebration.

"Well done, all of you," he said, his voice firm but tempered. "But save your strength. This was only a skirmish. They'll be back—and they'll come harder."

The rebels dispersed with quiet nods, tending to the wounded and reinforcing their positions as dusk deepened into night. Adrian and Darius climbed to the higher ground, surveying the battlefield from above. Below, the last of Elinor's soldiers disappeared into the shadows. Adrian's jaw clenched. The victory was theirs, but only for now. Elinor would regroup, and when she struck again, she would strike with precision and fury.

"Small victories," Darius murmured, placing a steadying hand on Adrian's shoulder. "They add up."

Adrian gave a brief nod, his grip tightening around the hilt of his sword. "They do. But don't forget—she knows that too."

As the last embers of battle faded in the distance, soft footsteps approached. Cecilia emerged from the dim light, her gaze sweeping over the darkened pass before settling on Adrian. Pride flickered in her expression, tempered by the weary concern that always followed bloodshed.

"You did it," she said, her voice cutting through the stillness. "Another victory for the rebellion."

He turned towards her, his hardened features softening slightly in her presence. "A small one," he replied. "But a win, nonetheless."

She stepped closer, her hand brushing his cheek as she met his eyes. "Even small victories matter. You've given them hope, Adrian. That's worth more than you realise."

He exhaled slowly, the last of the fight still thrumming through his veins. "It won't mean much if we can't hold this ground. Elinor's probing us—testing our defences."

"And you'll meet her, every step of the way," Cecilia said, calm but firm. She placed a hand on his shoulder, grounding him.

"But not if you burn yourself out before the real fight begins. Rest while you can. You can't carry this alone."

Adrian hesitated and then nodded. He allowed himself to lean into her touch for a moment, drawing strength from her steadiness. She stepped forward and wrapped her arms around him, offering an embrace that was more than comfort – it was resolve.

"I'm proud of you," she whispered. "And so are they. Look at what you've accomplished tonight."

He glanced over her shoulder at the rebels scattered across the field, some tending wounds, others reinforcing defences, but all of them heartened. Darius caught his eye and offered a subtle nod of approval, loyalty shining clear without a word.

"You're fighting for something bigger than yourself," Cecilia continued. "Never forget that."

Adrian met her gaze, his resolve hardening beneath the weariness. "I won't. But we're far from done."

She smiled, quiet confidence in every line of her face. "Then let's make the most of the time we have. The next battle is coming. Our allies will be here soon—and when they arrive, we'll be ready."

Her hand lingered on his arm, grounding him amid the weight of responsibility. "The fight that comes to Elinor will be one she never saw coming. And tonight proved it. We are stronger than she thinks."

Adrian let out a slow breath, some of the tension uncoiling from his shoulders. "It proved something," he admitted. "But we can't afford to get comfortable. She knows me too well. Every move I make, she'll try to counter."

"And you'll counter her," Cecilia said firmly, stepping closer. "You know her just as well. But now you're not facing her alone. You have an army that believes in you. People who would follow you into fire."

Her words settled into him, quiet but undeniable. For a moment, the doubt faded. He reached up and took her hand in his, a small, weary smile forming at the edges of his mouth. "You always know what to say."

"I've had plenty of time to learn," she replied, a hint of warmth in her voice. "Come on. Rest while you can. The night is ours—for now. But we'll need every ounce of strength for what's coming."

He nodded and let her guide him back towards the campfires. The glow of the flames danced across the faces of the rebels – exhausted, battered, but resolute. For the first time since the ambush began, Adrian allowed himself to breathe.

The war was far from over. But tonight, they held the upper hand.

And he intended to keep it.

Chapter 35

A Warning in Words

Elinor sat in the high-backed chair at the head of the table, the weight of her crown heavy, yet familiar. Before her, maps and figures lay strewn across the table's surface, detailing the mines, the roads, and the rebel-controlled regions. To her left sat Liora and her band of priestesses. Though they appeared composed, Elinor could see the fear behind their eyes. Were their positions reversed, she wasn't sure how she would fare.

To her right sat Bradley and Julian, the two she trusted most in the room. Then came General Lawson and Sir Edric, men she relied upon to win this war. Their knowledge and tactical skill were invaluable. She had the strength and the numbers, but she couldn't deny it – the failure of the recent attack gnawed at her like a dull, persistent ache. Still, Elinor wouldn't allow doubt to show. Not here. Not now.

The rest of her council stood in silence, waiting for her to speak. At last, she lifted her head, her eyes sharp with resolve.

"Well, considering yesterday's disaster, I believe a better approach is in order for our next move," she said, her gaze landing pointedly on her general.

"Yes, Your Majesty and we have one," General Lawson replied with a respectful nod. "After the failure of our initial strike, I admit I underestimated their strength. But now, I propose a confrontation." He gestured to the map spread before them. "This open field—here, just beyond the castle—is ideal. It favours our cavalry and archers while limiting the rebels' ability to exploit the narrow passes they prefer."

He traced the edges of the terrain with a gloved finger. "Flat and unobstructed ground. It gives us the advantage. The rebels lack the discipline and numbers to hold it."

Elinor studied the map, her brow furrowed. "And the castle? If we leave it lightly defended, they could bypass us altogether. With my son there—I want no surprises."

Sir Edric, Captain of the Guard, leaned forward. "Your Majesty, I suggest leaving a garrison behind—sufficient to hold the walls should the rebels attempt such a manoeuvre. But I doubt they will. With Adrian at their head, they'll be eager to face us openly."

Elinor looked around the table. "Where do we stand with the rest of our forces? I was promised aid from all corners of the realm."

General Lawson cleared his throat, his expression darkening. "Your Majesty, the reinforcements from the Western territories are delayed. Heavy rains have rendered key roads impassable. However, the South and Southwest have sent word—they will arrive within two days. The remaining banners should join us within the week."

"Good. Then we prepare—and ensure the rebels face us in open battle. They will not humiliate the crown and live to speak of it."

She motioned to her diplomat, her voice slicing through the thick air. "Take this down."

She began, her tone cold and measured:

"To Cecilia, styling herself queen of the rebellion:

You have stolen from my armies, defied my rule, and endangered your people. Your so-called triumphs will be your undoing. From one queen to another, I offer you this final opportunity to avoid the annihilation of your forces. Surrender yourself and your army, and I may yet show mercy.

You have already lost your husband and now your son to this reckless rebellion. James fell because he was unfit to rule. Jacob, because you refused to bend the knee to your rightful queen. You sent him to his death, chasing shards and vengeance. His blood is on your hands more than mine.

And now Adrian, once my most trusted ally, stands among your ranks. Do you truly believe he will save you? A man who couldn't remain loyal to his queen?

Know this: betrayal only begets betrayal. Treason demands a bloody price. And you, Cecilia, have only your daughter left to lose. How much more are you willing to gamble before you have nothing?

One week from today, we shall meet, queen to queen, on the battlefield. If you refuse my terms, I promise you this: there will be no quarter. The full weight of the crown shall bear down upon you and all who stand beside you.

Signed, Elinor, rightful Queen of Ethos."

The Diplomat's quill stilled at the final word. Elinor met his gaze. "Ensure this reaches her directly. Let her know negotiations are over."

They hesitated. "Your Majesty, if I may—does this not risk emboldening them? Giving them time to regroup?"

Elinor's expression didn't waver. "No. This forces them to choose between surrender and certain death. Let them prepare if they wish. It will only make their defeat all the sweeter."

That night, under the cover of darkness, the diplomat rode out, carrying with him an ultimatum that would shape the days to come.

***

A messenger arrived with word of an approaching rider. Cecilia stood at the entrance of the rebel camp, her chin lifted high despite the exhaustion etched into her features. The wind pulled at her cloak as the rider dismounted, offering her a sealed letter bearing Elinor's unmistakable insignia.

Adrian appeared beside her, his expression unreadable as he took in the scene. "She couldn't resist the theatrics, could she?" he muttered.

Cecilia broke the seal and unfolded the parchment. Her eyes scanned the words, her grip tightening with each line. The mask of icy composure cracked, giving way to simmering fury.

"She dares," she whispered, her voice shaking with restrained rage. "She dares to paint herself as righteous? To speak of mercy while threatening my daughter?"

Adrian's eyes dropped to the letter. "What does she say?"

Without a word, Cecilia thrust it towards him. "Read it for yourself. Your former queen remains as pompous and self-assured as ever."

Adrian scanned the missive, his jaw tensing. "She's baiting you," he said finally. "This isn't about peace. It's a power play."

"Of course it is," Cecilia snapped, her voice rising. "She killed James, stole everything from me, and now she believes she can crush what remains. She underestimates us."

Adrian hesitated, the unspoken doubt flickering between them. *Does she?* He glanced at Cecilia, then back at the letter.

"She's forcing your hand," he said. "One week. Ashenridge Plain. She's daring you to face her."

Cecilia's expression hardened, her fingers crumpling the parchment. "Then we'll meet her. But not on her terms—on mine. She thinks she's dealing with the grieving widow who fled her court. She's wrong."

Adrian crossed his arms, his voice lower, steadier. "You know what she's doing. Twisting the knife—mentioning Jacob, threatening your daughter. She wants you unbalanced."

Cecilia's lips pressed into a thin line. "My daughter is the reason I fight. If Elinor thinks threatening her will make me yield, she's more deluded than I thought."

Adrian gave a slow nod. "Then we prepare. If she wants war, she'll have it. But let's make one thing clear—we are not the ones who will kneel."

Cecilia turned, fury transformed into resolve. "Summon the commanders. They need to hear Elinor's demands—and that we reject them."

Chapter 36

Family Ties

Over the next few days, the rebel camp stirred with grim determination. The icy rain had lessened to a steady drizzle, but the ground had already turned to a treacherous mire, hindering preparations for the inevitable clash with Elinor. Her letter had left no room for doubt: surrender and live as her subjects or resist and face annihilation.

Cecilia paced near the central fire, the flickering flames casting restless shadows across her weary face. Scouts came and went with updates, their reports rarely encouraging. Entire contingents of rebel fighters had been delayed by the weather, their arrival uncertain. Each piece of bad news tightened the knot in her chest.

Still, some reinforcements managed to trickle in. Late on the third evening, a scout approached, his breath clouding in the cold air.

"Another group's arrived," he said. "You'll want to come."

Cecilia followed him, her boots crunching through the frost-laced mud. As they neared the edge of camp, her steps faltered. Standing among the new arrivals, clad in battered armour and a travel-worn cloak, was Aevah.

Her daughter. The daughter she had not seen in over eight years.

Cecilia's breath hitched. Aevah's auburn hair was streaked with ash and tied back, emphasising the sharpness of her features. Her green eyes, so like Cecilia's own, were tired but unflinching. She was no longer the child Cecilia had once kissed goodnight. She was a warrior now, shaped by hardship and loss.

Across the distance, Aevah met her mother's gaze, her expression unreadable. For a moment, time seemed to suspend, the sounds of the camp fading into stillness. Then, Aevah stepped forward.

"Mother," she said softly, the word heavy with years of absence and unspoken emotion.

Cecilia moved before her mind could catch up. She crossed the distance between them in an instant, throwing her arms around her daughter. Aevah hesitated for only a heartbeat before returning the embrace.

"You're here," Cecilia whispered, her voice trembling. "After all this time… you're here."

"I didn't know if I'd make it," Aevah murmured, her cheek pressed to her mother's shoulder. "There were moments—close calls. Times I thought the road would take me before I reached you. But I never doubted, Mother. I was always coming. I had to."

Cecilia pulled back just enough to search her daughter's face. "You've grown so strong," she said, her voice thick with pride and sorrow. "Stronger than I ever imagined."

"And you," Aevah replied with a faint, wry smile, "look just as determined as I remember."

A small, tearful laugh escaped Cecilia. "I've had to be."

The moment might have lingered, but a shout from across the camp snapped them back to reality. Cecilia's eyes darted towards the sound, relaxing only slightly when she saw Adrian already handling the situation. She turned back to Aevah and placed her hands on her daughter's shoulders.

"Come," she said. "Rest and have some food. We have so much to catch up on."

Aevah glanced over her shoulder at the figures waiting just beyond the firelight, then turned back with a small, knowing smile. "Before we do… there's someone I'd like you to meet. Actually—more than one."

Cecilia followed her daughter's gaze as several figures stepped into view. The first was a young woman with braided jet-black hair and warm, familiar features.

"Isabella?" Cecilia asked, surprise and relief mingling on her face.

Isabella offered a sheepish smile, brushing mud from her worn cloak. "Aunt Cecilia," she said with a respectful inclination of her head. "It's been a while."

"Far too long," Cecilia replied, pulling her into a fierce, brief hug. When she stepped back, her expression was tinged with both affection and worry. "I heard you'd joined the cause, but I never imagined you'd take such a risk to come here."

"I couldn't stay behind while our family's fate hung in the balance," Isabella said earnestly. "My father raised me better than that."

Cecilia cupped Isabella's cheek, a bittersweet smile rising at the mention of her family.

Before she could speak again, two young men stepped into the firelight, and her breath caught once more. The first was tall and broad-shouldered, his tousled brown hair lending him a roguish charm. His grin was wide and unapologetic, his eyes alight with mischief.

"Galrick," she said, disbelief softening her voice. "Is that really you?"

"The one and only," he replied with a cheeky grin, striding forward with the easy confidence of someone who'd always felt invincible. His armour gleamed in the firelight as he added, "Hard to believe, I know. I've been meaning to come show off for you, but… rebellion and all."

Cecilia shook her head, exasperation and affection mingling in her expression. "You've grown into quite the young man, haven't you? The last time I saw you, you were slipping frogs into my chambers."

"Frogs, worms—you name it," Galrick said with a wink. "But don't worry, my pranks are more refined these days."

Aevah let out a soft chuckle, but before Cecilia could retort, the second young man stepped forward. Nicholas stood quieter than Galrick, leaner, his posture reserved. His dark eyes flicked between the group, his expression calm, composed, but watchful.

"Nicholas," Cecilia said, her voice gentler now. "You've grown as well. You look so much like your father."

He dipped his head in greeting. "It's good to see you again, Lady Cecilia. I've tried to stay busy and useful."

Galrick clapped a hand onto his shoulder, grinning. "Don't let him fool you. He's the sharpest mind among us—always the one with a plan when I get into trouble."

Nicholas's lips twitched into the barest smile. "Someone has to keep you from getting yourself killed."

Aevah folded her arms, her gaze shifting between the two with a smirk. "They haven't changed much, Mother. Loyal to the bone—unlike their parents."

Cecilia's exasperation gave way to a rare, genuine smile. "It's so good to see you both. Truly. As for your parents… well, some people will always follow the wind. I knew long ago where their loyalties lay."

Her gaze moved over the group – Aevah, Isabella, Galrick, and Nicholas – all standing before her, older, changed, marked by hardship, yet still tied to her by blood, memory, and purpose. Despite the cold night and the storm looming in the distance, a quiet warmth stirred within her.

"Come," she said, straightening her shoulders. "Let's get you all something to eat and a place to rest. We've much to plan, and I want to hear everything you've been through."

Together they turned towards the heart of the encampment, firelight casting long shadows behind them. As they walked, Cecilia felt a flicker of hope kindle deep within her chest. Her family was coming back together.

Reuniting after so many years felt like a miracle.

They spoke long into the night, their voices rising and falling over the crackle of the flames. Tales of hardship and survival spilt into the firelight, some spoken hesitantly, others shared with blunt force. There were moments of stunned silence when words faltered, and memories spoke louder. Cecilia's hand often found Aevah's arm, her fingers trembling as though anchoring herself to the reality of her daughter's presence. In the soft glow of the fire, she saw it clearly – the spark in Aevah's eyes, so familiar, so undeniably her own. But in the unflinching set of her jaw, in the strength of her bearing, Cecilia saw James too. That fierce resolve, that quiet, unrelenting will – he had left his mark on their daughter just as surely as she had.

There was laughter as well, unexpected, bright, and welcome. It bubbled up between solemn moments, sparked by old memories and efforts to close the distance time had carved between them. But as the night wore on, a quieter sorrow crept in – a deep ache for the years lost, for the milestones missed, for what could never be reclaimed.

And yet, despite the weight of that bittersweet realisation, there was peace.

They were here now. Together.

And for Cecilia, that was enough. More than enough. It was everything.

***

The next morning, Cecilia stood at the edge of the camp, her cloak tugged gently by the early breeze as sunlight broke through the thinning clouds. The laughter from the night before still echoed faintly in her mind, a fragile warmth amidst the cold clarity of dawn. Reuniting with her loved ones had soothed something deep within her, but it had also stirred old wounds. Watching Aevah stand strong among her companions, especially beside Nicholas, whose quiet intelligence and steadfast strength shone so clearly, filled her with pride and sorrow in equal measure.

They had gained much. But they had lost more.

And some would never witness this fragile beginning.

Her gaze drifted beyond the camp to the valley below, where a sea of tents stretched across the land in rigid, ordered lines. Elinor's army lay spread out with chilling precision, their banners fluttering in the breeze, their movements coordinated and disciplined. It was a sight both awe-inspiring and heartbreaking.

Thousands of soldiers gathered there, each one a life with its own story, its own fears, its own stake in the coming storm.

Her own forces mirrored that formation, positioned just beyond the hill in grim symmetry. Their armour caught the morning light with a dull gleam, and the occasional clatter of weapons and shouted commands broke the stillness. They waited – nervous, resolute, prepared to follow her into battle. Into bloodshed. Into the unknown.

No matter how the story ended, one truth remained: lives would be lost.

Sons and daughters, brothers and sisters, lovers and friends – none were immune to the carnage that loomed ahead. Even victory would come at a price, weighed down by grief. For every banner raised in triumph, there would be seats left empty, voices forever silenced. The cost of defiance was steep. But so, too, was the cost of surrender.

Cecilia exhaled slowly, the weight of command settling once more on her shoulders. She turned towards the makeshift war tent where her generals awaited her. With only a day left before she had to decide – surrender to Elinor's ultimatum or go to war.

There was still much to prepare.

And even more to lose.

Chapter 37

No Turning Back

Elinor sat cross-legged on the plush rugs of her chamber floor, morning light streaming through the tall windows and casting the room in a golden glow. Her son, a chubby-cheeked infant with a tuft of dark curls, giggled as he gnawed on a carved wooden lion. Nearby, Bradley lounged with his weight braced on his elbows, watching the boy with a soft smile – a rare moment of peace settling over them.

"Where's my little warrior hiding?" Elinor cooed, lifting her hands to cover her face. She peeked out dramatically. "Peekaboo!"

The baby squealed with delight, clapping his tiny hands before crawling towards her with unsteady determination. As he reached her, she scooped him into her lap and pressed a kiss to his temple, his laughter ringing through the chamber.

But her smile faded, though her hold on her son remained firm and protective. Her gaze shifted to Bradley, her tone growing solemn. "There will be a battle, Bradley. When we meet Cecilia on the field, she won't surrender. Not with Adrian at her side, too. They'll fight to the last breath. One of us won't leave that field alive."

Bradley's expression tightened, his gaze dropping to the child nestled in Elinor's arms. He reached out, brushing a finger along the baby's grasping hand. "Then we'll make certain it's them, not us," he said, his voice low but firm.

Elinor studied him, lips pressed into a thin line. "More than our lives are at stake," she murmured, drawing the baby closer. "This castle, these lands… our son's future. If we falter, if we let this drag on, they'll bring the war to our doorstep. I won't allow that. It ends on the field."

Bradley nodded, his resolve mirroring hers. "We'll strike hard. Swift and without mercy."

Elinor straightened, her posture regal even with her child nestled against her. "The priestesses give us an edge," she continued, her voice sharpening. "Zara's belief that the others remain loyal to Cecilia will blind her—until it's too late."

Bradley leaned forward, elbows resting on his knees, his jaw set. "And if they uncover Liora's betrayal? Or that she's not the only one? Their retaliation could tear through everything."

"That's exactly why we move quickly," she replied, locking eyes with him. "By the time they realise the truth, the battle will already be lost. They won't have time to regroup."

The baby stirred in her arms, cooing softly, and she adjusted him against her shoulder. The motion was instinctive, her maternal care woven seamlessly with her commanding presence.

"This isn't just strategy. It's survival. I won't let them take what's ours. Not this castle. Not these lands. And certainly not our future."

Bradley exhaled slowly, nodding as her words settled over him. "We march, then. And we don't stop until Cecilia and Adrian are nothing but a memory."

Her expression hardened, her resolve like steel. "No mercy. This ends on the field, not at our gates."

Silence fell between them, heavy with shared determination and unspoken fears. The baby shifted again, a small fist clutching at Elinor's gown. Bradley reached out, his fingers brushing the fabric near the child's hand – a fleeting moment of tenderness in a room poised for war.

Elinor broke the silence, her voice quieter but no less firm. "Check in with the men. Make sure Liora knows her role and what's at stake if she fails."

Bradley rose, his shadow falling across them as he squared his shoulders. "She won't fail," he said with quiet conviction. "None of us will."

***

The day had arrived. Elinor stood in her chambers, the air heavy with quiet resolve. Each breath she drew carried the weight of what lay ahead. She remained still, arms outstretched, as her attendants moved around her with practised precision, fastening the clasps and buckles of her ceremonial armour.

Polished steel gleamed beneath the sunlight streaming through the windows, etched with the fierce symbol of a wolf's head – her house crest. Unlike the battle-worn armour of her soldiers, hers was a seamless blend of regality and function, a reminder that she was both sovereign and soldier. A dark cloak rested over her shoulders, its hem embroidered in gold thread that shimmered with each movement.

Bradley stood nearby, already dressed for war. His armour clinked softly as he adjusted his vambraces, every motion deliberate and calm. His eyes lingered on Elinor, unreadable at first glance, yet softened by the quiet affection reserved only for her.

"Do you think he knows?" she asked, her voice low, edged with hesitation. She cast a glance towards the corner of the room, where Lady Chloe cradled Eadric. The boy squirmed in her arms, reaching for her necklace with chubby, grasping fingers as Chloe murmured soothing words.

Bradley followed her gaze and shook his head. "He's too young to understand," he said, stepping closer. "But he'll feel our love. Even from afar."

Elinor nodded, grounding herself in his certainty. She turned to Chloe, her voice steady but gentle. "Keep him safe. Whatever happens today, stay within the castle walls. Do you understand?"

"I swear it, Your Majesty."

Elinor stepped forward, bending to kiss her son's forehead. Eadric gurgled in response, oblivious to the storm gathering beyond the stone walls. She forced a small, aching smile. "Be strong, little one. We'll come back for you."

Bradley knelt beside her, pressing a kiss to the child's cheek before rising. He met Chloe's eyes. "We're trusting you. You're his shield today."

Then Elinor turned to Bradley, resting her hand on his arm. Their eyes met – no words needed, just shared understanding. "It's time," she said, her voice firm with purpose.

They left the chambers together, the sound of armoured boots echoing through the corridor behind them. Lady Chloe stood motionless in their wake, holding the boy tightly as the queen and her consort walked into destiny.

At the military encampments, Elinor strode through what could only be described as controlled chaos. Around her, soldiers yelled orders, blacksmiths hammered steel, and scribes delivered messages with urgency. Armour was polished, blades sharpened, and supply carts packed with meticulous care. The sun had climbed beyond morning's edge, and though it was not yet noon, the air trembled with the anticipation of battle.

Elinor halted outside the command tent, her hands clasped behind her back. The past week had been relentless – drilling troops, reinforcing alliances, refining every detail of her strategy. The sting of defeat at the mines still lingered, but she wouldn't repeat her mistakes. Not today.

"Your Majesty."

She turned to find General Lawson standing at attention, his face drawn with focus.

"The men are ready. Scouts report clear roads to the battlefield."

"Good," she replied, her voice cool and commanding. "We set out at once. I want no delays."

He bowed and withdrew, leaving her to join Bradley and Julian. She mounted her horse and rode forward, the troops parting silently at her approach. Her presence demanded reverence, her calm command inspiring steadiness amid the storm.

When they reached Ashenridge Plain, Elinor paused, her gaze sweeping across the distant horizon. Behind her, the army advanced, a silver tide of steel and discipline. A glorious sight. A force summoned not just to wage war, but to defend the crown and the realm it safeguarded.

As the final ranks fell into position, the noise faded – the rhythmic thud of boots, the clatter of armour – all giving way to silence. Elinor urged her horse ahead, positioning herself before her soldiers. A queen. A warrior. Their leader.

"This rebellion has gone on long enough," she called, her voice rising above the rustle of banners and the whisper of wind. "Today, we march not only to secure the crown, but to remind these traitors of the price of defiance. Let no one doubt our resolve."

A roar of affirmation rose from the army, their resolve ignited by her words. With a nod to General Lawson, Elinor turned her gaze across the plain. There, arrayed against her, stood Cecilia's forces. And beside her, Adrian.

Elinor narrowed her eyes, her voice little more than a murmur carried on the wind.

"And now, we see what her fate will be."

Chapter 38

The Battle Begins

Cecilia stood still, eyes fixed on the vast force stretched across the battlefield before her. Elinor's army loomed like an unbroken wave – shields glinting in the sunlight, banners rippling in the breeze. The sheer scale of it was staggering. Her forces, loyal and steadfast, were dwarfed in comparison. The realisation pressed against her like a physical weight, but she accepted it without flinching.

She studied the precision of Elinor's formation – each contingent aligned with military perfection, statuesque and disciplined. This was no mere display; it was an army bred for war, commanded by a queen whose strategic prowess was as fearsome as her reputation. Still, Cecilia squared her shoulders, refusing to let the imbalance sway her. Battles were not won by numbers alone. They were won by grit, by unity, and the unyielding fire that burned within.

Across the field, Elinor's figure stood unmistakable, a pillar of authority framed against the steel-clad backdrop of her host. Cecilia's gaze lingered, calm and assessing. Then she exhaled, steadying herself as she felt Adrian's quiet presence at her side. It was time.

The wind swept through the grass, carrying with it the faint clink of armour and the whisper of banners, but Cecilia heard none of it. Her focus narrowed on Elinor – her rival, her mirror, her opposite in every way.

Adrian moved beside her, his hand resting lightly on the pommel of his sword, a silent assurance in the subtle gesture. On her other side stood Darius, unflinching as ever, their long history reflected in the quiet gravity of his stance.

As they approached the centre of the field, Cecilia took in the scene before her. Elinor stood flanked by Bradley, his expression stone-cold, and her knight, Julian Wood, a towering figure encased in polished steel, radiating silent strength. The contrast between the two groups was stark. Equal in numbers, perhaps, but worlds apart in spirit.

The two parties came to a halt, the heart of the battlefield falling eerily silent despite the armies amassed behind them. Cecilia met Elinor's gaze. Neither woman spoke. The tension thickened, stretched taut like a bowstring about to snap.

Cecilia's breathing remained measured, her expression unreadable. Adrian stood motionless beside her, a shadow of calm and readiness. Across from them, Elinor exuded confidence, a faint smirk playing on her lips.

At last, Elinor broke the silence, her voice slicing through the stillness like a blade.

"So," she said, mockery laced through every syllable, "are you going to address your queen, or do you need a moment to remember how to bow?"

Cecilia's brows knit together. "There's only one of us who should kneel," she said through gritted teeth, "and it isn't me."

Elinor's smirk deepened, eyes glinting with cold amusement. "Such boldness from someone with so little ground to stand on," she said smoothly. "You've always been stubborn, Cecilia. But stubbornness doesn't win wars. It only ensures your defeat is messier."

Cecilia clenched her fists at her sides, nails digging into her palms, but her voice was sharp and steady. "Defeat is something I've never known. And I have no intention of beginning now."

Elinor's amusement darkened, her gaze sharpening. She stepped forward, her presence pressing like a stormfront. "Then let me be clear," she said, her voice dropping into something darker. "Surrender now. Bow before your queen, and I may show you mercy. Refuse… and you die with the rest of your pitiful army."

Adrian bristled beside her, his body tense, but Cecilia raised a hand to still him. Her voice cut cleanly through the tension, each word laced with defiance. "I would rather die on my feet than kneel to you."

A heavy silence followed, the air thick with unspoken fury. Elinor studied her for a long moment, as if searching for any fracture in Cecilia's resolve. Finding none, her lips curved into a cruel smile.

"So be it," she said, turning away with deliberate grace. As she walked, her voice rang out behind her like a pronouncement. "Prepare yourself, Cecilia. You'll regret those words when you're begging for my mercy… with your dying breath."

Elinor disappeared into the ranks of her army, her cloak trailing behind her. Cecilia stood rooted in place, her chest rising and falling with the force of restrained fury.

Adrian leaned in, his voice low and ready. "Your orders?"

She turned to him, her eyes lit with fire. "We fight," she said. "Rally the troops. This isn't just survival—it's about making her regret every choice that led her to this moment."

As Cecilia marched back to her troops, her mere presence quieted the murmur of unease rippling through the ranks. She climbed a nearby rise, gaining a clear vantage over the gathered soldiers. All eyes turned to her – their leader, their anchor, their beacon of hope beneath the looming shadow of war.

She drew in a deep breath, steadying herself. When she spoke, her voice rang out – firm, clear, and unwavering – cutting through the ambient tension like a blade.

"Listen to me, all of you!" she called, her tone commanding. "Elinor has declared war. Even now, she marches towards us."

A ripple of apprehension passed through the crowd, but Cecilia raised a hand, her gaze sweeping across the sea of faces. "Do not fear her," she said, her voice resonating with iron conviction. "She may outnumber us, but her strength lies in size alone. Our lies in purpose—in unity—and in the fire that burns within every one of you."

Adrian stepped forward to stand just behind her, his steady presence a quiet reinforcement. She pressed one.

"Today, we fight for more than survival. We fight for freedom. For our homes. For a future free from Elinor's tyranny. We are not just soldiers—we are a force to be reckoned with. We fight because we must. Because surrender is not an option."

Her words struck like a flint, sparking something in the hearts of her soldiers. Shoulders straightened. Hands gripped weapons with renewed certainty.

"Arm yourselves," she commanded. "Ready your shields. Steady your hearts. Together, we will show Elinor and her army that we will not bow. Not now. Not ever!"

A thunderous cheer erupted in response, swelling across the encampment as fear gave way to resolve.

Adrian and Marcus mounted their horses and rode along the lines, offering words of strength and encouragement. They paused often, speaking directly to small clusters of soldiers, reminding them of their training, their strategy, and the purpose behind every move they would make. With each word, morale rose. Their presence breathed renewed life into the army, steadying nerves and sharpening focus.

From her vantage point, Cecilia stood unmoving, eyes fixed on the far horizon. Across the battlefield, Elinor's forces shifted into formation – banners fluttering with intent, soldiers tightening their lines, and the metallic symphony of war preparations echoing through the plain. The scale of it all pressed in, a daunting reminder of the challenge ahead.

Adrian returned, his horse halting just below the rise where she stood. "They're ready," he said, his voice calm, resolute. "The plan is clear. Their spirits are high."

Cecilia nodded but didn't take her eyes off the enemy. "Good," she said evenly. "Because Elinor's army looks like it's been waiting for this moment their entire lives."

"They may have numbers," Marcus added, guiding his horse alongside Adrian's, "but they don't have you."

He met her gaze, firm and unwavering. "That makes all the difference."

A faint smile tugged at Cecilia's lips, though brief and edged with grim determination. "Let's hope you're right," she murmured, her eyes fixed on the distant sea of Elinor's forces. Without looking away, she added, "Signal the archers. Let them know to stand ready. This fight begins the moment she makes her move."

Adrian and Marcus exchanged a glance, then nodded in unison before turning their horses and galloping off, their voices soon lost amid the rising hum of preparation.

Cecilia mounted her steed, a seasoned warhorse bred for the rigours of battle. Like the others, it had been trained not to flinch in chaos, a far cry from the panicked beasts that could turn a skirmish into a slaughter. She adjusted her grip on the hilt of her sword, the leather-wrapped handle familiar and comforting beneath her fingers. The wind shifted, carrying with it the scent of iron, earth, and the dread weight of what was to come.

Across the field, she caught a glimpse of Elinor at the head of her army, her posture radiating certainty. Their eyes met – two queens, two forces of will poised on the edge of war. For a single heartbeat, the world seemed to hold its breath. The air was thick with anticipation, a silent vow of the chaos about to unfold.

Adrian raised his sword in silent readiness beside her, while Marcus's gaze swept the enemy lines, his posture taut with expectation.

Then Elinor moved.

With a flourish, she raised her hand high, a signal, precise and theatrical. The battlefield cracked open. Behind her, Elinor's army surged forward, a tide of steel and fury crashing into motion. The sound of countless boots striking the earth built into a relentless crescendo.

Cecilia didn't look back. She didn't need to. Her army was ready. They trusted her just as she trusted them.

She leaned slightly towards Adrian, her voice low and resolute. "This is it. Let them come."

With that, she wheeled her horse behind the shield wall, positioning herself on a low rise just beyond the front lines. From there, she could oversee the unfolding battle, her vantage point affording her both protection and clarity to issue commands as the storm broke.

"Hold your fire!" Adrian shouted, his voice cutting through the roar of approaching footsteps.

The shield wall stood firm, soldiers shoulder to shoulder, their faces grim with determination. Behind them, archers stood ready, bows taut, waiting for the order.

Cecilia tightened her grip on the reins. Her gaze remained locked on the advancing enemy. Dust kicked up under their march, the thunder of hooves and war cries nearing with terrifying speed.

At the halfway mark, Adrian's sword dropped.

"Now!"

The sky darkened as a storm of arrows loosed from their bows, slicing through the air with a deadly hiss. A shriek of whistles followed, then the dull, brutal thuds of impact. Cries rang out from the front ranks of Elinor's army as the arrows struck home – shields splintering, bodies falling, momentum stuttering.

But the charge didn't break. It simply pressed on.

Adrian's voice rang out once more, clear, firm, and commanding. "Archers, ready!"

His men moved with the ease of repetition, each one nocking a fresh arrow and drawing back their bowstrings in near-perfect unison. Tension rippled through the line like a taut wire; every archer fixed on the advancing enemy as the space between them narrowed with terrifying speed. Adrian raised his arm high.

"Again!"

The next volley soared into the sky, arrows arcing over the field like a dark wave. A second later, they rained down upon the enemy ranks, cutting into the charge with brutal efficiency. Cries of pain pierced the air. Shields rose too late or shattered beneath the impact. Gaps yawned open in the forward ranks as soldiers stumbled, fell, or were dragged down by wounded comrades.

Still, the tide surged forward.

Adrian remained where he stood, an unmoving pillar at the heart of his line, his calm presence anchoring the archers. He cast a glance towards Cecilia, who watched from her rise beyond the shield wall, sharp-eyed and unreadable. She offered a small, almost imperceptible nod, her attention fixed on the flow of enemy movement. From her vantage point, she saw the disruption the arrows had wrought – fractures in Elinor's formation that, with the right pressure, could be turned into vulnerabilities.

"Hold steady!" Adrian bellowed, his voice cutting through the rising din. "Wait for my mark!"

The archers held their ground, muscles coiled, bows drawn once more. Their eyes followed the enemy's regrouping efforts – the press of soldiers trying to reknit broken lines, the renewed push towards the shield wall.

Cecilia's gaze swept the field, her mind racing with possibilities. She leaned towards a waiting messenger, murmuring a set of rapid-fire commands to be carried down the line. Each decision she made hinged on timing, and for now, Adrian and the archers were buying her the seconds she needed.

Adrian's arm rose a final time. "One more!" he shouted.

The last volley loosed as one – a final, thundering curtain of steel and feather. The arrows screamed through the air, descending on the enemy like a judgment. Men cried out. Horses reared. The momentum of the charge wavered.

And yet, even as bodies fell, the wave kept coming.

The clash was imminent – Cecilia felt it in her bones. The time for strategy was nearing over; now came the reckoning of steel and resolve. She straightened, her body taut with readiness, every breath steeped in anticipation. Adrian's commands had given them a crucial edge, and now it fell to her soldiers to hold that line and press it home.

She turned to Adrian, stationed only a few paces away. "Stay close," she said, her tone firm. "I'll need you sharp and ready."

Then, raising her voice so it carried to the nearest captains, she called, "Hold the line! Let them break themselves against us. We are the storm they never saw coming!"

"Hold the line," the cry echoed along the formation, taken up by captains and lieutenants alike.

Then the enemy crashed into them.

The collision was thunderous. Shields groaned under the impact. Bodies slammed into one another with brutal force. Steel clashed in a cacophony of shrieks and sparks. From her vantage point just behind the front, Cecilia saw the shock of impact ripple through her ranks, but the wall held. Her soldiers leaned into the surge, gritting their teeth, answering the chaos with unflinching resolve. The line buckled under pressure, but it didn't break.

Elinor's front ranks pushed forward relentlessly, their momentum like a tidal wave battering against stone. Cecilia could see it in their faces, the desperation, the furious drive to overwhelm. Blades rose and fell, but her soldiers met them with grim efficiency, their shields turning aside what strikes they couldn't return. Above and behind the wall, Adrian's archers continued to rain down arrows, their volleys slicing through the sky and sowing fresh confusion within the enemy's ranks.

The battlefield roiled with motion – shouts, screams, the clash of arms – all flowing like an ungoverned tide. Every moment was a struggle to hold, to withstand, to endure.

Cecilia's gaze swept the field, searching for cracks in the enemy's armour and for signs of strain in her own. Her heart pounded faster as her eyes caught a break forming on the eastern flank. A knot of Elinor's soldiers had driven through, threatening to unravel the line.

She turned sharply to a nearby messenger. "Send reinforcements to the east flank! Tell Marcus to hold the breach—whatever it takes!"

The messenger saluted and galloped off, weaving through the chaos to deliver her command. Cecilia tightened her grip on the reins, her knuckles whitening as she forced herself to stay focused. She couldn't allow the breach to widen; a single crack, left untended, could shatter the entire line.

Before her, the battlefield was a storm of motion and sound. Shouts and screams rose and fell like waves, clashing with the metallic ring of steel, the guttural cries of the wounded, and the relentless roar of men locked in the fury of battle. Her soldiers fought with grim tenacity, holding their ground against the relentless push of Elinor's forces. Through the melee, she spotted Adrian – his tall form unmistakable as he directed the archers with calm efficiency. His voice rose above the chaos, clear and commanding, guiding the rhythm of their volleys. Arrows continued to rain down, slicing into the enemy ranks and stalling their momentum with deadly precision.

Cecilia's gaze shifted to the opposite rise, where Elinor stood apart from the fray. Her posture was composed, her expression cool and unreadable. She watched the battle unfold like a strategist at play, her presence detached, almost clinical, calculating each move like a queen on a chessboard.

Cecilia's jaw tensed. This was war in its rawest form – a test of willpower, of endurance, of whose line would crack first.

She drew a steadying breath and raised her voice once more, firm and resolute. "Stand firm! Hold the line—push them back!"

Her words carried through the din, igniting a fresh surge of resolve. Her soldiers responded with fierce unity, their shields locking tighter, their boots digging into blood-soaked earth as they pressed forward. The enemy met them with equal ferocity, determined to punch through the wall that held them at bay.

Steel bit into steel. The tide swelled, and still, the line held.

Chapter 39

Holding the Line

The battle had raged for hours, and exhaustion was etched into every soldier's face. Adrian felt it deep in his limbs, a dull, relentless ache that made his sword feel heavier with every swing. The sun, now dipping low on the horizon, cast a burnt-orange glow across the field, painting the chaos in surreal, haunting hues.

What had once been a steady rhythm of combat had devolved into a frantic, desperate cacophony. Men stumbled as they fought, their movements sluggish, their strikes less precise. Blood soaked the trampled earth, and the air hung thick with the stench of iron and sweat. Adrian's breath came in ragged gasps, but he pressed on, his blade crashing against the steel of an enemy soldier. He had long since ceased commanding the archers – now he fought in the thick of it, shoulder to shoulder with his comrades.

Elinor's forces were gaining ground. Slowly but surely, they pushed forward, their formations tightening, their discipline unshaken. Adrian cursed under his breath as he parried another blow. Her troops were built for endurance – they had trained for this kind of prolonged combat, and it showed. His own men, valiant though they were, were faltering beneath the strain. He saw it in their eyes, heard it in their strained cries. They were giving everything they had, but even the strongest walls eventually cracked under sustained assault.

His gaze flicked towards the distant rise where Cecilia still held position. She stood resolute amid the chaos, a steady presence that anchored the wavering morale of their lines. As long as she remained unyielding, the soldiers would find the strength to carry on.

Twilight deepened, and with it, the tempo of the battle shifted. The change was unspoken but understood – both sides were tiring. Movements slowed, blows grew fewer, and the clash of steel became sporadic. Adrian knew pressing the fight into the night would only breed confusion and needless death. Retreat was inevitable, at least until dawn.

He deflected another attack, forcing his opponent to retreat with a grunt, then turned to his nearest captain. "Pull the men back," he ordered, voice hoarse but steady. "We regroup and watch the line until morning."

Even as he spoke, a trumpet sounded from Elinor's flank. Her army, too, was withdrawing. Both sides had evidently come to the same conclusion – any further combat tonight would be reckless.

As Adrian returned to camp, he made sure a contingent of patrols would rotate through the night. He wouldn't put it past Elinor to strike under the cover of darkness.

The camp was a patchwork of weariness beneath flickering torchlight, the day's bloodshed weighing heavily on every soul. Near the healer's tent, Adrian leaned against a crate, his sword resting beside him, its once-keen edge dulled from hours of use. His body ached for rest, but rest was a luxury none could afford. The enemy would regroup, just as they would. And with dawn, the slaughter would begin anew.

Around him, the camp stirred with quiet, determined activity. Soldiers limped to their tents or sat huddled in small groups, their faces drawn and hollow with pain. The air reeked of blood and sweat, broken only by the sharp, clean scent of herbs from the priestesses' work. Adrian watched them as they moved among the wounded, hands aglow with faint magic, offering quiet comfort and healing where they could. They didn't bear swords, but their presence was no less vital. Without them, many of these men would never see the next dawn.

His eyes landed on a young soldier – no more than seventeen – being tended by a priestess. The boy winced as her glowing palm pressed to a deep gash along his ribs, the skin slowly knitting closed beneath her touch. Adrian had seen him on the field, fighting with a courage that defied his age. But courage alone was no shield against the horrors of war.

At the heart of the camp, Cecilia's tent stood, its entrance marked by fluttering banners. Through the canvas, Adrian glimpsed her silhouette, bent over maps, absorbed in calculations and reports. Even now, she strategised, searching for a way to turn the tide. He admired her resolve, though it troubled him. She carried the weight of this war as though every life depended solely on her shoulders.

The sound of approaching footsteps pulled him from his thoughts. A messenger came swiftly, his expression grim.

"They've strengthened their perimeter," the man said, voice low. "But movement suggests they expect reinforcements by midday."

Adrian swore under his breath. Elinor wasn't finished. "Tell Cecilia," he said, nodding towards the command tent. "She'll want to hear it."

As the messenger disappeared inside, Adrian turned his gaze towards the fires where his captains gathered, voices hushed as they discussed the morning's strategy. Their next move had to be flawless. They couldn't afford to give Elinor another inch.

He rubbed at his temples, weariness pressing in from all sides. The night was far from over. Wounded still needed tending, sentries needed placing, plans needed sharpening. The priestesses' murmured prayers and glowing hands might soothe the body, but they couldn't mend broken spirits. Hope was harder to restore.

Catching the eye of one captain, Adrian gave a small nod and crossed the camp to join the others. It was time to talk tactics, to brace for what lay ahead. And though exhaustion gnawed at him and dread coiled in his gut, he held on to one fragile hope: that dawn would bring the turning point they so desperately needed, and that the reinforcements they awaited wouldn't arrive too late.

Together, Adrian and the captains entered the tent, stepping into the flickering lamplight to join a weary but unbroken Cecilia.

***

The light of dawn crept over the battlefield, pale and cold. Adrian stood at the edge of the camp, his armour streaked with the grime and blood of the day before. His sword hung at his side, newly sharpened, though it felt heavier in his grip than it ever had.

The morning air was still and biting, a stark contrast to the chaos that had roared through the valley only hours earlier. All around him, his soldiers moved with quiet determination – reinforcing barricades, inspecting weapons, and tightening straps with practised efficiency. The weight of fatigue clung to them, evident in every motion, but their resolve remained intact.

Adrian moved among them, offering brief smiles and words of encouragement. He greeted each face, familiar and new, with calm assurance. Men and women alike acknowledged him with silent nods before returning to their preparations. They were tired, bruised, but unbroken and ready.

His own body ached with every step, a dull pain lingering in his joints and muscles, a reminder of the brutality of yesterday's fight. But there was no time for rest. The coming hours would demand everything they had left – and more. Unless something tipped the balance in their favour, he knew they wouldn't withstand another full day of assault.

"Adrian, there you are."

He turned as Cecilia approached, Aevah at her side. Cecilia's eyes were sharp, her tone brisk.

"Are you ready?" she asked. "Our troops are already in position, awaiting your command."

Adrian gave a short nod. "I'm heading there now. Darius is already on the field, organising the formations and reinforcing the defences."

"Excellent. I'll be out there soon," Cecilia said. "But first, I'm helping Aevah and the priestesses prepare. After yesterday, we need to ensure we have enough medical supplies and resources ready."

Adrian nodded. "Good idea. Hopefully, we won't see as many casualties today."

"Here's hoping," Aevah added. "But we'll be prepared, either way."

Adrian watched the two women head towards the healer's tent, their silhouettes fading into the bustle of camp. He knew how much Cecilia valued having Aevah by her side. Though Aevah shared her friends' strength, she had chosen to serve with the priestesses rather than fight on the front lines. Her power, her gentleness – it was a different kind of strength, but no less vital.

Galrick and Isabella, by contrast, were made for battle, throwing themselves into the conflict without hesitation. Even Nicholas, though stationed behind the lines with the archers, had found his role and held to it with unwavering discipline. Together, they were a force of sheer will. Adrian only hoped they would all make it out of this alive.

As he neared the ridge overlooking the battlefield, he spotted Elinor's army forming ranks once more. Banners snapped sharply in the wind, the crisp morning air cutting through him as he scanned the enemy lines. At first glance, nothing appeared out of the ordinary, just the familiar, grim ritual of soldiers bracing the war.

Then his gaze caught on a figure emerging from the ranks – a tall woman clad in violet and gold, her bearing poised and unshaken.

Adrian's breath hitched.

"Liora," he muttered, the name falling from his lips like a curse. The High Priestess of Elinor's order.

He had heard the stories of her power, her unwavering loyalty, and the devastation her magic could unleash. Her presence here could only mean one thing.

Magic.

A bead of sweat traced a path down his temple despite the cold. This changed everything. His forces were already strained –

exhausted, bloodied, and undersupplied. They couldn't withstand both steel and sorcery without a counterforce of their own.

Spinning on his heel, Adrian strode towards a waiting messenger. "You," he snapped, his voice sharp with urgency. "Ride to camp. Now. Tell them we need the priestesses—every last one of them. No more healers in tents. If Liora's bringing magic to the fight, we'll need our own to stand a chance."

The messenger paled but nodded. "Yes, sir." Without hesitation, he mounted and galloped off, hooves pounding a warning across the ground.

Adrian turned back towards the field, jaw clenched tight. The weight of responsibility pressed down on him like iron. If Elinor's army gained the upper hand now, it could unravel everything they had fought to hold together. He had to buy time – for Cecilia, for reinforcements, for the priestesses to reach them.

"Form up!" Adrian's voice rang out across the camp, loud and commanding. Soldiers jerked to attention, their fatigue momentarily forgotten as urgency crackled through the ranks. He strode to the front lines, positioning himself among them.

"Elinor's bringing her magic today," he called, his voice carrying with grim certainty. "She's brought her priestesses, and they're likely to use their power."

A ripple of unease passed through the lines, murmurs and exchanged glances. The rules of the battlefield had changed, and they all knew it.

"But fear not," Adrian continued, raising his voice above the murmurs. "Our own are on their way. We hold the line until they arrive. No matter what."

In answer, the rebel army began to strike their swords against shields, a steady rhythm rising like a war drum. The pounding grew louder, echoing through the valley like a heartbeat. Sparks flashed where metal met metal. Despite the fear, defiance burned in their eyes.

Then came the advance.

Elinor's first wave surged forward, their war cries tearing through the morning air. Adrian braced himself, sword steady in hand, eyes fixed on the glint of movement beyond the soldiers. Liora and her priestesses stood at the rear, hands raised, their robes billowing like smoke in a breeze. Their formation was flawless, their movements synchronised, too precise, too practised.

A ripple of energy swelled across the field, and Adrian felt it hum through his bones.

Then it began.

Fire ignited from nowhere – searing orbs of flame shot through the air, streaking towards Cecilia's line. Adrian shouted above the chaos, ordering shields to be raised as fireballs slammed into metal and earth. Smoke curled in the air. The ground hissed where the flames struck, leaving scorched, blackened craters in their wake.

And then the wind came.

Not a breeze, but a cyclone – targeted, brutal, summoned by the priestesses' raised arms. It ripped through the front ranks, toppling men, snapping banners, and scattering debris in its wake. Arrows twisted off course mid-flight. Dust and grit stung eyes, blinding soldiers who tried to press forward.

Adrian turned, raising his sword high. "Hold the line!" he bellowed, his voice like iron through the storm. "Magic won't break us!"

The soldiers rallied, their formation tightening despite the elemental onslaught raging around them. They advanced with grim determination – shields angled against the fire, swords raised to meet the winds. Through the chaos, Adrian pressed forward, steel meeting steel while magic swirled and cracked around him.

It was a relentless rhythm – blade against blade, strike after strike. He spun, ducked, and dodged through the melee, taking more lives than he could count. His sword moved as if it were part of him, guided by instinct and sheer will. Faces twisted in rage and terror blurred around him, their screams merging into a jarring symphony of violence. Blood sprayed through the air, warm flecks landing on his skin. Adrian didn't flinch. He couldn't afford to.

Bodies fell all around, friend and foe alike. A young soldier collapsed nearby, clutching a gaping wound that bloomed across his tunic. Adrian recognised him. They had spoken that morning – he had offered a few words of encouragement. Now, that life was gone, extinguished in a heartbeat. But Adrian felt nothing.

There was no time to grieve. On the battlefield, hesitation meant death.

Fireballs continued to fall from the sky, streaking like comets and exploding against shields and the earth. The air reeked of scorched flesh and burning soil. Adrian's lungs burned with every breath, but he kept moving. Each swing of his blade was deliberate. Each step, a calculation. He was no longer a man, but a weapon – sharpened by necessity, forged in desperation.

Winds howled through the ranks, vicious and unnatural. They tore up dust and ash, stinging his eyes and stealing his breath. Through the haze, he glimpsed flashes: Cecilia's banner barely upright in the gale, an enemy falling to a comrade's strike, a broken shield spinning across the mud. None of it felt real.

Adrian moved as though in a trance, his body running on sheer muscle memory. Pain gnawed at his limbs, his arms trembling from the effort of holding his sword, but he ignored it all. One strike, then another. Duck, pivot, parry. The world had narrowed to the motion of battle – the rhythm of survival.

In the distance, he caught sight of Liora, her priestesses unmoved amid the carnage as they continued to unleash wave after wave of elemental fury. Rage flared briefly in his chest, followed by a hollow despair. But he shoved it aside. There was no room for feeling. He was a sword now, and the sword didn't feel.

And so he fought – mind blank, heart armoured, soul numbed.

Until the howling began.

Adrian froze mid-swing, his blade suspended above an enemy's neck. A strange silence swept the battlefield, as if the world itself paused. The howl rose again, low and mournful, like wolves echoing through a mountain pass. No one knew where it came from, or why, but every soldier turned to listen. The sound cut through the clamour like a blade through silk.

His breath caught. For the first time in hours, he felt the rhythm of his heartbeat, thudding loudly in his ears. Around him, weapons lowered. Eyes darted. Confusion spread like wildfire.

The howls grew louder. Closer.

Soldiers on both sides gripped their weapons tightly, gazes shifting towards the dark treeline that bordered the field. Murmurs rippled through the ranks – speculation, fear, disbelief. Wolves never came near battlefields. *What could have drawn them into this blood-soaked chaos?*

Adrian stood still, chest heaving, dread coiling deep in his gut. There was something unnatural in those cries – something ancient and unknowable. A tremor passed through him as the first of them appeared.

From the forest's edge, six shadowy figures emerged, sleek, voracious shapes that seemed to bleed in and out of darkness. The wolves moved with eerie grace, their black coats rippling like mist, their eyes aglow with pale silver fire. They didn't walk so much as glide, vanishing and reappearing as if reality itself couldn't contain them.

Gasps spread through both armies. Soldiers stepped back, uncertain whether to flee or fight. The wolves didn't attack. They formed a silent line between the opposing forces, phasing in and out of sight like restless spirits.

Then another figure stepped forward, and Adrian's breath caught in his throat.

Aevah.

She moved with quiet authority, the faint glow of her magic lighting her path. Behind her came the priestesses, calm and resolute, their presence grounding amidst the chaos. The wolves flanked them like guardians, forming a united front against the storm.

Aevah's eyes locked with Adrian's across the field. Something in that look, something steady and sure, pierced through the numbness. A flicker of hope stirred.

"Aevah," he breathed, lowering his sword slightly.

Murmurs swept through the ranks as soldiers recognised her, recognised the priestesses, and understood. These wolves were not a threat – they were allies. Magical, yes – but theirs. Reinforcements, sent not to destroy, but to protect.

Aevah stopped just short of Adrian, the faintest smile playing at her lips. "You called, and they answered," she said, her voice calm but heavy with meaning. She cast a glance at the shadow wolves, who stood poised and silent, their silver eyes sweeping over the battlefield. "They fight for us."

Adrian exhaled slowly, the tightness in his chest easing as her words sank in. He turned to his soldiers, who stared at the wolves in a mixture of awe and uncertainty.

"They're with us!" he shouted, his voice slicing through the quiet tension. "The wolves are on our side—fight with them, not against them!"

There was only a heartbeat of hesitation before the army rallied. Cries of relief and renewed determination rose into the air like a wave. On the other side of the field, confusion rippled through Elinor's ranks as her soldiers struggled to process what had just unfolded. Adrian turned back to Aevah, a faint smile tugging at his lips.

"Good timing," he said, his voice thick with gratitude.

"I thought so," she replied, her eyes gleaming with quiet confidence. "Let's finish this."

With fluid grace, Aevah and the priestesses advanced, their magic coalescing into waves of radiant light that surged across the battlefield. Their power collided with the tempestuous chaos unleashed by Liora and her priestesses. Where Liora's fury brought fire and storm, Aevah's magic brought balance, a shield that cut through the elemental maelstrom, hammering Cecilia's forces.

The tide began to turn.

The shadow wolves darted through the fray like living phantoms, striking with eerie precision and vanishing before retaliation could land. Panic spread through Elinor's ranks as the beasts tore through soldiers with silent efficiency. Emboldened by the shift, Cecilia's troops surged forward, their blades flashing under the moonlight. The battlefield rang with steel and echoed with the rhythmic thrum of clashing magic, while the wolves moved like whispers of death between the lines.

From a nearby rise, Cecilia watched it all unfold. Her lips curved into a faint smile. What had seemed impossible just hours ago was now within reach – Elinor's army was faltering, ground reclaimed inch by inch. Aevah's presence had anchored their defence; Adrian's unyielding leadership had driven their assault. Cecilia's gaze locked on Elinor, whose frustration now showed plainly, her forces buckling under the pressure.

By night's end, the battle was won. Elinor's troops fled, their banners vanishing into the darkness as they retreated towards their camp. Cecilia remained still, watching Elinor's figure retreat under flickering torchlight. Rage and resentment carved sharp lines across the enemy commander's face, a silent vow that the war was not yet over.

But for now, Cecilia allowed herself a brief, hard-earned moment of satisfaction. They had not only held their ground – they had taken it back.

As the field fell quiet and the soldiers returned to camp, Cecilia, Aevah, and Adrian met at the edge of the battlefield. The shadow wolves approached silently, their silver eyes glowing softly in the night's hush. Adrian lowered his sword, his face drawn with exhaustion but brightened by relief.

Aevah stepped forward, inclining her head respectfully. "You came when we needed you most. For that, we are grateful."

The largest wolf – tall, sleek, and formidable – met her gaze. "You called, and we came, as promised. It was an honour to fight beside you, young one."

Then, with a final nod, the wolves began to fade. Shadows rippled across their forms as they turned, melting back into the darkness from which they came. They moved without a sound, vanishing into the mountains like a dream dissolving at dawn.

To them, all the wolves' forms began shifting subtly as shadows flickered around them.

Adrian watched them disappear, his voice low. "They were… remarkable."

"They were," Aevah agreed softly. She turned towards Cecilia, who stood tall despite her fatigue, one hand resting on Adrian's shoulder.

"Today, we survived," Cecilia said. "Tomorrow, we fight again."

The three stood in silence, gazing out over the scarred earth as the first stars pierced the sky. There was still a long road ahead, but for now, they had earned this moment, and they held it close.

Chapter 40

The Cost of Power

The world lay frozen in the hush of early dawn, frost glittering like shattered glass across a battlefield steeped in loss. The air was crisp, each breath she exhaled spiralling into a fleeting mist before vanishing into the pale, cold light, a chilling reminder of the lives lost and the fragile resolve of her weary army.

Elinor sat at the head of her table in the command tent, her shoulders rigid despite the warmth radiating from the brazier nearby. The flickering fire cast faint shadows across her skin. She hadn't slept. Fury burned low and constant in her chest, kindled by the memory of yesterday's chaos – of Cecilia's army gaining ground, despite every tactic she had unleashed. But today would be different. It had to be.

The wolves, phantoms born of mist, and Aevah's priestesses had twisted the battle into something nightmarish, far removed from her meticulous plans. Even her vast power had met its match in those creatures of myth and sacred magic. The sting of humiliation still clung to her, sharper than the frost biting at the camp's edges.

The wolves gnawed at her still—not with teeth, but with memory. Childhood whispers made flesh. They moved with otherworldly precision, tearing through her soldiers one by one. She had tried to strike them down, her magic crashing against theirs like stone on water, rippling, but ineffective. The battlefield had become their domain, and she, despite all her power, had been reduced to a spectator.

She had made certain Liora understood what failure would mean if this day ended as poorly as the last. Elinor wouldn't tolerate incompetence. Not now. Not ever.

Still, she wouldn't yield. Today, her reinforcements were set to arrive. And with them, her victory.

Across from her, Bradley tore into a hunk of bread while scanning the latest reports. His posture was easy, his manner unshaken, a strange calm had settled over the camp, one she hadn't expected so soon after the slaughter. Despite the losses they had suffered, despite the wolves, the priestesses, and Cecilia's relentless advance, hope had crept back in. The men dared to believe.

For Elinor, it was a fragile reprieve from the fury that had kept her sleepless. The battlefield had tested her limits, both as a commander and a wielder of power, and the taste of failure still lingered bitter on her tongue. But watching Bradley's quiet confidence, she felt it too: the promise of victory.

“By noon,” she said, her voice bright with barely contained delight, “this shall be over. Cecilia’s forces will break under the next wave. Her defiance will finally end.”

Bradley looked up, a wry smile curving his lips. “Confidence suits you, my lady,” he said, chewing thoughtfully. “The men feel it too. They’re ready. One more push, and we’ll crush what’s left of her line.”

Elinor leaned back in her chair, letting Bradley’s words settle around her. She picked absently at a plate of fruit and cheese, the meal mostly untouched. Her appetite had been dulled by the electric pulse of anticipation running through her.

“And by mid-morning,” she murmured, her voice a velvet purr laced with quiet satisfaction, “Lord Stone’s troops will arrive—fresh, rested, and ready to grind Cecilia’s army into the dirt. She doesn’t have the numbers anymore. Not with Stone on our side.”

Bradley’s brows furrowed slightly. “And we can trust him?”

Her smile turned sharp. “With his daughter still in my clutches, he has no choice.”

He chuckled, the sound low and certain. “Then it’s done,” he said, nodding. “The men will feast tonight. And Cecilia—she’ll finally learn what defiance costs.”

Elinor’s smile widened as she reached for her goblet. The wine was dark and rich, its warmth blooming through her with each sip. Everything was falling into place. Weeks of planning, positioning, and relentless precision had led to this moment. She was winning – and soon, Cecilia's banner would fall.

The thought sent a delicious shiver down her spine. There had been moments, rare and fleeting, when doubt had crept in. Cecilia was cunning, resourceful, and a worthy opponent. But Elinor had always known she would prevail. And now, the final move was within reach.

Even with wolves and borrowed magic, Cecilia would be no match for the flood of soldiers at Elinor's command, nor the priestesses she had bent to her will – powerful, unwavering, and prepared to turn the tide. And when the final blow came, delivered by Elinor's hand, it would be swift, precise, and merciless. They wouldn't see it coming.

Outside, the camp stirred. Soldiers readied themselves for the assault ahead, the click of armour and the rasp of whetstones rising in rhythm with the cawing of ravens perched among the skeletal trees. It was a good day to win a war.

Bradley brushed the crumbs from his hands and leaned forward, his tone more measured now. "We should have a message ready for Lord Stone the moment his troops arrive. They'll need clear direction, and we'll need them to strike hard and fast."

"Of course," Elinor said smoothly, setting her goblet down. "Have the runners prepared. We'll attack from every side, overwhelm her before she can regroup."

She allowed herself a beat of silence, savouring the image of Cecilia's line breaking, her troops scattering, her proud defences crumbling beneath the weight of Elinor's fury. By midday, this battlefield would be hers.

And Cecilia, unyielding, infuriating Cecilia, would be nothing more than a memory.

***

Elinor stood atop the ridge, her breath curling into the frosty morning air. The sun had risen, casting a pale, wintry light over the chaos below. She drew her cloak tighter around her shoulders, her gaze sharp and unyielding as it swept across the battlefield. Blades clashed with the harsh ring of steel, while bursts of magic flared like distant fireworks, their glow dancing eerily over the frost-covered ground. It was terrible and beautiful. And it was hers.

Her plan was unfolding exactly as intended. Cecilia's forces were beginning to buckle, their defences cracking under the relentless onslaught. Wave after wave pressed forward, and with each surge, her enemy faltered further. The priestesses who had allied with Cecilia had proven to be a nuisance, but they were no match for the raw power wielded by Liora's group.

Aevah, notably, had yet to enter the fray, a curious misstep on Cecilia's part. Elinor knew the girl was formidable; her absence made little tactical sense. Perhaps Cecilia was holding her back for a final gambit. But for now, with the wolves conspicuously absent, Elinor's soldiers had turned their full attention to the offensive, tearing through the rebel ranks with ruthless precision.

A small, satisfied smile curved her lips.

Bradley stood beside her, one hand resting lightly on the hilt of his sword. “It’s nearly done,” he said, his voice low and calm. “Another hour, maybe two, and her line will collapse.”

Elinor nodded, her chest swelling with pride. “Indeed. And now that Lord Stone’s troops have arrived… Cecilia may have fought well, but numbers win wars—and she no longer has them.”

Her eyes shifted westward, catching sight of fluttering banners cresting the distant hills – Lord Stone’s army. Just as she had anticipated. A triumphant warmth bloomed in her chest at the sight. The reinforcements were everything she had hoped for: fresh, disciplined, and perfectly positioned to sweep across the battlefield and crush the rebels beneath their boots.

Turning back to the field, she watched with growing satisfaction as Liora unleashed another devastating spell, a storm of magical fire tearing through the enemy’s front line. Cecilia’s soldiers scrambled to respond, their priestesses weaving desperate barriers to stem the assault.

It was almost poetic; the battlefield itself seemed to bend before her will. Every piece was in motion, every move accounted for. Victory wasn’t just possible now. It was inevitable.

But then, the shift came.

Elinor's smile faltered as she caught a ripple of unease spreading through her ranks. Movements that had been swift and purposeful moments before turned sluggish, uncertain. A frown creased her brow as she scanned the field for the source of the disruption, and then she saw it.

Lord Stone's army had arrived. But something was wrong.

They weren't reinforcing her lines. They weren't moving towards Cecilia's forces. Instead, they were turning – pivoting with military precision – and raising their weapons against her troops.

The first strike hit like a thunderclap. A brutal wave of force crashed into her flank, sending her men reeling. Shouts of confusion and panic rang through the air as Stone's soldiers surged forward, cutting down her warriors with merciless precision.

Her heart pounded against her ribs, disbelief and fury churning in her chest. Her mind scrambled to make sense of the betrayal.

"No," she whispered, the word barely audible above the din of chaos. "No, this isn't—"

The sentence broke apart as she turned her gaze southward, and her blood ran cold.

Another force had crested the horizon. Rebel banners rippled in the cold breeze as soldiers thundered forward, shouting with grim resolve. They rushed to fill the gaps in Cecilia's faltering line, their timely arrival turning the tide of battle in a single, stunning moment.

"How?" she uttered, stunned. No one alive should have been capable of hiding an entire army from view, certainly not from her scouts, who had reported only Lord Stone's movement. No signs. No warnings.

She clutched the edge of the ridge, her knuckles whitening with the force of her grip. Everything – her strategy, her impending triumph – was unravelling before her eyes. Victory, once so close she could taste it, was slipping through her fingers like water.

She spun towards Bradley, her voice cutting like a blade. "Send word to regroup. Pull the men back—now!"

He hesitated, his face pale with shock. "But—"

"Do it!" she snapped, her command cracking like a whip through the rising storm.

Her gaze returned to the battlefield. Her forces were crumbling, squeezed between two fronts. Rage flared inside her – hot, volatile, desperate – but she shoved it down. She couldn't afford to lose control. Not now.

She needed clarity. She needed a plan.

Below, Cecilia's troops rallied with renewed strength, their momentum redoubled by the reinforcement from the south. Lord Stone's betrayal had driven a knife deep into her side, and the arrival of the hidden rebels twisted it mercilessly.

This was no battle. It was a trap. And she had walked straight into it.

But Elinor was not one to flee. Not yet.

She straightened her spine, eyes locked on the chaos below and stepped forward – into the storm.

The battlefield was hers – a brutal symphony of confusion, rage, and dominance. Magic clashed with steel beneath her command, and with every step Elinor took, the ground hissed and steamed, frost scorched away by the remnants of her power. Her long cloak flared behind her, its edges singed and smoking. Lightning crackled at her fingertips, and her lips curled into a triumphant smile as jagged bolts tore through the sky, striking with deafening force and scattering Cecilia's ranks in wild disarray. Fire followed in sweeping waves, roaring across the field, devouring everything in its path.

The enemy's shield wall faltered, then buckled entirely. Victory was no longer a possibility – it was certainty.

Each spell sent adrenaline surging through her veins. She was the storm incarnate. Soldiers collapsed around her, their screams lost in the roar of elemental fury. It was intoxicating, the way the tide of battle obeyed her will, the way the very earth seemed to bend beneath the weight of her power. Elinor let out a breathless laugh, exultant, as she hurled another wave of fire towards the crumbling front line.

But then it came.

A chill swept across the battlefield like the breath of winter, piercing through the blistering heat of her flames. Elinor froze. The euphoria drained from her limbs, replaced by something sharper, colder. Her spine stiffened. Instinct prickled at the edge of her awareness.

The battlefield stilled in a way that made no sense. The noise faded, and the smoke hung suspended in the air. The atmosphere shifted – no longer saturated with her magic, but tinged with something unfamiliar. Older. Other.

From the veil of smoke and ash, a figure stepped forward.

She was draped in tattered robes, her frame slight, almost fragile, utterly different from the ruin that surrounded her. Yet it was her eyes that rooted Elinor to the spot: ancient, piercing, brimming with a power Elinor didn't recognise and couldn't begin to fathom.

The battlefield seemed to bow beneath that gaze. Time itself held its breath.

Elinor's victorious smile vanished. Her heart twisted violently in her chest, a sensation she hadn't felt in years.

Fear.

It clawed at the edges of her confidence, coiling tight as the old woman raised a withered hand and, with effortless grace, unravelled the firestorm raging across the battlefield. Flames vanished into thin air, smothered by a force that Elinor couldn't see, let alone understand.

Lightning crackled in her clenched fists. The air shivered with the weight of her fury as she unleashed a bolt straight towards the woman. But the strike never landed. It fizzled out mid-air, absorbed by nothing, erased by something. Again and again, she attacked. Each surge of power was extinguished without effort, as though the very elements had been turned against her.

Every failed strike was a blow to her dominance. A mockery of her power.

The battlefield no longer bent to her will.

It bent to hers.

"What—" Elinor began, but the words withered on her tongue. Gritting her teeth, she summoned another volley of power, her hands blazing with fury. With a cry of defiance, she hurled the lightning again.

It vanished just like the others.

Her breath came in ragged bursts, panic rising in her throat. She clung to her magic like a lifeline, summoning more, pouring her desperation into one final, furious strike. But the old woman simply watched her, eyes ageless and unmoved, her faint smile deepening with quiet certainty.

She already knew Elinor would fail.

The lightning died before reaching its mark.

Around her, the battlefield dissolved into chaos. Her soldiers screamed and stumbled, overwhelmed by the renewed ferocity of Cecilia's forces. The enemy tore through her lines with brutal precision. And at the centre of it all, the woman stood untouched – her calm, unyielding gaze never leaving Elinor.

"No!" Elinor screamed, her voice cracking under the weight of desperation. She scanned the field, eyes wide, searching for anything – anyone – that could turn the tide.

But all she saw was ruin. Her army crumbled, betrayed and overrun, the proud ranks that once marched beneath her banner reduced to dying shadows under the blades of traitors and rebels.

Her chest constricted, the weight of failure crushing her from within. This wasn't how it was supposed to end. She was meant to be victorious. Untouchable.

Instead, she stood powerless, her world collapsing around her.

"Fall back!" she cried, her voice cutting through the cacophony. "Pull back to the castle—now!"

The order met with hesitation. Her soldiers faltered, uncertain. Bradley appeared at her side, his sword bloodied, his expression strained. "My lady?"

"Retreat!" she snapped, shoving him towards the rear lines. "We can't hold this ground! Get them behind the walls—now!"

Julian stumbled up beside her, his armour streaked with blood, face pale with disbelief. "Elinor, we—"

"Do it, Julian!" she sneered, voice trembling with the force of her fear. "Get them inside, or we are finished!"

As her forces began to withdraw in frantic disarray, Elinor's eyes returned to the old woman, still standing, untouched amid the carnage. And then, to Elinor's horror, the woman tilted her head, her smile widening by the smallest, cruellest fraction.

The sight shattered something deep within her. Her hands trembled. Her certainty splintered.

For the first time in her life, Elinor understood what it meant to be hunted. To be outmatched. Her power, her cunning – none of it mattered.

Not against this.

The woman's gaze told her everything she needed to know.

This was her end.

Chapter 41

The Tide Turns

Cecilia stood at the edge of the battlefield, her sword still in hand, the metallic tang of blood and smoke thick in the air. She could scarcely believe it. Victory, improbable and stunning, was within reach. Two allied armies had come to her aid, swelling her ranks and turning the tide of what had seemed an unwinnable battle. Elinor's once-dominant forces were now retreating, scattering into disarray as they fled towards the safety of the castle.

Her gaze drifted to the old woman who had emerged from the chaos, her presence commanding and otherworldly. Cecilia's heart quickened as recognition dawned. It was the same woman she had met at the inn, the one who had told her where to find her children. Mysterious then, but now – now Cecilia was certain she was no ordinary traveller.

She had watched the woman counter Elinor's attacks with impossible precision, wielding a power that defied comprehension. Lightning and fire had clashed in the skies, but the woman's command of the elements was absolute. Every strike Elinor unleashed was met, absorbed, and rendered meaningless. The sheer magnitude of her strength was unlike anything Cecilia had ever witnessed. It had left Elinor retreating, her once-unshakeable confidence giving way to something that resembled fear.

And yet, there was no time to dwell on questions. Cecilia didn't know who the woman truly was, but she knew enough to be grateful. The tide had turned, and she wouldn't squander the gift.

As the enemy fled, Cecilia raised her voice above the din. "Let them go!" she commanded, her tone resolute. "Hold the line and regroup. This is not over."

Her soldiers obeyed, pulling back to reform their ranks. The wounded were tended to, the weary given a moment's respite, but the tension remained thick in the air. The castle loomed in the distance, its stone walls a formidable barrier yet to be breached.

Adrian approached, his smile faint and laced with exhaustion. She turned to him.

"The old woman," she murmured, her eyes still fixed on the field. "Has she said anything?"

He shook his head. "No. But her power… I've never seen anything like it. Whoever she is, she sent Elinor running."

Cecilia nodded, though her thoughts spun with unanswered questions. She stepped towards the woman, who stood poised and calm, a gentle smile on her face as if she had been waiting.

"Hello," Cecilia began, her voice firm yet measured. "I wanted to thank you for what you've done. I am Cecilia, and—"

The woman lifted a frail hand, palm outward, stopping her mid-sentence. Her expression deepened, kind and serene, but imbued with an unspoken authority that rooted Cecilia where she stood.

"I know who you are," the woman said, her voice low and steady, carrying the weight of centuries. "There is no need for thanks."

Cecilia blinked, caught off guard. "But—"

The woman's smile softened. She spoke again before Cecilia could finish. "You and I will speak again, child. When the time is right."

Then, without a whisper of warning, she was gone.

Cecilia remained frozen, the world around her resuming its chaotic rhythm, yet she felt unmoored, as if a thread she hadn't known was tethering her had been suddenly cut.

What just happened?

Adrian's voice pulled her back. "Cecilia? What just happened? Where did she go?"

She turned to him, her expression unreadable, and shook her head. "I don't know." But even as the mystery lingered, she forced herself to focus. The battle wasn't finished.

She turned towards her army. Their banners mingled with her own, and as she scanned the crowd, her breath caught. Standing near the centre of the group was a man she hadn't expected to see – his greying hair and lined face unmistakable.

Walter.

A friend of her father's and a figure from her past, his presence struck her with unexpected force. For a moment, she hesitated, unsure if her eyes deceived her. Then he stepped forward, his expression softening into a warm smile.

"Walter," she said as she crossed the distance between them. "I'm so pleased you made it in time."

"Life has a way of bringing people together at the right moment," he replied, his voice steady, carrying the weight of years. "It's good to see you, my dear. Your father would be proud of the leader you've become."

She swallowed hard, his words hitting her with a bittersweet ache. "Thank you. That means more than I can say."

He smiled knowingly. "I've been travelling across the country, recruiting new allies to our cause," he said, gesturing to a figure stepping forward from the crowd. "This man will be unfamiliar to you. He comes from a secretive, hidden home in the desert. But your children know him well—he helped them when they needed it most."

Cecilia's gaze sharpened as she studied the man approaching. His features were weathered by the desert sun, his demeanour calm, and he exuded a quiet wisdom. There was something in the way he moved – with confidence and serenity – that marked him as someone extraordinary. Though she had never met him before, something about him felt reassuring.

The man inclined his head in greeting. "Cecilia," he said, his voice deep and steady. "It's an honour to meet you. I'm Isaac, from the desert. I crossed paths with Aevah and Jacob in their time of need."

Her brows drew together in interest. "You helped them?" she asked, her voice tinged with curiosity. "How?"

Isaac offered a faint, knowing smile. "Let's just say my people provided them refuge when they had nowhere else to turn. It's a longer story—one we'll speak about when time allows."

Before she could respond, Walter stepped aside, revealing a young boy peeking nervously out from behind him. The boy, no older than ten, clung to Walter's cloak, his wide eyes darting between Cecilia and Isaac.

"And this," Walter said gently, placing a reassuring hand on the child's shoulder, "is Timmy—the boy George left in my care. I've protected him ever since. But now… I thought it was time he came here. He needed to see the fight his family has been part of."

Cecilia crouched slightly, her expression softening as she addressed the boy. “Hello,” she said gently. “You’re safe here. George would be so proud of you.”

Timmy’s response was anything but shy. He grinned broadly and puffed out his chest. “Thank you, ma’am,” he said, his voice bright with enthusiasm and a boldness that defied his small frame. “I’m ready to help however I can. Gramps said it’s important to stand up for what’s right—and I’m going to!”

Cecilia blinked, momentarily caught off guard by the boy’s fearless resolve. Then a soft laugh escaped her. “It seems my father taught you well,” she said, rising to her full height. “You’ll grow into a fine young man, Timmy.”

Walter chuckled, resting a hand on the boy’s shoulder. “He’s got George’s spirit, that’s for sure,” he said, pride woven through his voice.

Turning back to Walter and Isaac, Cecilia’s expression grew resolute. “Thank you for bringing him here. And thank you both for standing with us. Your support means more than I can express.”

Isaac nodded, his gaze steady. “We all have our part to play. Whatever comes next, you won’t face it alone.”

Walter added firmly, “We’re here to finish this fight by your side.”

A spark of determination ignited within her. These allies, new and old, were more than reinforcements. They were reminders of what they fought for, of the lives and futures they hoped to protect. She drew a deep breath, her resolve solidifying.

"Then let's make it count," she said, her voice firm. "Together."

Her soldiers rallied at her words, their cheers ringing through the cold air, cries of defiance and fierce hope. For a moment, Cecilia allowed herself a breath of quiet optimism as she surveyed the blood-stained battlefield. Elinor had fallen back, but victory remained uncertain. The castle loomed in the distance, its walls casting long shadows across the broken earth. Breaching it would take more than courage. It would demand cunning, precision, and a unity that couldn't be shaken.

Knowing her army needed rest before the next battle, Cecilia called for them to stand down and make camp. Fires were lit, wounds were tended, and the low murmurs of tired voices filled the air as the soldiers settled in for a hard-earned reprieve. Yet even as her people regrouped, Cecilia's thoughts refused to quiet.

She made her way to the command tent, Adrian's steady footsteps trailing behind her. Inside, Aevah and the council stood waiting, their gazes fixed on the war table, already spread with maps and markers indicating Elinor's defensive positions and the castle's formidable fortifications.

Cecilia paused at the threshold, taking in the scene. The lamplight cast a soft glow over Aevah's sharp features, her expression unreadable, yet brimming with restrained energy.

"What are your thoughts?" Aevah asked, her tone direct.

Cecilia stepped forward, her eyes sweeping across the map. She inhaled slowly, then spoke, her voice low but sure, steady and commanding.

"I have a plan."

And as silence fell across the tent, she began to lay it out – every step, every risk – etched with clarity and purpose.

The main army would stage a false assault on the castle's front, drawing Elinor's forces to defend the most obvious point of attack. Meanwhile, a smaller, stealthier unit would slip through the city and navigate a long-abandoned escape route – one Cecilia herself had once used – to infiltrate the castle. Once inside, they would seize control of the gatehouse, open the main entrance and allow the full force of the army to surge in.

"There's one rule above all," Cecilia said, her voice sharp and commanding. "The city's civilians are not to be harmed. They are our people, and this is their home. We move carefully, swiftly, and with purpose. Our goal is Elinor—nothing else."

Aevah nodded, her gaze unwavering. Adrian folded his arms, brow furrowed in thought.

"It's risky," he said. "But if we pull it off—"

"We will," Cecilia cut in, her tone unyielding. "We must."

"And we shall," Aevah replied. Then her voice shifted, firm but controlled. "But I have one request. Elinor—she's mine to face."

"No." Cecilia's response came swiftly, her voice hard. "Leave her to me."

"Mother," Aevah said, not flinching, "she wields power you can't match. I've trained for this. I'm already bonded to two of the shards—just like her. We'll be evenly matched."

Before Cecilia could speak, High Priestess Zara stepped forward. "She is right," the priestess said calmly. "My sisters and I bonded with Elinor. We've seen her strength. You can't rival it. But Aevah can. Trust in your daughter."

Cecilia's jaw tightened, her gaze flicking between Aevah and Zara. Their words pressed against her pride, and the walls of the command tent felt suddenly close, suffocating. She wanted to argue, to reject the notion, to protect Aevah from the danger that loomed ahead.

But she couldn't deny the truth. Aevah was right.

Cecilia exhaled slowly, the resistance slipping from her shoulders. "Fine," she said at last, her voice low and reluctant. "But you don't face her alone. We confront her together—no matter what."

Before anyone could respond, Marcus stepped forward, his voice deep and resolute as it cut through the charged silence. "Then it's settled. For now, we rest. Before the sun rises tomorrow, we attack."

His words hung in the air, final and absolute. Around the table, the council exchanged nods, their faces set with grim determination. The tension began to ease as they quietly dispersed, leaving Cecilia standing alone amid the dim glow of the lanterns.

Tomorrow, it would begin and end.

Bone-weary and desperate for even a few hours of rest, Cecilia stepped out into the night and made her way towards her quarters. But before she could reach them, she found one last group of people waiting for her.

Chapter 42

Falling Apart

Elinor paced the castle hall, her footsteps echoing off the cold stone floor as the storm within her threatened to consume her. Her hands trembled, faint sparks of energy crackling at her fingertips – power she struggled to contain. Though she had retreated to the supposed safety of the fortress, the walls now felt like a cage. Outside, the inevitable attack loomed. Inside, her fury simmered on the verge of eruption.

Her soldiers scrambled to prepare the defences, their movements quick but disorganised under the weight of her palpable rage. The very air around her felt charged, like the heart of a gathering tempest. She turned sharply as a hapless soldier, trembling under her gaze, fumbled and dropped his weapon at her feet.

"Useless!" she snarled, raising a hand. Before the man could utter a word, a jagged arc of energy lashed out, striking him down where he stood. His body crumpled to the ground, lifeless. A suffocating silence descended, and the soldiers around her froze. None dared to move, as if motion itself might provoke her wrath.

Elinor's breath came in short, ragged bursts. Her chest heaved, the storm inside spiralling further out of control. Her gaze swept the hall, landing on a familiar cluster of figures. Liora and the other priestesses. They stood apart from the chaos, an island of irritating calm in the maelstrom of her fury. Elinor's focus narrowed, her rage honing to a singular point.

"You!" she cried, her voice sharp and venomous. She stormed towards them, power crackling in her wake. The soldiers parted like frightened sheep. "This is your doing! How is this happening? Who was that woman—who wielded that power?!"

Liora opened her mouth to answer, but before she could speak, Elinor struck. A pulse of raw energy burst outward, crashing into the priestesses and sending them to their knees. Their cries echoed through the hall as they clutched their heads, agony twisting their faces.

"You were supposed to help me," Elinor sneered, each word steeped in accusation. "You were supposed to make me invincible. And now you cower—cowards!—while my enemies draw closer!"

Her fury surged anew, and the magic in the air turned volatile, trembling with dangerous potential. Yet even through the pain, Liora lifted her head. Her eyes met Elinor's with a flicker of defiance. The sight only poured fuel on the fire. Elinor raised her hand again, laughter bursting from her lips – dark, cruel, and fraying at the edges with madness.

But she hesitated.

Her thoughts shifted, veering towards desperation as they searched for answers amidst the chaos. Abruptly, she turned to the nearest soldiers.

"Where is Lord Stone's daughter?" she demanded. "If he betrayed us, she must have escaped. Someone bring her to me!"

Minutes dragged by, heavy with dread. The tension in the hall was thick enough to choke on. Then, at last, Mistress Fleur appeared. Her steps were slow, hesitant. Her head remained bowed, and her every movement radiated reluctance.

"Your Majesty," she said, her voice trembling, "I… I don't know how, but Lady Rosalind—she's gone. I'm sorry, my lady. I… I truly am."

Elinor froze. The words hit her like a blow to the chest. Her lips parted in disbelief. For a breathless moment, all was still – a fragile, trembling calm.

Then it shattered.

Her laughter rang out, sharp and discordant, echoing through the hall like breaking glass. It was laughter, devoid of joy, manic and unsettling, each note drawing her soldiers further away, their faces pale masks of horror.

Abruptly, the laughter ceased.

She turned on Mistress Fleur, her expression twisting into something monstrous. "You useless bitch!" she spat. And before anyone could stop her, Elinor lunged forward, her hands closing around Fleur's throat with terrifying force.

She choked the life from her barehanded, watching as the woman's eyes bulged in panic, her fingers clawing at Elinor's skin. Blood welled beneath her grip, but she welcomed the sting – it fed the fire, sharpened the edges of her fury. Fleur's struggles weakened. Her limbs trembled. Her terror remained.

Then a voice broke through the haze.

"Elinor, stop. She is gone."

Bradley. His hand was on her arm, his voice low but steady. She stilled, her breath ragged, her gaze locking with his. Her eyes burned with rage, but behind it, buried deep, something else flickered – something uncertain, fragile, afraid.

The storm in her mind faltered.

Slowly, her thoughts cleared. The full weight of what she had done pressed down on her, and she turned towards him fully. Her fiery gaze met his, heat pulsing behind her eyes, wild enough to turn steel to ash.

But Bradley didn't flinch.

Her lips parted as if to speak, but instead she straightened, pulling her arm free of his grasp with a sharp motion. Rising to her full height, she seemed to command the very air around her, her presence crackling with barely contained power.

"Fortify this castle," she ordered, her voice steady and slicing through the thick tension like a blade. "Cecilia will not win." There was no trace of doubt in her tone, only fury. Her words landed like thunder, leaving no room for hesitation.

Without another word, she turned on her heel, the dark folds of her cloak sweeping behind her as she strode from the hall. Her footsteps rang out against the stone, each one a beat of defiance. She didn't glance back. She didn't acknowledge the uneasy silence left in her wake.

For a moment, her soldiers remained frozen, fear rooting them to the spot. Then, galvanised by her command, they erupted into motion – barking orders, dragging supplies, reinforcing the castle's defences with a newfound urgency.

Elinor's mind roiled as she approached her chambers. Torchlight danced across the stone walls, casting shifting shadows that mirrored her turbulent thoughts. The fury within her had not abated. If anything, it burned hotter, stoked by betrayal and the looming spectre of failure. She could not – would not – fail.

She stormed into her room, slamming the heavy door shut behind her. The echo rang out like a challenge. Her breathing was uneven, her hands trembling with the power surging through her. Her gaze immediately landed on Lady Chloe.

The young woman sat rigidly in a chair near the hearth, her face pale and drawn. Cradled in her arms was Elinor's son. The boy slept peacefully, oblivious to the chaos beyond the chamber walls. The sight brought Elinor to a sudden halt, her fury momentarily dulled by a surge of unexpected emotions.

"Your Majesty…" Chloe began, her voice barely above a whisper. She clutched the child tighter, her apprehension clear.

Elinor didn't let her finish. She crossed the room in a heartbeat and swept the boy from Chloe's arms. Holding him close, she dropped to her knees, pressing her face into his soft curls. Her body trembled. Her breath came in shudders. But the warmth of her son in her arms grounded her – if only for a moment.

"This is all for you," she whispered fiercely, her voice quivering yet resolute. She stroked his hair, her fingers brushing his cheeks as if to assure herself he was real. "I will not fail. I swear to you, my darling—I will not let them take what is ours."

Eadric stirred, murmuring in his sleep, his small hands curling gently against her. The flickering lantern light bathed them in a golden glow, softening the harsh lines of Elinor's face and illuminating the fierce determination returning to her eyes.

She rose and moved towards the edge of the room. Lady Chloe still sat motionless, her hands clenched in her lap. At last, she found the courage to speak.

"What happened, my lady?" she asked, her voice shaking.

Elinor turned, her gaze sharp and unyielding. "Cecilia," she said, spitting the name like poison. "She has the upper hand. Lord Stone betrayed us. Mistress Fleur let his daughter escape." Her tone darkened with every word, venom seeping into each syllable.

"But it doesn't matter. This castle will hold. I will not let Cecilia take what is mine. I will see her dead."

Chloe's eyes widened, her lips parting in shock, but she dared not speak further. The air between them hung heavy, laden with tension. Elinor's expression softened only slightly as she looked once more to her son, her fingers brushing gently through his hair.

"No matter what happens," she murmured, her voice quieter but no less determined, "you are to protect him. Swear it to me."

Lady Chloe nodded without hesitation, her voice firm despite its tremble. "I swear, my lady. With my life."

Satisfied, Elinor crossed to the bed. The weight of exhaustion and fury pressed heavily against her shoulders as she lay down, her son still nestled in her arms. She began to hum – a soft, broken melody that echoed like a lullaby through the quiet room, wrapping them in a fragile cocoon of calm. Her fingers traced his cheek as she sang, a promise woven into every note: safety, victory, a future untouched by war.

The door creaked open, and Elinor looked up to find Bradley stepping inside. He said nothing as he moved to the bed, lying down on the other side of their child. His presence was quiet, steady – a counterweight to the chaos raging beyond the walls.

Their son rested peacefully between them, his breath rising and falling in a rhythm that steadied both of theirs. Neither spoke. The silence was heavy, but it was shared. In that moment, they were not rulers or soldiers or enemies.

They were simply parents, watching over the only thing that still felt pure in a world on the brink of ruin.

Chapter 43

Breaking The Gate

Adrian stood at the head of the formation, his breath misting in the cold morning air as he surveyed the castle's looming walls. This was exactly where Elinor would expect to find him at the forefront, leading what looked like a full-scale assault. Every movement, every detail, had to sell the illusion. She needed to believe this was their real strategy.

Behind him, his soldiers stood ready, expressions steeled with determination. They awaited his command, weapons gripped tightly, banners fluttering in the breeze like defiant warnings. From the ramparts, Elinor's forces stirred, falling into formation as defences snapped into place. Good. Let them see. Let them believe the storm would crash against their gates.

Adrian's thoughts flicked to Cecilia and Aevah, already slipping through the hidden passage on the castle's far side. While he held Elinor's forces at the front, the real mission would begin in silence and shadow. The weight of the plan pressed down on him – its success hinged on flawless timing. One misstep, and the entire effort could unravel.

A flicker of doubt tried to worm its way in, but he crushed it. There was no room for second-guessing now. The moment had arrived.

He lifted his sword, its blade catching the weak light of dawn, and turned to face his men.

"Hold steady," he commanded. "We wait for the signal. When it comes, we give them a battle they'll never forget."

A low murmur rolled through the ranks in response. Adrian turned back to the castle, his jaw set, his eyes scanning the sky. Let Elinor think she held the advantage. He would play his part to the letter – and trust that Cecilia and Aevah would play theirs.

Then he saw it, a black raven slicing through the clouds like a silent omen. It soared above the battlefield, a dark arrow marking the moment.

His breath caught. This was it.

Adrian raised his sword high, steel flashing, and bellowed with all the force he could summon: "Now! Attack!"

The shout tore through the air, echoing over the ranks of soldiers already braced for action. In an instant, the army surged forward, shields raised as the first volley of arrows rained down from the castle walls. The thud of arrowheads slamming into shields and the cries of those less fortunate rang in Adrian's ears.

Still, he pressed on, shouting orders above the chaos as his forces advanced.

At the front, the lead unit charged with battering rams, their strides heavy against the earth. With a thunderous crash, they struck the castle gates, the reinforced doors shuddering but holding. Again, they hit – wood splintering, sweat glistening on their brows – while defenders above poured down arrows and boiling oil.

On the flanks, soldiers hoisted ladders against the walls, climbing with frantic determination. Steel clashed as they reached the ramparts and met Elinor's defenders head-on. The ascent was brutal, but they clawed their way upward, refusing to yield.

Adrian's focus never wavered from the gates. Each strike of the ram chipped at the defences, and with every blow, victory felt closer even as chaos exploded around him. The battering ram slammed into the doors once more. Splinters flew. Arrows continued to fall. His soldiers pressed on, shields locked, their grit unshaken by the rising toll of the fallen. The next strike landed with bone-jarring force, and finally, a deep crack split the wood.

A triumphant cry erupted from the soldiers manning the ram. They heaved back, bracing for another hit. But before the blow could land, the crack widened. With a groaning creak, the gates swung open.

Adrian froze for a heartbeat, breath catching. Cecilia's team had reached the gatehouse. The plan had worked. The way was open.

"Charge!" he roared, his voice cutting through the din.

Sword raised high, he surged forward, leading the flood of soldiers through the breached gates. Shields remained high, their formation tight as they poured into the castle like a living wave of steel.

Inside, the battle ignited anew. Elinor's forces scrambled to regroup, rallying in the inner sanctum. Adrian moved fast, issuing commands as his troops split into strike units, sweeping through corridors and courtyards, clearing the path ahead. His focus was unwavering. He had to reach Cecilia and ensure Elinor's capture before she could vanish into the shadows.

With single-minded purpose, he pressed through the fray, his sword a blur of motion. He struck down anyone who dared stand in his path, every movement precise, honed by years of discipline and hardened resolve. The clash of blades, the screams of the wounded – these became background noise. All that mattered was the mission. And he wouldn't fail.

Adrian moved with lethal grace – fluid, calculated, yet fierce – as if the chaos of battle bent to his will. The castle pulsed with mayhem: screams and shouted orders rebounding off stone walls, steel clashing in sharp bursts that split the air. Around him, his soldiers fought with grim determination, loyalty and purpose driving them forward despite the mounting cost. He spared them no more than a passing glance. His focus was fixed on one goal.

And then, through the blur of combat, he saw him.

Bradley stood ahead, tense and ready, sword drawn, as though he had been waiting for this moment. The sight of him ignited a fire in Adrian's veins – rage and purpose tangled in a storm of raw instinct. This was it. The confrontation he had long awaited. The reckoning.

A grim smile curled Adrian's lips as he advanced, cutting down another foe with effortless precision. He stepped over a fallen body, his gaze locking onto Bradley's. In that instant, the rest of the battle faded – the noise, the movement, the blood – as if the world had narrowed to just the two of them.

"So, we meet again," Bradley said, his voice slick with venom. The twitch at the corners of his mouth could have been a smirk or a sneer.

Adrian raised his sword, its blade gleaming as if it too hungered for vengeance. "We do," he said coldly. "And this will be the last."

He struck first. Steel rang as their blades collided, and the duel began.

They moved like predators, each strike a blend of practised technique and raw fury. Adrian was faster, his footwork sharper, keeping Bradley on the defensive. The clang of their weapons echoed through the castle halls, each blow more desperate, more precise. Sweat beaded on Bradley's brow as he blocked another furious swing, muscles straining, breath ragged.

Adrian's eyes blazed with focus. He pressed his advantage without hesitation, driving Bradley back step by step. His strikes were relentless, honed by years of combat and tempered by cold resolve. Bradley faltered under the onslaught, unused to true battle but unwilling to give ground.

Around them, war raged. Rebels and royal guards clashed in bloody combat, steel and screams mingling in the smoke-choked air. The castle trembled with the violence of it all. The cries of the dying echoed through the corridors, blending with the gut-wrenching sound of steel piercing flesh. Wounded men dragged themselves through blood-slicked halls, their efforts ending abruptly beneath a cold blade or a crushing blow.

Adrian and Bradley wove through the carnage, their duel threading in and out of the broader chaos. They stumbled over corpses, dodged wild strikes from nearby fighters, and battled on without pause. A guard lunged at Adrian from the side – he spun left, parrying the blow with a sharp deflection, then stepped into the opening and delivered a swift upward slash. The guard crumpled.

Adrian didn't break stride.

His blade sliced cleanly across the guard's chest, a spray of blood trailing the arc of steel as the man crumpled. Adrian didn't stop to watch him fall. He turned sharply, only to feel a sudden, searing pain flare across his shoulder. Bradley's sword had found its mark.

The unexpected strike forced a hiss through Adrian's clenched teeth. Pain radiated down his arm, but he forced it aside, whirling back to face Bradley, his eyes burning with renewed fury. Around them, the chaos of battle dulled to a distant roar. In this moment, only the two of them existed – locked in a duel that would end with one of them dead.

Adrian raised his sword, levelling it at Bradley. "This ends now."

Bradley sneered. "Yes. With your death at my hands."

Adrian struck first.

He moved with swift precision, each step and swing driven by a volatile mix of pain and rage. His movements were fluid, purposeful, and relentless. Bradley struggled to hold his ground, parrying blow after blow, each impact forcing a grimace as Adrian drove through his guard.

They were both tiring. Adrian could see it in Bradley's footwork, in the way his reactions slowed with every strike. But Adrian wasn't unscathed – the cut on his shoulder throbbed with each movement, blood seeping steadily down his arm. His strength was waning, but he had one goal: outlast Bradley. End this.

With a sudden burst of force, Adrian pressed forward, striking harder, faster, until he forced Bradley back, step by step, into the cold stone wall. He raised his sword for the final blow – but a clang of steel interrupted the strike.

Another blade slammed into his, knocking it off course.

Adrian spun instinctively as a second attacker joined the fray. The battle around them had surged back to life, and now more guards were closing in, weapons raised. Two lunged at him at once, forcing him to twist and defend from both sides.

He fought with practised ferocity, blade flashing, cutting down enemies with brutal efficiency. But for every guard that fell, two more emerged. He was surrounded – on the defensive, parrying one strike while dodging another, spinning to deflect, then counter. His sword found its mark again and again, but he was no longer untouched.

Blows landed, bruising thuds to his ribs, sharp slashes to exposed flesh. He could feel his strength bleeding away with every wound. He gritted his teeth, fighting through the pain, refusing to fall, but he didn't know how much longer he could hold out.

Just as the tide threatened to swallow him, a group of rebels burst through the corridor, weapons raised, shouting battle cries. They crashed into the guards with unrelenting force, cutting them down and driving the rest back. In the sudden lull, Adrian staggered slightly, breath ragged, blood soaking his sleeve.

His eyes scanned the chaos, searching – hunting.

Where was Bradley?

He turned towards the spot where his foe had last stood. But it was empty. The tapestry behind him was askew – pulled just far enough to reveal a hidden door, now slightly ajar.

"Fuck."

Chapter 44

Echoes of the Past

How long had it been since she last walked these halls? Everything still felt familiar. Each turn she took brought her closer to the topmost tower, where the last crystal shard was kept. Aevah was certain this was where she would find Elinor hiding. Against her mother's wishes, she had slipped away unnoticed, determined to face this alone.

The corridors echoed with chaos. Violence surrounded her – swords clashing, shields crashing, knives slicing through flesh. Men and women alike battled fiercely, their cries ringing through the stone passageways. Blood painted the floor, the walls, the very air. She tried to block it all out, to stay focused on her goal, but the screams and shouts were impossible to ignore. With every corner she turned, savagery confronted her anew, striking deep into her spirit. Never in her life had she witnessed such carnage. She didn't know what hurt more – seeing the dead strewn across the floors or hearing the wounded beg for help, or worse, for death.

Whenever she faltered, frozen by the horror around her, Nicholas was there with a gentle touch to guide her forward. Between him, Galrick, and Isabella, they kept her shielded as they advanced through the castle. More than once, they were ambushed by Elinor's soldiers – men who recognised Aevah instantly. But thanks to their swift response and the aid of rebels still loyal within the walls, they escaped each encounter unharmed. Still, Aevah knew it couldn't last. The deeper they went, the more enemies appeared. Though dangerous, it was a clear sign they were getting close.

When they reached the midpoint of the corridor, Aevah knew the next turn would lead to the staircase ascending to the chamber where the crystal was kept. She remembered it well – her father had often brought her here when she was young. Always at midday, when the sunlight poured through a narrow window, striking the shard and casting brilliant rainbows across the room. The colours had captivated her then, as had the stories he told – tales of power, sacrifice, and ancient magic. She never learned whether they were true. Even so, those moments remained among her most cherished memories.

Snapping back to reality, Aevah felt her nerves begin to fray as she stared down the hallway. This would be the first time she entered that room without her father – this time, not to admire the crystal, but to confront an aunt who wanted her dead. Before she could voice her fears, two guards stepped into view from the corner, swords already drawn and ready to strike.

"Julian," Galrick said curtly. "I take it your queen is not far away if you're here."

"Indeed," Julian replied. "And you'll get no closer. Hand over the girl and walk away alive."

Galrick turned slightly, murmuring to his brother, "Get Aevah to the room. No matter what." As he and Isabella moved to intercept the threat, Nicholas nodded and tightened his grip on his sword. Aevah's heart pounded; she knew of Julian's reputation and could only hope Galrick, with Isabella at his side, was enough to hold him off.

She had to believe.

They moved together, Aevah sticking close to Nicholas as the guards surged forward, striking with speed and precision. Steel clashed violently. Galrick met Julian blow for blow, while Isabella held her ground against the second attacker. Nicholas, though determined, struggled to keep pace. A gash opened across his right arm, and he was knocked back more than once, barely keeping his footing.

Then came a sharp blow to the chest that sent Nicholas sprawling to the ground. Aevah's breath caught – she thought it was over for him – until another blade intercepted the guard's, sparing his life at the last second.

Two rebels had appeared, joining the fight. One moved to assist Galrick against Julian, evening the odds. With the enemy momentarily distracted, Nicholas gritted his teeth, grabbed Aevah by the arm, and bolted down the hall. He looked back once, anguish written across his face as he glimpsed his brother, then forced himself to press on, pulling her around the final bend.

A door came into view at the corridor's end. Aevah slowed, her feet heavy, every fear she had rushing back at once. Her heart pounded as dread twisted deep in her gut. She turned to Nicholas, and her breath hitched. His arm was bleeding badly, the crimson soaking through his sleeve.

Without hesitation, she rushed to him, ignoring his protests. Tearing away part of her dress's lining, she used her power to rip it into strips. She knew she needed to conserve her strength for what lay ahead, but she couldn't let him bleed out – not now.

His protests faded as she wrapped the wound and stopped the bleeding. Only when she was sure he was stable did she return her gaze to the door. The knot in her stomach tensed once more.

Sensing her unease, Nicholas reached out and took her hand, giving it a reassuring squeeze. Drawing in a breath, Aevah turned the doorknob and slowly pushed the door open.

She had prepared herself for the sight of Elinor – the woman she had come to defeat.

But what awaited her inside was somehow far worse.

"Liora."

The name escaped Aevah's lips like a curse.

The one who had trapped her and her friends beneath the temple, forcing them to battle the ghostly spectres of their pasts just to survive. The one who had stolen the decoy shards and left her for dead. Aevah had endured the visions. She had clawed her way back through the torment, and now, with fury igniting every vein in her body, she was ready to make Liora regret ever crossing her.

She stepped further into the chamber, fists clenched, her knuckles white with rage. "You," she sneered, her voice quivering with barely restrained anger. "Do you have any idea what you put us through?"

Liora smirked, her posture relaxed but deliberate, like a predator toying with prey. "Oh, I know *exactly* what I subjected you to. Did you enjoy reliving your memories? A little tour through your life—the triumphs, the tragedies, the truth of it all. Clearly, it didn't break you. Otherwise, you wouldn't be standing here now."

Aevah advanced, each step a tremor of fury. "You think this is a joke? You played with our lives. You *left us to die* while you ran off with the shards."

Liora laughed – a low, cruel sound, dripping with mockery. "Ah yes, those *fakes*—a clever trick, I'll give you that. Sending me back to Elinor with nothing but dust and lies. She didn't take kindly to my failure." Her expression darkened as she stepped forward, voice edged with bitterness. "Do you know what she did to me?"

Aevah didn't flinch. "Whatever it was, you earned it. Your punishment isn't my concern."

Liora kept approaching, but before she could close the distance, Nicholas stepped between them. Though wounded, he raised his sword with grim determination, his stance steady despite the pain evident in his eyes.

"Not another step," he said, his voice low and unwavering. His gaze locked onto Liora's with a hard warning. "You'll face me first."

Liora's smirk deepened. Her eyes flicked to Nicholas, amused, then returned to Aevah. "Oh, how gallant," she retorted mockingly. "Wounded, bleeding, but still ready to throw himself in harm's way. Noble to the end. But I wonder…" She let the sentence trail off, her grin widening as if feeding off the tension.

She began to circle them slowly, every step echoing with a disturbing confidence. "You say I deserved my punishment," she said, her smile fading into a cold, venomous glare. "Well then—let's see what *you* make of it."

Before Aevah could react, a jolt of agony tore through her.

It began as molten fire in her veins, spreading like wildfire until every inch of her felt aflame. Her breath caught in her throat as her muscles seized, her skin searing with invisible flames. Then came the worst of it – the sensation of her bones shattering, one by one, as if crushed by some unseen force. She screamed, a raw, animal sound, collapsing to her knees as pain consumed her.

Through the red haze, she caught a glimpse of Nicholas.

He, too, was writhing – his sword falling from his grasp as he doubled over, his face contorted with suffering. His lips parted in a strangled cry, eyes clenched shut as his body buckled under the same unseen torment.

The sight of him, strong and steadfast Nicholas, reduced to this, ignited something deeper in her. Beneath the agony, beneath the fire and fear, a fresh wave of rage surged through her.

Aevah gritted her teeth, forcing herself to focus. She couldn't let Liora win – not like this. Summoning every last reserve of strength, she reached deep within herself, grasping the power that had always lingered, waiting. She embraced it fully, letting it surge through her body. With a desperate cry, she unleashed a wave of energy.

The force tore through the room, crashing into Liora, but the woman barely flinched. She only laughed, eyes gleaming with cruel amusement.

"You'll have to do better than that," she taunted, her voice cutting through the air like a blade.

Aevah's vision swam, but she refused to yield. She shifted her focus, her mind narrowing in on Liora's connection to the power. It was a tether – faint, pulsing, almost visible. She seized it, her will stronger than the pain clawing at her. She pushed forward, building a barrier in her mind, layer by layer, and she forged a shield around Liora. It solidified, encasing her in her power.

And then the pain stopped.

Aevah collapsed to the floor, gasping, her limbs trembling from the effort. Across the room, Liora's smug expression twisted into a mask of rage as she realised what had happened. With a snarl, she drew a dagger and lunged.

But Nicholas was faster.

He surged forward, sword slashing through the air with deadly precision. The blade found its mark, slicing cleanly across Liora's torso. Her eyes widened in shock. Then, without a word, she crumpled to the ground. Silence fell over the chamber like a shroud.

Aevah stared at Nicholas, her chest heaving. Her mind struggled to catch up with what had just unfolded. He stood over Liora's fallen body, sword still clenched tightly in his hand, his face pale but resolute.

"It's over," he said hoarsely, though his voice held firm.

"Not yet. We need to find Elinor." Aevah stepped in front of a large tapestry, running her hand along its edge until her fingers found a hidden latch. With a soft click, the tapestry shifted, revealing a narrow doorway behind it.

She glanced at Nicholas. He raised an eyebrow but said nothing, waiting for her to speak.

"This way," she said quietly, stepping into the hidden passage. Nicholas followed, his footsteps echoing faintly in the narrow stone corridor.

The air grew cooler, damp and tinged with the weight of forgotten years. As they descended the winding staircase, Aevah's heart ached. Memories collided with the present. She had used this passage once before, long ago, to sneak out with her brother on some childish adventure. Now, it led to something far more grave.

At the base of the stairs, a worn wooden door stood before them. Aevah hesitated, her hand resting on the surface. Then, with a deep breath, she pushed it open.

They stepped into what had once been her parents' chambers.

The room struck her like a blow. Though familiar, it had changed. Elinor had left her mark, ornate rugs, gilded furnishings, lavish decor that clashed with the simple warmth Aevah remembered. Her eyes moved slowly across the space. Her mother's favourite carved desk remained, her father's worn armchair still near the hearth. But the gentle blues were gone, replaced by harsh crimson drapes. The comforting scent of lavender had been smothered by sharp incense. This was no longer a sanctuary – it had been twisted into something cold, hollow, and calculating, just like her aunt.

"Your parents' chambers?" Nicholas asked softly, as if wary of disturbing the ghosts that lingered.

Aevah nodded and moved to the centre of the room. "This used to be the safest place in the world," she whispered. Her voice faltered before she continued. "Elinor's changed everything… even this."

Her gaze swept the space, catching on the scattered remnants of her childhood – faded, distorted. Grief welled in her chest, but she pushed it down, steeling herself.

Nicholas reached out, his hand brushing her shoulder in silent support. She grounded herself in the present, and then she saw the woman.

Standing across the room, a child clutched protectively in her arms, the woman's eyes flicked between Aevah and Nicholas. Her grip on the child tightened. The resemblance was unmistakable – the baby bore Elinor's features.

"We mean you no harm," Aevah said, raising her hands in peace. "We're here for Elinor, not the child."

The woman – Chloe – hesitated. Her expression softened, but her stance remained guarded. "You say that now. But how can I trust you?"

"Because if I wanted to hurt you, we wouldn't be talking," Aevah replied, her tone shrill with urgency. "I want to end this—to stop Elinor before she does any more damage. Please. Tell me where she is."

Before Chloe could answer, the sound of approaching footsteps echoed through the chamber. Aevah turned as a group of armed guards entered, their weapons gleaming in the dim light.

Nicholas instinctively stepped closer to her, hand drifting towards his sword.

"She's in the throne room," Chloe said quickly. "The guards will take you there."

One of them stepped forward, eyeing Nicholas's weapon. "Hand it over," he demanded.

Nicholas hesitated, jaw tensed. Aevah placed a calming hand on his arm. After a moment, he exhaled and slowly unclipped the sword, passing it over with visible reluctance.

The guards moved in, flanking them on either side. Their grip was firm, but not violent. Aevah felt an eerie calm settle over her. The rage and fear had quieted, replaced by unwavering resolve.

Each step brought them closer to the throne room. Closer to the confrontation she had long prepared for.

As they descended the final staircase, Aevah's heart hardened with certainty.

She would face Elinor, and no matter what it cost her, she would end her aunt's reign of terror.

Chapter 45

A Warrior's Stand

Galrick tightened his grip on his sword, knuckles whitening as he stared Julian down. The battlefield around them seemed distant, its noise dulled beneath the crushing weight of his exhaustion. He and the rebels had fought tooth and nail to reach this point, their numbers thinning with every hard-won step. Now, only he and Isabella remained to face Julian, the battle still raging around them.

The air hung heavy, charged with the tense anticipation of the impending clash. Galrick's breath came fast and shallow, his muscles aching with every movement, screaming for rest. But he refused to yield. Beside him, Isabella stood with her sword raised, her face pale but defiant. Their eyes met, and for a heartbeat, the chaos faded.

"This could be it," Isabella said softly, her voice trembling yet steady with conviction.

Galrick shook his head, his expression hardening. "No," he said firmly. He reached for her hand and squeezed it tightly, as if the gesture alone could anchor them. "This isn't the end. It's the beginning."

She gave a small nod, her grip tightening on the hilt of her sword as he let go. Together, they stepped forward, their resolve sharpening into a lethal edge.

A rebel charged past them, slicing cleanly through the neck of one of Julian's guards. The guard dropped without a sound – but before the rebel could take another step, Julian struck. His blade flashed with ruthless precision, piercing the man's abdomen. The rebel collapsed, blood pooling beneath him.

Julian smirked, his stance relaxed but predatory. "You should've stayed hidden," he said, his voice calm, calculating. "This will end poorly for you."

Galrick didn't answer. His eyes locked onto Julian's every move. He lunged, his blade slicing through the air, but Julian met the strike effortlessly. Their swords clashed, the metallic ring echoing through the din of battle as the duel began in earnest. Isabella darted to the side, aiming to flank him, but Julian adapted swiftly, his movements brutal and precise.

Galrick staggered beneath Julian's relentless assault, each blow chipping away at his strength. His limbs felt heavy, his vision blurring with exhaustion. Before he could recover, Isabella moved to intercept, her sword meeting Julian's in a desperate clash of steel.

"Is that all you've got?" she shouted, her voice strained but fierce. "You can do better than that!" Her words were a taunt, meant to draw Julian's focus, and they did.

Julian's smirk deepened. With calculated speed, his next strike caught Isabella off guard. His blade grazed her arm, slicing through cloth and flesh. Blood bloomed, but she retaliated without hesitation, her counterattack driven by sheer willpower. Around them, the chaos of battle blurred – the cries, the steel, the blood – all drowned beneath the singular, brutal struggle.

But Julian was faster. Stronger. Merciless.

With a sudden feint towards Galrick, he pivoted mid-strike and turned on Isabella. His blade carved across her side, and she staggered back, clutching her wound. Pain flashed across her face, but she refused to fall. Gritting her teeth, she stood her ground.

Julian didn't relent.

A second blow knocked her weapon from her grip, and with a swift, brutal kick, he sent her sprawling to the ground.

"Isabella!" Galrick's cry tore from his throat, cracked and panicked. He lunged towards her, his sword clashing with Julian's in a frenzy of wild, desperate strikes. He fought with everything he had left, fuelled by fear, fury, and the need to protect her.

Isabella lay motionless at first, her breath shallow and ragged. Blood soaked the dirt beneath her, seeping from the deep gash along her side. Her fingers clawed weakly at the stone as she tried to rise, every movement stabbing through her with agony. But she pushed forward.

With quivering arms, she forced herself upright, barely managing her knees. Her vision swam, but she kept her eyes fixed on Galrick – still fighting, still faltering under Julian's blows. She reached for him, her hand outstretched, fingers trembling, crawling forward inch by painful inch.

"Galrick," she whispered, her voice thin and broken, barely audible over the din of clashing swords. Her fingers scraped the ground, reaching – hoping – as though his presence alone could pull her back from the brink.

She never saw the soldier behind her.

He struck without warning. His blade plunged into her back, piercing through flesh and bone in one brutal motion. Isabella arched, a strangled gasp escaping her lips. The steel slid free with a sickening sound, lost beneath the chaos of battle. Her arms gave way, and she collapsed to the ground, motionless.

"NO!" Galrick's scream shattered the air, raw with anguish. He abandoned the fight, his sword falling from his grasp as he ran to her side. Dropping to his knees, he gathered her into his arms, holding her limp body against his chest.

Blood soaked through Galrick's hands as he pressed against the wound, desperate to staunch the flow. His touch was frantic, as though sheer will alone could hold her life in place.

"Stay with me," he pleaded, his voice cracking under the weight of his fear. "Please, Isabella—stay with me."

Isabella's gaze locked onto his, her wide eyes filled with fear and a flickering, desperate hope. "I don't want to die," she whispered, her voice fragile and trembling.

"You won't," Galrick said, forcing strength into his voice, though it quivered beneath the surface. "I'm here. My heart—it's always been yours."

He cupped her face with bloodstained fingers, his thumb brushing away a streak of dirt and blood, as if trying to cleanse the moment of its brutal truth.

He pulled her close until their foreheads touched, and for a breath of time, the world fell away. The screams, the clashing blades, the stench of war – all of it dissolved, leaving only the two of them suspended in that fragile sliver of peace.

"Galrick," Isabella whispered, her tears brimming, her voice trembling with emotion.

"I'm here," he murmured, broken and raw, his fingers gently tangling in her hair. "I'm here."

"Kiss me, Galrick," she said, her voice faint but resolute. Her words carried the weight of goodbye, a quiet plea to make this last moment sacred.

He leaned in, and their lips met – soft, slow, and aching. The kiss held everything: love, sorrow, longing, and the bitter ache of all they would never have. When they parted, he brushed a strand of hair from her face, his hands shaking as he cradled her cheek.

"We'll see each other again," he whispered, his voice hoarse with both hope and despair.

Isabella gave the faintest nod, her lips curving into a fragile smile. "Until then," she said, steady despite the pain, her eyes shining with the last flicker of life.

"Until then," Galrick echoed, pressing one final kiss to her forehead.

As he pulled back, her body sagged in his arms. A single tear traced a path down her cheek, and then she was still.

Galrick rose slowly, every movement hollow, as though he were no longer tethered to his own body. His eyes, once bright with life, had dimmed, vacant, and lifeless. In the silence of his grief, something else took hold. Deep within, a cold ember flared to life, fed by anguish, hardened into rage. A fire not born of life, but of loss. It smouldered in the ruins of his heart, fuelling what remained of the man who had loved her.

Galrick reached for his sword, the blade dragging against the stone with a harsh, grating scrape. The sound cut through the silence like a jagged whisper of vengeance, raw and unforgiving. Each step he took echoed with purpose, his resolve hardening with every movement as he turned to face the soldier who had taken everything from him.

He levelled the weapon with deliberate precision, his grip unwavering despite the tempest roaring inside him. His voice, low and deadly, rang across the battlefield, weighted with finality.

"It's just you and me."

He began to circle, his pace slow, controlled – the rhythm of his footfalls matching the pounding of his heart. The blade's dull scrape along the ground sang an ominous song, a prelude to blood. The path he carved into the earth was a scar, mirroring the one etched into his soul.

His eyes never left the man before him. Predator and prey.

The soldier adjusted his stance, his fingers tightening around the hilt of his sword. Sweat clung to his brow, trailing down his cheek as he tried to steady his breath. Every rise and fall of his chest betrayed the fear he fought to contain. He swallowed hard, the weight of the moment pressing down like stone.

Galrick remained still, coiled and ready, his movements deceptively calm – each step a warning, each pause a threat. He was baiting the soldier, daring him to make the first mistake.

Then, the slightest shift – the soldier's foot twitched, his balance adjusting. A tell. Galrick saw it. He didn't move, didn't blink. He simply waited, the tension in his frame palpable, vibrating with restrained fury.

"Make your move," Galrick said at last. His voice was ice – cold, quiet, and razor-sharp. It wasn't a challenge. It was a verdict.

The soldier lunged.

Steel clashed in a burst of motion. Galrick met the attack head-on, his blade slicing through the air with ruthless precision. The soldier staggered, thrown off balance by the force of the counterstrike. Galrick advanced, his movements fluid and relentless, each blow driven by anger honed into discipline.

The two clashed in a brutal rhythm – strike and parry, lunge and dodge – yet Galrick held the upper hand. He fought with the fury of grief and the clarity of vengeance, each strike guided by loss, each step by love turned to wrath.

The soldier faltered.

His back slammed against the cold stone wall, his eyes wide with panic. Galrick didn't hesitate. He closed the distance, his sword raised, its blade catching the flicker of torchlight like a shard of judgment. His breath was steady.

And in that moment, everything stilled – save for the fire in Galrick's eyes and the weight of the justice he was about to deliver.

But in his focus on the soldier before him, Galrick missed the flicker of movement behind.

Julian stepped forward, a cruel smile curling at the corners of his lips. His blade moved without a sound – silent, deliberate – a predator striking from the shadows. The steel pierced through Galrick's side, driving deep into his lung.

The pain was immediate. Sharp. Searing and all-consuming.

Galrick gasped, the breath wrenched from his chest as his sword slipped from his grasp and clattered against the cold stone floor. His knees buckled beneath him, but he refused to cry out, even as Julian twisted the blade with cruel precision before yanking it free.

He staggered, one hand clutching the wound as blood poured between his fingers. Still, he turned, just enough to meet Julian's gaze. The smirk on Julian's face was a mask of cold satisfaction, his eyes gleaming with victory.

"This is where your story ends," Julian said, his tone low and mocking. "And hers."

He stepped closer, savouring the moment, his blade still wet with Galrick's blood.

Galrick's breath came in ragged gasps, each one more difficult than the last. Pain burned through his side, but his hand drifted downward, fingers searching, trembling, until they found the hilt of the dagger at his belt. His grip tightened.

"And yours," he rasped, his voice raw, but resolute.

Before Julian could react, Galrick surged forward with the last of his strength. The dagger drove deep into Julian's chest, striking true. The blade sank in with brutal finality.

Julian's eyes widened in disbelief, the triumph draining from his face. He stumbled back, his sword slipping from his hand as blood poured from the wound.

Galrick's hand trembled as he withdrew the blade, crimson coating his fingers. Julian collapsed to his knees, eyes dulling, breath faltering. For a fleeting moment, satisfaction flickered in Galrick's gaze.

But the effort had taken its toll.

His legs gave out. He collapsed beside his fallen enemy, the dagger slipping from his grasp as darkness crowded the edges of his vision.

He lay motionless at first, his chest heaving, the world reduced to blurred shapes and muffled noise. He tried to rise – his body barely responding. Blood trickled from the corner of his mouth as he propped himself on one trembling arm, eyes flickering downward in bewilderment, as if trying to comprehend the wound that would claim him.

A wet, rattling breath escaped him.

Then, through the haze of pain and blood and grief, he saw her.

Isabella.

She lay just feet away, still and silent. The sight of her reignited something within him – something broken, but not yet extinguished. His heart, shattered and dying, found one last flicker of purpose.

Dragging himself forward, he clawed at the stone floor, nails scraping, tears mixing with the dirt and blood smeared across his face.

"Isabella…" he whispered, the name cracking in his throat. Each syllable tore from him like glass, his voice frayed and fading.

Inch by inch, he crawled through the agony, every movement a defiance of death itself. Finally, he reached her. Galrick collapsed at her side, gathering her into his arms with what little strength remained. His body shook violently as he cradled her, sobs wracking him.

"I'm here," he whispered, forehead pressed to hers, tears falling onto her blood-streaked face.

His breathing grew shallow. His vision dimmed until there was only her. Only Isabella. The woman he had fought for. Bled for. Loved beyond life.

With his final breath, he spoke her name once more, lips brushing her ear. "Isabella…"

Then he stilled.

The battlefield fell into silence, as though the very world paused in mourning. Two souls, bound by love and loyalty, now lie side by side. And in death, as in life, they had given everything for each other… and for the kingdom they could never live to see saved.

Chapter 46

The Threads of Prophecy

The throne room shuddered as the castle groaned beneath the weight of battle. Dust drifted from the vaulted ceiling with every distant clash reverberating through its ancient walls. At the room's centre stood Elinor, her figure radiant with raw, unrelenting power. Sparks of dark energy flickered at her fingertips like embers on an inferno waiting to be unleashed.

Before her stood the High Priestess Zara, her golden robes torn and dirt-streaked, her staff faintly glowing as it drew from the waning magic within. She met Elinor's gaze with a strange mixture of defiance and weariness.

"So, you dare show your face, priestess," Elinor said, her voice cutting through the charged air.

"I would have come sooner," Zara replied evenly, "but you locked yourself behind these walls."

"For good reason!" Elinor snapped. "You and your band of rebels, with your fake prophecy, sought to unseat me—to drag me down from the throne I earned!"

Her voice quaked with fervour, and the darkness in the room pulsated in rhythm with her rage.

Zara's expression hardened. "Earned?" she repeated. "You murdered your brother and stole his crown. You earned nothing. And as for the prophecy—it's not false, Elinor. It simply does not favour you."

Elinor's eyes blazed, twin flames of fury and denial. "I did what was necessary," she hissed, her voice sharp enough to split stone. "I saved this kingdom from his weakness! He would have led us to ruin. Just as you are trying to do now. Prophecy be damned."

Zara stepped closer, her robes trailing through the dust of the crumbling room. "Weakness?" she countered, her voice rising. "He ruled with wisdom and mercy—virtues you twisted into scorn. Your ambition blinded you. It still does."

"You dare?" Elinor retorted, the dark magic crackling at her fingertips. "You stand there cloaked in righteousness, spewing your sanctimonious lies? You betrayed me, just as he did."

"We betrayed nothing," Zara said, her tone steady. "We tried to protect the people from the darkness we saw blooming inside you. And now, as I stand before you, I see that shadow fully realised. The woman I once knew is gone, consumed by her lust for power."

Elinor laughed – a cold, hollow sound that echoed through the chamber. "You speak of betrayal while justifying treachery? Spare me. The throne is mine, and no one—not you, not your feeble rebellion—will take it from me."

Zara's grip on her staff tightened. "This rebellion rose from your darkness, Elinor. We only tried to stop what we feared you might become. Even Bradley saw it. He came to us, begging for our help before your coronation."

The name struck Elinor like a dagger to the chest. She stepped forward involuntarily, shadows curling tighter around her hands. "Bradley?" Her voice cracked. "You dare invoke him in your lies?"

"It is no lie," Zara replied, her tone calm but unrelenting. "He came to us because he feared what unchecked power would do to you, to the realm. He acted out of love. You know that."

Elinor's hands curled into fists, power flaring around her. Her voice trembled, not with fear, but with rage. "Liar! You poisoned his mind, as you've done to so many. Bradley would never doubt me."

"Questioning is not betrayal," Zara said, her voice low but firm. "He cared for you, Elinor. That love is what made him act. But it is not his shadow you fear—it's your own."

The air crackled as Elinor's power surged outward, shadows spilling across the chamber like a rising tide. "Enough of your poison! You will not manipulate me as you did him."

Zara stepped back, raising her staff defensively as the magic thickened between them. "If you can't face the truth, you are no queen—only a tyrant drunk on power."

At those words, Elinor lashed out. Tendrils of shadow burst forth, surging towards Zara with blinding speed. They struck her ward with a soundless force, the protective magic flaring in resistance. The air hissed and snapped, the clash of their powers setting the room trembling.

"You dare call me a tyrant?" Elinor's voice boomed, undercut with an otherworldly resonance. She advanced, black tendrils curling around pillars and slithering across the stone. "You, who've sown chaos and rebellion in my kingdom? You twist Bradley's name to poison my mind, but I see through your lies."

Zara's face was pale, her features shadowed by Elinor's unholy power. Still, her grip on the staff held firm. "It's not lies that shake you—it's the truth. Bradley feared the very thing you've become. Your anger proves it."

The tendrils struck again, hammering Zara's wards and sending a shockwave across the chamber. The throne room groaned, ancient stone cracking beneath the strain. Elinor's eyes glowed with dark fire, the shadows thickening and coiling, feeding off her fury as they reached for Zara like predators drawn to blood.

Zara raised her staff high, mustering her strength. A burst of violet light exploded from its tip, slamming into the oncoming shadows. For a moment, the throne room was lit with the brilliance of battle – light against darkness, hope against despair. But the glow faltered. Zara's strength was waning.

Elinor saw it – the weakening stance, the tremble in Zara's limbs. A cruel smile curled her lips.

"You've fought for so long, Zara," she said, her voice heavy with power. "But look at you now. A relic clinging to a cause already crumbled."

Zara gritted her teeth and forced one last surge of light. It struck the shadows, scattering them, but they reformed almost instantly, darker and stronger. They lashed out, coiling around her arms, legs, and staff, wrenching it from her grasp.

The High Priestess gasped, struggling against the tendrils, but it was futile. Elinor raised a hand, and the power lifted Zara from the ground, suspending her like a marionette cut loose from its will. Her staff clattered to the floor, its light extinguished.

Elinor stepped closer, her aura pulsing, her voice low and cold. "You thought you could break me. But you were weak. You could never stand against me."

Zara's gaze locked on hers, defiant even in the face of death. "You've already lost, Elinor," she whispered. "You just don't see it yet."

Elinor's face hardened. "Then let me show you what losing truly looks like."

With a flick of her wrist, the tendrils hurled Zara across the room. She slammed into a pillar with a sickening crack, her head snapping back as blood spattered the stone. Her body crumpled, lifeless, a dark pool seeping around her.

The shadows ebbed, receding as if appeased by her wrath. Elinor stood still, her chest heaving, eyes locked on Zara's broken form. The chamber had fallen silent, save for the distant cries of war beyond the throne room doors.

"Your Majesty."

The voice sliced through the quiet. Elinor turned sharply. In the doorway stood her guards, their armour streaked with soot and blood. Between them stood a young man and woman, their faces stark. The man's gaze was steady. The woman's hands trembled, though her eyes held firm with determination.

Chapter 47

The Last Stand

Aevah and Elinor stood face to face across the throne room, the air between them alive with tension. Elinor's brow furrowed as she studied the young woman before her, confusion momentarily clouding her gaze. For an instant, uncertainty flickered in her eyes, but Aevah caught the precise moment recognition took hold. Elinor's stare hardened, her brows knitting into a scowl.

The chaos surrounding them receded to a distant murmur in Aevah's ears. The clash of steel and the cries of warriors faded into the background, eclipsed by the confrontation now commanding her full attention. Smoke drifted in lazy spirals near the frayed tapestries lining the walls, and the throne – crooked, battered, and scorched – stood as a broken monument to a power long fractured. Yet none of it mattered. Aevah's entire world had narrowed to Elinor.

"Aevah," Elinor said at last, her voice smooth and sharp, like a blade sheathed in silk. She tilted her head slightly, a faint smirk tugging at the corners of her mouth. "It's been many years."

She stepped forward with deliberate poise, her presence both regal and menacing. Her tone dripped with cruel amusement. "You are every inch your mother's daughter. Everything about you screams Cecilia—especially that scowl." A low, wicked laugh escaped her, echoing through the vast chamber like a chilling wind. "Oh yes, I've seen that look on her face more times than I can count."

Aevah's lips thinned, the muscles in her jaw tightening. "Don't you dare speak her name," she snapped, her voice laced with venom.

Elinor's laughter cut off abruptly, though its malice lingered like smoke in the air. Her eyes narrowed, a calculating gleam sparking within them. "Ah," she murmured, more to herself than to Aevah, "the fire runs deep in her blood too." She took another measured step forward, closing the distance between them. "Tell me, Aevah—did your mother also pass down her talent for betrayal? Or is that something you've perfected all on your own?"

The accusation struck like a blow. Aevah's eyes widened for a heartbeat before she forced her features back under control. But it was too late. Elinor had seen it – the smallest fracture in her carefully guarded façade.

"You don't know anything about me," Aevah shot back. Her voice was forceful, a shield thrown up in haste, but the slight tremor beneath her words betrayed her unease.

Elinor's smile curled faintly and cruelly, her eyes gleaming with quiet satisfaction. "Oh, my dear, you're right," she said, her tone deceptively soft, almost kind. "I don't. But I know enough to see the war tearing you apart from the inside." She leaned in slightly, her voice dropping to a conspiratorial whisper. "Tell me… which side is winning?"

"Ours!" Aevah cried, releasing her magic in a furious burst. Power surged from her hands in a blinding wave.

But Elinor was faster.

With a flick of her wrist, she conjured a barrier of shimmering energy. The attack struck it with a force like a hammer on steel, sending sparks crackling into the air. The blast rebounded, slamming into the stone wall behind with a deafening boom that shook the throne room to its bones.

"Predictable," Elinor said coldly. She brushed an invisible speck of dust from her sleeve with an air of detached disdain, as though the assault had been nothing more than an inconvenience. "You have power, I'll grant you that. But do you know how to use it?"

Aevah's hands trembled as she steadied herself, her breathing ragged. The air still vibrated with the remnants of her magic, a charged hum of unfinished violence. She squared her shoulders, her voice sharp despite the strain that edged it. "I know enough."

Elinor tilted her head, her lips curving into a slow, cruel smile. "Sufficient to challenge me, perhaps, but not to win." She stepped closer, her words falling like venom. "Power without control is a dangerous thing, child. And you…" She leaned in, her whisper ice-cold. "You're far more dangerous to yourself than to me."

The words cut deep, sharp and merciless, but Aevah stood her ground. Her spine straightened, her jaw clenched. She locked eyes with Elinor, and though the storm within her still raged, her voice rang steady. "We'll see about that."

She struck.

Raw energy exploded from her hands, a blazing torrent surging towards Elinor with untamed fury. It hit hard, catching the queen off guard. Elinor staggered, her composure cracking as pain twisted her elegant features – a fleeting glimpse of vulnerability beneath the mask.

But only for a moment.

She recovered swiftly, her expression snapping back into cold precision. Her eyes blazed with fury. Another blast flew towards her, but this time she was ready. With a swift motion, Elinor deflected the attack, redirecting it with ruthless efficiency. The magic slammed into a nearby column, shattering it in a thunderous explosion. Stone fragments rained down on the chaos below. A soldier flinched, raising an arm just in time to shield himself before diving back into the fray.

Elinor's eyes blazed with fury, the brief crack in her armour replaced by an icy, venomous glare. "Oh, you think you understand pain?" she snarled, her voice cutting through the din of battle like a blade.

“It’s not enough to know the command,” she hissed, stepping closer, her presence pressing down on Aevah like a storm. “You have to mean it—every ounce of it—when you let it loose. Like this.”

With a flick of her wrist, searing agony erupted in Aevah’s veins, fire tearing through her like dry tinder catching flame. She collapsed to her knees, a raw scream ripping from her throat as Elinor’s power surged through her, merciless and unrelenting. The throne room’s chaos dimmed into a distant murmur – the clash of steel and cries of war drowned in the silence of torment that enveloped them both.

Elinor advanced, towering over Aevah like a predator over wounded prey. Every movement she made was deliberate, sharp, and cruel. The distant sounds of battle became little more than a backdrop to the cold, calculated laughter spilling from her lips.

“Can you feel it?” she whispered, her voice brushing against Aevah like poison on the skin. “That’s what it means to wield true power.”

A piercing cry shattered the moment, raw and desperate.

Nicholas.

He broke from the ranks, sword in hand, fury etched into every line of his face. “Aevah!” he bellowed, charging towards Elinor with reckless abandon.

Elinor turned, her gaze snapping to him, disdain flickering across her features. With a single motion, she unleashed a wave of force. Nicholas flew backwards as if weightless, his sword clattering to the floor. He struck the stone wall with a sickening thud, his body crumpling on impact. Blood trickled from a cut at his temple as he slumped, unconscious, to the ground.

Elinor let out a soft, humourless laugh and turned her attention back to Aevah, as if Nicholas had been nothing more than a passing nuisance. "Another traitor to the crown dealt with, and nonetheless a son of a loyal lord," she said with a sneer, brushing a lock of hair from her face. "So eager to play the hero. So pitifully outmatched."

Aevah writhed, her body convulsing under the unrelenting power coursing through her. Pain consumed every corner of her being.

"You're resilient," Elinor admitted, her voice rising above the din. "But resilience won't save you."

With a flick of her wrist, she lifted Aevah into the air. Her magic snaked around the girl like invisible chains, binding her limbs, squeezing the breath from her lungs.

Aevah gasped, her limbs thrashing, her vision blurring at the edges. Elinor stepped closer, her eyes gleaming with triumph.

"It's time to die, little one," she whispered, her voice thick with malice. "You've fought well, but this is where it ends."

Aevah's consciousness began to slip. The throne room dissolved into a haze. Steel rang and warriors screamed, but it all melted into a crushing silence. Her limbs grew heavy. Her mind drifted.

Then, through the fog, came a scream. A raw, desperate cry, sharp as shattered glass, tore through the air.

It broke the magic's grip.

Aevah fell, slamming into the cold stone floor. The jolt of impact tore her back from the edge. Pain still throbbed through every nerve, but she forced her eyes open, her vision swimming before it settled.

She caught a glimpse of Elinor, now staggered, her once-imperious poise broken, her expression twisted in fury and disbelief.

Aevah's strength waned. Her body trembled, her breath ragged. Darkness pressed in again, heavy and irresistible. As the chaos of the throne room roared back to life, her eyes closed, and the world slipped away once more.

***

Cecilia's heart pounded as she tore through the castle's winding hallways, the distant thunder of battle spurring her onward. Each step was fuelled by desperation, a raw and primal urgency to reach Aevah. The thought of her daughter in danger clamped her chest like a vice, driving her into a breathless sprint.

The clash of steel and screams of the wounded grew louder with every stride. Crumbling stone and splintering wood echoed through the corridors, a grim symphony of destruction. She reached the throne room, its massive doors shattered and hanging from twisted hinges. She burst inside, her breath catching at the sight before her.

Elinor stood with her back to the entrance, her focus consumed by the girl writhing in midair before her, Aevah.

She hadn't noticed Cecilia.

Cecilia moved like a shadow, crossing the space in a heartbeat. "Oh, no, you don't," she shouted, her voice slicing through the chaos like a clarion call. Her chest heaved as she faced her old enemy, years of grief, rage, and loss surging into a single, unshakable moment of resolve. "This is for James, Jacob, and every soul you've destroyed."

Her words rang like a judgment.

She lunged.

"For them," she cried, "and for my daughter."

The dagger flashed in her hand, and with every ounce of strength she had left, she drove it into Elinor's chest.

Elinor's eyes widened with fury. Her face twisted into something monstrous as the blade sank deep. Blood spilt from the wound, soaking into the gold of her robes. But pain didn't stop her – rage eclipsed it. With a feral snarl, she lashed out, magic surging from her like a black storm.

Cecilia was struck full force.

Darkness slammed into her, shadows coiling like serpents around her limbs, her chest, her throat. Agony exploded through her, white-hot and unrelenting, and her legs buckled beneath her. She crashed to the stone floor, her breath ragged, her body shaking as Elinor's power raked through her soul.

It was agony unlike any she had known, merciless, consuming, and designed to break. Her strength faltered beneath it, the hand that had wielded the dagger now trembling uncontrollably. And still, through the searing pain, Cecilia refused to look away. Her eyes stayed locked on Elinor.

Elinor loomed above her, face twisted in defiance, but Cecilia saw it. A flicker. A fracture. The tiniest tremble in her hand, the faintest wince at the dagger still embedded in her chest. Her power remained immense, but her control was slipping.

Cecilia clawed at her throat as Elinor's magic constricted like a noose. Her vision blurred. Darkness gathered at the edges, and for one agonising heartbeat, she thought this would be her end.

But then – weakness. A falter. Elinor's breathing hitched. The shadows pulsing from her began to thin.

The grip around Cecilia's throat loosened. She slumped forward, gasping, her lungs straining for air. Her vision swam, but she forced it to steady, blinking against the haze clouding her sight. Slowly, painfully, she raised her gaze once more, fixing it on the faltering figure before her.

Through blurred vision, Cecilia watched as Elinor sank to her knees. One hand clutched the dagger still embedded in her chest, the other braced against the cold stone floor, as if she needed it to keep from collapsing. Her head bowed, shoulders trembling, and for the first time, she looked burdened, crushed beneath the weight of her unravelling power.

Elinor's gaze met Cecilia's one final time, fury and disbelief etched deep into her pale, stricken face. Her lips parted as if to speak, but no sound emerged. The strength that had carried her through years of cruelty and dominance drained away in an instant. Her knees gave out. She toppled forward and crumpled to the floor, the sound of her fall echoing through the throne room, heavy, conclusive, and absolute.

And then, silence.

The chaos of battle seemed to dissolve, the clash of steel and the roar of voices fading into an eerie stillness. Cecilia forced herself upright, her entire body trembling with exhaustion, her mind numb with disbelief. The pain dulled, but the ache in her chest only deepened as her eyes found the motionless form lying nearby.

Aevah.

She lay sprawled across the floor, unmoving, her stillness a blade that pierced Cecilia's heart. Tears spilt down Cecilia's cheeks, carving trails through the dust and grime. She reached out with a trembling hand, her fingers brushing Aevah's, seeking connection, grounding herself in a world that suddenly felt like it might collapse around her.

At her touch, something stirred.

A flicker. A twitch of Aevah's hand.

Cecilia froze, her breath catching in her throat. The tears still streamed, but her expression shifted from grief to a spark of hope. That faint movement shattered the despair threatening to engulf her.

"Aevah," she whispered, her voice ragged and soft.

Then, louder, the desperation rising in her chest, "Aevah!"

She leaned closer, brushing a tangle of hair from her daughter's face, her hands trembling. "Please, my darling, open your eyes," she pleaded, pouring every ounce of love and fear into her words.

Aevah's eyelids fluttered. Her chest lifted in a shallow, quivering breath. Slowly, painfully, her eyes opened.

"Mother…" she rasped, her voice barely more than a breath, fragile and hoarse.

With immense effort, she began to sit up, her movements slow and unsteady. Cecilia didn't hesitate. She gathered Aevah into her arms, holding her tightly, protectively, as fresh tears streamed down her face.

Relief crashed over her like a wave, washing away the fear, the agony, the despair. She stroked Aevah's hair, her voice breaking as she whispered, "It's over, my darling. It's over."

Aevah slumped against her mother's shoulder, her body weak but her spirit clinging to the warmth of that embrace. Around them, the world receded – the wreckage, the blood, the battle – fading into distant noise. For a moment, there was only this: the quiet, aching certainty that they had survived.

Together.

Chapter 48

Blood in the Moonlight

Bradley saw now that there was no winning this war. Retreating to the castle had been the final blow – the moment it became undeniable that the rebels held every advantage. Their sheer numbers overwhelmed his dwindling forces, and their skill in battle rivalled even the fiercest warriors on his side. And then there was the channeller Cecilia had unearthed, an unpredictable force that even Elinor's formidable power couldn't match. Yet Elinor refused to admit defeat, her conviction unshaken even as the enemy closed in.

Bradley had pleaded with her to flee, to take Eadric and escape while they still could. But she wouldn't listen. She remained convinced they could turn the tide. Nothing he said could sway her. That morning, he had left their chambers, putting what little he could in place to aid her should she change her mind. But he had no intention of staying behind.

With everything arranged and a final message dispatched, urging Elinor to come with him and begin a new life elsewhere, he made his way back to his quarters. On the way, he crossed paths with Adrian. The encounter had nearly killed him. The bitter taste of defeat still lingered on his tongue – only a desperate manoeuvre had allowed him to escape with his life. Now, he moved swiftly through the shadowed passageways, his breaths sharp and shallow, heading towards the chamber where Lady Chloe protected his child.

Elinor might still believe she could shift the tide of battle, but Bradley knew better. The rebels' victory was inevitable, and staying would mean not only his death, but hers – and perhaps their son's as well. He couldn't allow that. Fleeing was the only option left, even if it meant leaving behind the woman he loved.

He had sent a raven to the docks, where his sister's ship awaited. She had warned him this would come. She had seen the danger in his union with Elinor long before he did. He had been blind. A fool. Now, as his world collapsed around him, he had one purpose left – to save his son. Whether Elinor chose to follow or not, he had to act.

Adina should already have been on her way to the hidden exit with the carriage, ready to take them to safety. The plan was fragile, a thread in the storm, but it was all they had. And Bradley would see it through, no matter the cost.

He stepped into the royal chambers through the secret passage, greeted immediately by the guards stationed inside. Their hands moved instinctively to their weapons before recognition dawned. They lowered their blades with respectful nods. Bradley offered a curt acknowledgement, his mind too consumed to bother with courtesies.

"Back to your posts," he ordered. "Keep watch. Ensure no one enters."

They hesitated, then obeyed, retreating to their positions. No one could know what he was planning. The fewer eyes on him, the better. As they moved away, tension bled from his shoulders. He couldn't be certain Elinor hadn't instructed them to keep him from Eadric, suspecting what he might do. She likely thought it was just an idea, a desperate threat he wouldn't dare carry out.

Turning to the room, Bradley's gaze landed on Lady Chloe. She sat slumped in an armchair, her head tilted to one side in uneasy sleep. He stepped lightly, careful not to wake her.

At the cot, his breath caught. His heart clenched as he looked down at the child, his child. Eadric's small face was peaceful in sleep, untouched by the storm gathering outside these walls. Bradley reached down, lifting him with aching tenderness. The infant stirred, a soft whimper escaping, but Bradley rocked him gently, whispering until he calmed.

He moved quickly after that, snatching a satchel from the corner and filling it with whatever he could find – Eadric's blanket, a carved wooden rattle, small comforts for the uncertain days ahead. At the dresser, he opened a gilded trinket box and rifled through its contents, pocketing gold coins, rings, and a jewelled brooch. He would need every resource he could carry – enough to buy safe passage far from this crumbling throne.

Lastly, he threw on a dark cloak, pulling the hood low over his brow. The weight of the satchel on his shoulder and the warmth of his son pressed against his chest grounded him. With one last glance at Chloe, still unaware, he slipped out of the chambers, his footsteps vanishing into the shadows of the passageway.

If Elinor was fool enough to keep fighting, so be it. But he wouldn't sacrifice his life, or their son's, for anyone. Not even her.

Bradley moved swiftly through the narrow, dimly lit corridors, his cloak trailing behind him. The air was thick with tension, pierced only by the distant clang of steel and muffled cries of battle. The secret hallways were nearly empty, save for the occasional figure darting past – members of the household, lords and ladies clutching what little they could carry as they sought their paths to safety. No one stopped him. No questions lingered in their hurried glances. They were all driven by the same grim purpose: survival.

The cries and clamour of the battle pressed against Bradley's ears, a cruel reminder of the time slipping through his fingers. Each desperate shout and clash of steel drove him onward until he reached the final doorway. His heart pounded. He paused just long enough to steady the infant in his arms. Eadric whimpered softly, nestling closer, as if he too could feel the fear surging through his father.

Bradley pushed open the heavy door, and the cool embrace of night met him like a whisper of freedom. Darkness stretched before him, the world beyond the castle shrouded in shadows. He stepped out cautiously, the chill biting at his face. The roar of battle faded behind him, but its weight clung to him like a shroud.

Just beyond the rubble-strewn courtyard, the outline of a carriage emerged, its form faint but unmistakable. Beside it stood his sister, her stance rigid with tension as her eyes scanned the gloom. At the sight of his silhouette slipping from the shadows, she stiffened, one hand flying instinctively to the dagger at her waist.

"Adina," he called softly, his voice low but urgent.

Recognition dawned, and she relaxed, though the lines of worry remained etched across her face. "You've made it," she whispered, relief tempered by the danger still looming.

She stepped forward to take Eadric. Bradley handed her the satchel first, his hands trembling as they brushed against hers. Then, gently, he passed the child into her arms. "Take him," he murmured, his voice hoarse. "Get inside."

He ushered her back to the carriage, catching a glimpse of Fleur waiting silently within. Adina nodded, her expression unreadable, and climbed in, cradling Eadric against her chest.

Bradley scanned the dark courtyard one last time and moved to follow – but a sharp, searing pain tore through him. He staggered. An arrow had struck his back, slicing through muscle and bone. His breath hitched as his knees buckled beneath him. The world tilted. Another arrow struck – then another. Each impact drove him closer to the ground until he could no longer resist gravity's pull.

"Bradley!" Adina cried, reaching for him, desperate to drag him to safety.

He pulled away, blood leaking through his cloak, staining the gravel beneath him. "Get out of here," he choked.

"Not without you!" she snapped. "Get inside the carriage—now!"

"No… It's too late." He collapsed to his knees, the cold gravel biting through the fabric of his trousers. Blood pooled beneath him, warmth spilling into the night. "Go," he rasped, barely audible but filled with desperate urgency. His blurred gaze met hers. "Go now!"

She reached for him one final time, but the whistle of another arrow split the air. It landed inches from her face. She recoiled, a sob breaking from her throat as tears streamed down her cheeks. The anguish in her eyes was unmistakable. She looked at him one last time, her heart breaking, before turning towards the carriage.

"Let's go," she cried to the driver.

With a jolt, the horses surged forward. The wheels groaned and crunched over the gravel, carrying the carriage – and his son – into the shadows, away from the chaos he could no longer outrun.

Bradley collapsed fully, his strength spent, his blood dark against the stones. The world around him dimmed, the cold creeping in as everything slipped away.

Chapter 49

A New Beginning

Those around them fought on, unaware of what had just transpired. Cecilia, assured that Aevah was safe for the moment, rose slowly to her feet. Her heart pounded as she looked down at Elinor's lifeless body. The queen's hand still clutched the dagger embedded in her chest, her wide, disbelieving eyes fixed on nothing as death claimed her.

Cecilia stood frozen, her ragged breaths mingling with the cacophony of battle. The clash of steel, the cries of the wounded – it all pressed in around her, yet she remained rooted, her gaze locked on the woman who had wrought so much destruction. All around, Elinor's warriors fought on, oblivious to the shift that had begun to ripple through their ranks.

It began with a single soldier. His gaze drifted towards the fallen monarch, and his weapon faltered mid-swing. Realisation struck him, his arms losing strength as his sword dipped. "The queen…" he murmured, voice unsteady. Another fighter turned, their expression slackening as they too saw the unthinkable. The news spread like wildfire through the battlefield.

One by one, the soldiers ceased fighting. Swords once lifted in fierce loyalty fell from trembling hands, the metallic clang of steel striking stone echoing through the throne room. The rebel fighters stood poised but watchful, their breaths held as Elinor's warriors began to surrender. They dropped their weapons and raised their arms, conceding defeat – to the rebels, and to the woman they had once called queen.

Cecilia remained at the centre of it all, her chest rising and falling as the weight of the moment settled over her. Behind her, the ornate throne loomed, a cruel monument to all she had fought for and all she had lost.

Elinor's body lay sprawled at her feet, a lifeless contrast to the shattered grandeur of the once-opulent room. Bloodstained marble floors caught the firelight with a dull gleam, while torn tapestries swayed limply in the smoke-laden air. Around them, the chaos of battle slowly ebbed.

The rebels – her army – moved with swift precision, disarming the surrendering soldiers. Those loyal to Elinor were gathered under heavy guard, bound and subdued. Some knelt with defiance still burning in their eyes, casting glances between Cecilia and the fallen queen as if willing Elinor to rise again. Others surrendered in hollow silence, their hands raised in a quiet plea for mercy. Beyond the throne room doors, the clash of steel and distant shouts still echoed, but within these walls, the tide had turned.

Cecilia's voice cut through the oppressive silence like a blade.

"Spare those who yield," she commanded, her tone firm but tempered with restraint. Her gaze swept over her army – men and women who had fought, bled, and sacrificed for this very moment. "But know this: there will be justice. For every drop of blood spilt in her name."

Her soldiers nodded, their movements precise and unwavering as they moved to secure the defeated forces. Cecilia's gaze lingered on Elinor's broken form for a moment longer, the lifeless body a grim symbol of the cruelty that had plagued her kingdom. But then her focus shifted.

Her eyes found her daughter.

Aevah sat amidst the wreckage of battle, one hand rubbing her throat where angry red marks stood out against her skin, vivid reminders of Elinor's grasp. Tears stung Cecilia's eyes, but she blinked them away. There was no room for weakness. Not yet.

"Aevah," she whispered, her voice hoarse with exhaustion. She stepped forward cautiously, as though afraid the image before her might vanish. Aevah's wide eyes met hers, and for a heartbeat, the chaos around them seemed to fade away.

"I'm fine," Aevah rasped, her voice unsteady with lingering pain. She lowered her hand from her throat and lifted her chin with quiet resolve. Her gaze drifted to Elinor's body, then to the rebel soldiers who moved swiftly to disarm and contain the last of the enemy. A faint, tremulous smile touched her lips. "You did it, Mother. You saved us all."

"No. Not just me," Cecilia said, her voice thick with emotion. "All of us. Every rebel who stood and fought made this happen."

Relief surged through her, sharp and unsteady. Her knees felt weak beneath the weight of what had been won. Drawing in a deep, trembling breath, she placed a hand gently on Aevah's shoulder.

"This is our moment to rebuild," she murmured. "For us. For everyone."

The throne room had fallen eerily quiet, save for the low murmur of voices and the clatter of weapons being gathered. Cecilia turned her gaze to the defeated soldiers. Many knelt in silence, eyes cast downward in shame. Others stared back at her, unyielding and defiant, refusing to accept the truth of their defeat.

"Take them to the lower halls," she ordered, her voice firm once more, laced with command. "They will face judgment. But we are not executioners. Their fates will be decided by their actions, not by vengeance."

Her army moved with practised precision, the sound of boots striking shattered ground echoing through the chamber. The rebels disarmed and bound Elinor's loyalists, escorting them to one side under vigilant guard. As the last of the enemy fighters were led away, Cecilia allowed her gaze to sweep across the throne room – a place that had once stood as a symbol of her family's legacy, now reduced to ruin. Death lingered in every corner. The acrid scent of blood clung to the air, and the broken remnants of marble and torn tapestries whispered of devastation.

Though they had triumphed, the victory rang hollow. The silence that had descended upon the castle was not peace; it was weighty, oppressive, a stillness filled with loss. Cecilia's legs felt like stone as she took in the wreckage, her thoughts drifting to the faces of those who had fought beside her. Too many were missing. Too many would never rise again.

The grandeur of the throne room had crumbled beneath the cost of their defiance. Blood stained the once-pristine floor, and smoke curled in lazy spirals above the shattered columns. The throne itself sat crooked, fractured – no longer a symbol of power, but of what had been endured to reclaim it.

She exhaled, unsteady and quiet in the hush.

Adrian's hand touched her shoulder, gentle and grounding. His fingers, rough with calluses, anchored her in the moment, pulling her back from the storm within. She turned to him, their eyes meeting. Exhaustion radiated from him, etched into every line of his face, but it was the quiet understanding in his gaze that unravelled her.

It broke through the fortress she had built around her grief. The walls she had held so tightly began to crumble.

The tears came without warning, hot and unstoppable. Her knees gave way beneath the weight of it all – the grief, the relief, the guilt. Adrian caught her with ease, pulling her into his arms.

He held her close, steady and sure, and she clung to him as if he were the only thing keeping her from sinking completely. Her fingers twisted into the fabric of his tunic. The dam had broken, and with it came the flood, the full, unrelenting tide of everything she had held back.

Her kingdom. Her people. Her failure to protect them.

Through the blur of tears and trembling breath, she heard Adrian's voice rise above the silence, steady, clear, and commanding.

"Listen up!"

The words rang out, sharp and sure. The scattered murmurs died away. Even the most distracted turned to listen.

"Spread out. Send messengers to every corner of the kingdom. Let them know—the war is over. Elinor is gone. Victory is ours."

A ripple of subdued agreement moved through the throne room. Boots shifted against broken marble, weapons clattered as they were collected. The soldiers stirred into action, driven by his words and the weight of what they had achieved.

When Adrian turned back to Cecilia and Aevah, the edge in his expression softened. Despite the exhaustion that clung to him – his ash-smeared face, his hunched posture, the raw fatigue in his eyes – his focus was sharp. He studied them both carefully, searching for signs of deeper harm.

Cecilia straightened under his gaze, though her limbs ached with weariness, and the pull of sorrow still threatened to drag her down. She steadied her breath and forced her shoulders back.

The war was over, but her people still looked to her. And they would need her strength now more than ever.

"Have either of you seen Bradley or the child?"

Adrian's voice cut through Cecilia's thoughts, low and urgent. The question landed like a stone in her chest.

She turned to Aevah, searching her daughter's face for any flicker of recognition, any sign of hope, but Aevah only shook her head. Her pallor, the stiffness in her posture, betrayed the shock still gripping her.

"No," Cecilia said, her voice quiet but weighted with concern.

The implications settled over her like a shroud. Bradley had vanished in the final moments of the battle, and the child – the thought of him stirred a knot of unease in her gut. She could feel Aevah tense beside her, her jaw set, lips pressed into a thin line that mirrored her apprehension.

Adrian's jaw clenched. His gaze moved between them, assessing and calculating. Then, with a swift pivot, he called to one of his men. His voice was quiet, but the steel in it left no room for doubt.

"Send word—discreetly. Find them both. Bradley must be brought in by any means necessary. But no harm is to come to the child. Do you understand?"

The soldier nodded and vanished into the swirl of motion around them.

Still, the tension in Cecilia's chest refused to ease. The war had been won, but shadows remained – threats hidden in the aftermath. Bradley. The child. The fragile, uncertain peace. One thing was clear: Bradley had to be found. Had to be stopped. If not, everything they'd fought for might still unravel.

With the fighting behind them, Cecilia moved through the castle's familiar halls. It was a strange, bittersweet return. Each step stirred memories, some heavy with grief, others filled with stubborn hope. As she passed, soldiers and castle staff paused to acknowledge her. Some bowed their heads, murmuring thanks or soft words of praise. Others simply stared, their expression etched with fatigue, shock, and sorrow.

Cecilia met them all with quiet nods, a faint, solemn smile tugging at her lips. This victory wasn't hers alone. It belonged to them all – the wounded, the fallen, the survivors who had held the line.

She paused in the great hall, where the wounded lay in rows, tended by healers and volunteers. The air was thick with the scent of blood and poultices, heavy with moans and whispered reassurances. Yet beneath it all was life. Enduring. Breathing.

She knelt beside a young soldier, his arm tightly bandaged, his skin pale with pain, but his eyes clear and steady.

"Thank you," she murmured, meeting his gaze. "Your courage made this possible."

He offered a faint smile and nodded.

Cecilia rose and moved on, her footsteps echoing through the stone hallways of her reclaimed home.

Eventually, she climbed the winding stairs to the battlements, where the remnants of her closest circle awaited. The cool night air struck her as she stepped onto the open platform, its quiet sharpness a stark contrast to the heat and noise of the throne room below. The castle grounds sprawled beneath them, scarred by war – tents still smouldered, and weary figures moved slowly through the wreckage. Yet beyond the chaos, the horizon held the faintest glimmer of dawn.

Adrian, Aevah, Darius and a few others turned as she approached. Their faces reflected the same mix of emotions that stirred in her chest – triumph tempered by exhaustion, uncertainty shadowed by grief. For a moment, they stood together in silence, gazing out at the ravaged world they had fought to reclaim.

"It's over," Adrian said at last, his voice low. "But there's still so much to rebuild."

Cecilia nodded, her eyes fixed on the pale line of light blooming on the edge of the sky. "The hardest battles come after the war," she murmured. "We've won, but now we must mend what's been broken."

The first light of dawn crept across the land as the hush between them broke. Footsteps approached – measured and hesitant. A group of her soldiers came forward, their faces solemn. One of the captains stepped ahead, his posture stiff, gaze lowered with the weight of what he carried.

"Your Majesty," he began, his voice tight with restrained emotion, "the death toll is higher than we feared. Many fought to the last breath… but there are names you'll want to hear."

He paused, swallowing hard before continuing.

As he read the list, each name struck with painful familiarity – men and women she had known, had trusted, had fought beside. But two names cut deeper than the rest.

"Galrick and Isabella… they didn't make it. I'm so sorry."

Cecilia's breath caught in her throat. The words hit with brutal clarity, carving fresh wounds in an already battered heart. Gone.

A heaviness settled over her chest – sorrow tangled with guilt, with gratitude, with the bitter truth that their sacrifice had helped bring about this fragile dawn.

"There is another you must know of."

The captain hesitated, glancing at Cecilia as if weighing the weight of what he was about to say. "Bradley."

At the name, a ripple of tension passed through the group. Fatigue was momentarily forgotten as backs straightened and eyes sharpened. Adrian's jaw clenched, his expression hardening.

"What about him?" he asked, voice low and taut.

"He's dead," the captain replied. There was no sorrow in his tone, only grim finality. "He was struck down while trying to flee the castle grounds. But…"

Cecilia's gaze sharpened. "But what?"

The captain shifted uncomfortably. "The child—the boy—escaped. We believe Bradley managed to get him out through the hidden passages before he was killed. We're still piecing it together, but… there's no trace of him. He's gone."

A heavy silence settled over them.

Adrian exchanged a glance with Cecilia, his features drawn, contemplative. "So the child is missing," he said quietly. "Bradley and Elinor's heir."

A fresh weight dropped into Cecilia's chest. Her breath came slowly, deliberately, as she tried to steady the tightening coil of dread within her.

"If he's out there," Adrian continued, "he could return one day—claim the throne."

Cecilia nodded slowly, the truth bitter on her tongue. "We have to find him before anyone else does. He's just a child—innocent—but his bloodline makes him dangerous. If someone decides to use him… this kingdom could fall into chaos all over again. I won't let that happen."

Another guard stepped forward. "We also have Lady Chloe in custody. She's under guard and awaiting interrogation."

Cecilia's lips pressed into a thin line. "She was fiercely loyal to Elinor, but her resolve might crack now that the queen is dead. We need answers—and fast. Before word of the boy spreads."

Aevah's voice cut through the stillness, soft but firm. "Do you intend to raise the child, Mother? If we find him, I mean."

The group stilled. All eyes turned to Cecilia, as though the future hinged on her response.

She met Aevah's eyes without hesitation. "Yes," she said. "He is innocent. Whatever his parents were, he doesn't deserve to live under the weight of their sins. If Elinor and Bradley are truly gone, then we have the chance to shape him into something better. Someone who can strengthen the kingdom… not tear it apart."

Adrian's brow furrowed. "Not everyone will see it that way," he said. "There will be dissent, especially if the boy ever learns who he is."

"Then we'll deal with it," Cecilia replied, her voice firm, though a quiet tremor of doubt stirred beneath the surface. "We have no choice but to try."

Scouts were dispatched at once, slipping into the early morning gloom in search of any sign of the boy. Meanwhile, the group remained on the battlements, cloaked in a silence heavy with grief. They mourned in quiet company, surrounded by the weight of absence.

Nicholas sat apart from the others, his head bowed, hands clasped tightly together as if holding on to the last pieces of his brother's presence. Aevah moved to his side, her sorrow etched plainly on her face. She rested a hand on his shoulder, light and grounding. When she spoke, her voice trembled, but her words carried strength.

"Galrick fought so hard for this moment," she said. "All he wanted was to make sure we survived. He and Isabella both."

She paused, her hand remaining steady on Nicholas's shoulder. "They would be smiling down on us now, glad to see we made it."

Nicholas released a ragged breath, lifting his gaze to meet hers. His eyes were red rimmed, shadowed by grief, but Aevah's words seemed to reach him, if only slightly.

"They gave everything for us," he murmured, his voice cracking. "I'm going to miss them. Jacob, too," he added, the name thick with emotion. He knew that Aevah carried her loss – that the ache in her heart mirrored his.

Aevah's fingers tightened gently around his shoulder. Tears shimmered in her eyes, but her voice was resolute. "We won't forget them," she said. "Galrick, Isabella, Jacob… They believed in what we were building. They fought for it, died for it. We'll make sure their sacrifices meant something."

Across from them, Cecilia sat in silence, her hands folded tightly in her lap, her posture composed but brittle. The names rang through her mind – Jacob's most of all – alongside the faces of so many others who had given everything. Grief settled in her like a second skin: inescapable, and somehow still incomplete.

The group exchanged quiet glances, the flicker of resolve returning despite the exhaustion etched into every movement. Gradually, they turned their attention to the future – reparations, justice, and the delicate task of uniting a kingdom torn apart. Cecilia listened, contributed, but even as they spoke of rebuilding, the ache in her chest persisted.

This was the moment she had fought for. And now it was hers to carry.

Then she felt it – a shift in the air, subtle but unmistakable. The atmosphere seemed to ripple, energy curling through it like a sudden wind. A strange stillness fell over the group.

Cecilia turned, her heart quickening.

A figure stepped from the shadows.

The old woman emerged with fluid grace, each step light and deliberate, almost too effortless for someone who had stood on the battlefield mere hours ago. Not a scratch marked her skin, not a hair lay out of place. Amid the weary, bloodstained survivors, she seemed untouched, an illusion of calm in the wreckage of war.

If Cecilia hadn't seen her unleash her fury on the battlefield, she might have thought the woman had arrived late, missing the chaos entirely.

The old woman's serene smile held something strange, otherworldly. Her eyes gleamed with a knowing light, ancient and unreadable. For a moment, Cecilia felt as if the ground beneath her had shifted, as if time itself paused in deference.

"You've done well," the woman said, her voice soft, yet threaded with quiet command. "The battle is over, but much remains to be done."

Chapter 50

The Divine Spirit

Cecilia glanced between her companions before extending a hand to the old woman, her gesture calm and resolute. "Thank you for your aid during the battle," she said. "You helped turn the tide in our favour, and for that, I will always be grateful. But… I can't shake the feeling that our meetings weren't by chance. Adrian and I—we've seen you before."

"Yes!" Adrian stepped forward, urgency in his voice. "You're the woman who vanished from the inn!" His eyes widened as recognition dawned. "I didn't realise it at first, but now it's clear. That was you."

The old woman regarded them with a serene smile, her features softened by their words. "Indeed, it was me," she said, her voice rich with an ageless calm. "Every meeting we've shared has had purpose, though not in the way you might imagine."

Cecilia hesitated, curiosity filling her tone. "Purpose? What do you mean?"

The woman shifted, her movements graceful despite the frailty of her frame. "I have walked among you in many forms—each one chosen to guide when guidance was needed most. I introduced myself as Elara to all of you. To you and Adrian, I was the old woman who offered comfort. For Aevah, I was her mentor and confidant. Each face was shaped with care, tailored to the needs of those I encountered. Even through Zara, the High Priestess, I offered counsel. The prophecy she bore—it was mine. A message meant not for control, but for warning. And for hope. It was always meant for this day, when the shards would reunite, and I could become my true self once more."

Her voice faded into the stillness, and the air around them stirred, as if the earth itself exhaled. Energy shimmered, unseen yet palpable, like the first breath of dawn.

"My name is Indra," she said. "The Divine Spirit of this land. You were not fighting my battle, but I was here to guide you in restoring balance. Without your actions, the fragments would have remained scattered. And I would still be lost."

Cecilia stared at the figure before her, unable to look away. The woman – no, the Divine Spirit – radiated a presence that defied all mortal comprehension. She was ageless yet ancient, her skin glowing like sunlight dancing on water. A living paradox, she was everything and nothing, a being beyond the limits of understanding. Her presence was overwhelming – brilliant yet comforting; immense, yet profoundly still. Even the world itself seemed to hold its breath as she spoke.

"When the crystal broke," she began, her voice resonating with a depth that stirred the soul, "my connection to this realm was severed. It was my tether, my anchor to the physical world. Without it, I was cast into limbo. My essence scattered, my strength faded. For thousands of years, I existed only in fragments, able to reach your world only briefly, and only through borrowed forms. I offered what guidance I could, but my true self remained just out of reach."

She lifted her gaze, the light around her seeming to pulse with her words.

"But as the shards began to reunite, so too did my power. With each piece, my presence strengthened, the bond reforged. Now that the crystal is whole, I am whole as well."

She paused, her gaze sweeping over them, her eyes meeting each of theirs in turn.

"I have watched you fight and sacrifice. I have seen your courage, your doubt, and your grief. Now, I am here to mend what was broken—not only the crystal, but the bond it represents. Together, we will link the power of the shards to the new royal line and ensure that it is wielded with wisdom."

Her words hung in the air, heavy with promise and purpose. For a long moment, no one spoke, each of them stunned beneath the weight of revelation and radiance.

At last, Cecilia found her voice. "This doesn't feel real," she said softly. "But… why now? Why us?"

The Divine Spirit's smile deepened, warmth blooming through her luminous form.

"Because now, the balance can be restored. The shards have chosen their bearers. The battle against Elinor has ended. What comes next is the beginning of something new."

She turned to Aevah, her glow softening as she stepped closer. Each movement was slow and deliberate, granting the moment the reverence it deserved. Then, with quiet grace, she cupped Aevah's face in her hands. Despite the divine aura around her, her touch was warm and grounding.

"You are the one," she said, her voice threaded with absolute certainty. "The shards have chosen you, Aevah. The bond is yours to wield. And tomorrow, once rest has restored your strength, we will begin."

Aevah's breath caught in her throat. Her eyes widened as the words sank in, and she gave a small shake of her head, as if trying to cast off the weight of it all.

"Me?" she whispered. "But surely… surely there's been a mistake. How can I—how can I possibly—?"

Before Aevah could finish, Nicholas stepped forward, his voice steady and sure. "You've always been the one, Aevah. Everything you've endured—every step of this journey—has led you here."

Cecilia nodded, her gaze unwavering. "It's true. The shards wouldn't have come together without you. They're bound to you now, because this was always meant to be yours to carry forward."

Aevah looked between them, her lips trembling as she struggled to speak. But the significance of their words left her mute. Finally, she swallowed, her voice barely above a whisper. "I… I don't know if I can do this."

"You can," said the Divine Spirit, her voice low and resonant, filled with a quiet strength. "And you will not walk this path alone. Together, we will mend what was broken."

Cecilia watched her daughter closely, heart aching at the storm of emotion etched into her face. Aevah's breaths came unevenly, her eyes distant, as though searching for clarity in some far-off place.

Stepping closer, Cecilia softened her voice. "I know it's hard to make sense of it all," she said gently. "But I know you. I've seen your strength, your heart—your courage—even when you couldn't see it yourself. And I believe in you."

Aevah's hands trembled at her sides, her mouth tightening as she tried to hold herself steady. "I… I'm just not sure I'm ready for this," she admitted, her voice cracking under the weight of her vulnerability.

Cecilia placed a hand on her shoulder, her touch firm, grounding. "You don't have to be—not yet. None of us was ready when this began. But that didn't stop you then, did it?"

Nicholas stepped forward again, his voice soft but unwavering. "We trust you."

Adrian echoed him with a nod. One by one, those gathered on the balcony stepped forward or lifted their chins, offering quiet smiles, solemn nods, and silent support.

Aevah looked around, gratitude warming her chest. She turned to the Divine Spirit, her voice hushed but clear. "I don't know if I'm worthy… but I trust your judgement—and theirs."

The Divine Spirit's radiance softened. Her presence was still vast but now more intimate, more human. "Worthiness is not something we are born with," she said, her voice like wind through leaves, calm and resonant. "Nor something we seize. It is forged through the choices we make, the hardships we overcome, and the strength we uncover when all hope seems lost. You have already proven yourself in ways you have yet to understand."

Aevah's gaze shifted to the crystal shards glowing softly at her side, then back to the faces of those who stood with her. Their belief held her steady, even as doubt lingered at the edges of her heart. She nodded, hesitantly at first, then with growing resolve.

"I'll try," she said quietly. "I'll do everything I can."

Nicholas clapped a reassuring hand to her shoulder, offering a warm grin. "That's all any of us can do, Aevah."

Cecilia stepped beside her, her eyes bright with pride. "You're not alone in this. We're with you. All of us."

The Divine Spirit inclined her head, her expression unreadable, yet imbued with a deep, quiet approval. "Tomorrow brings a new journey. Rest now. You'll need your strength, for what lies ahead will demand more than courage. It will demand unity."

As the group slowly dispersed, the weight of the moment lingered like the sun breaking over the horizon. Cecilia stayed, watching her daughter from a few paces back, pride swelling in her chest. Yet beneath it, a shadow of concern stirred. The road ahead wouldn't be easy, but if anyone could walk it, it was Aevah.

Their eyes met across the quiet. For a long moment, neither spoke.

Then, with her gaze fixed on the broken land below, Aevah whispered, her voice fragile but rising with quiet strength, "I'll be ready."

Chapter 51

Recovery

Weeks had passed, yet each morning, Cecilia awoke feeling tethered to the echoes of the past. For a fleeting moment, she was back in the heart of battle, fighting desperately to survive. The memories clung to her like shadows, unrelenting and vivid. But soon the present would reclaim her, reminding her that they had endured. A soft, unbidden smile would stretch across her lips.

Across the room, Adrian was already awake, his movements deliberate as he dressed for the day. She watched him for a while, quiet admiration settling in her chest. He had become the Queen's knight, protector of the realm and confidant to Aevah, her daughter, the new queen.

Cecilia's days had grown simpler, yet no less meaningful. Though the crown now rested on Aevah's brow, she had found renewed purpose in her role on the royal council. Here, her experience as a former queen lent weight to her words, her voice a steadying presence amid the trials of rebuilding a fractured kingdom. It was a role she had never envisioned for herself, but one she had come to cherish.

The kingdom hadn't forgotten its losses, nor had she. Funerals had been held for the fallen, solemn moments of unity that bound the people in shared grief and gratitude. The priestesses had returned to their sacred duties, weaving faith and tradition into a tapestry of hope. The air remained heavy with remembrance, but it also carried a quiet resolve – to honour those who had given everything for a future worth believing in.

As Cecilia dressed, her thoughts turned to Aevah. The young queen had embraced her role with a strength and grace that stirred deep pride in Cecilia's heart. Every time she saw her daughter speak before the people, that pride swelled anew – quiet, steady, and profound.

Adrian's voice drew her back, warm and familiar. "All set to face the day?" he asked, fastening the final clasp of his armour.

She looked up at him, her smile deepening. "As ready as ever," she replied, her heart lighter than it had been in months.

Together, they stepped into the world they had helped rebuild – a realm where hope, at long last, had begun to bloom once more.

When Cecilia reached the royal hall, the sight before her gave her pause. Sunlight streamed through the tall windows, casting golden beams across the chamber. Repairs had been underway for weeks, and the room now looked nearly restored. Fresh drapes and tapestries softened the remaining cracks, while the pillars gleamed with newly set gold. The space radiated quiet grandeur, each gilded line a testament to resilience, transforming the scars of battle into something luminous. Where once there had been fractures, now golden seams shimmered in the morning light. The hall hadn't forgotten what it had endured – it honoured it, its very foundation gleaming with the weight of survival and rebirth.

Atop the steps, Aevah sat upon the restored throne, her presence both radiant and composed. Beside her, the Divine Spirit hovered, a shimmering figure, at once ethereal and deeply grounded. They spoke in low tones as Aevah practised channelling her newfound power. The air was charged with energy, as though the chamber itself held its breath in reverence.

Linked to all four shards, Aevah had become a symbol of unity and strength for their people. Cecilia's heart swelled as she watched her daughter, so composed and determined, embrace her role as queen. For the briefest moment, she saw the little girl Aevah once had been, darting barefoot through the castle gardens. And yet here she stood now, a monarch shaping the future of their kingdom.

Adrian approached the throne, his posture relaxed but ever alert. Cecilia walked just behind him, her gaze still fixed on her daughter, a gentle smile playing on her lips. As she reached the base of the steps, Aevah's eyes met hers.

"Morning, Mother," Aevah said, her voice warm and steady.

The Divine Spirit turned as well, her radiant form bowing ever so slightly in greeting.

"Good morning," Cecilia replied, stepping closer. "How fares your training today?"

Aevah smiled, a glimmer of humour in her eyes. "Challenging, as always. But I think I'm beginning to understand the balance."

The Divine Spirit spoke then, her voice melodic and resonant. "She learns swiftly. The shards are powerful, but Aevah's heart is steadfast. She will wield them with wisdom."

Cecilia nodded, pride glinting softly in her expression. "Of that, I have no doubt."

Aevah descended the steps, her movements graceful and sure, as though the weight of her crown had settled easily upon her shoulders. She reached for Cecilia and embraced her, and Cecilia returned the hug with quiet strength, her heart full.

Cecilia held her close for a moment, then gently pulled back, studying her daughter's face. "Have you thought more about what we discussed?" she asked, her voice calm, though curiosity flickered behind her eyes. "The new lords and ladies of the land?"

Aevah nodded, quiet certainty settling in her features. "Yes. I plan to share my decisions at dinner tonight with our friends." A hint of a smile touched her lips. "Though I have already spoken to Lord Stone."

Cecilia arched a brow, intrigued but not surprised. "And how did he receive the news?"

"With great consideration," Aevah replied, a respectful note in her tone. "He understands what it means—for the kingdom, and himself."

Cecilia hummed softly, approval warming in her chest. Aevah had stepped into her role with grace, learning not only how to command but to listen, to weigh decisions with care, to judge with wisdom rather than impulse.

She knew what a difficult choice Lord Stone had made. Allowing him to retain his title wasn't simply a gesture of forgiveness – it was a calculated act of rebuilding trust. His past actions had left scars on the realm and his reputation alike, yet in the final hours, he had chosen differently – chosen loyalty, chosen change. Aevah's decision to let him keep his lands reflected not only maturity but a deep understanding of what the kingdom now required. Strength, yes – but more than that, faith. Trust was the foundation upon which lasting peace must be built.

After the battle, the Divine Spirit had spoken to Lord Stone and Rosalind. The torment Rosalind had endured under Elinor's hand had left its mark, but with Indra's power, much of the damage was healed. Not long after, they had returned home, determined to rebuild alongside their family.

Most of the lords and former rebels had departed by the end of the first week, their duty to the fallen honoured through solemn funerals and shared mourning. But Cecilia's closest companions had remained, offering their strength to help Aevah shape a new future. Their presence had become a quiet reassurance – a reminder of bonds forged in fire and loss.

Soon, though, even they would return to their lands and lives. But not before one final gathering, a farewell dinner to honour those they had lost, to embrace the promise of what lay ahead, and to mark the roles many would soon assume. It would be an evening of remembrance and renewal, a gentle turning of the page from one chapter to the next.

Change had been inevitable. Many former lords had forfeited their titles willingly. Among the first were Lloyd and Victoria Roberts, who had vanished without a trace before the final battle. Whispers told of their escape by ship from Darlington, abandoning their queen in her hour of need. With their whereabouts unknown, Aevah had no difficulty stripping them of land and title. Their absence spoke louder than any defiance they might have offered.

Then there was Christopher Malins, who had served Elinor until the bitter end. Refusing to surrender, he poisoned his entire family before taking his own life, an act carried out in front of the guards sent to apprehend him. His name, his holdings – everything – was erased from the records, as though he had never existed.

Lord and Lady Bennett proved a more complicated matter, given their long-standing ties to the former queen and their connection to Nicholas. Despite the personal cost, Nicholas agreed that his parents must face justice. Their titles and estate were stripped and transferred to him. Yet he chose not to reside in the family home, instead remaining in Carraton by Aevah's side.

Though Nicholas permitted his parents to stay in their former residence, they now lived a far simpler life. Their wealth had been seized, and their movements carefully monitored. Aevah's love for Nicholas may have softened their sentence, but mercy didn't exempt them from accountability. The rule of law remained firm, even for those closest to the crown.

The last matter concerned the Woodlock family. With Bradley gone and his sister's whereabouts unknown, their mother was taken into custody. She surrendered her rights with surprising ease, as though she had long accepted her downfall. There was no protest, no plea for clemency, only quiet resignation, as if power had already slipped through her fingers.

Rather than a prison sentence, Aevah decreed that she would live out her remaining days in the temple, dedicating herself to a life of humble service. Stripped of status and wealth, she faded into obscurity among the priestesses, her past reduced to a whisper, her future devoted to contemplation rather than influence.

These decisions left many positions vacant across the realm, making it all the more compelling for Cecilia to see whom Aevah would appoint to fill the gaps. Fortunately, Lord Stone and Lord Bishop remained, both seasoned leaders, well-versed in the responsibilities of governance. Lord Bishop, in particular, had become a figure others could look to for guidance, Aevah included. He and his family had stood by her until the very end, their loyalty unshaken and their counsel invaluable in shaping the road ahead.

Confident that her daughter had matters well in hand, Cecilia turned to the rest of her day. Several meetings with council members awaited her – discussions that would ensure the transition of power continued smoothly. Though the crown had passed on, her role remained vital. She was no longer queen, but she was still a steadying force – an anchor amid the ever-shifting tides of change.

Chapter 52

A Legacy Reborn

Aevah stood before the mirror, adjusting the delicate embroidery along the cuffs of her gown. The weight of the crown remained unfamiliar, but the responsibility it carried had begun to feel natural, an extension of everything she had fought for. Tonight was more than a night of shared memories; it was a celebration, a gathering that marked the dawn of a new era.

Beyond remembrance, beyond farewells, this dinner stood as a symbol of change – a testament to the kingdom's renewal. Aevah wasn't merely hosting a meal among friends; she was ushering in a future where tradition no longer dictated power, where ladies stood as equals to lords, their strength and wisdom recognised without question.

She inhaled deeply, smoothing her hands over the fabric of her gown. Turning, she let her gaze drift over the familiar room. The royal chambers. Now hers. She had insisted her mother take them, after all, they had once belonged to her, but the former queen wouldn't hear of it. As queen, the chambers were Aevah's by right. She wasn't yet entirely accustomed to the title, but with each passing day, it became a little easier to bear.

She and Jacob had left royal life behind when they were only eight years old. The return had come with a steep learning curve. Their grandfather, George, had taught them the essentials, but court etiquette and royal formality were skills she had to reacquire. Aevah exhaled softly. Being here without either of them – Jacob or Grandpa George – was a quiet ache she carried every day.

Her fingers drifted over the intricate carvings of the vanity, the familiar patterns worn smooth with age. The memories here were heavy, echoes of laughter and mischief. She and Jacob had often hidden in this very room to avoid bedtime, giggling behind curtains or beneath furniture. Their grandfather had always played along, pretending not to notice before scooping them both up, one child balanced on each hip, as he carried them off to their chambers, ending the night with a story or two.

A knock at the door drew her from the memory. She straightened, composing herself before calling, "Come in."

The door creaked open to reveal one of her ladies-in-waiting, eyes filled with cautious concern. "Your Majesty, the guests are gathering—and young Lord Nicholas is here to escort you."

"Let him in. I'm ready."

Nicholas entered with a warm smile, bowing deeply as he stepped into the room.

"My queen," he said, offering his arm. "May I escort you to dinner?"

Aevah laughed, the sound light and unrestrained. "Really, Nicholas. You, of all people, don't need to bow to me." She accepted his arm with a smile. "But I would be delighted to accompany you. I've been looking forward to tonight."

And she meant it. After everything they had endured, she could finally see the light ahead, and she wanted nothing more than to share that light, that new beginning, with the people who had stood beside her.

Together, they walked towards the private royal dining chambers, where friends and family awaited them. The palace hallways were rich with the scent of roasted meats and spiced wine. From beyond the doors drifted the hum of quiet conversation, the occasional laughter mingling with undertones of solemn reflection. Tonight, titles would be given not out of tradition, but as a promise, a vow towards a better future.

As they entered the dining room, Aevah saw that many of her guests were already seated. Some began to rise out of respect, but she halted them with a small wave and a faint frown.

"Please, keep your seat," she said gently, moving to the head of the table.

Nicholas took his place at her left, and Aevah took a moment to look around. Her heart swelled at the sight of those she called family – some by blood, others by bond, all irreplaceable.

Edward and his wife, Sage, sat beside Bryne and Isaac. The four of them had stood as pillars during her and Jacob's darkest days, offering kindness and shelter when the world had turned cold. Because of them, she had found a family she never knew she needed – and a safe haven when fear and uncertainty had loomed large.

Nearby sat Walter and young Timmy, along with Erica and Trysten. Though her time with them had been shorter, their stories had become a part of her own. Without their courage and sacrifice, the war might have ended far differently. Erica, Damon, and Trysten, in particular, held a place of deep significance in her heart. They had fought for Jacob until the very end. Though they hadn't been able to save him, they had given everything they had, and the memories they carried of him were a gift beyond measure.

Further down the table, beside her mother and Adrian, sat Marcus, Darius, and Fiona. They had worked tirelessly behind the scenes, chipping away at Elinor's power, undermining her at every turn. Their loyalty and courage had helped turn the tide of the rebellion. Aevah respected them deeply, not only for their actions, but for the constancy with which they had stood beside her cause.

Even Adrian, once a figure she had regarded with suspicion, had grown on her. Knowing how his journey began and how hard he had worked to make amends had allowed her to see the truth of his remorse. He was no longer just a relic of the past; he had proven his loyalty, time and again. And though she wouldn't say it aloud, seeing how happy he made her mother softened her view of him even further.

And then there was Nicholas. What could she possibly say about the man who had stolen her heart? When they had reunited, love had been the last thing she expected – but there she was. He had been her constant, her steady presence in the chaos. He understood the heaviness she bore, not just as a queen, but as Aevah: the girl who had lost, who had loved, and who had fought for something greater than herself. He never saw only a ruler or a warrior; he saw *her*. And that had made all the difference.

She turned to him now, catching the warmth in his gaze. It was a look that spoke of quiet devotion, of a promise unspoken – a vow that, no matter what lay ahead, they would face it together.

Aevah smiled softly, her fingers brushing against his beneath the table. The gesture was simple, but it said everything that words never could.

Knowing the moment was as bittersweet as it was significant, she rose to her feet and lifted her glass.

"Thank you," she began, her voice steady but full of emotion. "Each one of you, in this room. Without you, we wouldn't be here today. Though we have won the war, we have each lost someone along the way."

She paused, lowering her head in solemn remembrance. Around the table, others followed suit.

"Their sacrifice wasn't in vain. And they will not be forgotten. Please, let us raise a glass. To those gone but never forgotten."

"To those gone but never forgotten," came the chorus, voices unified as glasses were raised high and then touched to lips in reverent silence.

Aevah looked around once more, her smile touched with both gratitude and grief. "Please, everyone, we have a wonderful feast before us. Dig in."

At her word, the room stirred to life. Plates were passed, laughter bubbled up again, and the heavy stillness gave way to warmth and celebration.

The table was filled with plates of roasted meats, fragrant and tender, their juices pooling beside golden-crusted breads. Steamed root vegetables, rich with butter and herbs, were handed from one guest to another, accompanied by bowls of spiced grains and sauces that carried the comforting scent of home.

Goblets brimmed with amber wine and honeyed mead, candlelight catching the glass and casting a soft golden glow over the gathering. Conversation rose and fell like gentle waves, and laughter once again found its place among them.

It was a feast – not just of food, but of resilience, remembrance, and the lives they had fought so fiercely to protect.

As the evening wore on and the main courses dwindled, dessert was brought out, trays lined with delicate pastries, fresh fruits, and sugared confections. Aevah's gaze drifted over the spread, casual at first, until something familiar caught her eye.

At the centre of the dessert table sat her mother's honey cakes.

Her breath caught, a small smile tugging at her lips. Those cakes had been a symbol of warmth and comfort in simpler times. Her mother had baked them for birthdays, celebrations, and quiet evenings when the world felt too heavy. For Aevah, they were more than just a sweet treat – they were a reminder of home, of love, of safety.

And now, here they were again, nestled among the delicacies of a feast meant to mark the beginning of something new.

She reached for one, fingers brushing the soft, golden surface. The scent of honey and warm spices enveloped her, bringing with it a flood of memories: laughter in the kitchen, flour-dusted hands, her mother's soothing voice humming over the clatter of pots. Moments that had once seemed small but now meant everything.

She turned, meeting her mother's gaze across the room.

"I see you still can't resist my cakes?" Cecilia said knowingly.

"Of course not. They're divine," Aevah replied before taking a bite and then promptly reaching for a second.

"Are they really that good?" Timmy asked, eyeing the tray as he took one for himself.

"The best," Aevah said and gave a knowing nod.

Timmy took a bite, and his eyes widened in delight before he quickly stuffed the rest into his mouth. The sight sent a ripple of laughter around the table, and soon, everyone reached for a honey cake of their own. Conversations resumed, turning now to childhood favourites and nostalgic treats.

"I always loved my grandmother's spice loaf," Bryne admitted, shaking his head as he savoured a bite. "But this might be stealing the crown."

"Nothing beats warm berry tarts, fresh out of the oven," Sage said with a grin, reaching for her goblet of mead. "With a dollop of cream—absolutely heavenly."

"You're both wrong," Darius chimed in, grinning broadly. "Caramel-dipped apples after the harvest feast. The crunch, the sweetness—perfection."

Aevah laughed, listening as the light-hearted debate unfolded. There was something deeply comforting in the simplicity of it all – in the way old friends and new shared pieces of their past without fear or hesitation. For the first time in a long while, it truly felt like a state of peace.

Her gaze flicked to Nicholas, who had been quietly watching the exchange, an amused smirk playing at the corners of his lips. He caught her glance and nudged her playfully.

"And what about you, my queen?" he asked. "What was your favourite?"

She smiled, considering for a moment. "Well, my mother's honey cakes, of course. But if I had to choose another…" She paused, tapping a finger thoughtfully against her goblet. "Jacob and I used to sneak into the kitchens at night and steal handfuls of sugared almonds. I swear, they tasted better stolen."

Laughter burst from around the table, her mother shaking her head in mock disapproval.

"And to think," Cecilia said, feigning scandal, "I raised such a troublemaker."

Aevah laughed with them, warmth spreading through her chest. This – this was what tonight was meant to be. A celebration. A moment of healing. A reminder that even after great loss, there was still sweetness to be found in life.

As she looked around the table, watching the joy and laughter ripple through the people she loved most, she knew the time had come.

She straightened slightly in her seat and raised her voice just enough to carry. "If I may have everyone's attention."

The room quieted at once, all eyes turning towards her.

"I have gifts to offer each of you," she said, her voice steady and sincere. "Should you choose to accept them. These are not simply tokens of gratitude, but promises—recognition of what you've given, and what you may yet help build."

Her gaze shifted first to Marcus, Darius, and Fiona, her expression softening with respect.

"You three have fought not only for victory, but for justice—for the people who look to us for guidance and hope. Your courage, loyalty, and unwavering resolve have shaped this battle. And now, I ask you to help shape what comes next."

She paused, letting her words settle.

"I offer you each a place of highest honour within the Queen's Guard—not merely as protectors, but as leaders, strategists, and symbols of the kingdom's strength."

Her eyes found Marchus first. "Marcus, I offer you the mantle of Commander. You will train and guide those entrusted with the defence of our people."

Then to Darius. "Your mind for strategy, your understanding of battle and terrain—you've been invaluable. I would have you serve as Master of Intelligence, ensuring no threat escapes our notice."

Finally, to Fiona. "Your dedication is unmatched. I would trust no one more to stand at my side as my guardian. Fiona, I name you Shield of the Queen."

She met each of their gazes in turn, allowing the weight of her words – and the significance of the offer – to settle fully.

"If you accept," she continued, her voice clear and steady, "know that this is more than a title. It is a vow, a responsibility. It is the next step in forging a future where the kingdom stands not through fear, but through trust and unity."

Marcus rose first, followed closely by Darius and Fiona.

"My queen," Marcus said, his voice rich with respect, "you honour us all. I accept this role with gratitude and resolve."

Darius inclined his head, a rare smile curving at the edge of his mouth. "This is more than we ever expected. We have fought for the future, and now you entrust us with safeguarding it. I, too, accept this role."

Fiona pressed a hand to her heart and bowed low. "I would be proud to serve at your side, Your Majesty. I accept this with everything I am."

One by one, they resumed their seats, the weight of the moment settling over them like a solemn benediction. The room remained still, quiet for a breath, as those gathered absorbed the gravity of what had just taken place. Then, slowly, a ripple of murmured approval moved through the table – nodding heads, soft smiles – a shared acknowledgement of the trust Aevah had placed in them.

She exhaled gently, her eyes returning to each of them in turn. "Thank you," she said. "Each of you has proven not only your strength but your heart. I believe in you—now and always."

Turning next to Edward and Bryne, she stood once more, raising her glass in their direction, a warm smile playing at her lips.

"Edward," she began, "your steadfast leadership, your wisdom, and your unwavering commitment to protecting those in your care have made you invaluable. You have given so much, and now, I entrust you with the stewardship of the kingdom's ports. It will be your task to ensure trade and prosperity flourish under your watch. And with this duty comes an honour you have long since earned: I name you Lord. Of course, your home,

Dunes Rest, shall remain yours, a sanctuary for you and your family—always."

Edward inclined his head, his expression composed but deeply moved. "It would be my honour, my queen."

She turned then to Bryne, her voice no less warm, but firm with conviction.

"Bryne, your devotion to your people, your quiet strength, and your unbreakable bond with those who fought beside you speak volumes. Because of all you've done and all you are, I grant you Adlington. You will oversee its lands and citizens as Lord, shaping its future with the same care and loyalty you've shown throughout this journey."

Bryne exhaled slowly, the weight of the honour settling across his shoulders. "I shall serve as best I can," he said respectfully, the sincerity in his voice unmistakable.

Aevah's gaze shifted, coming to rest on Erica, Trysten, and Damon. "And knowing the bond between the three of you, I can't separate those who have fought as one."

Her voice carried with it a note of warmth and finality as she continued, "Erica, Damon, Trysten—you have stood beside those who needed you most. Your courage has never wavered, your sacrifices too great to be measured. For that, I offer you Ravenswood Manor, to hold together, near Adlington, where you may continue to work alongside Bryne."

A hush fell across the room as her words settled over them, heavy with meaning.

"You shall all hold the titles of Lords and Ladies," she said, her gaze sweeping across them, "not for tradition's sake, but because your actions have earned them. You have shown what true leadership looks like."

A ripple of approval moved through the room, quiet and reverent, as Edward, Bryne, Erica, Trysten, and Damon rose to their feet. Each bowed their heads in solemn acceptance.

"To new beginnings," Edward said, lifting his goblet high.

"To new beginnings," Aevah echoed, her voice strong with conviction.

The room burst into celebration once more, a wave of laughter and cheer spreading through the table as goblets were raised and voices rose together in joy.

Once the noise settled, Aevah spoke again, her tone clear but composed. "Lord Bishop and Stone will retain their lands and titles. And I have also chosen to bestow the titles and holdings of Lord and Lady Bennett to their son, Nicholas."

She turned to him then, warmth flickering behind her gaze, the moment stretching between them with quiet certainty.

"Nicholas has chosen to remain here, in Carraton Castle, by my side. It's no secret that our bond has deepened over time, and that the future ahead of us is one we will build together."

A murmur of understanding passed across the table, gentle and approving. Aevah allowed herself a soft smile before continuing.

"For all that we have endured, and all that lies ahead, I know this: Nicholas and I stand as one. This kingdom is ours to shape, to nurture, and to lead—with trust, with strength, and with love."

Nicholas reached for her hand then, his fingers wrapping gently around hers. The unspoken intimacy of the gesture grounded her, a touch that spoke of certainty and promise.

"Whatever the future holds," he said, his voice low and sure, "we will face it together."

Some guests exchanged knowing glances, whispers of marriage stirring softly among the tables. But Aevah chose not to entertain them, at least, not yet.

With measured grace, she shifted her focus, her eyes settling on Adrian.

"Adrian," she began, her voice steady and clear, "your journey has not been without fault. We all remember the choices you once made, the betrayal that nearly cost us everything."

A hush fell over the room. It was not a silence of judgement, but of recognition, a shared acknowledgement of the past.

"But just as we now stand in the light of a new beginning," she continued, "so, too, have you fought to rewrite your path. You didn't ask for forgiveness. You *earned* it—through action, through sacrifice, and an unwavering dedication when it mattered most."

Her gaze flicked briefly to her mother, then returned to Adrian.

"You have already accepted the title of Knight of the Realm, but your service doesn't end there. Like Fiona, you will serve as a personal guard—entrusted not only with the queen's safety, but with the safety of the realm itself."

She took a breath, her next words carrying a deeper weight.

"Your duty will extend beyond me. You will divide your time between protecting me and protecting my mother, Lady Cecilia—ensuring that neither of us stands unguarded."

Across the table, Cecilia met Adrian's gaze and gave a quiet, knowing nod. Whatever had passed between them – the betrayal, the reconciliation, the long road of rebuilding trust – was understood in that single, silent exchange.

Adrian didn't hesitate. Rising to his feet, he placed his hand over his heart and bowed his head low.

"I don't take this honour lightly," he said. "Nor do I forget the past. But from this day forward, I vow my loyalty—not just in word, but in deed. I stand to protect, to serve, and to prove that redemption isn't spoken. It is lived."

Aevah held Adrian's gaze for a moment longer before offering a solemn nod.

"Then let it be known, Adrian stands as Knight of the Realm and Guardian of the Crown and Lady Cecilia."

Cecilia inclined her head in gratitude. Murmurs began to stir again among the gathered, but they faded as Aevah's voice rose once more.

"Now," she said, her tone reverent, "I wish to honour the priestesses who fought beside us, and those we lost along the way. With every fallen sister, they, too, have grieved. And yet, even in mourning, they have chosen to rebuild, assigning new positions within the priesthood."

Her voice carried across the hall, unwavering, filled with the weight of respect for those who had given all for the realm's salvation.

"As decreed by the priestesses themselves, Nala shall take the mantle of High Priestess and guide their order into this new era. Though they are not present tonight, their wisdom remains with us, and their sacrifices shall never be forgotten."

A pause followed, a moment of collective remembrance. Aevah let her gaze travel across the room, giving space for reflection before continuing.

"There is another presence I must acknowledge—one who has guided me on this journey, shaping not only my path, but the very balance of this kingdom."

A hush fell, deeper this time, as she spoke.

"The Divine Spirit has walked beside me, teaching me, strengthening me, and ensuring I was prepared for the trials to come. Now, as peace begins to settle across the land, the priestesses rejoice in her return."

She allowed the significance of the words to sink in before speaking again, this time with even greater reverence.

"They have waited long for this moment. In the years ahead, they will work alongside her, restoring what was lost and preserving the sacred bond between the land and its people. This is more than a victory. It is renewal."

Murmurs of agreement rippled through the hall. The return of Indra wasn't just a spiritual triumph – it was a sign that healing had truly begun.

With a gentle smile, Aevah drew a breath, her focus shifting as she prepared to address those who had served with quieter strength.

"There are some among us who seek neither title nor reward," she said. Her voice, though gentler, rang no less true. "Walter. Issac. You have both served with unwavering devotion, asking for nothing in return. Though such efforts often go unseen, I see you, and so does this kingdom."

She looked to them with quiet pride.

"The Crown is forever in your debt."

She lifted her goblet, her gaze steady as it swept across the room. "I offer you no lands, no titles—but my eternal gratitude. If ever you are in need, simply ask and it will be yours."

A ripple of approval stirred among the gathered. Walter gave a humble nod, while Issac offered the faintest of smiles, accepting her words in the quiet, unassuming manner that had always defined them.

Then Aevah's expression softened as her attention shifted to a smaller figure at the table. Her eyes lit with warmth, and the corners of her mouth curved into a knowing smile.

"I've heard whispers," she said playfully, "that someone here dreams of becoming a Knight of the Realm one day."

Timmy's face turned a brilliant shade of red as laughter rang out across the room, affectionate and full of delight. But Aevah wasn't finished.

"A dream like that," she continued, "should never remain only a dream.

She inclined her head slightly, her voice gentler now, but just as certain.

"So tonight, I offer you Carraton Castle, my home, and with it, the opportunity to train alongside the very best."

For a moment, Timmy could only stare, eyes wide, lips parted in disbelief. He glanced between Aevah and the others, as if trying to confirm that he hadn't imagined it.

"You mean it?" he asked softly, voice barely above a whisper.

Aevah's smile deepened. "I do."

A stunned silence fell over the room, just long enough for the moment to settle. Then came the roar of cheers and applause – hearts lifted, hands clapping, voices rising in celebration of a young boy's first step towards knighthood.

With roles bestowed, honours accepted, and the kingdom's future firmly set in motion, the final weight of ceremony lifted.

In its place came joy – undiluted and overflowing. Laughter spilt from every corner, goblets clinked in toast, and conversations blossomed – some filled with nostalgia, others with new beginnings.

Music soon rose above the din, its melody threading through the hall like a welcome breeze. It called to the people not with pomp, but with familiarity, drawing them towards the open space where dancing had begun. The rhythm was light, the steps well-worn and beloved, not performed for tradition's sake, but for the sheer joy of being alive, together.

Aevah lingered on the edge for a moment, letting the scene wash over her. These were her people, the ones who had fought, who had lost, who had endured, and who now, finally, could begin to heal.

Then, with a soft breath and a knowing smile, she stepped forward – into the dance, into the light, and the first true night of peace in far too long.

***

As dawn broke across the horizon, Aevah stood atop the highest tower, her gaze fixed on the light cresting the world. The sun's rays struck the newly restored crystal, casting brilliant rainbows that danced along the stone walls in a kaleidoscope of wonder.

Power surged through her veins, the crystal calling to her with its ancient rhythm. She opened herself to it without hesitation, and warmth flooded her being. Golden tendrils of light encircled her, wrapping her in radiant energy.

In that moment, she was no longer just queen or conduit – she was one with the power, one with the land. Equal in spirit. The golden light swelled around her, rippling outward in gentle waves that rolled across the kingdom.

The world answered.

Flowers bloomed where none had dared to grow, as though waking from an enchanted slumber. Rivers surged with crystalline clarity, their waters renewed. Even the air itself felt lighter, as if it had finally exhaled centuries of sorrow. The kingdom, scarred and scattered, was whole again.

Beside her, a soft presence emerged. Indra stood with her, woven from light and stillness.

"Aevah," she said, her voice warm and resonant. "You have healed what was broken. This power answers only to purity, and in you, it has found harmony. The land is healed. The cycle begins anew. And in return, it offers you its truth."

Aevah felt it all – every heartbeat within the kingdom, every whispered prayer carried on the wind, every fragile hope trembling into life. She was no longer separate from her people. No longer apart from the land. She was part of it. As it was part of her.

Indra reached forward, her luminous hand pressing gently to Aevah's chest.

"Lead with an open heart," she said, "and this world shall never fall into shadow again."

Aevah closed her eyes, allowing the truth of those words to settle deep within her. She accepted the gift, the bond, and the responsibility it carried.

And when the last shimmer of light faded, she turned towards the horizon – towards what lay ahead.

A new era had begun.

Epilogue

"What just happened?" Adina's voice was a bare whisper, raw and fractured. The world had slowed, splintered. Bradley had been alive only a moment ago, and now he was gone. Just like that.

Her arms tightened around Eadric, cradling him against her chest as if she could shield him from the brutality of the night. The weight of his small body, warm and steady, was the only thing anchoring her. Everything else had shattered.

She was dimly aware of Fleur beside her, the gentle way her wife took her hand without a word, offering presence without intrusion. Fleur didn't speak at first. She simply reached out, her fingers brushing the back of Adina's hand, grounding her.

Adina swallowed hard, her throat burning. She turned towards Fleur, and the sight of her – soft, steady, with grief shimmering in her eyes – unravelled something deep within.

"He's safe," Fleur murmured, her voice quiet but sure, as she gently stroked Eadric's head. "I wish Bradley were here, too. But his son is safe—with us, with you. That's what would have mattered most to him."

The words settled into Adina's bones, threading through the ache and loss, fragile yet real. She closed her eyes and exhaled unsteadily, letting herself lean into Fleur's touch.

The rest of the trip to the docks passed in a blur. The rhythmic jostle of the carriage did little to ground her. Her mind remained trapped between the past and the present, replaying the moment Bradley fell – the way his body crumpled, the way there had been no time to mourn before they had to flee.

Eadric stirred against her, his tiny fingers flexing before settling again. Still unaware. Still safe.

She felt Fleur's gaze on her – warm, steady, watching over her as she always had through every storm before this one. Adina drew in a deep breath, the salty scent of the docks creeping in as they neared their escape.

"We're almost there," Fleur said, her fingers brushing through Adina's hair in soothing strokes. Adina gave a faint nod, not trusting her voice. Grief would have to wait.

The docks were quiet, mercifully empty. No guards. No delays. Soon they would be on the ship, and then, perhaps, she would let herself break.

But for now, she remained steel.

The carriage lurched to a stop, and Adina moved first, holding Eadric close as she stepped out onto the worn wooden planks of the pier. Fleur followed at her side, silent and steady, as they strode forward and locked eyes with the waiting crew.

"We leave now," Fleur commanded, turning to her first mate. "Make sure everything is ready—no delays." There was no room for hesitation.

"Aye, Captain."

As they boarded the ship, the scent of salt and sun-bleached wood enveloped them, a sharp contrast to the blood-soaked ground they had fled. The deck creaked underfoot, but Adina hardly noticed. Eadric was still nestled against her chest, his small breaths calm, unaware of how his life was about to change.

Fleur led the way to their quarters, her presence firm and reassuring. There was no need for words, and the crew knew their roles. The escape was already in motion. There was no desire to linger, no reason to watch the ship come alive beneath them. All that mattered was leaving.

Adina cast one last glance over her shoulder. The ship's hands moved with purpose, casting off ropes and unfurling sails. The first mate's voice rang out, crisp commands steering them forward. A jolt beneath her feet signalled the ship's departure, cutting through dark waters, each wave a breath of distance from what they had left behind.

Only when the coast began to fade into shadow did Adina allow herself to breathe.

She lay Eadric down on their bed, brushing a hand over his cheek. A quiet resolve took root inside her. She wouldn't let anything harm him. Not now. Not ever.

Adina turned towards Fleur, her eyes steady as they met the intensity in her wife's gaze.

"We need to leave Ethos behind," she said. "Completely. We forget the life we had and continue the one we built. We raise Eadric as our own—no ties to his past. Only the future we make for him."

The words hung in the air between them. For a long moment, Fleur didn't speak. She simply stepped closer, her touch gentle as she cupped Adina's face, eyes searching hers.

"We start again, as our own family. And we teach Eadric all there is to know about life at sea."

She kissed Adina then, slow and sure, a promise sealed in salt and silence. When she pulled back, there was a new light in her eyes. Not just determination, but freedom. A quiet exhilaration for the life still unwritten.

Adina exhaled slowly, grounding herself in Fleur's gaze, in the strength of her touch. She lifted her hand, covering Fleur's, holding it there as if anchoring herself to that promise.

Beyond the cabin walls, the ship groaned and swayed. The salty breeze slipped through the window, cool against her skin. Adina turned, watching as Ethos shrank into nothing more than a shadow on the horizon. Once, that country had been her world

– her duty, her family, her future. Now it was just a silhouette. And she didn't mourn it.

Fleur came to stand beside her, their shoulders brushing, hands still linked.

"This is home," she said softly. "It always has been."

Adina squeezed her hand in silent agreement. The past had been left behind. What lay ahead was vast and untamed, written in the waves, carried by the wind in their sails.

No return. No regrets.

Only the open sea, the life they had chosen, and each other.

Acknowledgements

It's hard to believe this is it – the final book. After years of immersing myself in this world, creating these characters, and following them through every twist and turn, it feels surreal to be writing this section one last time. What began as an obsessive idea centred on one character named Elinor has evolved into something much larger than I ever imagined, and now here we are at the end. Or at least, this end.

The tale of Ethos may be ending, but I have a feeling there's another story waiting to be told.

To my readers – thank you. Truly. Your support, messages, and excitement have meant everything to me. This world belongs to you just as much as it does to me. You've laughed with these characters, cried with them, and maybe even yelled at them (I know I have way too many times). Thank you for joining me on this journey and for making Ethos feel as real to you as it is to me.

To my husband, family, and friends, thank you for being my constant. Your love, support, and belief in me have carried me through to making this trilogy a reality.

To my editor, Carien, thank you for being such a steady and brilliant presence throughout this series. Your insight, encouragement, and care have helped shape these books into what they are. I'm so grateful we crossed paths.

And finally, to the characters who've lived in my head and heart for so long – thank you for allowing me to tell your story (or rather, for allowing me to tell your story through me). You've surprised me, challenged me, and reminded me why I love doing this.

This may be the final chapter, but it's not goodbye. Stories have a way of lingering and finding new life in the hearts of readers. So, if you've laughed, cried, or felt even a flicker of magic while reading, then Ethos will never truly be gone. I hope its story stays with you forever.

With all my love and gratitude,

Abigail Mader

About the Author

Since completing her debut trilogy, Abigail Mader has been diligently working on new stories. Saying goodbye to the world of Ethos was bittersweet, but it has also opened the door to fresh characters, new adventures, and even more emotional chaos (the good kind).

Abigail continues to explore the indie publishing world with curiosity and passion – connecting with fellow writers, engaging with readers, and building a creative life that blends storytelling, community, and a touch of magic. Whether she is drafting her next novel, designing bookmarks for her online bookshop, or collaborating with other indie authors, she is always in pursuit of inspiration.

When she is not writing, you can find her enjoying nature, tackling her never-ending TBR pile, or spending time with family and friends. She believes that the best stories are the ones that evoke emotion, and she's just getting started.

To follow Abigail's journey and discover what's next, check out the links to her social media on the next page.

Connect with Abigail on:

Website

www.abigailmaderauthor.com.au

Instagram

https://www.instagram.com/abigail.mader_fantasy_writer/

A Picture of Us

Marine Biologist Mia dreamed of something more—so when a job offer from a remote island marine conservation centre arrives, she jumps at the chance. With a new home, new role as lead biologist, and her girlfriend Tash beside her, it feels like life has finally fallen into place.

But even paradise isn't perfect.

When a journalist twists her words into a divisive headline, the small-town trust she's built begins to unravel. Forced to lay low while the storm passes, she turns inward, until her girlfriend Tash reminds her that she needs to breathe, and spend some time back in nature, doing what she loves. It's shared chips on a dock, windblown sketches, and the slow, surprising pull of something magical beginning.

Between reef dives, small-town politics, and windswept sketches that capture more than just sea life, *A Picture of Us* is a heartwarming novella of salty air, soft kisses, and second chances—perfect for readers who still believe in the magic of a happily ever after.

www.ingramcontent.com/pod-product-compliance
Lightning Source LLC
Chambersburg PA
CBHW030602310726
48979CB00003B/544